THE SWEET ROWAN

Keira Dominguez

PRAISE FOR KEIRA DOMINGUEZ

Her Caprice

"It has been a long time since I have stayed up to the wee hours of the morning with a book I couldn't put down. This book was totally worth the groggy sleepy day I had today. I won't give away any of the details but it was a really great read. I can hardly wait to read Keira's next novel. I hope I don't have wait too long." ~a Girl and a Boy

"I loved this book! I stayed up entirely too late at night reading and I have no reservations in saying that I couldn't put it down. One of my favorite parts were a few end of chapter sentences...they were so good that I often read them twice. In truth, my only complaint was that I wanted more." ~Carrie

"I'm an avid reader, so being surprised by "newness" is a delight to me. The time period was obviously thoroughly researched, and the book was free of the glaring cultural inconsistencies so often found in Regency romance. The author stayed firmly within the bounds of the time period. I truly enjoyed this book and look forward to more offerings from this author! Write quickly, Keira!" ~The Book Gramma

"This book is absolutely wonderful. Almost like a thriller, a regency romance with lots of wit and gutsiness. The secret is surprising and totally original (have never read it anywhere else, fact or fiction!). The hero and heroine seem very real and totally lovable. The other characters largely likeable. The villain is more villainous as the book progresses, so the danger increases to a gripping finale. I finished reading it on a flight and didn't notice that the plane landed or that hours had passed, so absorbed was I in this book. Highly recommend." ~AM

"I love finding an author who has done something a bit different with the Regency romance, while still maintaining its best traditions. The characters in 'Her Caprice' are delightful, the writing is excellent and the tension was at times so great that I had to stop reading to catch my breath. I'm really looking forward to reading more from this author." ~Lian Tanner

"What a unique and interesting fairy tale Beatrice has a secret and feels it will stop her from normal life. This story deals with parents fear and how they plan to hide the issue. No matter what happens fate has another plan. I loved the beautiful twists and it was written brilliantly too. Keira Dominguez is a new author for me and I enjoyed her story will be on the lookout for other works by her." ~VineVoice

The Telling Touch

"This book was everything I didn't know I needed right now. A sweet jewel of a regency that warmed my heart and made me smile. I absolutely loved the banter between Meg and Nick. The plot was deep and rich and wonderful. The characters were complex, robust and realistic. And the love story was both tender and transcendent. I loved every single thing about this book. READ IT! And follow the author on Instagram @keiradominguezwrites - she makes me smile with her wry commentaries on life's profound miscellany." ~Andreajanel831

"The Telling Touch was a book I could not put down. I read under the covers. I read while cooking dinner. I may even have read while sitting at stoplights! (I was careful, I promise.) Meg and Nick are beautiful, yet flawed and utterly relatable. Their slow burn romance is full of sparks and witty dialogue and delicious misunderstandings. Just like Beatrice in HC, Meg has a bit of inconvenient magic that gets her into trouble more than once, but which she learns to harness and use in a new and really great way, literally turning her weakness into a great strength . . . a theme that is ultimately so powerful. Well researched and thoughtfully written, I am happy to recommend this book to everyone who loves a good romance." ~Afton Nelson

"I love the author's use of paranormal abilities in historical romances - it just heightens the social tensions of the time and it is so clever. Well-written and I equally appreciated the awfulness of the villain and the humanity given to the character. Meg is a favorite of mine. She was very lovable and I liked seeing her through Nick's eyes. I enjoyed the complexity of her relationships - it helped make her character even richer. Nick was great too. I loved the last scene." ~Sarah C.

"This author is fabulous! I love the way she has combined sweet and whimsical with a touch of sensual. My grown daughter "Eeeked!!!" out loud when she spotted this book on my bedside table. I loved

'Her Caprice', but this book just kicked it up a notch with Meg's spunk and attitude :) I can't wait for the next one!" ~T. Hunsaker

"This book robbed me of a good night's rest! I couldn't put it down! I highly recommend both the author's books. Trust me you won't be disappointed!" ~momof2

"Meg has been in love with Nick since she was fourteen years old, but when her sister elopes with Nick's uncle, an aged earl, all the scandal seems to fall on Meg. In the six years he was gone Meg became an outcast people could barely tolerate. This was a beautiful story with characters I loved. Meg was an amazingly brave character who, despite the times, followed her own heart." ~Linda Tonis, Paranormal Romance Guild

www.BOROUGHSPUBLISHINGGROUP.com

PUBLISHER'S NOTE: This is a work of fiction. Names, characters, places and incidents either are the product of the author's imagination or are used fictitiously. Any resemblance to actual events, locales, business establishments or persons, living or dead, is coincidental. Boroughs Publishing Group does not have any control over and does not assume responsibility for author or third-party websites, blogs or critiques or their content.

THE SWEET ROWAN

Copyright © 2021 Keira Dominguez

All rights reserved. Unless specifically noted, no part of this publication may be reproduced, scanned, stored in a retrieval system or transmitted in any form or by any means, electronic, mechanical, photocopying, recording, or otherwise, known or hereinafter invented, without the express written permission of Boroughs Publishing Group. The scanning, uploading and distribution of this book via the Internet or by any other means without the permission of Boroughs Publishing Group is illegal and punishable by law. Participation in the piracy of copyrighted materials violates the author's rights.

ISBN 978-1-953810-39-7

To Zac, the demon baby of Bethany

ACKNOWLEDGMENTS

When I began writing Penny and Malcolm's story, I had no idea it would be so on the nose. Skeptical woman homeschools too many children during a global disaster, which keeps everyone indoors much of the time. Because of the unusual situation around the world between early 2020 and now, I had to get creative about writing, fitting it in after sessions of teaching fractions and supervising Zoom lessons.

My undying thanks go to Jonah, Jane, Spencer, Zac (who really made up the word "slinch"), and Maren for being interesting and delightful people to be with day in and day out. I had no idea I would be doing so much real-life research for the life of a governess, and many of my feelings made it into the book.

Still more thanks go to my husband Nathan who bravely carried on as I suffered the ultimate betrayal when my local Chick-fil-A franchise stopped carrying cheese sauce in the middle of the pandemic. He has spent more of this year on the phone with insurance adjusters than anyone should have to. I am thankful he absorbs so many of our domestic calamities.

Thank you to my critique partners and beta readers Afton, Christine, Marianne, Paula, Kylene, Donna, Jessica and Debbie (who read this book at least three times) for their priceless feedback and encouragement.

Thank you, dear reader, for diving into *The Sweet Rowan* with me. If you loved it, please consider writing a review on Amazon, Goodreads, and telling your best friend and every rando you know on Instagram.

THE SWEET ROWAN

Chapter One

January 1816

Penny smelled smoke.

Weak winter moonlight slanted through the windows and she jerked upright, bracing herself against the groaning walls of the travelling coach as it rocked through the deep mud. The lamps had gone out hours ago, and she took in the dark mound of fur rugs sheltering Mama and Papa sleeping on the opposite bench. Squinting through the window, Penny searched for menacing flames lighting the blue and black shadows of the countryside. Nothing.

Then she sniffed, getting a nose full of it, and muttered a sharp German curse under her breath.

Perhaps it was only a bonfire...in the dead of night. Perhaps Papa should investigate. Or the coachman. Anyone besides a tired young woman who had finally achieved a degree of comfort, nestled into the fur. She wanted to stay comfortable.

She rubbed her eyes and threw the rug off in a flurry of decision. Banging a gloved fist against the driver's box, she shouted loud enough to wake the dead. She sprang from the door before the coach had come to a halt, leaving her parents shouting after her. Landing hard on a rocky verge, she followed her nose, stumbling up a sharp rise with Papa on her heels. Icy wind slipped under the collar and cuffs of her pelisse. "Can you smell it?"

"Other side of the hill," Papa huffed after her.

"Yes, I—" Then her words choked off as the scene unfolded below them. Smoke poured from the open doors of a large stone stable as shouts of farm hands volleyed over the pop and crack of flames. Horses screamed wildly, dragged from the flying embers and released, bucking and frenzied into, the paddocks.

"Stay back," Papa shouted, charging down the hill, but Penny charged after him, her gaze tracking over the barn and the yard, searching for a way her talents might be of some use. Before she could decide on any course, Mama grasped her arm. "The water brigade. No heroics. They need us there."

Penny's mouth set, but she saw the truth in Mama's words. A chain of women—most of them too young or too old and strung out along the courtyard—struggled with the buckets, sloshing half of the precious water onto the muddy earth. She added her strength to theirs, wordlessly using her long arms to narrow the gaps, working alongside her mother, restless for something more to do.

The fire raged, licking up the beams and catching hold of the roof while an endless stream of men drove out draft animals, pigs, and then a farm dog making frantic high-pitched whimpers. Women doused the nearest flames.

"Give her the whelps and get her back," a man shouted, pulling three little dogs from his coat.

"It's enough," roared an older man stumbling from the smoke. He fell to all fours and a woman rushed forward to wrap her arms around him. "Let the damned thing go up and thank God the house is saved."

A stunned, exhausted silence followed before he limped off, wrapped in a woman's shawl, leaning heavily against her. Penny felt Mama at her side, heard the weighty breaths of bone-weariness that left her body. "Come along, Penny. We're not five miles from home."

More shouts carried over the yard as guards were posted between the house and the barn to watch as it burned down to its last cinder. The rest of the household, muddy and soaked, began to find their rest where they could get it. As she must.

Penny rubbed the dull pain in her neck, recollecting the list of aggravations they had encountered on the journey from Vienna. The axle breaking on the road to Munich. No blacksmith for miles. The Rhine having the temerity to flood. Even the greasy inn at Bruges while they waited for the weather to clear. She could see herself adding to the list. Conflagration in Dorset.

She traced a diagonal path up the hillside, stumbling in the strange light while trailing her mother. It was when she had almost reached the crest of the hill her head jerked around, eyes narrowing on the rear of the structure. "Did you hear that?"

Papa, his coat slung over his arm, bearing hardly any resemblance to the celebrated diplomat he was, stared at the inferno. "What?"

The crackling blaze pierced the roof and lit up the night sky. Tendrils of flaming hay drifted from the loft and the stinging acridness of smoke invaded Penny's nose and eyes.

Mama stumbled onward but Penny couldn't move. There it was again. A small sound—the smallest sound she had ever heard. It might've been the ancient structure wailing in the inferno. Then she knew it wasn't.

She tried to keep her balance during her headlong rush down the hill, racing across freezing pools of water, and clambering over a wall. She waded through mud, not stopping until she stood beneath the large bay doors of the hayloft raining fire. No one to see what she was about to do save for the silent, terror-stricken shadow of Mama racing to catch her. Penny took no heed, summoning her magic with the ease of long practice, bidding thoughts of lightness to fill her mind. *Ash floating on the night air. Hot air balloons lifting from a grassy field. The sun pulling free of the horizon.* Power flowed through her veins, gathering in her belly until her toes lifted from the ground and she rose into the sky.

It felt so good to rise, so right, as though she were a fish gasping on a riverbank, suddenly returned to race the wild stream. Sodden skirts slapped against her legs and she stepped through the opening of the loft with a grin on her face. Mama would be preaching sermons about the risk of being discovered for weeks to come, with all the intensity of a Calvinist pastor.

But it was worth it.

Hissing sparks were doused on her sopping dress. She held an arm across her face, peering into the smoky enclosure. The fire would devour this soon enough, but she was in no danger. Her magic would keep her safe. It always had.

"Here...dog." She tried to whistle but her throat erupted with a cough. Eyes stinging, she crouched beneath a flaming beam. "Here little one."

The fire sounded different than what she was used to, unbound by the neat, bricked walls of a chimney, banked carefully behind a grate. Here it raged in her ears, groaning and snapping like a rampaging giant, the structure screaming under its own weight. "Here, pup," she called, moving swiftly along the loft with urgency.

In the distance Mama was calling her name, cutting through the roar of the fire, drowning out the little noise Penny could hear if only Mama would stop. Instead of quietness, there came an ominous crack and she crouched defensively.

"Last chance," she said, fear coloring her tone, feet inching back towards the door.

Out of the darkness, the little beast launched itself into her arms in a flurry of sharp nails and soft fur. Another crack sent sparks raining onto her hair, skipping over the skin of her face and neck, but Penny ignored the pain and spun, stumbling as she cradled the creature tight against her bosom. She tripped around crates and ropes, sighting the open doors as smoke shifted between them. Almost there. Almost there.

Tongues of flame licked up through the floorboards, pitting her path, and she sprang forward, reaping her magic as she went. *Ash on the night air. Flaming straw drifting from a fire.* Her speed was greater now as she sailed past pockets of fire, floating inches above the rapidly disappearing floor. Even in such danger, her veins raced with excitement.

Almost there.

The gaping doors were rimmed in fire and Penny slid to a stop at the opening of the barn, gathering her thoughts as she stared down into the upturned faces—Mama, Papa, but strangers, too. She must not use her magic too obviously, now. *Dust motes dancing in sunlight. Dandelions blown—*

The crack of a beam hit her ears a second before it caught her across the back, searing heat and blunt force. She fell into Papa's outstretched arms and knew no more.

Chapter Two

April 1816

Penny's scar itched where the soft wool fabric of her dress rubbed across her back. She placed her fingers between the neckline and her skin, looking up to the ceiling of the round, high-vaulted building—her practice gymnasium—and released a shaky breath.

A thick layer of straw covered the floor, swallowing up the sound of her footsteps as she paced to the center. Morning light slanted through the high-set windows and settled on her hair, tamed in a coil against her neck. She closed her eyes, her mind conjuring images of lightness. *The twirl of her skirts in a Viennese waltz. A leaf drifting on a breeze.*

She waited for lightness to suffuse her being. She waited to feel herself grow as airy as thistledown. She waited and waited and waited.

She screwed her eyes tighter shut and felt beads of sweat rise on her forehead. She fisted her hands at her sides and clenched her jaw. She felt only the sensation of tightening ropes banding her chest and shoulders, squeezing her, and holding her down. There was a scrape of a key in the lock and she gave a wild, desperate cry that echoed against the rafters.

She sank to her knees and a puppy, far larger than he had been when she pulled him from the burning barn three months ago, bounded through the straw to lick at her hand.

"Your trunks have been brought from the attics," Mama said as she entered. Her words were pleasant and informative, but her gaze slid along Penny like a ship's captain assessing the seaworthiness of his vessel. "Where shall you go?"

The choice was Penny's, for which she ought to be thankful. Mama may have learned the vocabulary of compromise and grace over the last several years, but she still spoke it as though it were a beastly foreign tongue.

Penny scrubbed her hand under Fritz's jawline, and he wriggled onto his back to give her greater scope. She smiled at the sight of his belly where the pink blurred into patches of grey and white, and got to her feet. *I want to stay and learn to rise again. Demand my magic return to me. Find the way back to how I was.* That's what she chose.

Mama touched the tip of a finger. "London."

Godmama had written weeks ago to say she was prepared to manage a Season for Penny. There would be balls, parties—as many trips to Hatchards as she could wish for. She was of age to make a match.

A muscle in Penny's jaw jumped. A match might be a fine thing, but far less important than her magic.

Mama touched the tip of a second finger. "Beatrice."

Penny clamped her lips tight. To spend the better part of six months with her sister—someone who could rise into the sky as easily as taking a breath—seemed a form of torture.

Mama touched the third finger. "Or you may come with your father and me."

Penny supposed that would have to be it. Papa had got himself a knighthood for his diplomatic service in Vienna, but the strings that came attached would tie her parents to the demands of Lord Liverpool for months. The gentleman wished for them to take a tour of the counties east and north, reporting on towns and villages riven by hunger and want since the end of the war. If Penny went along with them, she might do some good.

She wrapped her shawl around her shoulders and moved to stand in the open door of the gymnasium. Fritz padded over to lean heavily against her skirts.

"Isn't it dreadful?" Mama asked, slightly behind her.

A sharp wind stirred the tree branches across the paddock like a furious Belgian cook whisking eggs, and the idea of it sent a smile feathering across Penny's mouth. She glanced to Mama with a little hopeful twist on her lips.

"Miss Starling is down in the village," she said. "If I could stay at Thorndene, she would be my companion."

There was a long silence, and a tightening in Mama's neck. "Your healing was miraculous."

To anyone else it might have been a non sequitur, a black sheep wandering among a flock of white, but not to Mama. Like enthusiasm for a London Season, it fit neatly under the category of Things Penny Ought to Feel.

An icy flood of frustration filled Penny's insides. If anyone knew how close she had been to death—how the putrid fever and flaming wound had clawed through her, scratching out her magic and shredding it from its moorings—she did. She knew it was a miracle to be pronounced in perfect health by every physician from here to London. Deep in her bones she knew it.

But she wasn't healed. Not entirely. Penny Thornton was a magical creature, and, without the return of her magic, her healing was incomplete.

She took a breath and gazed over the fields once more. "Miss Starling and I get along beautifully. I'd even let her finish teaching me Latin if you like."

Mama stepped into the doorway and leaned against the opposite doorpost. She opened her mouth and Penny could see her rearranging the words before they left her tongue, cooling them. Then she fished a missive from her pocket, showing it to Penny.

The address read, "Miss Starling, Morton's Cross, Dorset, England."

"You can't stay with Miss Starling," Mama said, turning the square in her hands. "I received this sealed inside one from your sister, who asked I send it on. Your old governess will be getting a new job."

"Beatrice's children can't be old enough for a governess. Charlie is—" Penny fumbled.

"Three," Mama supplied. "The request is not for Beatrice. Lady Ainsley has a cousin who lives in Scotland. A widower."

"A Scottish widower?" A shiver shook through Penny's veins and her eyes widened. It was cold—too cold for April—and perhaps she was catching a chill. "It sounds like the beginning of an ominous Gothic tale."

A breath of a smile passed over Mama's lips. "Nothing of the sort. The gentleman had to dismiss his governess and will require a replacement of impeccable character."

"Miss Starling has that. How many children?" Penny asked, as she bent to pat Fritz. Excitement prickled through her skin as the cords which seemed to bind her, trapping her earthbound, loosened around her chest—loosened and reached. Oh Lord, here it was.

Her heart raced and she closed her eyes to greet the return of her power. *Thistledown. The spray of an alpine waterfall.* Her concentration spun through her mind and body, reaching for her magic only to find an empty harvest.

Confusion lined her brow, and slowly she opened her eyes.

No lightness gathered in on her. No impulse to rise.

Still, there was a shivery longing, which seemed to coil away from her, wrapping around the plain, square missive in Mama's hand, filling Penny with a fierce need.

No lightness, only wanting for a simple letter. Penny lifted her fingers and felt the invisible bands loosen by degrees. The letter. The letter would cut her fetters loose—of that she possessed a strange, unaccountable certainty. She only needed to get her hands on it.

"There are only three," Mama explained, glancing back to Penny, unaware of the forces shaking through her daughter's frame. "The two boys are old enough to have instruction and then there's a nursery maid to look after the little girl. Do you think Miss Starling is too old to manage them?"

Penny smiled as a plan began to form in her mind like a tightly packed snowball rolling downhill, picking up speed and mass as it went. Of course, Miss Starling was too old. Chilblains had laid her low this year with all the cold. "Of course, she's not," Penny said.

Mama pocketed the letter once again and every nerve in Penny wanted to leap at it, tearing it out of her hands.

"So, you see, staying at Thorndene is impossible." Mama gazed out at the storm, and Penny followed her eyes. Trees that appeared so rigid and obstinate in ordinary weather, twisted and bent in the wake of such wind.

Penny smothered her sharpened nerves and mirrored Mama's contemplative stance. Mama would give her an opening.

"When your sister first got her magic," Mama began, "we spent months believing if we read the right books or repeated the right words, Beatrice would go back to being the person she was before. We wasted years wishing it away—" Mama exhaled sharply, and then pulled her voice under rigid control.

Penny could hardly attend her, the insistence in her mind too loud to ignore. *Get the letter. Get the letter.*

Mama went on. "I wasted seven years praying my daughter would come back to me." She turned and reached for Penny who drew away from the wall, tucking her hand in the crook of Penny's arm. "I don't want you to be as foolish as I was, chasing after things that are gone. Putting off happiness until the world rearranges itself to your satisfaction. Do you understand?"

Penny nodded, her smile tight, obedient. "Sussex," she whispered. "I choose Sussex. I'll start for Beatrice's house next week."

Mama pressed her hand, touched her cheek. "I wish we could afford to send you off ourselves, but Lord Liverpool is anxious for us to depart and there is so much to organize."

Penny smiled once more and wondered how Mama could not see how false it was. "Let me run the letter down to Miss Starling. I'll save you an errand."

Mama gave her an approving look. Admiring her, perhaps, for accepting her losses at last. "I should write to your sister."

"Oh no, Mama," Penny answered. "I'll manage that too."

Chapter Three

From the hackney, Penny jumped into the sheeting rain of Edinburgh, her sturdy half-boots sinking into the mud, the icy ooze encasing her ankle, spilling over the edge and down her foot. She closed her eyes for the briefest moment before whispering, "I'm in hell."

"No, miss. You're in Scotland." A young man, sounding unforgivably cheerful, jostled against her in the posting house yard as he collected her trunks from the carriage, the squelch of his boots flinging thick black sludge in irregular arcs around him. "You wantin' a room?"

"No," she called, clenching her teeth against the cold. "Only a place by the fire."

Though her cloak was thick, wind sneaked between the seams of the dense felted wool, shaking her shoulders. She turned to collect her little dog, doubling his lead over her hand and folding him securely to her breast. Lord help her if she lost him.

Fritz poked his head from her cloak and measured her progress to the inn. Seeing ghastly weather, he wisely ducked his head back again. Lucky dog.

What on earth had possessed her to come to Scotland to try on the role of a qualified governess, concealing she was a young lady from the highest society?

The answer loomed as large as the thundercloud overhead. Magic.

Had it been magic? The memories of Mama in the gymnasium were indistinct, recalled as a quickening along her veins and the sensation of the invisible, tethering bands, which had become a shade less constricting. Weeks later, the recollection was as faint as the sound of a tiny dog yelping over a raging fire.

On the strength of those feelings, she had organized everything. Through two carefully worded letters and even more careful silences, Mama thought she was with Beatrice. Beatrice thought she was with Mama. Her employer expected her soon, and Miss Starling knew nothing at all.

Such was Penny's genius for carrying out her wishes with speed and competence. Before her ship had sailed from Weymouth, she was comparing herself favorably to Wellington and lamenting the fact she had been born a girl. Now, a soaking, white-faced wretch, she resembled a piece of driftwood cast up on a Scottish shore.

She made straight for the fire in the common room, sat on a stool, and huddled before its crackling warmth. Pride was an awful thing, she thought, slipping off her gloves, holding them to the dancing flames. It could choke you. It could lay in your stomach like a greasy stew until you were praying for death. It could teach you you were not an excellent traveler, venturing across the world without a hair out of place, but an ordinary woman suffering from *mal de mer*.

Within a tiny ship's cabin, Penny's idea of herself had been razed, brick by brick. She was not magic, and she was not a good traveler. Not when she couldn't use her magic to lift herself a fraction of an inch above a muddy road so she never got dirty, to lift herself high above a swelling ship's berth so she never suffered sea sickness, or slightly above the incessant rocking and jarring of a coach so she never felt a moment's discomfort.

A faint thread of her magic had remained alive enough to lead her to Scotland. Penny let the realization sink deep into her bones, searching the crannies of herself for some answering, magical echo. She waited the space of a minute and exhaled roughly, disappointment filled the emptiness and pressed against her throat and eyes. Within her, all was as still as the dish of water laid for her morning wash.

She kissed the top of Fritz's head as he nuzzled her neck. Then, squeezing a measure of water from her cuff, she stood, resolving to remedy the worst of her situation. She was halted by the bang of the door, and the barman, loud enough to be heard over the low drone of voices, calling, "Did you get a good price?"

"Enough," came the answer in a Scots burr to which her ear had not yet become accustomed. "But it was as I feared. Too many cows at the market in a country without enough turnips to keep them. Has the English woman come?"

Penny released Fritz and whipped around. The question had come from a large man shaking rain from his hat.

The innkeeper laughed, his voice carrying. "How am I tae know an English lass? Sour-looking? Helpless? Mean as a hungry stoat? We havenae seen one of those."

A low-answering rumble of laughter washed across the bar, as thick as the fog of tobacco smoke and wet clothing clinging to the dark beams of the room. Penny felt her blush extend to the tips of her ears.

Pride was a wonderful thing, she thought. It could color your cheeks. It could straighten your spine. It could make you stand even if you wanted to sink through the floor.

Fritz pranced at her feet, but Penny would not be moved.

The large man slapped his hat on the bar. "Can I trust her native good sense, d'ya think, to make her way to the inn? She'll drown out there, as like as not."

"Native good sense," the barman repeated with an amused judicial flourish, "There ye have your problem. She's English."

Heads bobbed in accord around the room, punctuated by *aye, aye*.

Penny drew herself up to her not insignificant height and broke in, every vowel drenched in Miss Starling's precise tones. "Is the joke supposed to be I'm too stupid to get out of the rain?"

Her words silenced the room, but the man with the hat unfolded himself from the bar and turned slowly, regarding her with laughing blue eyes. He was several inches taller than she, and that wasn't something most men could boast. Dark brown hair thatched over his forehead as though groomed with a hay rake rather than a comb, and heavy brows flanked two deep grooves above an impressive nose. But, as though nature had decided to mitigate these strong features, there was a dimple set in each cheek even though he was not smiling.

"Miss Starling, I presume?" he asked, and her heart thudded hard to hear the name. To know this would be the first lie she uttered.

"Yes." She crossed an invisible threshold. She was Miss Starling now.

She did not ask his name, and later, when the fright of embarking on her masquerade had dulled, she blamed the lapse on his outerwear. He was dressed in plain, serviceable clothes and sturdy boots. Obviously, he was a farmer or laborer of some kind—selling cows. That's what he'd been speaking of, and she felt the satisfaction of placing him so neatly in his pigeonhole.

His deep blue eyes appraised her, and he lifted his brow. "You're dripping wet." His accent had moderated, smoothing out. Not English sounding, but easier for her. Perhaps it was one he used to speak to his betters. "Did you not think to change?"

Miss Starling. Miss Starling. Miss Starling. What would her old governess say?

Penny could not conceive of Miss Starling being foolish enough to sit even one minute in mud-begrimed clothes when a remedy was at hand.

Penny might not be magic anymore and might be the worst traveler ever to board a ship, but she was the daughter of Sir Charles and Lady Thornton. She was still an heiress and a gentlewoman.

Her chin notched higher. "I'm presentable enough to meet the present company."

A universal grunt of approval by the patron-adjudicators greeted her retort, and she heard the smooth click of a scorekeeping bead slide across a track. Though it was bad form to conduct a conversation within hearing of an entire inn, Penny glowed with triumph. She had scored a hit, and even the dark giant seemed to recognize it.

His blue eyes gleamed. "We look a pair of wet hens," he said, his self-deprecation carrying a barb for her alone. "I know that well enough. You must be freezing."

She opened her mouth to tell him she'd never been toastier in all her life when a hard, betraying shiver shook through her. Imperiousness was a cold refuge, but she would take it.

"You may see to my things while I tidy myself," she said, almost certain a governess would outrank a— Her mind fumbled for an occupational title. Certainly, smooth blue wool would have some authority over rough broadcloth. She crouched down to attend Fritz.

"Excuse me, lads" the man drawled, slowly enough she turned her head. He was sharing a grin with the company. "I have to collect some baggage."

Baggage. How dare he call her such a thing? This time the laughter from the common room was louder.

When the man came closer, he crouched down to scratch the puppy under the chin. She hoped for a moment that Fritz would have the good sense to take the giant's hand off, but the traitorous beast rolled onto his back and presented his belly for more attention.

"Yours?" he asked, directing his astonishingly blue eyes to her face again.

"Yes," she said, settling onto the stool, which brought him closer, and she immediately wished she had remained as she was. "I wrote the people at *Coille na Cyarlin* regarding the conditions of my employment," she said, saying at the name of her future home with more confidence than skill.

"And gave them no chance to reply," was his answer. From here she could see the length of his eyelashes, as long as her little finger was wide. She gave herself a silent scold and looked away. "We've quite a journey ahead of us. You best go on and tidy yourself."

A rosy blush stained her cheeks. "I've recently arrived," she said with the sort of crushing haughtiness she had observed in her mother. It would put this man—hired help, after all—in his place, but it felt like playing dress-up in ill-fitting clothes.

"No time like the present," he answered, more amused than crushed. "I'll order a meal."

He lifted a hand to the innkeeper, and she followed a servant up the stairs. "No time like the present," she muttered as she went.

He'd spoken to her as though she was an ordinary servant. A burble of laughter escaped her lips. She *was* an ordinary servant, and she ought to remember it. This brash man had somehow achieved a position of trust with their employer, Mr Ross, and it would not be wise to antagonize him.

She emerged from the room a short while later, restored in some measure by dry clothing and tidy hair, and was directed to the private room where a simple meal of cold meats, cheese, and bread was laid out. The smell of it pulled her forward. For the first time in more than a week, the thought of food did not turn her stomach.

"We've no time to waste," he said, giving her a cursory look and scooting her chair in with a thump before taking his own seat. Fritz stood from his rug by the fire, shook off his tiredness, and curled at this man's feet.

"I took only a little time," she murmured, buttering her bread, and taking a bite. Her eyes drifted closed. Heaven.

"We leave directly after you've taken some nourishment. There will be no time to titivate yourself with weather like this." Heaven was ruled by an impatient angel.

"I wonder what passes for titivation in Scotland," she said, piling food onto her plate with gusto. "A comb? A washcloth behind the ears?"

He grunted and she smiled at the top of his bent head before tucking in, profoundly thankful she was no longer riding the howling North Sea.

The Scotsman ate with efficiency, casting his knife down when he finished and reached for his ale, his posture communicating a desire to be off and away the moment she wiped her lips.

"Aren't we going to wait for the weather to break before you take me to *Coille na Cyarlin*?"

His features twisted into a grimace. "*Coille na Cyarlin*," he repeated for her benefit, his voice lilting over and into the syllables, giving the name a strange beauty. "If we wait for the weather to soften, we might wait all year."

A rolling clap of thunder and hard gust of wind shook the panes of the window. "More than ten miles in this weather? Are you trying to kill us?"

"Nae. I'm trying to get us home before the snow."

"It is the middle of April, sir." The food in her stomach seemed to rekindle her spirit. "Snow is impossible so late in April."

He gave a grunt and Fritz lifted his jaw for a scratch. Traitor.

The man sat back and regarded her narrowly. "I brought cows down to market and got a fraction of their worth. It was hard frost that killed our turnip crop, and so went the fodder for the cows. It's a backward year, Miss Starling. You must be prepared to expect anything."

Grimly, Penny stood. She lingered long enough to tuck a few more slices of bread into a handkerchief and wished there was a way to bring the pot of marmalade. Soon he had her bundled in a snug gig behind which her trunks were strapped. "Not a coach?" she asked, willing the dismay from her voice. But she evidently hadn't willed it far enough.

"Much too heavy on these roads. You might pray for the horses, however. The wind will be at our back and the hood will protect us from the worst of it."

He placed her snugly under a heavy fur rug and an oil cloth blanket, with Fritz tucked by her feet. She chanced a look into the glowering sky. If she had her magic she could rise above the clouds. There would be no rain there, only wind sailing her along to *Coille na Cyarlin*.

She smiled. In her thoughts, at least, she had achieved some fluency, no longer mangling the name of the house to fit her English ear, but hearing his voice speaking it as it should be.

The carriage dipped, and he inserted his tall frame beside her, lifting the blankets to share them, throwing them into close proximity. She wriggled on the bench, turning to tuck her side more securely.

Laughter rumbled through him. "We can't wage a land war across this bench, Miss Starling. For now, we must be allies." Then he flicked the reins, pulling into the road.

Uneasy allies, she thought, leaning away from the sheer vastness of him, the press of hip and thigh and shoulder. She had never been in such contact with a man—a stranger, and a Scotsman at that—her nerves tightened as she began to pray the horses would grow wings.

Narrow streets gave way to tidy farms, which, in turn, gave way again to long stretches where there was nothing to be seen but a few sheep, and a distant, lighted window. The wind buffeted the hood and darkened the skies, but she was surprised to realize the Scotsman was warm and solid, reassuring.

"You know I am the new governess?" she asked, lifting her voice above the groaning of the wind.

"Aye." The man was laughing again, heaven only knew why.

"Can you tell me about the children? I don't suppose you have much to do with them."

"Oh, I see the children. Everyday."

Perhaps he gave them riding lessons. It seemed rude to ask when she hadn't bothered to before.

"Ewan is the oldest. He's eight. Then Robbie is seven, and little Kathleen is four. You'll not be expected to teach her."

"Your master?" she asked. If this man had pronounced himself her ally, she was going to get something out of it. Papa would approve of such strategic thinking. "What is he like?"

Did she imagine his hands stilled on the reins? "Bit of a lad, really, with his easy manners and dashing good looks."

"Oh," she croaked, the future spilling out beyond her reach like a tangled skein of yarn. She had not figured a lecherous employer into her calculations. "I imagined him differently."

"How so, Miss Starling?"

"You won't tell?"

"Upon my honor, it will never leave this carriage."

Good enough. "I thought he would be a sober, dour sort of gentleman. Scotsmen have that reputation, you know." He nodded gravely, inviting her confidence. "The letter said that he needed someone trustworthy and I thought—"

"*Are* you trustworthy, Miss Starling?" His lips had twitched, but it was the wrong question to put her at ease. Asking about trust. Calling her by a false name. Guilt seeped through to her bones.

"The children will be safe in my hands."

They travelled a distance before he said. "You're not what he will expect either."

A shiver of apprehension shook her. "What does he expect?"

The man's eyes twinkled, and he transferred the reins to one hand, slipping his other into the front of his coat, drawing out a missive, flicking it open. The skies were dark, and it was difficult to make out the words over his arm. "My cousin Margaret wrote that you were—" He peered more closely at the page as a slow-dawning horror began to overtake Penny. What had she said at the inn? With an anxious swallow she began to pick over their first meeting. A thin crust of nausea crystalized in her stomach. Lord. She had been horribly impertinent, saying such things. A fresh wave of embarrassment broke against her skin.

"Let's see," he continued. "Highly competent, educated, and able to manage yourself under any circumstances. I thought I was getting a combination of Joan of Arc, Flora MacDonald, and Mary, the mother of Christ." He paused for a moment, expressing his doubts more eloquently than an accusation. "I thought you would be a good deal older than you are."

Penny shut her eyes for a moment. She would crawl into a hole but could not imagine one dark enough or deep enough to hide her mortification. Not even if she dug all the way to China.

"You're Mr Ross," she said, taking sanctuary in the accusation. "You knew all along that I thought you were—"

"I make it a habit," he laughed, "of stepping off the road when the English are riding by on their cocky high horse, Miss Starling."

Malcolm Ross flicked the reins once more and Penny wracked her memory for a time when Miss Starling had allowed herself the joy of delivering a set-down. The more she wracked the less happy she became. There were no such examples. Miss Starling served at the whim of the rich and powerful. It was likely she never answered back.

Penny dipped her head and took a composing breath. "I am sorry, sir."

He turned a laughing glance at her. "You are not. And I am not, either. I dare say we will laugh at this, by and by."

"By and by," she muttered. "You're laughing now."

The dimples on his cheeks deepened. "Let it be some relief to you that I've never been one to chase women around the furniture, begging for a kiss. You'll be safe with me."

Even in the dim light she could see the twinkle of amusement in his eyes and spent the next quarter of an hour practicing Mama's exceptionally good posture and wondering if she could afford to hate him with every fiber of her being. She had to abandon such thoughts when the apocalyptic skies screamed for attention.

Mr Ross gave the horses a sharp whistle as thunder rumbled across the sky and through her chest. The horses strained to pull the light carriage through the tenacious mud while, at her feet, she pressed Fritz's flanks with her boots, nestling him securely in place even as the wind swirled from every direction, ripping the front edge of the hood from its metal frame.

This was no time for propriety. She dove into the cavity between Mr Ross and the bench and he leaned forward, making more room, shielding her at his own expense. The oil cloth loosened, flapping in the gale, and he reached for it, tucking it around her hips. She burrowed into his considerable bulk, wrapping her arms around his chest and holding on for dear life. With each turn of the wheels, they rose higher into the hills, raindrops pinging the damaged hood of the carriage like icy grapeshot.

When she began to think the journey would never end, a shard of lightning broke from the sky, followed by a crack of thunder. She shot upright and watched as a large tree fell across their path. A scream tore from her throat as the thick branches bit into the road, tumbling toward them. The horses reared and plunged and Mr Ross sawed at the reins, the carriage lurching out of the way and slithering sideways to a stop.

"We can't go on like this," she shouted, raising her voice against the rough wind. Her heart was beating out of her chest. He put an arm around her shoulders, pulling her lips to his ear and she repeated, "We have to stop."

He shifted and then it was his lips to her ear, wrapping her in warmth. "There's a cottage ahead."

She nodded, feeling the unexpected scratch of his whiskers against her skin, feeling amused at the primness, long-abandoned now, that made her worry about sharing a close carriage bench with the man. When he released her, she did not hesitate to wrap her arms around him once more, pressing her face against his shoulder and inhaling the comforting scent of tobacco.

His hand covered hers for a moment, she thought, and returned there often as he continued the harrowing drive.

As had been her habit for many years, her mind turned to her magic, looking for a way to aid him. She would hold onto the carriage and lift the entire load a few precious inches, easing their way around obstacles. *A leaf in a stream. Champagne bubbles.* There was nothing. She could not even lift herself.

She felt the uneven jolt of the carriage moving across uneven ground and the icy splash of accumulated rain as they pushed through an overgrown track.

When they stopped, she unwound from her employer's person to see a simple shepherd's hut and tumbledown stable, nestled in a grove of trees. Mr Ross jumped down to push the doors of the rough stable open, and though she missed his warmth, she did not wait for his return to lift the reins and steer the carriage through the doors.

In a moment the wind was extinguished. She heard the flick of a flint and a weak light filled the space, taking on a warmer glow as he found a lantern.

"Is this Scotland, then?" she said, turning exhausted, eyes to him. The ghost of a laugh escaped her.

He raked his fingers through his hair. "It's our protection against foreign invaders. We greet them with a squall, and they run away to softer lands," he chuckled, reaching up to swing her from the carriage.

His hands spanned her waist, and as she gripped his shoulders an odd warmth seemed to bloom under her fingertips. Her eyes widened, but before she could explore or categorize the sensation, he stepped away quickly.

Chapter Four

The girl sneezed and Malcolm lifted his head. “We should get you into the cottage.” He reached for the oil cloth to shelter her, but she stopped him in those precise English tones.

“I shall need my trunk. The one on the bottom.”

A shadow of a smile passed over his face. Though she knew now who he was, she hadn’t stopped giving orders. With frozen fingers he unstrapped the trunk and swung it from the carriage, not bothering with the oil cloth.

She raced at his heels, ducking under the tails of his long coat, the little dog behind her.

“I have to see to the horses,” he reminded her, before she could order him to build a fire and forage food for her dog. He set down the trunk with a thump, glancing at her dubiously, and cast his gaze around the rough room, ice-cold and gray with cobwebs already sticking to his face. This one would demand to return to the docks at first light, unless he missed his guess, carrying tales of the heathen Scots back to England.

He took his time with the animals, digging out clean straw and rubbing them dry as he sang a low, calming song. He fought through the rain again, prepared to do such service for Miss Starling as she needed to calm her skittish nerves and settle her.

As the door swung back, he saw a glow filling the room. His mouth tightened in surprise. The English girl had managed a good deal more than he expected. She was not standing stock still terrified in the dark. A well-laid fire burned in the hearth and in the corner a pile of refuse lay beside a half-broken broomstick. Bisecting the room, a long piece of twine stretched from one wall to the other and on it hung three petticoats and the gown she had been wearing that morning.

Miss Starling glanced up from the low stool as her dog sniffed interesting things in the crannies of the floor.

"You made a fire," he said stupidly.

"There was a broken chair," she answered. "I dashed it to pieces."

His face must have registered surprise because she turned her eyes up to him and notched up an eyebrow. "Don't you remember? Educated, able to manage myself in difficult circumstances."

He startled himself with a laugh. When he had set out this morning to collect an Englishwoman, he had not expected her to contain even an ounce of good humor.

While she prodded the fire, he settled on the floor and found himself examining the young woman more closely. She had pleasant features, if not precisely beautiful. Picked out against the firelight, he noted the sweetly curving lips, a pointed chin, and curling hair that looked to be fair—reddish. Her brows were mobile, arching delicately, but when an answer displeased her, they tended to descend swiftly, ordering themselves into straight, determined lines. Her grey eyes were glowing crescents when she smiled, as she was doing now. All in all, her expressions were so absorbing he could not keep his eyes from following them.

She swung a battered pot over the fire, the flames picking up the amber lights in her hair. Miss Starling was young, for all her imperious ways. Why had she agreed to come all the way to Scotland? The letter from his cousin failed to mention the reason.

He leaned forward, arms resting on bent legs. "Dare I hope that contains a hearty stew?"

"You can hope all you like." Again, her mouth curved into a smile before twisting apologetically. "But you'll be far happier if you prepare for the inevitability of tea."

"Really?" he asked, brightening. "Where on earth did you find tea?"

"I brought some in my trunk."

"Then I want tea."

"What luck," she smiled. "I have toast, too, if you're not particular about the shape." She turned and presented a couple of lumpy pieces of bread, skewered on sticks, handing him one. "You must hold it to the flame if you want to crisp it up. If yours drops in the fire, I'm not sharing."

He smiled, toasting his bread over the fire, listening to the comfortable hiss and crackle of it. The children dreaded her coming.

He had dreaded it. Perhaps they had been too hasty. He dug into his pocket and exhumed a pipe, showing it to her with a lift of his brows.

She nodded and he packed the bowl of tobacco, lit it, and drew smoke. They were in a world quite their own, and the little dog paced to his side, setting his head into Malcolm's lap. Malcolm broke off a piece of toast and gave it to the beast, looking up to encounter her clear, keen eyes.

A faint reverberation went through his chest like the ring of a bell, echoing on and on and then he blinked, pushing that feeling—at once familiar and unwelcome—away from him.

He cleared his throat. "You are quite young to be abroad in the world, Miss Starling," he observed, his tone kindly, disinterested.

"Nineteen," she answered, "this year. I know my job, Mr Ross. You needn't worry."

Ten years his junior, he thought, immediately measuring her against himself. Nine years younger than Jean would have been. He pulled on the pipe and thought of her scampering around with the children if she gained their trust. He felt old.

"Was it always your ambition to become a governess?"

Her brows leveled above her soft grey eyes, and her hair, escaping from her braided bun, formed a fuzzy halo around her head. "That's a silly question. Show me the woman who dreams of being a governess."

"Then what did you dream of becoming?"

Her answer was silence and then he heard the creak of the hinged arm over the fire. She lifted the teapot from the hook and set it on the hearth with more care than needed.

"Hand me those mugs," she directed. He brought then down, and she used the hem of her skirt to dust them out. Then she poured him hot, sugarless tea and he held the earthenware mug in his hands, feeling the warmth seep into his skin.

"Can you tell me about *Coille na Cyarlin*?" she asked.

Malcolm's lips twitched. She had stopped saying *Call-ee na Cyarlin* and was attempting to mimic his own speech. It came out as *Cullyeh na Cyarlin*. Close, but the girl had a thick English tongue and still mangled the sound of it. He kept his corrections to himself, recognizing a desire not to wound her feelings. He recognized, too, he was no longer certain she would run away home as soon as she could.

"What does it mean?" She dipped a bit of toast into her tea and gobbled it down.

"It means Woods of the Witch."

Her brows rose and he waved a hand to stave off her interest. Too late. "Don't let the children be telling you we're haunted. We are *not* haunted."

"Your defensiveness has roused my suspicions." Her mouth curved and he dragged his eyes away from it, focusing on scratching the dog behind the ears.

"Is that why you had to send for a governess from England? No one who speaks Scottish Gaelic would come?"

"The name is harmless enough. We've a stand of old forest on the property and it pleased my great-grandfather to choose a suitably spooky name. I cannae blame a woman for being afraid of witches."

She leaned forward, resting her head on the folded arms crossing her knees. She yawned. "Not all witches want to gobble up little children. Not all magic is black."

"A sensible outlook," he said, clinking his mug against hers.

Their glances held long enough that it was a relief when a shutter banged open. He hastened from his seat and closed the window, stuffing the crack with a rag.

"Snow," he said, returning to the fire, plucking his travelling blanket from a heap on the floor and laying it near the hearth. "This will be for you."

She nodded and yawned again, taking it as her right she should be warm and protected while he was cold and watchful.

Stretching out long arms, she stood and then saw to the business of her drying petticoats, turning them over and arranging them more closely to the flames. Malcolm kicked a spot near the wall free of leaves and debris and settled down, crossing his booted feet, tugging his waistcoat, and crossing his arms over his chest. It was bound to be a miserable night, he thought as he watched Miss Starling settle near the fire with hooded eyes, making out the gentle curves of her hip and shoulder.

Who was the real Miss Starling? The imperious lass who ordered him about, or the gamine dipping bread in her tea? Would Robbie be safe in her hands? The thought turned his blood cold.

If only Jean hadn't died, began the familiar litany. He had been walking through a wilderness since she went, searching for answers, holding his small family together with the rough tools a man could yield. If only the previous governess had been as kindly as she looked. If only he hadn't made such a muck up. The list of regrets piled like snowflakes into a heavy drift.

He sighed, the sound hardly carrying to his ears, and another litany began. He could not change what was past. He could not mourn over it still. It was time, and then some, to accept things as they were.

Things as they were. An estate in the throes of an endless winter. Three children who seemed to shoot up every time he poked his head into the nursery. Work to fill his days. It was enough. Enough. He had no reason to look back.

The image of Jean rose unbidden. There would be no recovering what he lost.

Near the fire, Miss Starling began to snore gently, scattering the ghosts who haunted him. He smiled at the sound and drifted off to sleep.

Malcolm woke to a nudge at his shoulder. A mug of tea was thrust into his hands before he was fully aware of Miss Starling's form bending over him.

"Good morning, sir," she called brightly, already retreating. He scowled, every muscle stiff as he staggered upright, glancing at the crack in the window.

"A light wind, but the snow is melting."

Her petticoats were already folded away, and she'd combed her hair into order, re-braiding and coiling the mass to present a neat appearance. What did it look like down?

She stood winding the long piece of string around her hand and elbow. Then, tucking it into her trunk, she turned expectantly.

"You carry twine as well as tea, Miss Starling?" he asked, tossing back the last of the tea and setting the mug out for another traveler. "Exactly how uncivilized did you expect us to be?"

She looked around the room, at the cottage, which looked more tumbledown and neglected than it had by firelight and raised her brow. "A woman of sense prepares herself for any eventuality."

"There it is," he grinned, brushing past her and swinging the case over his shoulder, enjoying the momentary puzzlement on her face.

"I wasn't certain you were fit to be a governess but if you have a ready store of platitudes..."

She followed him into the chilly morning with a chuckle. "You want a good deal of correction, Mr Ross."

"I'm sure you're the governess to do it, Miss Starling," he answered, his voice low, his eyes watching for his words to land in her ear and watching, too, for the planes and features of her lively face to reflect some new emotion. It was like setting a rush light to a well-laid fire and seeing it catch the kindling and burn brightly.

He turned to strap the trunk on the carriage, occupying his hands. This was not flirting, only a wee bit of wordplay. The will to tease a response in a lass's laughing eyes had died with his wife. One could not rake over coals so cold.

They set off, bundled up as before, but the weather did not require her to shelter against his back and he found he missed the contact. Instead of the straightforward route he'd hoped for, they encountered washed out roads, wind blowing like a rapier from the north, more downed trees, and a miles-long detour through the narrow river valley. It was near dusk when they came to the outer boundaries of his land.

There he slowed the carriage and hopped to the ground, kneeling with one knee in the slush to roll the cold earth in his hand and cast it down. Almost May and there was snow. This weather would ruin him.

He returned to the carriage, and Miss Starling took a fortifying breath as her gaze roamed over his mud daubed trousers, gamely lifting the oil cloth for him. He tucked both sides around her.

"This is what passes for titivation in Scotland," he said with a wink.

"You will forget my impertinence," she commanded.

"I doubt that," he replied, liking the way her lips pursed when she did not get her way.

It was not long before he spotted the house at last, rising out of a broad, tree-lined meadow to meet them. Great-grandfather had commissioned a building in the Palladian style, and with all its uncompromising symmetry and sharp angles, it presented a forbidding and austere aspect in the fading light. Still, he loved the old place.

"Welcome to *Coille na Cyarlin*," he said, pulling up before the entrance and dropping from his seat to help her from the carriage, careful this time to offer her a steadying hand instead of swinging her down in his arms.

She tilted her head back as Fritz relieved himself on a grassy verge. Her probing gaze ran all over the house. She chewed on her lip, her brows in a thoughtful line.

"There's a garden around the back," he went on, explaining away the austerity as though a governess needed to be impressed.

"*Coille na Cyarlin*," she said, still not getting it right. "I expected something with turrets and moats."

He laughed. "I'm certain ghosts would be more interested in it if we had a moat. I told you there wasn't a speck of magic in it." He expected her to laugh with him, but she only nodded, her mouth pinching on one side.

Was she disappointed? Before he could ask, his housekeeper burst from the front doors.

"Naughty boy," she exclaimed with all the familiarity of an old nanny.

For all her tiredness, Miss Starling suddenly grinned up at him, devilment in her eyes. "Are you in trouble?" she whispered gleefully.

"We thought you might be dead," Birdie said, reaching up to kiss his cheek, scrubbing it away briskly. "We were wondering what delayed you, Master Malcolm. Oh, you look dreadful."

Surely, Miss Starling found this hilarious, but Malcolm did not chance a look at her. Within the shadow of *Coille na Cyarlin*, he seemed to be once more absorbed in its conventions and virtues. A man of this house would not share smiles with a young woman under his roof.

He trained his eyes up the stairs, straightening his waistcoat and began calling out orders to the assembling footmen as he went into the house. "See to the governess's baggage and see that Miss Starling has all she needs to be comfortable. Have the children gone to bed?"

He left the girl far behind, striding to his own rooms where his valet held open the door, and felt his servant's troubled examination as he passed.

"Have a tray sent up," he ordered, "and I'll retire."

"A tray and a bath," the valet amended.

Tiredness rolled between his shoulders like a grist mill, grinding him into a fine powder, but he steeped in the bath and let his mind wander. Little surprise his thoughts returned again and again to Miss Starling. The strange day and night he and the English girl weathered together had blurred the lines between governess and guest. Between landed gentleman and hired help.

With a sigh he slipped between the sheets. They had returned to the world as it was, the lines must be drawn and redrawn between them until the sound of her gentle snoring sending him off to sleep last night faded from his ears.

He woke to find Robbie digging through his bed sheets, rolling him out of the warm, soft cocoon so the boy might take his place. "Morning, *Athair*," he said.

Malcolm yawned, making a little room for the knobs and elbows of his middle child. "Morning, Rob."

"You were gone a long time." Robbie's hand stroked Malcolm's scratchy chin like a cow rubbing her long belly along the rough slats of her pen. "Are we doing anything fun today?"

"I brought the governess back from Edinburgh."

Malcolm felt the little body tense and he reached for his son, holding him so close that the tightness was absorbed into his arms and Robbie's body relaxed again.

"I don't need to know my letters, *Athair*. Not if I join the Navy."

"Captains have to write out the ship's logs, Rob. Sailors have to write letters home. Try another one."

The lad would. Tomorrow he would come wriggling under the covers, talking of another occupation that prized illiteracy and ignorance. Thus far he had been disappointed by the scope of careers requiring him to make sense of the letters which skipped like crickets on a page.

Malcolm slipped from bed, sending a glance out the high window frowning at the view–grey skies, heavy clouds, and biting wind. Not weather fit to sow delicate seeds, but they must get the crop into the ground soon. He whacked the counterpane lightly. "It's time we were up, Rob. We have to teach Miss Starling our ways."

Robbie's muffled voice came from under a mountain of blankets. "Will you be close by?"

Malcolm heaved a breath. "Aye."

Chapter Five

When Malcolm Ross strode off without a backward look, Penny fought the urge to throw something at his head. It wasn't the bad weather or even having to doss down in a ramshackle cottage overnight that had worn on her nerves—she had experienced less than ideal circumstances more than once on her travels. No, it was the house. The obviously-not-magical house. She cast a look over the relentlessly severe lines and tried to feel any scrap of magic—tried to find a spring of enchantment trickling from between those closely fitted stones.

Damn and damn. A folded square of paper in her mother's hand had given her a stronger sense of magic than this.

"Not good enough for ye, Miss Starling?" Birdie snapped, and Penny blinked, scrubbing her face of disappointment and confusion.

"No, ma'am. It's grand."

"Come along, then." The woman trotted up the steps at a good clip and Penny scooped Fritz into her arms dashing after her. At the door, the woman spun.

"You're not bringing the dog."

"I am—" she began.

"Nae. He'll be taken to the stables."

A vivid scarlet vision of the last time Fritz was in a stable rose before Penny and residual panic made her voice come out in a croak. "Fritz will stay with me, in my quarters."

Mrs Birdie planted her fists on her hips and gave a snort. "Your quarters? No, miss. There are no dogs given leave to come inside the house. The master will not allow—"

"But he did," Penny declared, sounding unequivocal even though the master had said no such thing. With these lies, she was overseeing the construction of her mansion in hell, brick by brick. What a fine, sprawling residence it would be. "It was part of the contract."

Mrs Birdie turned and snorted again. “Contract,” she muttered, jerking her head as a sign that Penny must follow. She found herself in a spacious hall with nary a cobweb or broadsword in sight.

One of Papa’s diplomatic tactics was winning over locals, undercutting the natural disadvantage of fighting on enemy territory. She employed it now, asking brightly, “How long have you been the housekeeper here, Mrs Birdie?”

Another snort and the woman turned on the stair tread. “No. Just Birdie.”

There was nothing for it but to shut her mouth and pray for deliverance as the housekeeper led her up two flights of stairs, each narrower and less ornate than the last, and then down a long hall to her quarters.

Penny took in the spare, clean room with a narrow bed, side table, wash basin, and window. She turned to Birdie with a rueful smile. “Fritz can’t stay here all day.”

Birdie offered a clipped nod. “He will remain in the stable yard and join you after the children are finished with their instruction.”

That would do. Penny smiled and pivoted in the small space and peeled off her gloves. “What I wouldn’t do for a bath.”

An icy silence cloaked the room and Penny glanced over her shoulder. “Mr Ross did say he wished me to be comfortable,” she clarified. Helpfully.

The housekeeper’s eyes widened still further. “A bath,” she said, pressing a hand to her bosom. “Noo bath,” she intoned, pressing hard on the “o” as though it was a stubborn button being worked through a tiny hole. The sound seemed to make a word that meant more than *no*. “You’ll get a pitcher of hot water and a towel. A girl will fetch it for you in the morning.”

Penny, remembering Papa’s diplomacy, nodded. “Thank you. That will be lovely,” Penny said, feeling herself a step nearer saintliness and perfect self-denial.

Birdie went on. “The nursery is two doors down and there’s the schoolroom betwixt. In the morning, I’ll escort you to the master,” she said, making way for the footmen who bumped through the door with her cases.

“Your meals will be brought to the schoolroom on a tray, morning and evening, as well as midday tea.”

“I’m not to join the rest of the staff in the kitchen?”

"We're not half grand enough for a fancy English governess, Miss Starling," Birdie said, lifting her nose as she went through the door.

Penny was relieved when a tray arrived and she consumed her meal in silence, breaking apart a bun for Fritz. *If Mama could see her now.*

Penny shivered, divesting herself from her dress and going to work to put a few things to rights. The task distracted her for a time, but when her head touched the pillow and she was perfectly still on the narrow bed, thoughts that had been held at bay rushed in. She had disappeared into the wilds of Scotland and nobody knew where she was. The thought, which ought to be reassuring, brought a current of fear. She was on her own.

"Not for long," she whispered, and Fritz raised his head and set it down again. She was fine. In the morning she would set about to discover some lead to her magic—reading what she could, putting her hand to everything in the house she could, waiting for that wellspring within to move as it had in her gymnasium—and, before too many days had passed, she would find the whole of it. She was fine. Still, warm tears trickled onto Fritz, tucked up under her chin.

When morning came, before she opened her eyes, Penny could hear the rain beating on the glass of her small window. Her gaze lit on the twine that ran in a diagonal across the room, fashioned into a makeshift drying line for her petticoats. Mama always told her not to travel without a bit of string. Of course, Mama had always meant it to be an anchor when she slept—a small cord to keep her from floating.

No need of that now. *Soon.*

A knock sounded on the door, revealing a maid with a basin of water. Penny allowed the girl to take Fritz away and set herself to washing with brisk efficiency, dipping her cloth in the clean water, scrubbing at the grime of travel and rinsing it into a waiting basin. She bared each limb in its turn, covering it quickly as it dried, and though this method cleaned her well enough, she felt a childish wish to stomp her heels against the floor until she was given the sinful extravagance of a German spa.

That would not bring back her magic.

Penny put her hair up into a knot, taming her curls with abundant hairpins, racing through her preparations with thorough economy.

When Birdie knocked on her door, Penny was able to present a serene picture in a dark blue wool dress, whose military braiding under the bust had been neatly removed to reflect her new station. She followed the housekeeper through the halls and asked gently, "Did you sleep well, Birdie?"

"I have no sins to keep me awake."

Penny's smiling mouth set, but she tried again. "How is Mr Ross this morning?"

"You'll see for yourself, soon enough, and be meeting Mrs Stuart, too."

"She is…?"

"The master's mother-in-law."

Penny nodded briskly, her curious mind probing for a polite question. "Is Mrs Stuart a guest or a member of the household?"

Birdie turned down the final stairs. "She's family," was her answer, the broad Scots accent kicking up. "And that's the long and the short of it. You make peace with Elspeth Stuart and you've made peace with Malcolm Ross." Birdie turned a mulish eye on Penny. "He would be better if he hadn't fetched an Englishwoman from Edinburgh for the better part of two days. He must've been up all night when you were out in the wilds."

Penny clamped her lips shut. Malcolm Ross hadn't been awake the whole night long. If she closed her eyes, she could still see his long legs crossed at the ankle and his dark head tipped to his chest. She could still feel the warmth of his hand on hers.

"At least he slept last night."

"Robbie won't let him sleep for long," Birdie stated with a smile so soft Penny halted for a moment. The gorgon had a weakness.

"Robbie," Penny trotted forward. "The middle child."

Birdie shot her another unaccountable scowl and stopped by a door, scratching the surface of it lightly.

A deep voice sounded from within, and Penny lifted her chin as the door swung wide. Warm air greeted her, mixing with the cool air at her back, pushing her forward into the dark, paneled library where Mr Ross stood by the mantel regarding her with the polite, distant eyes of a stranger. No dimples grooved his cheeks. His eyes held no ready wink. He was not laughing at her pretensions.

He no longer looked like a laborer either, He filled the room with his freshly shaven face and dark blue coat, the image of a civilized country gentleman. Well, not entirely civilized. His hair, she decided, was too long in the front, thatching across his forehead. Her fingers itched to comb it into order.

She held his gaze until his glance darted away and he indicated a figure sitting near the fire, her back bowed under a shawl, hands knotted with the telltale cords of rheumatism resting in her lap.

"Elspeth, may I introduce you to Miss Starling, who promises to save us from simple-mindedness and stupor." Penny's eyes narrowed reprovingly. "Miss Starling, the children's grandmother, Mrs Stuart."

Penny dipped a curtsey worthy of an archduchess. "Ma'am."

Mrs Stuart pursed her lips and stared so long that Penny wanted to fidget and apologize for some imagined crime, stopping herself with a sharp reminder that she, like the true Miss Starling, was educated and qualified.

Organize your face, Penny. Put away the young girl hungry to remember her lost magic. Sweep aside loss and grief. By infinitesimal changes, she adjusted her expression to one of benign inquiry.

"She's young," Elspeth Stuart accused, her strong voice at odds with her frail figure. She had dark hair streaked with brilliant silver, and her eyes were a deep pansy brown. Her jaw was square, and she looked at Penny as though she was a rock to be inspected for flaws under a jeweler's loupe.

"Yes ma'am. Almost nineteen."

"Heaven help us," Mrs Stuart muttered, "Are you untried too?"

"Elspeth." Mr Ross gave a gentle rebuke.

Penny smiled. Barely. "I'm perfectly willing to offer you a mathematics demonstration, or to translate a French text into English or German. My Latin is regrettably spotty, but good enough for an eight-year-old boy."

"We were hoping for someone—" Mrs Stuart tilted her head one way and then the other before exhaling audibly. "Malcolm?"

"I am convinced our Miss Starling is highly-competent, educated—"

Penny tossed him a frown and she caught a fleeting dimple brushing his cheek. The heavy cloak woven of fear and worry lifted a little.

He drew a chair forward and she sat.

“Mrs Stuart and I hope to see you succeed with the children,” he said, “but there is something we need to address. A request we would ask of you.”

Request. Penny’s gaze shifted. “Better tell me at once.”

“When you instruct Ewan and Robbie, Mrs Stuart will be your companion in the schoolroom.”

“Pardon?” Penny’s brow steepled. Her own governess had ruled the schoolroom like it was a minor kingdom, entitled its own natural rights and dignities. Her parents would no more have thought of intruding on the lessons than they would have thought of declaring war on a neighboring estate.

Mrs Stuart did not waste her breath going over the same ground twice. “If my health does not permit me to sit with you, you will administer lessons under the guidance of the nursemaid.”

Penny held up her hand and felt anxiety unspooling in her abdomen. Elspeth was going to watch her be a governess. Yes, Penny knew the necessary things she must do, but there would be no rehearsals, no going over lines and getting them right before the audience would be brought in to judge the performance.

Penny’s thoughts spun. If Mama had known of Penny’s charade and approved of it, she might tell Penny to stand on her dignity and refuse. Papa would say that every offer contained the seeds of a satisfactory negotiation.

“Why?” Penny blurted, choosing neither negotiation nor dignity. She breathed through her nose, releasing her next words calmly. “I mean to say, shouldn’t a governess have a free hand if she is to build a rapport with the children?”

There was an acrid taste coating her mouth that came with the knowledge she didn’t care about building rapport and being a governess. Not really. It was magic she wanted.

Mrs Stuart tugged the shawl closer to her body. “Building rapport is your own business, Miss Starling. Protecting the children is mine.”

“Protecting them from me?”

The answer came like a shot. “Aye.”

Penny felt the rough edges of doubt scrape across her tender skin. This house was a block of uncompromising stone and the people in it made of flint. The skies were cold and leaden She’d spent days being assaulted by gales of wind and rain and snow. How, in heaven's name could there be magic in this dismal, joyless place? To be watched as closely as she would be, how would she have a spare moment to find it?

She turned inward, searching like a miser along the familiar tracks of her magic, desperate for some confirmation she had done right to uproot herself and follow a fading trail to Scotland. Nothing.

"Am I to know why I am to have a warder?"

"Warder is too harsh a word, Miss Starling." He smiled at his mother-in-law and leaned forward, lacing his fingers together. "Elspeth will be your guardian."

The smile sent a pang through Penny, a sharp reminder that she was his employee now and the easy companionship that had arisen in the shepherd's cottage had been put away. He would smile at Mrs Stuart, but not at a mere hireling.

"Have I given you any reason to mistrust me?" she asked, speaking before she remembered she was here because of lies. In time she would accustom herself to the sick rush of guilt that occurred when she spoke them. Not yet.

Mr Ross ran a tired hand through his hair. He stood and leaned against the mantel. "Did you not wonder why I was so anxious for a trustworthy governess, Miss Starling? Why I would go to a good deal of effort to secure one?"

She flushed, dropping her gaze into her lap.

"Our last governess, a woman who claimed much experience, came to us on the recommendation of a kinswoman. We accepted that recommendation and did not look further."

"She always had a smile for me," Elspeth muttered. "I should have slapped it off her face."

Penny's eyes widened.

There was no disapproval in Malcolm Ross's answering grunt. "I gave her what you termed 'a free hand.' It was a mistake I willnae make again. My boys have not been the same since." His words, so softly spoken, opened up deep, treacherous gullies of meaning.

Penny inhaled sharply.

"It should not surprise you," Mrs Stuart said, "to know that our sex is as capable of cruelty as the other."

Penny shook her head from side to side. "I wouldn't—"

Mr Ross's hand sliced across the air, silencing them both. His voice was firm. "I don't know what you're capable of, Miss Starling, and I don't intend to find out. Will you accept Elspeth in the schoolroom as a condition of your employment, or will I ready the carriage?"

"You should have written, waited for my reply—"

His eyes glinted. "You arrived too quickly for the niceties to be ironed out, Miss Starling. May I remind you, you didn't wait for a letter before bringing your dog."

"She has a dog, too?" Elspeth exclaimed. "For the love of Queen Mary's wig."

"We'll keep him away from Rob," Mr Ross assured, turning back to Penny with a question still unanswered.

Penny's brows knit. "I'm sorry for the trouble you've had."

"But—?" he prodded.

"But don't be surprised if the children don't take to me. They'll know you don't trust me and won't give it themselves."

Mr Ross gave her face an all-over look, weighing her up. "Have I set you an impossible task? Do you want to run away?"

Why did it sound like he was daring her?

He went on. "If the children prove too much for you, I will send you home at once, no bitterness on either side. I would not blame you."

The words were generously spoken, and she allowed herself to imagine the day of rough travel into Edinburgh, waiting at an inn for the right ship, followed by a terrible week of sailing home. She could be back in Dorset before the fortnight was out. Safe. Comfortable. Away from these people who looked at her like she was a worm inching in from the garden.

Mama and Papa wouldn't know she hadn't gone to her sister's house. She could join Beatrice or bury herself at Thorndene. It was a comfortable picture but there was no hope of magic in either of those places. Not even the tiniest tug. But here...

She dredged up the feeling of that paper against her palm, the inexplicable longing that had invaded her bones when Mama had turned it over in her hands and spoken of the Scottish widower and the three young children living far away in the north. She wanted to curl herself around that feeling, protecting it like a flame in a gust of wind. That was her task. To get the feeling again—get it and keep it. If she could manage that, then she would be herself again.

She smoothed her skirts. “I look forward to having your company, Mrs Stuart. Perhaps you could assist me by giving the children their lessons.”

Mrs Stuart sat up as straight as she could in her chair, the knots of her knuckles rubbed under the palm of her hand. “I cannae teach them what I do not know,” she stated. “If you are, as Malcolm says, an educated young woman, you can get the job done.”

“We are decided, then?” he confirmed. “You are staying?”

Penny gave a nod.

“Thank you.” Mr Ross straightened. “Will you come meet the children?” he asked, reaching for her hand and lifting her to her feet.

As their fingers touched, a thin veil of magic settled upon her skin, as delicate as mist over the meadows. She looked up with startled eyes, but he was already striding from the room, unaware that the confirmation she sought had come to her at last. A smile brushed against her lips.

There you are. Magic. Despite the austere symmetry and the flat grey stones, there *was* magic at *Coille na Cyarlin.*

Chapter Six

Penny tripped along after Mr Ross even as hope welled in her throat. Magic was here. She wanted to stop and shout it to the rafters. She blinked away the threatening tears and tried to feel it again, scrambling up the staircases. Of course, it wasn't to be felt. The magic was shy, and indistinct as a soft cloud and as easily burned away. But it was here.

"Sir," she called, turning after him on the final flight. "There is an amendment I wish to make to our agreement."

He halted on the stair, a hand curled around the carved bannister and looked down.

She meant to be ladylike and deferential toward him, but, added to her other sins, she was not made for meekness. If she must make her home in this dismal house, coaxing her magic from the shadows, she would have to make herself as comfortable as possible.

"Why did I think that was the end of it?" He pinched the bridge of his nose.

"You called it an impossible task," she said, taking great liberties with his meaning, "teaching the children, but having no authority."

"Did I?" he answered mildly.

She stepped up to his stair and then stepped up again, putting her eyes level with his. "I would like the children to know, within reason, the schoolroom is my domain. You could help with this. First impressions matter."

His brow lifted, and she nodded her head with such vehemence one of the locks sprung loose from her topknot and brushed against the back of her neck. "For instance, when you first saw me, I was shivering by the fire. It hardly helped to establish a proper footing between us when I was so desperate and alone."

She twisted the curl up around her finger and probed her hair for a pin, pulling it free and securing the wayward lock by pressing it back again. Though his expression did not change, she felt his eyes take in the swift movement of her arms bent over her head and she flushed.

"Desperate and alone," he scoffed. "No, Miss Starling. You were never that. Even sopping wet you did not present such a pitiful sight."

She shook her head. "Though I accept Mrs Stuart's...companionship, I would ask that the decisions in the schoolroom be left to me."

"I will tell Elspeth to stay out of your way." His hand sketched an apology. "We've not had much luck with governesses here, but you gave me an opportunity to see your true character out there in the storm. We will learn to trust you, I wager."

Her true character. That was twisting the knife. She had done nothing but lie to him from the moment they met.

She gave a short laugh. "I'm not certain you will, if those moments were evidence of my true character. I order everyone about and like my own way." Cold and lost and without her mother's moderating influence, it had been difficult to remember to be mannerly and kind.

"Resourceful, uncomplaining, and prepared for upsetting circumstances, too."

She looked up, a little surprised at the pleasure which flooded through her at his words. He could be forgiven for using his position to cut her down to size, but he wasn't doing that at all.

He glanced up the stairs when a sudden burst of noise descended upon them, young voices coming from the nursery. These were her charges. She tried to pick out the sounds and make sense of each voice.

"Scared?" her employer asked.

Terrified. Penny had always been at home in the company of adults, tagging along after older sisters for much of her childhood, interacting with babies and children only during nursery teas or for a quick embrace after the child had been topped and tailed, likely to smell fresh.

But she gave an *of course not* snort and swept past Mr Ross—the way she had once watched a group of Russians plunge into an icy lake—getting the worst of it out of the way at once. Chin up. Shoulders back. Mr Ross quickly outpaced her, stopping at the nursery door, and bracing his arm across it. She caught herself before she cannoned into his solid frame.

"Allow me to go in first," he said. "I must prepare them for you."

Her resolution to be cool and calm was upset at his proximity. "Will they think me a dragon?"

His answer was fair, measured. "I can never tell what they are going to do. You said, yourself it would be a challenge to win their trust in these circumstances."

His head tilted, his expression assessing, and she felt like a stage actor whose costume had caught in a door frame right before the soliloquy. This was a moment when Mr Ross must believe her pantomime of the competent governess or send her away.

In Vienna there had not been anyone she had failed to charm—soldier, traitor, king, or servant. Wariness and skepticism had been daubed on every wall of every palace like a spring whitewash, but Miss Penny Thornton had been an asset wherever she went. Certainly, her charm would work on three Scottish children.

"I expect they'll be like all the other students I've managed," she assured him, a little impressed at her ability to skirt a lie. "They are going to love me."

They had to.

Mr Ross smiled at her declaration and backed through the door. He disappeared into the room and she bent her ear to the wall, waiting for his voice to issue a sharp command for silence. But the tumult of the children's voices merely rose to an ear-splitting clatter, punctuated by a wild, piercing squeal of joy.

Finally, Mr Ross bellowed, "Kathleen, love, you're going to make me deaf."

Penny pressed the door ajar and peered through the crack she had created. Malcolm Ross had become a many-headed hydra as his form, sliced up and down by the narrowness of her view, slid forward and back. A child was dangling from his neck, while another wrapped herself around his boot, clinging to it with four limbs, dark plaits swinging, jam-faced and squealing with delight. A third child was tucked under one arm like an umbrella waiting to be unfurled at the chance of rain.

Here was the heart of *Coille na Cyarlin*. Not in the relentlessly square lines of its architecture, or the baldness with which it stood on the green meadows to meet its visitors. Not in the barren fields or wind-scoured façade.

"Who's that?" piped a little voice.

Penny jerked upright. Mr Ross hadn't had time to tell them about her, but now, his hair more unruly than ever, he gasped, "You may as well come in, Miss Starling."

She pushed through the door, not spying anymore but declaring herself a patent fact in their lives.

"Shall I have the nursery maid mop Kathleen up, or would you rather meet the wild Scots all in one go?"

"I'll meet them now," she said, and the happy squeals drained away as surely as if a stopper had been pulled from a basin.

Now that she could see them fully, untangling her jumbled impressions, they looked ordinary enough. Reflexively, she had created two columns in her mind, labeling them neatly: True Impediments and Small Obstacles. Into this second column, the Ross children were consigned. Tending them might delay the return of her magic but they were too tiny to hinder her for long.

She advanced across the room, assuming a mantle of pleasant authority. Mr Ross was not smiling but had the air of someone who found her attempts at dignity amusing.

The neck child and the boot child disentangled themselves from their father, scrambling to an imaginary line on the rug and stared at her with hard eyes. The little girl tucked her small jammy hand into her brother's larger one and he whipped out a handkerchief tucked into the waist of his trousers to clean her.

"Miss Starling," Mr Ross began. "May I present Ewan," he indicated the eldest boy who gave a stiff bow, heavy with the implication that he was performing it under duress.

Then Mr Ross gestured to the little girl at his side. "Kathleen."

The girl performed an awkward curtsey, glancing up at her brother.

Then Mr Ross said, "This is Robbie." Mr Ross's hand went to his son's head, cradling it as the boy's knobby legs wrapped about his waist.

Penny dipped into a brief curtsey and saw little Kathleen echo the brisk movement with another curtsey of her own. Ewan glared at his sister and she began sucking her thumb, whispering, "Forgot," around the red knuckle.

Ever so slightly, Penny began to shift the children into another place, inventing a new column labeled Unfortunate Setbacks.

Penny's lips pinched together. She had come, knowing her life would be proscribed. Her circle hardly extending beyond her charges and all the servants she could win around. By necessity, these would be her first and best sources of information as she searched for something as elusive and invisible as magic. She had planned for this.

Now she caught the militant eye of the oldest lad and wondered if she would find beetles in her bed.

"Mary is the nursery maid," Mr Ross said, drawing Penny's attention to a moon-faced girl of sixteen or so standing in the corner with some mending wadded in one hand.

"A pleasure, miss." She bobbed a curtsey and turned to her employer. "Will you want the boys in the schoolroom now, sir?"

Mr Ross stroked the back of Robbie's head. "This afternoon is soon enough. You reprobates can have the whole morning to wallow in ignorance."

Ewan smiled and breathed out a laugh at his father's joke. Kathleen, looking up at Ewan, laughed too. Robbie's shoulders merely eased.

"Your governess will have to get settled and used to her surroundings. She asked for my permission to allow your grandmother to sit in on your lessons." The children did not clap or cheer, but there was a fluttering of relief that went through the room. "Be sure to show her what you can do in repayment of such kindness."

The master of the house nodded at Penny and disentangled himself from his son, then followed her into the hall. As soon as the door was shut, the shouts of the children started up again and she turned to find Mr Ross leaned up against the door jamb, watching her.

His head tilted slightly. "What did you think of them?"

She lifted her shoulder, a French habit, but Mama was not here to correct her. "I have never failed to bring my charges around," she said, walking a narrow path of truth, brushing against lies and stirring their scent. "I expect we will settle down soon."

"Robbie won't always—" His words trailed off and she finished the sentence for him.

"Treat me like I'm some English Medusa, ready to freeze him if he so much as peeps at me?" She strove for lightness though the child's obvious dislike stung her pride.

"Forgive him," Mr Ross replied. That was all. But she thought she saw the same protective feeling she had when Fritz had leapt into her arms those many weeks ago.

Then he shifted, crossing his arms over his chest, and smoothed the emotion that tugged against his mouth. "He likes people. He'll come around."

She made no answer but stood near the opposite wall, weighing up her position. Things had been simple in Dorset. She would come on a crusade to get her magic back—only that. It was her first and only aim as she suffered the privations of travel and separated herself from her parents. Here, in this cold, hard place, she was not blind to the struggle this man had on his hands, and it complicated things that this family could ill afford to suffer fresh alarms.

Penny felt again the sudden relief of a tiny body hurling itself into her arms, fleeing from a fire—the last time she had tasted her power. She wouldn't lose anything in aiding Malcolm Ross's cause by answering his need for a good governess to teach his children, be patient, and forgive. It might not require her to step even a footfall off her chosen path. It would probably cost her nothing.

"I will be the best teacher he's ever had."

His mouth tucked in a smile and her breath caught. He was another creature when he smiled. "You're confident, Miss Starling. I like to see it."

She shook her head. "Confess. You like to witness a tumble, sir. Especially if it's taken by some cocky Englishwoman."

His smile deepened the tuck in his cheek, warming the narrow hall, and his voice dropped to a teasing whisper. "You do ride a very high horse."

Her heart beat hard in her throat, and dimly some part of her recognized that this sparring between them belonged in a moonlit garden or a ballroom. She wasn't Miss Thornton anymore to laugh at his words and wield her fan hoping for a dance. She was Miss Starling who would collect her wages on the next quarter day.

With an inaudible sigh, she dipped her chin. "I will practice a greater degree of modesty," she said, as correct as the true Miss Starling would wish.

She hated what the words did to his smile. The way it broke apart, piece by piece, reforming into pleasant, distant lines, any hint of deviltry gone. It was like throwing a rock and dashing out a stained-glass window.

Yet, it was for the best.

Chapter Seven

She spent the morning ordering her room, unearthing books and papers which would guide her teaching. She shook out her small clothes and petticoats. Two dresses were next, the deep brown and dove grey fabric denuded of the rich trimming, which would betray her station.

Three dresses in all. Her fingers brushed the fabric, and she felt a feathering of longing for the smooth satin and spidery lace she would have worn if she'd travelled with her parents as an honored guest in the great country houses of England.

A tide of grief and resentment slipped up her body, up and up, crashing over her head, buffeting. *Why me? Why not Beatrice who hardly ever rises at all? Why, when I can do such good with it?* Questions crested and smashed on her neck until she took a deep, shaking breath and slowly unclenched her hands. The tide slipped down again, as silently as it had come.

In its wake, she felt weak and bruised, even as some dull noise beyond the walls roused her to her task. Poor souls who survived a shipwreck must rise to their feet and shake off their weakness, joining the world once more. As she would. Penny set the frocks on the hooks.

Midday tea was a solitary affair and she told herself she preferred it that way. The little maid who brought it bobbed a short curtsey and stammered and fidgeted during the brief questions Penny had put to her. It was as though she didn't think of Penny as a hireling, equal to what she was. Yet, she didn't consider her a guest, either. Penny was to be at home neither here nor there, neither up nor down, but rather like a coin suspended in a Christmas pudding.

She took a tentative bite of a round biscuit and chased the dry, grainy portion down with a swallow of tea. She stifled a cough and eyed the long table in the center of the room. There she had set out fresh pens, matching inkwells, paper and primers suited to the boys' ages. Despite the complications actual flesh-and-blood children would bring, her fingertips tingled in anticipation.

Even as deer raced their moors, and martens darted through their woods, Penny Thornton was most truly at home in a schoolroom. It had been easy to evade Mama's intense scrutiny and constant strictures by burrowing inside a book.

Over time she'd learned to love botany, history, and languages for their own sakes. When she had grown out of reading lessons with the real Miss Starling, the knowledge she had accumulated had given her the power to make her comfortable at parties and dinners, which included accomplished, well-travelled men and women.

Penny brightened, brushing the crumbs from her lap as she imagined herself as some cherubic spirit bestowing these gifts on children deprived of the same atmosphere of discipline and inquiry Miss Starling had given her.

The delight and confidence grew in her as the moments passed, and hardly thinking, she played at gathering lightness, thinking rising thoughts. *Cobwebs strung through a forest. Sparks flying up a chimney. Malcolm Ross's unruly hair.*

Her concentration snapped, conjuring her employer as he had been in the hall, the memory of his smile pushing all thoughts of rising from her mind. She frowned. He should stop doing that—intruding in her well-regulated thoughts. In what manner her magic might be won around again, surely it would require a degree of study and application.

Penny stood, lifting the bell that would bring a halt to the merry noise coming from the nursery, and gave it a vigorous shake. She positioned herself neatly in front of the battered schoolroom table. As the boys stumbled in, they were followed by their grandmother, her gait proud and halting.

"Good afternoon, Mrs Stuart. Mr Ross has informed you of our arrangement?"

Mrs Stuart eased her rigid frame into a sofa by the fire, holding her crooked hands to the flame, and gave the same smile Death might wear as he swung his scythe. "I would not interfere for all the world, Miss Starling."

Penny swallowed hard and turned to the boys "Good afternoon, Master Ewan, Master Robbie."

"Good afternoon, Miss Starling," Ewan muttered, nudging his brother to look up.

"Noon," Robbie muttered.

Ewan took the seat nearest to Penny, unblinking, and Miss Starling's voice sounded in her head. *Begin as you mean to go on.*

Penny consulted the schedule, written on a crisp sheet of paper tacked to the wall, and rang the bell once more.

Mrs Stuart jerked in alarm and sent Penny a scowl. "Has someone died?"

The noise brought Robbie's eyes up to her face. They were a rich, deep brown, she noticed. Nothing like his father's bright blue.

She said with a brisk clap, "We will begin by composing a short essay."

Ewan drew a piece of paper forward, then not waiting for further instruction, he drew another one forward for Robbie and placed the pen in his brother's hand, folding his fingers until the grip was correct.

"Ten minutes. Any subject of your choosing," Penny said, watching this process with a sinking feeling. She glanced at the clock. "You may begin."

In a bid to avoid Mrs Stuart's basilisk stare, Penny turned to the set of books, as battered as the desk, and pulled several likely volumes from the shelves, leafing through their contents.

The hair on the back of her neck prickled in awareness. Was there nothing to distract the old woman from training her undivided attention on Penny? Mrs Stuart seemed to read no books, she could manage no bit of sewing or bundle of knitting. But her dark eyes worked fine.

Penny glanced up. "Set down your pens," she said, turning around. Ewan set his quill aside and Robbie squashed his paper against his shirt front.

"Now then, Ewan," she said, well-pleased to make out that the boy had written in a juvenile, but even hand. "You will stand and read your selection aloud, please."

His lips set in a hard line as he held up his page.

"I hate starlings," he began. Penny's eyes widened and a strangled cough emanated from the sofa.

The childish voice was firm. "They eat fat worms and scuttling insects. They like it. Starlings push in where they aren't wanted.

They break houses to make their own. They chase other birds out of their holes. Starlings are meaner than devils. Starlings trick you. They can sound like other, better, birds. They look nice, but they're not."

He looked up, half-defiant, half-frightened, his glance flicking to his grandmother. No word of censure came from that quarter, and Penny's face flamed.

In the silence Robbie piped up, "Tha's a nice poem, Ewan."

Penny wished to rip the paper into a thousand pieces and scatter them out the window. Ten minutes into her first lesson and she was already having to think up punishments. What would Miss Starling do?

"Now that I know you can write so well, Ewan, I will ask more of you." The boy's face reddened, but he did not drop his eyes. She tapped the paper he had laid on the table. "You will fill an entire page describing as many animals as you can. Mind your penmanship. You may retire to the desk in the corner."

He bundled up his materials and slunk away. Penny's heart slowed almost to normal. This had been her first hurdle, but she was over it. The rest of the race could be taken in stride.

"Now, Robbie, show me what you have."

The little boy held his paper to his chest.

"I must see what you've done so we know how to proceed," she explained, softly, coaxingly, the way she had called Fritz into her arms that long ago day.

"No," came his short, unequivocal reply.

Penny could almost feel Mrs Stuart's gaze on her back, feel the tension as she watched Penny struggle. For a moment she imagined trying to wrestle the mangled paper from the lad's grip. She held her hand out and prayed that the paper would appear in it.

Penny held her breath until, his little mouth in a flat, displeased shape, Robbie scooted the page across the table. Penny's exhale was one of relief. She turned the page around to see one word was written on it, the ink so light that it might have been sketched out by a ghostly hand. Well, he was only seven. His penmanship would improve under her tutelage.

"*Sssslllllinch*," she sounded out. She tried to be polite. "I don't know that word. What does it mean?"

"It's Scots," he said. "Secret language the English don't know."

Penny tipped the paper to the light. The letters were scattered across the page. “Use it in a sentence, please.”

Robbie looked down at the table. “I put a *slinch* of butter on my oatcakes. Slinch.”

“Everybody knows that word,” Ewan cut in. “I cut a slinch of cheese. Even Kathleen knows Scots. What can you teach us if you don’t even know that?”

“Languages, Geography, Mathematics, and History.”

“Imagine not knowing Scots,” Robbie murmured.

“Imagine,” Ewan echoed.

“Attend to your composition, Ewan,” Penny ordered, “or be prepared for me to double it.” How would a child his age be able to manage so much? The threat had spilled from her mouth without thought, and she hoped desperately Ewan would be wise, that she would not have to carry out her words.

Penny inhaled sharply and picked up a book of rhymes, avoiding Mrs Stuart’s intent gaze. “I would like you to read to me now, Robbie.”

Before they could settle themselves at the table, Kathleen banged through the door holding a sheaf of papers that scattered as she walked. “I’m coming to school.”

“Kathy,” Mrs Stuart scolded.

“This is my classroom, Mrs Stuart,” Penny interjected. The lady hadn’t come to her defense earlier. Why allow her to start now? Penny strove to make her voice level and plain. “You will leave the ordering of it to me.”

She glanced to the pristine schedule written out in her own hand and pinched her lips. At the rate they were going, they would have to forego the Introduction to Mineralogy. “Robbie, will you return your sister to the nursery?”

“Back in a slinch,” he said, sliding from the stool. “Come on, baby,” he said, tugging Kathleen’s chubby hand.

That was when all hell broke loose.

Chapter Eight

He ought to check on the schoolroom.

Malcolm set down his quill and pushed aside his ledgers, glancing up at the clock. It would take no time at all.

The boys would be bent over some bit of schoolwork and he could lean his head around the door and assure himself Miss Starling was comfortable and had all she needed to perform her duties. He would lift his brows. She would nod her head. That would be it.

To enact his role as a conscientious employer and caring parent need only take a few minutes. There. Two exceptionally good reasons for setting aside his work and going to the schoolroom.

He scraped his chair and stood.

Some residue of the younger, less respectable Malcolm mocked this sober plan as he strode from the room, peeling away his rationalizations like a heavily wrapped man coming in from a blizzard.

It was *not* that he wanted to see Miss Starling, he frowned as he mounted the stairs. He had seen plenty of her on the road from Edinburgh.

Malcolm continued his ascent until he heard Kathleen's ear-splitting shriek and tripled his speed, heart slamming in his chest. He burst through the door and into a melee.

Robbie had Kathleen by the ankle and was trying to drag her across the floor. His daughter had clamped her chubby hands around the leg of the table and with each scoot Robbie made, the table lurched across the wood with a low, shuddering scrape.

"Come 'ere," Rob shouted as Ewan stood on a desk in the corner, bellowing the words of an incomprehensible song at the top of his lungs.

Malcolm's mind kept trying to sort it out, mashing a word into a form he understood. Slinch? Elspeth grinned like a demon as Miss

Starling, ringing a tiny silver bell, shot him such a withering glare he ought to be a sizzling husk.

He couldn't help smiling, but, taking pity, he shouted, "Order. Or-der," he called, drawing the command out until the last of the childish clamor had gone. Papers drifted from the table like a spill of apple blossoms. "What is going on?"

Robbie, dropping his sister's foot with a thump, volunteered an answer. "We are getting along with our new governess very poorly, *Aither*. We should send her back to England."

"Wait a slinch, Robbie Ross," Miss Starling said. "I'm not going anywhere."

There was that word again.

"Slinch?" Malcolm asked, his voice mild.

"Did I use it wrong?" she asked, biting her lip. She was dressed in a sensible blue dress with her cuffs rolled back. That hair of hers was plainly coiled on her head, the intriguing curls barely abiding their confinement. There was nothing whatsoever about her person to excite the least reaction.

"Slinch?" he repeated, hearing the roughness in his voice, giving it a short, pungent rebuke to get in line.

"Yes," she confirmed. "I took it to mean a measure of something, A little bit. Was I wrong? Does it only work with food?"

She passed Robbie's paper to him and Malcolm smiled. "Another of your Scots words, Rob?"

"Aye, *Aither*," the boy answered, crossing the room, and detoured around his governess, giving her a wide berth.

Malcolm settled in a chair, which creaked beneath his considerable weight and Robbie climbed into his lap, hooking an arm around his neck as was usual. Malcolm held the paper up so they both might view it. "That's a fine 'S,' Rob."

"It wanted to be a dragon, but I kept it a letter. See how it wiggles on the page."

Malcolm looked on the "S," static and stationary. Robbie's letters often liked to gallop across the paper. "It's a fine 'S.'" He dropped a kiss on Rob's head and beckoned his other children around the table. Kathleen gripped the edge of it and rested a mournful face on her hands.

"I never thought to see my children behave with such rudeness."

Kathy burst into tears, but then she was always bursting into tears. He held his arm out and she clambered onto his other knee to wail into his coat.

He fixed his stern eyes on his sons.

"Miss Starling is our guest, and her mind, I am given to understand," he said, allowing a shadowy smile to pass over his lips as he glanced at the lass, "contains more treasures than a pirate's lair."

"A rich pirate?" Kathy murmured, smearing tears and snot across the sleeve of his coat.

"Aye."

Miss Starling gave her head a tiny, exasperated shake, aiming an expressive look to the ceiling. He tore his eyes from the sight with some effort.

"Ewan, would I be a fool or a wise man if I happened upon such a treasure and traded it away?"

"A fool, Papa."

"A fool and an ingrate. Have I raised fools and ingrates, Rob?"

"Maybe," Robbie considered. There was a long pause. Malcolm would wait. "No, *Aither*."

"What example do you set for your sister, Ewan, when you treat a lady in such a manner?"

Ewan's mouth was hard for one so young, but he still spoke the right words. "I expect a bad one, Papa."

"Aye, son. A bad one."

Malcolm looked up and caught Miss Starling looking at them all as though they were a column of sums that would not tally. The afternoon sun lit her proud features and he felt like an invisible length of twine bound them together, winding tighter the longer he was in her presence. He would lose her if he did not take care.

He blinked the thought away and felt some relief when he found a safe explanation. The woman would abandon them all if he could not get some cooperation from the children. The weather was too bad, the roads too treacherous, to think of dropping her at the Edinburgh docks to make her way home. Then there would be the trouble of finding her replacement.

He frowned at her and she frowned back. He almost laughed and felt the twine tighten again.

"Kathy," he began, putting his cheek against her dark plaits. She leaned into the hollow of his shoulder.

"I want to learn my letters," she said, in such a sorrowful tone that he hugged her.

"You don't," Robbie declared. "'Tis torture."

Miss Starling caught her lip. The children would have to apologize. Perhaps he should as well.

"Help your sister and brother pick up, Ewan. Prepare your grandest apologies. When your governess returns to her duties tomorrow morning, I expect you will be ready to attend her. Miss Starling," the governess gave him a flinty glance, "if I might have a minute of your time?"

She nodded and followed him into the hall, halting. He reached past her to pull the door shut, realizing too late it brought them nearly in contact. She smelled nice. There was nothing particular about the scent, aside from a general air of floral young womanliness, but in *Coille na Cyarlin* it was an exotic, tantalizing smell.

He stepped back swiftly, and a soft pink color rose from the high collar of her chemisette, staining her neck.

Malcolm cleared his throat and looked down the hall at safer vistas—floorboards and chair railings. "You didn't pack enough twine or tea to be prepared for our wild ways."

"No one could be that prepared," she said, turning her neck and glaring at the schoolroom door.

"Have the children put you off teaching?"

Her look was direct. "I'm not sure they haven't put me off children."

He laughed then, letting slip a thread of the amusement, which always seemed to want to escape in her presence. Perhaps tomorrow would be soon enough to remember how to be bland and avuncular. She did not share his amusement and turned stern, governess eyes on him. He wiped his face free of smiles and became placating.

He lifted his chin towards the door. "I will make certain that doesn't happen again. I think part of the problem must be the weather. This dashed winter won't lift, and their spirits are restless."

Miss Starling nodded, gazing abstractedly out the window, working the side of her thumb slowly up across her bottom lip.

"They aren't quite ready to endure another governess. Tell me, sir, was she like me, the other governess? Do I remind them of her?"

"No. She was a round-faced woman in her forties. She looked as harmless as a bun, but she was tyrannical." He exhaled and ran a hand through his hair, trying and failing to wring any comfort from the words he often repeated to himself. "I didn't know. Elspeth never suspected."

"Then how—?"

"Mary bathed them and saw marks on Robbie's back and arms."

"Robbie?" Miss Starling's eyes narrowed.

"Scholarship doesn't come easily. He hardly knows his letters." Malcolm locked his arms across his chest at the familiar rage that boiled through his veins, and as the familiar pain of guilt hit his stomach. Malcolm's visits to the schoolroom had caused more problems for his children rather than less, each stumbling recitation a reason for whispered threats and hidden punishments. Rob's stumbles were the greater, so too were the consequences. "I think her idea was to beat the alphabet into him."

Miss Starling spat a short, foreign-sounding word and he looked up, surprised at the outraged expression on her face. "He's only seven."

"Too old not to know how to spell his last name, especially one as simple as ours. You'll find that he signs each page 'Rob.' Not 'Robbie.' or 'Robert."

Her thumb worked against her lip again and he had a sudden wish to capture it and press a kiss against the pad—the kind of husbandly gesture he used to make and missed.

"Because there are fewer letters to work out," she guessed.

His gaze explored the seams in the ceiling, looking for damp. It was a safe occupation and would yield better results than noticing this woman not three paces from him. "Aye."

"That's quite clever."

She understood that much, did she? Rob had plenty of native intelligence if one could only see it. His gaze returned to hers as he had known it would, and a slow smile crossed his face.

She smiled back and his breath stuck. Damn. Here they were again, staring at each other across the gap in the hall, attended by some awareness of one another, which seemed to hover on the edge of his consciousness. Perhaps looking at every woman, even the most unsuitable specimens, with a kind of weighing up was his body's way of telling him it was time to look for a wife again.

Perhaps that was it.

"If there is anything I may do to make your stay with us more pleasant, you will not hesitate to ask," he said, choosing something to say that seemed proper, distant, and ringed around with benevolent, if vague, interest.

Her hand half lifted. "Please, there is one thing," she said, and he found himself slightly frustrated by the Englishness of her. If she had been a Scots lass, he could tell by the sound of her accents where she had come from, what kind of upbringing she'd had. He could place her manner of dress in a particular class. Her expressions could be read at face value instead of run through a rough translation of what might be expected of a girl from the south. He would know so much without having to ask.

Her chin came up. "I wondered if I might borrow books from time to time. The library looked like quite a good one."

Was she surprised that it was? "Of course, Miss Starling. It is no bother. Take what you like."

He glanced to the end of the hall and his gaze fell on the window. "The rain is holding off. While I restore some order, you ought to take a walk with your little dog."

Miss Starling brightened and dipped a curtsey. He nodded. They were again on a proper footing he thought with some relief, until he caught himself watching her skirts making a provocative swish as she went down the hall. Malcolm drank in every last drop of the view, calling himself a fool in English, Scots, and some of Robbie's nonsense words.

He returned to the schoolroom to find all the books were put away, the children quietly occupied. He settled himself across from Elspeth and gave her a long look.

"You were able to put things right rather quickly," he observed, his voice low.

"The children will listen to the voice of authority. They ran circles around her." Her tone was innocent, but he knew better.

"And you watched."

"She insisted that she would have a free hand in her schoolroom. I merely saw to her wishes."

"You're a fiend when you want to be Elspeth Stuart."

His mother-in-law smiled. "She's not going to last. An English flower way up here in Scotland. Not hardy enough."

A vision came into Malcolm's mind of Miss Starling sitting on a low stool in a shepherd's cottage, making a fire, fixing tea, and never uttering a word of complaint despite being soaked to the skin, the firelight drawing flames in her hair. Maybe she wasn't for here, but it wouldn't be because she was too delicate for discomfort.

Malcolm grunted. "Miss Starling is merely a governess. We don't need her to belong here, but we do need help with the children." He shifted under the weight of Elspeth's speculation, and cleared his throat. "I need you to make peace with her."

Elspeth exhaled sharply and then nodded. She smoothed her skirts, her fingers at sharp angles to her palm.

How difficult it was to remember she had been whole once, and not so long ago. She had danced at his wedding, as merry and lively as Jean.

"How are your bones?" he asked, knowing the cold and rain would send daggers of pain lancing through her joints.

Elspeth sighed, but answered. "Not so bad today. I have been too busy watching that proud miss try to manage a room full of naughty children. I almost split my stays trying not to laugh."

He smiled. "You're the naughty one, Elspeth. I wish you would find a way to help her."

"That is asking too much," his mother-in-law said, her face twisting in pain, the mask of rigid stoicism slipping away for a moment to show the agonies she bore in body and spirit. "I want nothing to do with that girl. It's Jean who should be here watching things, ordering the education of those two rogues."

Bless her, Jean would hardly have been able to see the boys past basic arithmetic and reading. She had not been a lass who sat still long enough to learn anything that came from a book. Still, she had a talent for happiness, quick to slip a hand through the crook of his elbow and jostle him out of his worries. When she was alive, the house had been one of laughter.

He rubbed a tired hand over his face. "Jean's spirit will haunt me if I do not look after her children and see them properly raised. I'll ask again if you have any help to offer Miss Starling."

Elspeth fought a battle with herself in those brief moments before she spoke. But, at last, she said, "I won't throw a party for her. That one is so determined to dictate in her schoolroom, I wouldn't presume to throw a bucket of water if it were burning."

"Get ready with your bucket, Elspeth, for me and for the boys. The last thing we need is a conflagration on our hands."

She gave him a grudging nod, generous in her way.

When he returned to the library, he opened his pocket watch and stepped from the terrace into the small, formal garden. The clouds had broken up with a brisk, piercing wind coming in from the northwest, and he found the outdoor thermometer damp from the recent downpour and reading a temperature of 39 degrees. He opened a small notebook to jot the observations when his head jerked up in surprise.

It was Ewan's song, filled with Rob's nonsense words, sung from the lips of Miss Starling. Her pitch was wildly inaccurate, and he smiled as she flung a stick from the terrace. Her little dog raced away for it. The dog must have been deaf because he raced happily back to her side, dropping the stick and wagging his bottom like Kathleen when she attempted to jump the garden steps.

Miss Starling laughed and the sound called up a memory.

He had not spoken truly when he told her *Coille na Cyarlin* hadn't a speck of magic. When Jean had been alive it had seemed to burst from the windows and chimney pots, filling the house and reaching every nook.

Miss Starling wore a look of concentration for a moment and leapt down to the garden steps in one go, scowling briefly when she landed on her feet. Then she darted around the corner of a yew hedge after her dog.

Malcolm didn't move.

Instead, he listened to the sound of a woman's laughter.

Chapter Nine

After more than a week of governessing—a daily exercise in exhaustion and futility—Penny rubbed Fritz between the ears and slipped from her bed. It was almost May and she could still see her breath.

"Where would you look for my magic?" she asked the little dog as she donned her flannel petticoat. He turned his head and yawned, his curling pink tongue stretching out. "It's not in the schoolroom, that much is certain. I've touched every surface, every book, and I feel no magic." She sniffed against the cold and Fritz turned up his limpid eyes with an expression both wise and sympathetic.

She smiled. Fritz understood the Ross boys were impossible. Fritz knew Mrs Stuart was composed of equal parts ice and granite. But Fritz never seemed to know what to do about it.

The morning lessons proceeded as they always did, with barely contained mutiny followed by Mrs Stuart finally asking, "D'ye need a hand?" as though she meant it.

This time Penny met Mrs Stuart's eyes, dancing with the same detached amusement she wore when she intervened enough to keep the children's outrages below a certain level and breathed hard through her nose. "No," she replied, longing to throw her books and papers out of the window and leave this house forever. This was too much work for too little magic.

She moved behind Robbie, reaching to reposition the angle of his pen, and his hand jerked across the page, smearing his ill-formed letters. Well, letter. Just one. "M." Over and over. He scooted off his chair and upset the page, knocking the inkwell as he jostled away from her.

It was beautiful, she thought, the arc of the liquid before it spattered across the table, bouncing among composition papers, spraying across reading materials Penny had brought from Dorset, across her pristine, wildly optimistic schedule, before landing with a benign thunk as the remainder of the ink glugged from the top.

Ewan acted first, stepping swiftly between her and Robbie. "It was my fault," he said, daring her to disbelieve him. "I'll clean it up."

Her eyes darted to Mrs Stuart, flailing wildly for her walking stick until she rocked from the sofa. "You've no need to bother yourself with this, Miss Starling. I'll see to the boys."

Penny felt the lightest racing in her veins, the indistinct slip and shiver of magic. She wanted to stop everything and savor it, but the ink was glugging, and the magic wanted out. It wanted to rush from her. Penny brought her hand up and Ewan turned his face and scrunched his eyes closed.

Too late she realized he was poised to take a blow. This is what these people thought her capable of. The magic, if indeed there had been any, vanished and her voice broke with disappointment. "No," she enjoined Mrs Stuart, pressing the air with her harmless gesture, willing her to settle back on the sofa. "I will manage this."

She dropped onto the chair and regarded the boys. Who wanted this? Frustration crowded her throat and eyes, dragged at her mouth. The children hated her, and her magic could find no purchase within her bones. Reasons enough to let Mrs Stuart take the brunt of this calamity while she ran to her room and screamed her head off.

Penny Thornton might have done so. Mama might've knocked gently on the door with a pot of chocolate and told her it was entirely sorted and nothing she need upset herself about. Mama might be calm and sensible and happy to manage the entire mess, and Penny might let her.

Penny Starling released a shaky breath. She was a governess, and governesses must shift for themselves.

"Robbie, this was your doing." Ewan tensed but said nothing. "How would you like us to help you put the table to rights?"

Though so much of what she had said and done in the last week had been wrong, this seemed to be right. Robbie directed Ewan and Penny, keeping his distance from her, but working at a common aim.

The ceasefire did not produce angelic students and a satisfied governess. As one week bled into a second, she could not claim to have made peace in the schoolroom or any progress in regaining her magic.

One day, as the noon hour approached, Penny glared at the clock with an increasingly desperate edge. “And...” she said, dragging out the word as the timepiece shivered toward the hour, “that will be all.”

The boys shoved their stools back with a harsh scrape and shot a look at their grandmother to confirm, yes, a few courtesies would still be required of them. They gave the slightest of bows before they ran for the door, as anxious to see the back of the schoolroom as Penny was.

Penny rolled her shoulders and scooped up the papers scattered across the desk, listening to Mrs Stuart’s uneven gait as she went. When Penny was quite certain she was alone she sat heavily on a stool, putting her elbows on the table and cupped her chin.

The real Miss Starling would’ve never tolerated such untidiness, such careless manners. Miss Starling would not put up with—

She dragged a paper over. One of Ewan’s. She had set him to reading a collection of children’s verses, and he had scribbled his improvements in the margin. Poor rhymes about English invaders meeting grisly ends in boggy marshes mingled with rather good sketches of small creatures.

At least he was writing.

She had made no headway with Robbie. The lad had somehow grown more difficult over the course of the week, transforming from a staring, silent figure into a pugnacious boy, answering back as often as not.

Even given the simplest of tasks, Robbie managed to break several pens and pretended to fall asleep, a puddle of drool blotting his paper.

Though she had spent the last fortnight replicating Miss Starling’s precise, orderly lessons and applying them with as much faithfulness as another human being possibly could, the children resisted being brought to the fountain of knowledge. If the learned and redoubtable Miss Starling couldn’t reach them, what hope did Penny Thornton have?

A maid brought her tea tray and Penny ate the simple meal quickly, chewing the biscuit with a determination born of desperation. The sooner she could manage to swallow the oatcake, the more time she had to look for some clue to her magic before she had to be back at the head of the table to teach children utterly determined to continue on in ignorance their whole lives long.

Not even an hour.

She tossed the remnant of the oatcake into the banked schoolroom fire and made her way to the library. She hadn't known where to find her magic, but it made sense to conduct her search in the place that held the most information.

A week of this had yielded few results.

She poked her head around the door and gave a little sigh. Though her father conducted all the estate business within the library at Thorndene, Mr Ross must have duties that took him elsewhere. He seemed to be within the confines of the home hardly at all, until she heard his voice through the walls of the nursery as the children took their dinner. It was good—yes, most decidedly good—that he was not.

Far simpler for her.

She could go about her business undisturbed by his masculine presence, even if her eyes sometimes wandered over the desk in the center of the room as they did now. Her steps checked as she made her way to the shelves and she cocked her head. No one was about. What would a tiny investigation hurt?

Nearing the desk, Penny touched a small pouch of tobacco slouching against a well-worn pipe. It must be this habit that gave the room its warm, rich scent tinged with sweetness—the scent that clung to him when they passed in the hall or on the stairs. She brushed her finger along a chipped teacup that held a few coins and her hand rested on a ledger lying open on the blotter. No magic in any of it.

Quickly, she perused the revenue and expenses of *Coille na Cyarlin*—the tiny sum for the cows he must have sold in Edinburgh, the purchase of extra feed, and strange, overlarge outlays for lumber, glazing, and masonry when there were no repairs on the house.

She moved on, touching a book he had set aside, the only sign it had been disturbed was the bookmark she had noticed digging deeper through the pages with each passing day.

She returned to the shelves, trying to put out of her mind the details which told her as much about his habits and temperament as if he had conducted her on a tour of his personal effects.

Penny began to focus her mind on the books. It was a good library, she thought, trying and failing to add an asterisk. It was especially good for what one would expect in rural Scotland. Travel had a way of upsetting one's notions.

He was learned, and so, too, must his family have been, for filling the library had been the work of generations. The mahogany shelves, polished to a warm, glossy finish, contained every type of literature Penny could imagine. Philosophy and family bibles sat cheek-by-jowl with fifteen pocket-copies of *Much Ado About Nothing*. Outdated agricultural treatises occupied the same shelf as a first edition of *The Wealth of Nations*. Histories. Novels.

As the clock ticked gently on the mantel, she took each book from the shelf as she came to it. Some warranting several minutes of perusal, some given only a few seconds as she fanned through the pages.

Then she came to the poetry—a surprising amount of poetry.

She began to explore a shelf that contained a riot of Shakespeare, Herrick, Pope, and Burns. Her quick examination had her noting with delight, many of the books opened of their own accord to pages marked up by generations of Rosses, each adding their thoughts and opinions like layers of sediment in a rock formation.

She laughed. At least Ewan had come by his habit of vandalizing books honestly. Even his father was within these pages. Penny looked for his hand—the strong M she knew stood for Malcolm and the scribbled questions he wrote.

She perched upon on a library ladder, sweeping her skirts to the side, hardly remembering it was unlikely her magic would be found pressed between the pages of a book of poetry like a love token. She devoured the verses as she came to them, feeling their enchantment weave around her until her attention was broken by a sound.

Penny's head jerked up and she watched as the door swung open, pushed by a woman—young still, but older than Penny—of remarkable loveliness carrying a basket. Her dark brown hair parted severely under the rim of her bonnet and framed a face that seemed as pale and soft as lilies. Until coming to Scotland with three plain wool dresses, Penny had liked to follow the current styles and she judged in an instant that this lady's black dress was worn and faded, the fashion several years out of date.

She had not spotted Penny sitting on the ladder in her grey woolen dress, and there was something in the way she stopped, cocked her head, and moved swiftly to the desk, that caused Penny to say, her voice ringing with authority, "Good day, madam."

The woman gave a yelp of alarm.

Chapter Ten

"Might I be of service? Perhaps you are lost," Penny said, forgetting a servant would bob a curtsey and wait for instruction. There was none of Miss Starling in her tone now. No readiness to please. With Penny Thornton's eyes she had observed the furtive motion of the unknown woman crossing the library.

Penny was not entitled to answers. She remembered so when the woman's gaze lingered on Penny's plain gown and simply dressed hair. She arched a brow, amusement touching the lines of her face.

"An English girl," she began appraisingly, her own accent refined and unmistakably English. Then she took half a step closer, eyes widening in surprise. She raised a finger at Penny. "I know you."

It was not an accusation, but a cold wave rolled up from Penny's toes, brushing her skin into gooseflesh even with the flannel petticoat. Swiftly she slid from the ladder, her eyes taking in every facet of this woman's appearance, trying and failing to match it to an image with which she was already familiar. The pace of her search speeding and speeding, threatening to throw her dizzily into a ditch. She planted her feet firmly on the floor and ran the tip of her tongue over suddenly dry lips.

"I don't think I've had the pleasure of meeting you before, ma'am." Penny dropped her eyes and bobbed a deep curtsey—deep enough to make up for the tardiness of it.

But the humility had not won her a reprieve from the woman's probing eyes, her laughing mouth. "I love a mystery." Her brow furrowed and she fondled a gold locket hanging from a chain around her neck, tapping it against her lips. "Let me see. We would not have met here." Her head tilted at an assessing angle. "You're not old enough to have been in London when I reigned. Oh," she said, drawing the word out like an executioner who may take all the time in the world to strike the killing blow. "The Thornton girl. Mrs Gracechurch's little sister. Poppy or Peggy or—"

"Penny." Her name came out in a rough whisper.

The lady insinuated herself into a chair, dropping a small basket at her feet, a look of triumph on her face. "That's it. It would've been a few years ago, but our paths crossed in Sussex. I suppose you were visiting your sister." She paused slightly and then frowned. "I'm Lady Ainsley. Do you really not remember?"

Penny shook her head. "I've met Lady Ainsley many times. Meg is my sister's dearest friend. You're not—"

Her nose crinkled in distaste. "*Dowager* Lady Ainsley, then."

Ah, so this was the merry widow. Fleeting impressions rushed in on Penny as she dredged her memory. Isabelle. That was her name. She had married the old earl when she had been hardly out of the schoolroom, and there had been enough of a scandal about it, she had been kept from hearing the details. Indeed, most of what Penny guessed had been gleaned from the long silent pauses and darting glances following the lady's name.

Other small scraps of information Penny was able to sort through in these suffocating moments, told of no particular virtues. Oh heavens. Her plans were scattering like a tower of cards, and every nerve screamed for her to leave. Run. Steal the pocketful of small change from the desk and fly away before she was unmasked in the presence of the entire household.

Mr Ross's image rose in her mind, his mouth bracketed in stern lines, ice cold fury in his eyes. A pale shadow of such a look had crossed his face when he spoke of the former governess and the idea that it should be turned on her— Her insides slid.

Penny held onto a rung of the ladder, willing her shaking limbs to still, and said with a thin, butter-scraped composure, "Your memory is excellent. Far better than mine."

Lady Ainsley lifted an elegant hand. "I don't forget people, Penny Thornton," she said, repeating the name. "It doesn't pay."

Penny started forward, alarm stiffening her sinews. "Please—" she whispered, stumbling over her words. "Please do not call me by that name, Lady Ainsley. I am the new governess here and known as Miss Starling to the household."

Lady Ainsley's eyes widened. "More surprises."

Penny opened her mouth to explain, to plead, to beg, but snapped it shut again when her employer swung through the door, bringing the smell of rain with him, halving the size of the room, and sending her shrinking back into the dark shadows.

Mr Ross was dressed much as he had been that first day, in a soaking coat and worn britches, but she did not mistake him for someone of no account as she had then. Indeed, looking at him now, she wondered how it had ever been possible.

"Isabelle," he exclaimed, taking his hat from his head and shaking a hand through his hair. Droplets sprayed the carpet, the floor, and Penny bit into the soft flesh of her lip. What did he mean, calling Lady Ainsley by her Christian name?

Her mind twisted down a strange corridor, shooting off before she knew what it was about. Isabelle was a far lovelier name than Penny, elegant and beguiling where the latter was young and playful. A thoroughbred standing next to a puppy. He'd spoken the name so easily—nothing secretive about it, no whisper. The name and the woman were welcome here.

She yanked hard on her thoughts, pulling them back in order. Why should she care?

She did not.

She could not.

Lady Ainsley was no interloper. At any moment, she might turn and tell Mr Ross he was harboring a fraud.

"What brings you out in this weather?" he asked. "And looking so well, too, cousin."

From her corner of the library, Penny released a breath she didn't know she was holding and would not have acknowledged even if she had.

Lady Ainsley flicked a glance to the shadows. "This dreary weather, if you must know. I've hardly seen a soul in weeks. You've not been by, nor brought the children for tea and cake."

Mr Ross leaned against the desk. "The path from the big house to Foxglove Cottage is long and muddy," he answered, his accents flatter.

"Curiously, it's not a step farther than the path from Foxglove Cottage to the great house, nor a drop muddier. Yet here I am."

Penny darted a look to the open door, not twenty paces away and began to move under the cover of Lady Ainsley's admonishments.

Mr Ross spread his hands. "You are a woman of great intrepidity. A pity I was not here to greet you when you came."

Penny took a long step. Breathed. Took another.

Isabelle laughed. "Oh, but I found the most charming companion. Penny, don't scuttle off."

Penny froze as Malcolm—Mr Ross—swung around, half-crouching. She unfolded herself and a pulse beat hard in her neck. Lady Ainsley would tell him now, flinging the truth at his feet.

"Miss Starling, forgive me." Mr Ross gave a bow and he looked at her as he often had in the last fortnight, as if there was a high hedge between them and a moat besides. "I didn't see you."

Penny's mouth began to form the beginnings of several words, discarding each. When would Lady Ainsley speak? Her heart raced, but the lady did not say anything, merely shook her head, gave a soft smile, and gave a conspiratorial wink behind Mr Ross's back.

Was this mercy? Relief shook through Penny's veins, weakening her knees.

"I must get back to the children—" she began, a book held loosely in her hand. Had it been there all the time? She moved swiftly to the door.

"Don't go," he stopped her. "I was about to offer my guest tea. She would enjoy the pleasure of speaking with a fellow countrywoman for a few minutes, I think."

"Indeed, I would," Isabelle said, and Penny returned, each step taking her near a precipice. Malcolm offered her a chair and under the light patter of Lady Ainsley's conversation she glanced up to find him looking down at her, his mouth set, the blue eyes making a slow perusal of her face.

"You can help me draw out the time before my cousin pushes me out into the storm again," Isabelle teased. Malcolm blinked, straightening away from Penny.

"I have business to attend to, but I'll send you home in a carriage."

"Business," Lady Ainsley scoffed, sliding a confiding look to Penny. "You would not believe what he calls business."

Penny tilted her chin, and he answered her unspoken question.

"You recall the river we forded on the final push toward home? I'm building a village on the other side."

Her brow puckered. “Are villages built? I thought they simply grew.”

“Not this one,” Isabelle said with a chuckle. “Every stick and stone of it will be planned—and paid for—by Malcolm Ross. The greatest folly these hills have ever known.”

Folly. Penny smiled at the word. That’s what the villagers called the round, high-walled building Papa had built for her at home. Thornton’s Folly, where she used to practice her rising, discover her powers, and shave away its limitations. They thought it the whimsy of a rich and foolish man and declared it would be a hay barn in the end. But, while Lady Ainsley might think Malcolm’s village a mad impulse, Penny had too much experience of follies to think that they arose without reason.

“There are perfectly good dwellings dotting the countryside,” Penny noted, a puckish spirit overtaking her. “Abandoned shepherd’s cottages and such.”

His lips twitched. “Ah, but they’re in a terrible state. Not fit for dogs. A gently bred woman such as yourself would be shocked at the condition.”

Her eyes widened innocently. “I daresay.”

She was rewarded with one dimple and his look lingered on her until Lady Ainsley broke in, pulling apart the cobweb thin strands that seemed to bind them.

“Do not let him prose on about clearances and conditions, and the plight of the rustic farmer, Penny.” Penny tensed at her name, but Lady Ainsley did not seem to notice. “I hope you do not mind me calling you Penny,” she continued, as Birdie brought the tea tray and set it on the table. “Please, you must call me Isabelle. I’m the only gentlewoman for miles.”

Birdie snorted as she left the room, muttering darkly about pestilences.

Though Penny drank with outward composure and nibbled on cake, the likes of which she had not seen in weeks, enjoying the conversation of grown people who already knew their sums, she fretted. Isabelle had been kind, but Penny’s whole life—the right to find and capture her magic—was now in the hands of someone she hardly knew.

After a quarter of an hour, Malcolm set his plate aside.

"I suppose that means it's time for me to go," Isabelle declared, standing, and bringing the others with her like puppets on invisible stings.

"It was lovely meeting you, Penny," Isabelle murmured, reaching her hand to touch Penny's briefly. Isabelle's smile faltered but she recovered quickly, fussing with her shawl, with the locket at her neck. "I would so like to have you drop in on me from time to time. You can follow the path through the witch woods, not more than a mile. It's a muddy bog as often as not, but I promise to ignore your grubby petticoats and we can gossip together in our native tongue."

Isabelle turned and picked up her basket again and now Penny could see that it was full of long, springy yarrow stalks. The tiny clusters of flowers had been lopped off by a thick, curved pruning knife resting atop them.

Yarrow. There was nothing as wholesome as an herb that could ease a toothache and stop a flow of blood. The sight of it settled Penny a little.

Isabelle curtseyed to Mr Ross, but said, laughing at Penny as she drifted towards the door, "You feel as much relief as I do for hearing your own accent again." Tugging her gloves on, she gave her cousin an arch look. "Far better than the dreadful Scots."

It was meant to be a little joke, but Penny frowned at her back. The accent wasn't dreadful. When she passed unseen, the voices in this house rang out in such rich, energetic cadences, she found herself stopping in the hall or on the stairs, lifting her head to hear them a little while longer, wishing she had the right to join them.

That was not why she was here. She must remember. Penny plucked up the book she had laid aside and made to follow in the wake of her ladyship.

"Miss Starling," Malcolm commanded, taking a position by the fire and leaning his broad shoulders against the mantel, "if I might have a moment of your time?"

His thick accent had returned, and she released a breath, walking calmly forward to stand, like the servant she was, receiving her orders.

His cheek tucked with a smile—two dimples—and, looking at them, Penny had the strangest notion. She had given some thought to the man to whom she would join her life when the time came to choose. His image was bright in her mind. He would work for the Foreign Secretary, of course. Probably some young officer in the diplomatic corps she could mold into the right material. One of the faceless, beardless subordinates attached to Papa's mission in Vienna. Then she would spend her life travelling from New York to Paris to Bombay, learning languages, holding salons, facilitating negotiations over a tea table.

Standing here, her head tilted back slightly to meet his eyes, she felt the list of requirements lengthen.

He must smile at me like that.

"Do you borrow books often?"

She glanced down at the volume she held in her hand. "You did say I might."

"I did." He slid his hands under the book and turned it over as she held it, their fingers almost brushing as he examined the spine, their heads tilted down at the same angle. Her lungs filled with the smell of him. "You've chosen well if your aim was to flatter these flinty Midlothians you make your home with," he chuckled.

He will have to laugh in such a way.

She looked up as he did, their noses a breath away. A warm blush travelled up her neck and she straightened. "Midlothian." She traced her mind for lessons in geography and supplied an answer. "A man from Edinburgh," she said.

"Or thereabouts. You've chosen Allan Ramsay. Did you know you're in for a rare treat?"

"Am I?"

"You doubt me." His blue eyes shone with merriment and his voice tilted low as he began to recite, his voice full-Scots now, no ragged remnant of enunciated English. Almost music. Yes, exactly that.

"*There's up into a pleasant glen, A wee piece frae my father's tower, A canny, saft and flow'ry den, Which circling birks has form'd a bower...*"

Dimly she knew she was in a squared-off room in a fine country house while rain lashed the windows, and cold wind gusted through the cracks under the door. She knew these things, but his words were magical, calling forth from her another kind of knowing. In them she saw a golden day, heard fat bees drunk on nectar buzzing through the woods as she felt the buzzing in her veins. She could almost see sunlight winding lazily through the leaves, and wished she would never, ever move from this spot. She closed her eyes to see it more perfectly.

"When e'er the sun grows high and warm, We'll to the cauller shade remove..."

Penny's lungs tightened and then there was a harsh sound—the scrape of his boot against the floor as he moved away.

Penny swallowed, blinking her eyes open, half-surprised to find a patterned rug beneath her slippers.

Malcolm offered a rueful half-smile, blinked, and was distant once more.

"I can't remember the rest."

Chapter Eleven

"...There will I lock thee in mine arm, And love and kiss and kiss and love."

The master of *Coille na Cyarlin* had done well to halt his recitation, but even several days removed, Penny wanted to fan herself with a loose bit of paper. Malcolm Ross would get himself into trouble if he made a habit of quoting such poetry to the governess.

Malcolm.

When had she stopped thinking of him as Mr Ross? She had no friends at *Coille na Cyarlin*, she reflected, swallowing hard past the hard lump forming in her throat. Was it any surprise her mind should invent a closer connection to the one person who seemed...to like her? No. He didn't always look as though he liked her. He had shown her kindness. There. That was it.

A thought—not an encroaching thought, but one that lingered like a gnat on the edge of her consciousness—surfaced briefly. Since the moment the poetry had woven between them, she was avoiding the library, and had no reason to.

Penny curled on the battered old schoolroom sofa with the volume of Allan Ramsay she ought to have returned as soon as she knew it did not contain any particular insights into the magic of this place.

Some of the poems were rough and well-nigh unintelligible, until she fell into reading them in Malcolm Ross's accents. They had come alive then, the words like leaves slipping over river rock on their journey to the sea, cushioned in chill, bracing liquid. Poems of gentle wooing and daring men, the words warm enough they could light a fire in her own cheeks and for a hundred years on.

When she read these passages, she could not think of him as Mr Ross but as Malcolm, the man who'd sheltered the night in a cold shepherd's hut, his strong profile softened by the bristles on his chin.

He had added some notation to nearly each poem, and she found herself murmuring her replies as though he were reading them aloud from the other end of the sofa. Arguing with him about the rewards each boldly drawn character had merited. Listening as he repeated favorite passages.

She tucked the bookmark between her knuckles and tipped the book open to a simple military ballad, an adventure-bound soldier parting from his girl. Whole stanzas were simply underlined and initialed by the same hand she knew as well as her own.

Farewell my Jean,
No tempest can equal the storm in my mind
Tho' loudest of thunders
On louder waves roar
That's naething like leaving my love on the shore

Jean. His wife.

Only an underlined passage and one letter but Penny glanced briefly away from the page as though she had been caught reading a private missive. Finally, she picked up a pencil and read the poem again, encountering another word she had never seen. *Maun.*

She added it to a list she had begun on her bookmark, an exercise, she now saw, which would require more room than one folded scrap of paper.

slinch
pawky
carle
oxter
bickey

The last was another Scots word Robbie had spelled out for her this morning, supplied with a definition. "Bickey," he'd said, impatiently, as though teaching patent facts to a toddler. "It's when the clouds look like an overstuffed pillow." The clouds were *bickey,* the sun had shone in places, and he had wanted to go out.

Penny snapped the book closed and went to the stables, anxious to make the most of the decent weather. She rambled through the grounds over stiles and through distant meadows, with Fritz racing ahead and around her. She watched fieldhands pace through the cold, freshly-plowed fields, scattering seeds from grain sacks slung across their bodies, too late in the season.

She doubled back when she judged her free time had been spent and shivered as a gust of wind blew from the tops of the nearby hills. A wind like that might blow a seed from the ground before it took root. It might freeze it before the green bud could unfurl from the husk.

When she neared the garden, she crossed paths with the nursery party, surprised to see Mrs Stuart had joined them. Here the path narrowed, and she stood aside, smiling at Mary who returned it as she herded Kathleen forward like a mother duck with her duckling. Ewan kept his eyes trained entirely on Fritz while Mrs Stuart gave her the smallest nod.

Then it went pear-shaped. As soon as he saw the dog, Robbie shot up the nearest topiary, holding onto the sculpted shape at the top, swaying dangerously. Penny rushed forward, intent on rescue as the soft wood began to bend. Tripping her up, Fritz barked and yipped in wild abandon at her feet.

Then, as quick as she could breathe, everyone seemed to move between her and the boy, forming a battlement, cutting her off from any means of assisting the procedure. A muscle in Penny's cheek jumped, and Mary disentangled Robbie from the shrub, pulling him on her back. His dark gaze darting towards Fritz.

Ah. Understanding dawned at last. Penny tightened her hand on the lead and gave Fritz a sharp command that he only half obeyed, settling onto his rump as his front paws danced. "He won't hurt you," she began. Silently, Robbie hooked a knobby leg over Mary's shoulder, determined to let no part of himself touch the ground.

Penny turned to Mrs Stuart, anxiousness in every word. "Perhaps if he could see that Fritz is no threat."

Mrs Stuart exhaled sharply. "The sooner you leave, Miss Starling, the sooner we will have all in hand."

Dismissed. What else was there to do but take herself back to the schoolroom? But her nose stung as she climbed the winding servant's staircase, pausing to tidy her appearance and pinch some color into her cheeks. She blinked several times and breathed out, gauging her reflection for signs the scene in the garden had hurt. She smoothed her hair and tucked away a wayward curl. There were no marks of it, and yet she felt bruised all over.

Hope had sustained her in the black days after she woke from the fire. When the bright scar crossing her back oozed, and dressing it had been an agony. Hope had carried her through the alarms of a tumultuous voyage, and the shocks of being around mulish people all day, each day. These difficulties were the price she must pay for the return of her magic. That was the trade she had worked out in her mind.

What if it never returned? Although there had been moments of fleeting, ghost-like sensations, the brief touches of magic seemed no stronger, no more memorable than a chill shivering down her spine.

Penny turned her head in the looking glass. One would think losing magic would show on a person's face, too. Perhaps she should take to wearing a black ribbon in her hair or dyeing old frocks the color of mourning. It was common when one suffered a loss.

She closed her eyes and breathed in, out, in, out, until the roar of failure faded a bit. Plucking up her courage, she rang the bell, listening for the familiar sound of the boys slamming out of the nursery and into the hall. They banged through the schoolroom door and dropped onto their seats with Mrs Stuart following in their wake, without her cane.

The afternoon lessons were hardly worse than usual. One child on the other side of the wall pleaded to get in the schoolroom and two who were within behaved obstinately until they were let out. Today she was attempting to teach Robbie arithmetic, and his proficiency in that subject was, if anything, perched upon a boggier foundation than his reading and writing.

"How many fingers does your hand have?" she asked, abandoning the paper and pen entirely.

"Five," he squinted.

"Yes. Excellent. Now add three. How many do you have?"

"I told you I only have the five," he stated, thumbs stuffed into his ears while his pinkies flipped his lower lip again and again. "Haven't heard of anyone with more'n six on a hand. Are the English misshapen?"

In that moment Penny wished to flail and scream, to throw herself on the ground exactly like Kathleen and drum her heels on the floorboards. Such a small setback, but the ordinarily thick cushion between feeling in command of herself and feeling as though the riders of the Apocalypse were mounting their steeds and drawing straws for the pale horse, was fast dissolving.

Again, she drew in a deep breath. She had crossed hundreds of miles to be in this house. She had lied to her mother. There had to be something more she could do if only she looked for it.

She glanced to the carefully wrought schedule lying innocently on the desk, a mute reminder of the gaping chasm between what ought to be and what was. It was of Miss Starling's devising, but some innovation would be needed.

Penny turned her head looking for any lifeline, discarding Mrs Stuart and Ewan as hostile to her cause. Her glance caught the volume of poetry and she brightened. The Scots words Rob had been supplying for her.

She drew a paper forward. "Let's put away our sums, Robbie. I wondered if you might help me with a project I've been worried over."

"Yes, miss."

"I ought to know more Scots words and thought you could help me make a list of all you know. Of course, we'd have to get the spellings just so."

Out of the corner of her eye she saw Ewan put down his book and Mrs Stuart lean forward. This was a genius idea. Small wonder they were impressed.

The words began to roll from his memory.

bragubrah

maunka

ayefton

owzleweip

farisal

They worked at it far longer than Robbie had worked on any project and, though she was certain his spellings were haphazard, she breathed a happy sigh of satisfaction when the page was filled.

"You've done wonders, Robbie. I'll have a lot of studying before I master the words." A tender feeling for the boy caught her by surprise and she had to suppress the startling desire to ruffle his hair. A whole hour of work. She had not known he was capable of it.

Penny creased the paper and rang the bell. The boys ran off with their usual stampede but this time there was laughter, and a smile touched her mouth. It was getting better. It was.

Now if she could only win Mrs Stuart around.

Penny shelved a stack of books and came to perch lightly on one end of the sofa. “You have no cane, Mrs Stuart. May I fetch it for you?”

“Not today,” the woman said, shifting forward to stand in a relatively fluid motion. “The pain will return,” she continued, snapping off the hopeful thoughts, which must’ve shown on her face. “There is never any real improvement.”

Penny ought to have subsided, having won a meager victory with even this much conversation, but she didn’t. She would spend another evening by herself with only the muffled sound of voices beyond the wall to keep her company. “Would you care to join me for tea, Mrs Stuart? I brought a blend from England. It’s...it’s quite good, and I fear I am in danger of becoming a recluse up here in my schoolroom.” As she asked, Penny lifted herself slightly onto her toes. More hope.

Elspeth Stuart halted. “No, Miss Starling. I fear my tastes are too plain for rich English blends.” She nodded a stiff farewell. “I shall see you tomorrow.”

She still hoped. “Perhaps you will be able to entertain yourself with some handicraft or a...a book.”

Mrs Stuart notched her brow up, every inch a dour Scot. “Much like Robbie, I am no reader.”

“He will be a reader after I’ve had him for a time.” A flame of pride glowed in her breast and she wanted to shout her success from the walls of *Coille na Cyarlin*. “Did you see how interested he was in teaching me the Scots words? All that effort. If I can shift his interest to English, why then—”

Mrs Stuart choked on a laugh and Penny’s pleasure checked. “You dinnae think those words are real Scots?” She chuckled again. A light laugh, which seemed to eviscerate the last shreds of Penny’s dignity. “It was all nonsense. Robbie’s been spinning his tales for the better part of an hour.”

Dimly, Penny heard the scrape of the door as the bitter metallic taste of Mrs Stuart’s mockery flooded through her. Ewan and Robbie’s too. Their laughter took on a malicious edge in her memory. Her smile wobbled, and she began to fear that tears would spill from her eyes. They balanced precariously against the well of her lashes. Damn and damn and damn.

“Miss Starling, are you—”

Malcolm. Penny took a breath with a smile that was half-grimace. Another breath and the smile righted itself. Shame washed through her bones, drying the tears in her eyes, kindling a fire so hot they burned away.

Was it shameful to want something so small, so simple as company and friendship? It was certainly shameful to find them so out of reach.

She curtsied, not daring to look away from the floor.

“Excuse me.”

Chapter Twelve

Penny raced through fields dotted with freshly scattered seed; the wind whipping the betraying moisture from her eyes and cheeks. All the while she imagined the words that would put this cursed house behind her and send her winging to the safety of Edinburgh and home. *To the devil with Coille na Cyarlin,* spoken through clenched teeth as she stepped into a hired carriage. Those would be good words.

She had failed here, and it was best to admit that now before… She didn't know what lay ahead or why it should worry her so, but the word slotted neatly into her mind. Before.

Eventually Penny found herself following the rough directions Isabelle had sketched out, tearing through a narrow, muddy track in the woods, the stately trees whispering as she flew past them. Her lungs burned with cold and exertion, but she lifted her grey wool above her ankles and dug her feet into the dirt, feeling the earth pound against her heels.

bragubrah

ayefton

bickey

When she spotted a cottage clearing, she slowed, swallowing air as she took in her surroundings. Had she planned to come? She didn't think so. But Lady Ainsley had been kind to her once.

Penny dug a fist into her side where a stitch of pain radiated, unable to take her eyes from the cottage. Isabelle lived in a tidy, well-kept dwelling, but the house was ringed about by ancient trees resembling stooped giants, their backs broken by rough work. These forest spirits seemed to be kept in abeyance by a low stone wall and a garden gate that squeaked when Penny swung it open.

Along the flagstone path, beds were full of dark soil, well-spaded and ready for planting, and around the back there was a tiny glasshouse that would capture as much light and heat as this dark spot had to offer. A lazy scarf of smoke unwound from the chimney, and the thought of a good fire quickened her pace. Penny's toes were as cold as strawberry ice.

She rapped on the door and a maid escorted her through a narrow passage and into a warm, comfortable parlor, nothing as grand as she might expect from a dowager countess. The furnishings were a mix of styles that might have once been elegant, but were now faded and patched over, and a poisonous smell of decay and age hovered in the air. Something rotting in the room that looked out on the garden.

Penny sniffed and her gaze glided along the fitted bookshelves stretching the length of one wall. Not rot, she diagnosed. Only age, dust, and treasure. Penny drew closer to the shelves, her breath sticking in her throat as she read the titles. An illuminated manuscript of a book titled *Solomon's Magicians*. Beside it sat *The Compleat Guide to Sympathetic Magic*, and further down the shelf, *Herbs and Their Uses*.

Her heart began to race as fast as it had when she ran. She'd been searching the library at *Coille na Cyarlin* for weeks only to find it was full of ordinary things—novels and poems and household history. But these were magical books—grimoires—that whispered and argued the secrets of enchantment and sorcery. Not the ten or twelve Papa had collected after Beatrice rose, but an entire wall. She put a fist to her chest and felt the laugh trapped in her lungs.

All these weeks of making do with weak flutterings and vague impressions—poor replacements for true power, but the only things which compensated her for the thankless hours in the schoolroom. Yet, all the time, this was where her magic meant to lead her. It must be.

A hesitant fingertip traced the spine of *Malleus Maleficarum*—Hammer of Witches, she translated in her childish Latin. Another volume lay open on a nearby table and Penny ran her finger down the page, reading in a whisper.

"In days long past, our magic was whole, possessed by one being, but then there was a scattering of magic, of that there can be little doubt. We know not whether it was caused by a celestial meteor crashing from the sky, or through divine purpose as with the multitudes cursed at the Tower of Babel. The wholeness of magic fractured, but shards and fragments are to be found to this day reflecting the light in thousands of ways…"

"I wondered when you would come."

Penny whipped around at the sound of the voice, her heart hammering her throat.

"Lady Ainsley," she gasped, dipping a curtsey, and regaining some of her composure with a slowly released breath.

"Isabelle," the lady corrected, moving with a feline grace past Penny and subsiding into a chair by the window, the diffused light enhancing her features. "To what do I owe the pleasure of your call?" She flicked a glance at Penny's petticoats and smiled.

"You said I should come," Penny answered, taking the seat Isabelle offered. She shifted her skirts to hide the wreckage of mud and rainwater on her petticoats. "Particularly when I wanted to hear my own accents."

"Poor thing. Is the schoolroom so ghastly?"

Thoughts flitted across Penny's face, she knew they did, and she struggled to master them. "What an enormous understatement, my lady. It makes me wonder if my former governess had such a thin time of it, or if I am a particularly miserable specimen."

The maid entered with a tray of tea, and Isabelle poured it out, her movements precise and methodical. Only when she was finished did she take a sip from her own cup and ask, "Were you wondering if I would keep your identity a secret, Miss Thornton?"

The air seemed to shiver between them, and, for the moment, the pull of the grimoires was forgotten. Penny dug hard into her memory, hoping to unearth some new nugget of information about a person who could ask such a thing without turning a hair.

There was nothing. Isabelle was as she had been long ago, still wearing her widow's weeds, the black of her dress an elegant contrast to her pale, blue-veined skin. Why was she in Scotland? Why was she in relative poverty? Why did she have books on the history, art, and science of magic?

These questions remained unspoken.

"I *was* wondering why you already have. You could have unmasked me to Mr Ross. I am not your kinswoman. You do not owe me any duty or loyalty."

"No, but you are a fellow Englishwoman, and you looked so desperate. It would've been like shoving a drowning person back under the water when I had the power to pull them to shore. You are going to tell me why you needed such aid, I hope."

Isabelle's expression held concern, but Thorntons didn't speak about their magic. Beatrice had only told her husband when the only other option was death. It was doubtful she had even spoken of it to her best friend.

"I have a particular reason to be addressed by the name of Miss Starling," Penny stated, "and wish you would oblige me by using it. I have no nefarious reasons, I assure you. I am not an adventuress."

Isabelle's brow arched as smoothly as a stretching cat and Penny was eaten up with jealousy. She hadn't the knack to do anything half so elegant.

"That is a pity," Isabelle replied. "Miss Starling, the world would be a great deal more amusing if we had more adventuresses."

At the sound of her alias, Penny released a slow breath and took a sip of tea. It was only her mother's excellent training that kept her nose from wrinkling at the musty brew. Isabelle must have spent every coin of her widow's jointure on those books.

"Still, I cannot help but wonder," Isabelle began, "why an heiress should take a position as a common governess."

"I would not do it for a lark."

Isabelle smiled. "Ah. It is a significant thing. Are you angling for a match with the master of *Coille na Cyarlin*? Is dressing in drab woolens and locking yourself into the schoolroom some clever way to insinuate yourself into Malcolm's life?" She took a sip of tea and winked. "Too clever for me."

Surprise gripped Penny by the throat as the image of Malcolm Ross's face—of his bright azure gaze holding her own—stirred her mind, setting off reactions that were becoming as regular as winding a clock. Her cheeks flushed and warmth gathered in her belly. She raised the tea to her lips before setting it aside with a little snap. The smell was unforgivable.

"I cannot work it out," Isabelle continued, dragging Penny roughly back from thoughts she was not prepared to foster. "The house is adequate, but nothing out of the common way. Malcolm is so... Encumbered. The ragged tenants, the obsession with his village, those children, the old woman. Is *Coille na Cyarlin* sitting atop a diamond mine I don't know about? Or does madness run in your family? For I can see no other reasons for your interest."

"When I look for a husband," Penny declared, her lips suddenly dry, the words tumbling from her mouth, "he will have to suit my requirements."

"And those are?"

"Certainly not to be found here."

"No? There are few treasures to be found in this part of the country. I suppose a dilapidated widower and his ravenous estate might be considered one of them."

Dilapidated. The word raked across Penny's skin and her throat ached with the effort of holding in a swift denial. Is that how his cousin saw him? Broken down and penny-pinched? Oh, but when he smiled. That smile made her wish he was what she needed him to be—a diplomat's son, his tongue proficient with four languages or five, willing to be loved slightly less than she loved her magic.

She shook off the thought. "I have no interest in Mr Ross," Penny stated, her voice firmer, the words drummed into her head. She did not have any interest in Malcolm Ross. She could not. "You are utterly wrong."

Isabelle chuckled. "No need to overset yourself, child. I'm only teasing."

Penny took a deep breath and set her tea aside, motioning to the shelves, "I've never seen anything so wonderful as your books, Lady—Isabelle."

"You could not keep your hands from them."

Penny's unease slithered back. Though Isabelle's face was laughing, the words were baldly spoken.

"I meant no offense," Penny smiled, striving to hide her thoughts behind a polite façade. She reached a hand to a nearby table and plucked up the volume she had studied so closely. The spine, picked out in scarlet letters, read *Origins of Power*.

Isabelle leaned forward and touched the brittle pages. "They are of great use in the still room."

"Are you a healer?" Penny asked, lifting her eyes.

Isabelle's smile broadened. "Oh, yes." She waved a hand at the shelves and Penny could almost hear them groaning with magic. "Each of these contain a kernel of truth, and I do my best to discover it. Have they piqued your interest?"

"Very much."

"You surprise me. I supposed a woman of reason and education such as yourself," Isabelle's brow lifted softly and Penny nodded the answer. Her education was no lie. "would find my interest in enchantment and divination rather quaint."

Papa was the diplomat, able to dance around subjects and skate over obstacles with geniality and good humor. It was far more difficult when Penny attempted to wield those tools. "Not at all," she said, a delighted smile on her face. Too delighted. "The illustrations are breathtaking even if the tone is a little—"

Isabelle tilted her head and Penny brushed a light finger over the book. "Ancient tales of scattered and lost magic." The idea brought a sparkle to Penny's eyes. If magic existed as fragments, it could be found again in the most unlikely places. Even in a Scottish cottage. But when she spoke, Penny tried to sound like a young woman of reason and education. "It's a charming story."

Isabelle's laugh was more full-throated. "Charming? Magic is not charming. You can't buy it for a shilling in a fortuneteller's tent. Not if it's real."

"Real?" Penny tilted her head in a passable show of confusion as a wave of goosebumps washed down her flesh.

Isabelle placed her cup on the saucer, putting both aside. "Come now, Miss...Starling. I'm not an easy person, but I am honest, and it goes hard against my nature to be false in any way."

Penny froze, each nerve on end as the silence soaked into her bones. Then Isabelle leaned forward, a sympathetic half-smile on her mouth. "What if we didn't pretend you know nothing of magic?"

Penny's breath circled her lungs, the pressure building up, her mouth open to utter more lies.

"I can feel it radiating from you."

Isabelle lounged against the back of her chair, empress of this tatty parlor, but panic beat hard inside Penny's breast and a voice sounding remarkably like her mother's told her to push over the tea table and run as fast and as far as she could. Get the hell out of Scotland and race back to England where people don't know and can't guess. Hide away behind the nigh impenetrable walls of money and rank.

However, there was another voice whispering too. *Stay, stay.* Isabelle could sense the magic, which meant that Penny hadn't imagined the stirrings in a fit of grief and longing. She still had magic.

"It's faint," Isabelle assured her, running her locket up and down the chain. There was nothing in her tone that said she was discussing anything more distressing than the latest fashions or the state of the weather. "You needn't worry anyone else might notice, but I felt it the first time I touched you."

"I have no magic," Penny said, the bands which seemed to anchor her to the earth growing taut and constricting. For too long Mama had drummed secrecy and caution into her head, and the voices warred within her, one loud, another inexpressibly soft. Penny was already beginning to stand. The room was too close, the fire too warm, the musty rot of the grimoires filling her nose with a sickly, sweet scent. It had been wrong to come, and now she would do anything to escape, to leap through the window and rise into the air.

"If you admit you have magic, we can do something about it." Isabelle sounded so dashed ordinary, her whole manner reminding Penny of an exhausted parent coaxing a button out of a child's mouth.

"Did." The word was ragged and ghostly as it squeezed from Penny's throat, but it set off a cascade, unloosing the dam. Her voice broke. "I did. I don't have magic anymore. I did, but I don't now."

"There," Isabelle said, and she looked proud of Penny. The rustle of her dress seemed a sigh, but Penny's stomach roiled. Loss twisted her features, and she caught a faintly enquiring look on Isabelle's face.

"You must have magic too," Penny gasped out. "If you can sense mine. What is it?"

Isabelle placed her elbows on the arms of the chair and tented her fingers. "I haven't any magic, aside from brewing little tisanes and tinctures. Any magic that isn't inborn—any that you find in a book—is weak, full of limitations and compromises, but I come from a family with a bloodline of magic stretching back generations. Oh, yes," she said, at Penny's start of surprise. "My little sister Margaret can read the minds of those she touches. She's probably read your mind," she added, spilling her family secrets as easily as emptying a reticule.

"You must have magic. You touched me. You read—"

Isabelle spread her hands. “Hardly anything at all. I don’t *have* magic, but I do own it,” she said, leaning forward and cupping her locket in cool fingers, running a light touch over the delicate scrollwork. “The cost was quite dear. Would you like to hold it?”

She began to unfasten the clasp and soon it was coiled in her palm, the dull metal shining in the sunlight. This was not familiar magic and Penny tensed. Her own magic had been an extension of herself, as familiar and comfortable as her stays, but this was strange, metallic, alien.

I’m not an easy person but I am honest…

Penny extended her arm and Isabelle held her wrist, dropping the object into her hand. The metal felt cold to the touch, far colder than it should have been resting against Isabelle’s skin, but soon there was a pleasant warmth suffusing the gold.

In a quick movement, Penny released her wrist and dumped the jewelry back into Isabelle’s hand, a little disappointed. This was magic far weaker than her vague quickening. “It’s interesting.”

Isabelle held the item in her hand, furrowing her brows in an expression that was there and gone faster than quicksilver. Then she fastened the locket once more around her slim neck. “It warms up when I’m around magical creatures long enough. Did you feel that?”

“A little. I told you, my magic is—” She spread her hands and then a thought struck her. “Is Mr Ross magic?”

It would explain much about her reactions to him. The breathlessness. The awareness of every subtle shift in his face. The way her fingers itched when he was near. Oh, what a relief. She leapt forward, a nimble doe bounding forward with theories and conjectures until Isabelle spoke.

“Not a bit. I cannot think of anyone less magical than Malcolm Ross. No doubt, if he had it, it would go wandering from brain to liver to kidneys looking for something to repair or organize. It must have skipped a generation when it landed on the children.”

“The children?”

Isabelle peered over the rim of her teacup with a slightly wicked expression, “Well, one, anyway.”

A laugh squeezed from Penny’s lungs. “Impossible. No. You must be wrong. I’ve been looking for magic for more than a month and I would have noticed if it had been in the same room. The children are many things,” she said, her mouth tightening on the memory of Robbie's list of Scots lies, "one of which is profoundly ordinary."

"Nevertheless," Isabelle insisted.

"Which one?" Kathleen, likely.

Isabelle's lips crumpled in frustration. "I'm not certain which one of them has it yet. Their magic isn't strong enough to trace, and I haven't spent nearly enough time with any of them. But I have every confidence I will discover the answer as it grows. I'm working on a theory." She waved at the shelves. "Magic works like a seed, sort of rattling around for a while until it begins to sprout. It's why we don't have babies prophesying the weather or turning their mash into cake. The seed is there but it hasn't taken root."

Penny's thoughts turned inward as she measured the idea against her own experience. Is that what had happened? The old magic had been cut down and the new hadn't regrown? "Will we wake to find Kathleen transfiguring her dolls?"

"If you see such a thing, I expect to be the first to know." Isabelle offered Penny a slice of cake, the familiar rhythm of the visit clashing wildly against the talk of powers and enchantments. At least Penny had found someone with whom she might speak freely.

Her mouth tightened against the familiar rush of grief. "I could rise into the sky as high as I wanted to go."

"You could fly?" Isabelle tilted her head.

A ghost of a smile touched Penny's mouth. From the first day of discovering her powers she had bent her mind to the task of discovering the reach and breadth of her magic, restless until she understood the scope of it. She always meant to discover a way to fly. "No," she said, brushing over the endless variations of movement she had perfected. "I could rise and fall as I wished."

"I'm certain it was quite pleasant," Isabelle said, the faint praise doing more than outright derision in conveying her feelings. Then her gaze sharpened. "I've never met anyone who lost their magic. How did it come about?"

Penny's mind flooded with memories. The fire, the billowing smoke, the fear that had been born inside that barn. Her hand reached to her neck, to touch the scar where it rubbed against the neckline of her gown. Her brow wrinkled as her fingers found no raised or irregular skin and she surreptitiously slipped the pad of her forefinger below the fabric, encountering its familiar shape. She had survived. She must not forget.

"I was in an accident, and afterward I was sick for weeks and weeks with a fever. My mother sat at my bedside for more than a month. They thought I might die and when I woke—" Penny swallowed back bile and wrinkled her nose against the stinging behind her eyes. She shook her head briskly.

Instead of the perfect stillness of unexpressed sympathy, Isabelle almost ran to the bookshelves. "A sickness? This is marvelous," she exclaimed, running light, exploring fingers along the spines. She murmured as she went, "*Books of Mystery*, *Le Petit Josue*… Here. *Whispers of Enchantment*."

She pulled the volume from the shelf and set it on a table, leafing quickly through the flyspecked pages. When she stopped Penny stood over her shoulder, her glance taking in the bold medieval hand.

Isabelle tapped a finger on the page. "Read from here to here."

The spellings were haphazard, but Penny worked them out as she read aloud. "A woman's magic is shy and skittish, as she who bears it. Upsets and alarms will whisk it from a body, sending it flying to more fertile ground. This may be a great mercy, but if the loss is regretted, tricks abound for coaxing it home."

"That is an interesting piece of the puzzle." Isabelle leaned against the bookshelf and regarded Penny with a long, searching look. "Upsets and alarms drove your magic out. It wasn't done by some other magic practitioner," she added, narrowing her eyes, lost in thought.

Penny turned the page, frowning as she read on. Until it failed to materialize, she could not have said what she expected to happen when she found another thread that might lead her to her magic. A shivery excitement would travel every vein, lightness would suffuse her, perhaps there would be some supernatural certainty. She would feel as she had when Malcolm had pulled her from the library that first day when she met the children—reaching forward, breathless with wonder and hope.

There was nothing but the hiss and pop of the fire in the grate.

Her eyes darted over the text. "I don't want a cure for itchy feet," Penny exclaimed, flipping the page between her fingers.

Isabelle took the book, closing it with a snap. "Grimoires are frustrating things. Enchantments offered in tiny scraps alongside potions for grippe and scabies." She smiled. "I can help you get your magic back. That's why you came to Scotland, is it not?"

It was disconcerting to have one's motives laid bare. "Why would you help me?"

Isabelle waved a hand over the shelves. "Magic interests me—the origins, uses, limits. Having found one clue in these books, I'm certain I could find another."

"I could help you read through—" Penny reached for the volume, but Isabelle shelved it quickly.

"Let me do this thing for you," Isabelle said, steering her back to the tea tray. "What have you tried, thus far?"

"I've been searching the library for something magical. There haven't been many promising texts, but I did find a history of the local villages. The old folklore might be illuminating. I've touched every item I can lay my hands on at *Coille na Cyarlin*, looking for a talisman. I've also been attempting to call my magic at least twice a day, working on the theory it might return if given enough practice."

Isabelle's look was arch. "How methodical. You do it standing each morning in your stocking feet and nightdress, I wager."

Penny flushed though she nodded. Every morning and every night in the stillness and quiet, she gathered thoughts of lightness and willed herself to rise from the ground.

"A fever and a fire forced it out of you. If you really want it back, you should try something more dramatic. A real leap of faith. Do let me watch, if you do."

Penny didn't let her. She didn't even know she meant to try until she left Isabelle's cottage, taking another track leading through the woods and found a wide meadow where the ground dropped away to the river below, fifty feet or more. Not such a great height but enough.

She stood there for several long minutes observing the roll of the hills and signs of Malcolm's village, willing herself to step off the precipice, coaxing and then prodding and finally raging at herself that she must trust that her powers would return, or they never would. When not even her most scathing denunciations would move her feet, she turned away, ashamed, and saw the tree.

It was a dead oak tree spread on the edge of the meadow, the bark torn away to reveal the twisted heart, with branches that reached like witch's fingers to the sky.

Penny's heart caught in her chest, but she ran to it, and before cowardice could call her back, she threw her cloak over her shoulders and jumped for the lowest branch. She reached for the next limb, and the next, rough bark scraping her knuckles as she climbed higher and higher. The branches thinned and she felt the familiar sensation of wind tugging at her hair.

She closed her eyes, clinging to the trunk, her face turned up to the sun as though she was standing in a crow's nest at the top of a mast with the wide green ocean undulating beneath her. I'm home. I'm home.

Was this magic? Almost. It was so very like it had been.

She only needed to let go of the branch to be fearless again, to command the sky and know her place in it. She only had to step forward to begin to believe again the story of herself. *Penny Thornton is magic. She can rise into the sky and drift on currents of air. She can do anything she wants.*

Then she looked down and her stomach slipped into her shoes. Thirty feet. Tears pooled on the edge of her eyes and she looked up, blinking them away, her mouth shaking in a silent cry. Thirty feet was nothing, hardly an exercise, but it terrified her as it never had before.

Let go.

It was too high. She clambered down several branches, tugging her cloak loose, dragging her skirts away from snags. Stopping halfway down, she judged the distance and swallowed. It was a terrible distance to drop from, but her powers would save her. They would.

With perfect faith, she closed her eyes and fell.

Chapter Thirteen

Malcolm glanced at the sky and sent the children inside to have their wash up and supper. It hadn't been properly bright in months, but there was still plenty of time to ride out to the village before the smudgy blue skies faded into twilight.

Perhaps the ride would distract him from thoughts of Miss Starling's mobile face, struggling for composure. She had been shattered when she left the schoolroom, brushing past him as quickly as a hare, hanging onto her self-possession by the slimmest of threads. If he had stopped her, he was certain she would've said that all was well and would've been lying through her teeth.

Thoughts of her chased after him as he galloped his mount between the soil-blackened fields. He wondered if she wished she had never come to Scotland. Wondered if she always read poetry. Wondered what her hair would feel like between his fingers. When he halted on the stretch of land rimming the ridge he read himself a stern lecture.

Malcolm Wallace Ross, you will leave the lass be.

All the sternness in the world was insufficient to banish the image of the English girl racing through the fields. Her strong figure running across the ground caught at his throat, making his neckcloth feel too tight. A true gentleman of the sort his mother had raised did not chase after petticoats, particularly if they belonged to a governess under his protection. Even if it was the first time he'd wanted a woman since—

Don't.

Malcolm cut the thoughts out as though he wielded a knife, cold reason sharpening the blade. The girl was English. She had no love for Scotland, his children or him. She would grow tired of the cursed weather and would run back to England soon enough.

Malcolm forced himself to survey the view of meadows and woods, and river below him, along with the bright slash of newly constructed cottages. More than cottages. A couple of streets, a village green, a pub, a grocer, a smith, and, further on, following the curve of the river, a paper mill waiting to be roused to life like a sleeping giant. He smiled.

At this hour, the tools were silent, and the workmen had dispersed to their crofts until morning. His horse danced, and he reached his hand to pat the mare's neck. From this distance, he couldn't see the empty window frames, the well that collapsed this morning with the rain, the walls needing pointing with lime mortar. From this distance, the progress which seemed so glacial resolved itself, sharpening a blurred line the closer he got.

This is what he should be concerning himself with. Planning this village had sustained him through the black days of his grief, when there had seemed no escape from sorrow. It would surely prove ample to the task of putting a foolhardy, inexplicable curiosity in its proper place.

When he had tidied things in his mind, he gathered the reins again and heard a scream.

Malcolm wheeled his horse and saw her falling. Saw her body strike the ground below the dead tree. Saw her fair hair, bright against the green grass. He dug his heels hard into the mare's flanks and raced over the turf, the sound of galloping hooves no match for the thundering of his heart.

"Miss Starling," he bellowed, halting the horse so swiftly it almost sat on its hindquarters. He slid from the back and hit the ground at a run.

Another cry. It was a pitiful sound, which tore at his heart. He followed it and fell to his knees. "I'm here." Throwing his gloves aside, he cradled her face in his hands. "Look at me," he begged. "Look at me. Are you hurt?"

Her face twisted, and when she tried to speak, she let out a whimper, nodding as a shudder racked her body. He ran his hands over her limbs, testing with a kind of desperate concern he could not understand. He had seen injury before. Death. He was level-headed and cool in a crisis. Only now he didn't feel cool.

"What happened?"

"I fell. A few branches up," she breathed, the words coming in choppy gasps.

“A few branches,” he muttered, his hands gentling the moment he witnessed a spasm of pain cross her face. It was her arm, twisted at an unnatural angle, and he could not leave this point of agony, but must continue his inspection. He must bring more pain. He grimaced as he felt the scrape and grind of the bones, felt the separation, and heard the wild cries she stifled in her throat.

“It’s broken,” he pronounced, and she released a shaky breath, her pallor chalk white. A whisper of amusement laced her words, even if her brow was damp with sweat. “You can stop wearing that expression. You’re not the one in pain.”

Lord, was she really trying to coax him into a better frame of mind? He could not laugh now. Faith, he felt as though he *was* the one in pain, and he let the relief that she was safe—that she was going to be safe—wash through him. “Anywhere else but the arm?”

She shook her head.

He helped her sit up, slowly, carefully.

“A clean break, I think,” he said, tugging at his cravat, unwinding the cloth. “I only saw half that fall, and it was bad enough.”

Ten minutes. Was it only that long ago he had been telling himself to leave her alone, to let her occupy a space in his life which attracted no more notice than a scuttle of coal or a mantelpiece figure? Now, here he was touching her, looking for frailty, for fissures in her bones and agonies he would mend if he could.

He sat back on his heels and rubbed a hand over his face. He’d aged ten years in ten minutes. Glancing up again, he measured the distance. Fifteen feet or more. The thought that she had been within a hair’s breadth of killing herself hammered its way past his clenched teeth.

“What possessed you?”

A stricken look crossed her face.

Damn it. Blast and damn it. Tears gathered in her eyes, and without thought, he pressed his cheek against hers, hand cradling the delicate bones of her jaw as she mangled his lapel. He held her until she spent her tears, her floral scent working into his coat and onto his clothes, her smooth skin rubbing his scratchy chin. He tried to hold her like she was one of the children with a skinned knee. He tried.

A shudder shook through her and she bit hard into her lip as he drew away. He’d hurt her again. “I’m sorry,” he said, finishing with his cravat, feeling the sudden chill as the gusting wind curved around his neck. The setting sun would soon turn the sky into flames of rusty orange, scarlet, and pink. “Forgive me.”

She nodded, though she didn’t turn her grey eyes on him.

“This is going to hurt,” he said, as she sniffed away a residue of tears. He folded her arm against her chest and bound it tightly, ignoring as much as he could, the flinching of her jaw.

He scooped an arm around her waist. “Steady on,” he said, easing her upright. “I’ll have you to the doctor in no time.”

“You will not let me fall, sir,” she instructed as he set her atop his horse, her tone taking him back to a frigid morning in Edinburgh when he’d found an empress seated by a common room fire.

“You may kick me if I do,” he teased. Perhaps if she were annoyed at him, she would not feel it so much. He led them down the track, but what should have taken a few minutes became an agonizing half hour until they reached Doctor Bell’s home.

“You were a Trojan, Miss Starling. I would be wailing in your shoes,” he said, sliding her into his arms when they arrived, allowing himself not the tiniest pleasure in holding her.

As soon as her slippers touched the paving stones, he let loose her soft figure and held his arm out to assist her. A mocking voice came from the recesses of his mind. Maybe he had taken the tiniest pleasure.

Her determined chin came up. “I never wail,” she insisted, a falsehood if ever there was one. He still smelled the scent of her, soft as worn ivory, clinging to his neck and coat, and still felt the span of her strong back as she shook with tears.

“Not only can you teach the children math and science,” he said, rapping on the door, “but your talents are far wider. Climbing trees. Stoicism. Mendacity.”

“Are you enjoying this?” she grouched, her pinched lower lip expressive. He had never wished to be an artist before but found himself wanting enough mastery of charcoal and paper to capture the shades and planes of her expressions. To tuck them away and take them out when he had a solitary hour.

He raised his fist to pound the door again and it swung open. When the maid ushered them into the front parlor, Miss Starling eased onto a straight-backed chair.

“Are you quite well?” he asked, crouching at her side, and taking her hand in his.

“No worse,” she breathed. “Exhausted. I’ve never felt so tired.”

Dr Bell entered, his cropped blond beard bristling along his jaw. He wasted no time on pleasantries. He unwrapped Penny from the binding, peppering her with questions.

Malcolm supplied the answers, his eyes narrowing on the blunt hands moving assuredly over Penny’s injury.

“You’re being quite rough, wi’ her,” Malcolm said, when he had taken all he could bear. The old man would do the girl some injury moving at that pace.

“This is how I do it, lad,” the man admonished. “I’ll not bend my methods to anxious maidens.”

“The maiden isn’t anxious,” Penny ground out, though her eyes were closed tightly, and her chin was pulling.

“Aye,” the doctor agreed, “but that one is.”

Even in her agony, a tiny laugh puffed from her lips. Her eyes opened and they trained on his for a long moment. Then her breath hitched, and she squeezed his hand in her smaller one.

“You’re doing grand,” Malcolm said, wondering how this handclasp could unnerve him so.

“It’s not broken,” Doctor Bell said, scooting away slightly and slapping his thighs. He moved to a decanter of whiskey and poured out a measure. Malcolm dragged his eyes from Penny’s face.

“It is broken,” he insisted. “I felt the bones wiggling under my fingers. I could even hear the pieces grating —”

“Don’t be disgusting,” Penny grimaced.

“They were your bones, Miss Starling. I’m not one of your pupils, wanting correction.”

She gave him a look that said otherwise.

“If the doctor can’t find a break, you could be pleased.” The doctor gave a chuckle and offered Penny the glass. “For the pain.”

Penny sniffed the strong spirits and shook her head. Doctor Bell turned and raised it towards Malcolm. When he declined, the old doctor grinned and tipped it down his own throat.

“I am pleased,” Malcolm said. “Check again.”

The doctor set the glass down with a thunk and put his hands to Penny’s arm once more, moving quickly, his attitude one of aggrieved tolerance. "I've set more bones in my time than you have bricks in your chimneys, lad," he muttered. "It's not broken."

"It's right under the bruise," Malcolm said.

Dr Bell perched his spectacles atop his head and crossed his arms, pointing with the flat of his palm. "What bruise?"

Malcolm turned Penny gently toward the light. "That's impossible."

"Would you prefer to be the doctor, Mr Ross? You certainly have no need of me. Now, child," he said, turning his back on Malcolm. "Can you wiggle your fingers. Aye. Now your wrist. Good, good. Elbow…"

Penny flexed and stretched her arm at his bidding while Malcolm watched, unable to match the tentative but flexible movements with the feel of bones under his fingers. Shifting. Separating.

"You're in no pain?" the doctor asked.

She smiled. "None at all."

"She's a terrible liar," Malcolm insisted, his eyes dancing when she narrowed hers at him. "I would make up a powder for her, if I were you."

"If I were you," the doctor muttered. "Do you need one?" he asked Penny.

"It's aching abominably," she conceded, "but no worse than that. Truly."

"Well, then, I'll make one up for you and Elspeth. She must be running low in all this cold weather. I can bring it up—"

Malcolm's mouth eased into a smile. "She's been in excellent health, Doctor. Hasn't needed any of your powders for weeks."

The man scratched the back of his head. "Even with the cold and the wind and the rain?"

"Even then. For Elspeth, spring came early."

Chapter Fourteen

They walked the distance to the big house, the air dense with rain that had already fallen and would yet fall. As *Coille na Cyarlin*, a dark rectangle set against a sky painted like a travelling caravan, rose into view, her will failed her.

What had the misadventures of the day wrought? Very little. There was the promise of help from Isabelle, but all else—

"You feel well?" he asked. He stopped to examine her, and she stopped too, turning her face. Sun struggled through the clouds. A golden rim lined the slight stubble on his chin.

"I'm well enough," she replied, continuing on the track. She brought her hand to her arm. It burned still, like a hot coal had slipped under her skin to smolder until it died away. It was agonizing, but her bones were not broken.

How was that possible?

She focused on the question, the better to distance her thoughts from the man who had set his pace to match hers, his horse trailing behind him held by the reins in his left hand.

How had she survived the fall? Try something dramatic, Isabelle had said, and, like some fool she had done it without thought or preparation or care.

"Why were you climbing trees, Miss Starling?" Malcolm's deep voice tugged her attention.

They had gained the gravel drive now, the crunch of booted feet and hooves muffled in the night air. "I needed some respite from the schoolroom."

"I noticed that." He was even with her now, his dark frame inches from her elbow, the horse following slowly in their wake. "Elspeth explained about Robbie's Scots."

"I have tried several things with him," she said, clamping her mouth shut in case she cursed with great fluency. The fluency would shock him. It would shock a sailor. When the crisis passed, she continued. "He's grown more obstinate under my care. I'm not doing anything for him."

"You think you're failing?" His surprise sounded genuine and she glanced up at him. The fading light made his expression unreadable, but his voice took on the quality of twilight, dark and soft. "He grew so strangely obedient when the last governess had him, and after, when she left. He was scared."

"I can't blame him for being scared, for not trusting me."

A laugh. "You don't understand. Robbie's prank today was a welcome surprise. He trusts you, Miss Starling, enough to know when he's high spirited and fiendish, you won't lift a finger to harm him. He is practicing on your good nature, and I'll have another talk with the lad, but you're managing the boys far better than you should be." What delight she took in his words was immediately punctured by, "Have you and Elspeth settled amicably?"

Penny lifted her chin at the sudden image of Mrs Stuart's eyes, narrowed in malicious laughter. Even remembering that moment sent a sharp painful tug through her chest.

"That answers that," he supplied as her silence stretched. "I expected better of Elspeth, but I ask for your understanding. Jean, my wife," he added roughly, "was her only child. We were shattered after she died. I don't mean for you to cut your feet on our sharp edges."

It must be the deepening sky that invited confidences he wouldn't have shared in sunlight, and she felt a push and pull of emotions. Pleasure that he should speak to her so. Pain— She could not understand her pain.

They carried on towards the house.

"I saw your village," she said, thinking to find an easy topic.

"Ach," he exclaimed. "What did you think of it?"

Penny had hardly been thinking of anything up on that cliffside beyond what a frightened child she was. But she scraped her memory. "It looked quite well-ordered."

"'Tis that," he answered, pride in his voice.

"Why are you doing it?" She didn't much care what his answer was, only that he kept talking, moving him further and further from asking about the tree and her fall.

"Dotted along the river were tiny villages—no more than a few cottages to them. In the last fifty-odd years, the land turned to grazing, and the new ways of farming chewed away those small holdings. Then the villages began dying: Skelpit Maun, Wryborne, Scunner, Wee Scunner, Lour.

"So you'll build another one?" She gave a low laugh. "Is this an example of that economical and canny Scots thinking I hear so much about?"

"Wretched woman. I saved your life."

She gave an un-governess-y giggle. "I'm not even scratched."

"About that—"

"Why are you building a village?" she rushed on.

"I hope to lure the crofters to work at a paper mill down the river a mile when they leave their holdings."

Penny wrinkled her brow. Lure. "Why would they leave their homes?"

"They don't have a choice. They'll have to leave sometime and—"

Her voice tightened. How could he speak of this so calmly when lives would be upended? "Aren't they paying you high enough rents?"

There was a sudden spray of gravel and his hand caught her lightly by the arm—the good arm, she noticed—and his touch set off an answering warmth she seemed to have no control over. Isabelle was wrong about Malcolm having no magic. It might have been too small to trace, but Penny felt it every time he touched her.

"I don't need money," he said.

"No?" Penny recalled the numbers in his ledger book, how much was going out, and how little was coming in. She shook off his hand with a small movement, releasing an aggravated breath.

She had been to enough dinner parties in Vienna to know how things were decided. The most noble families took pride in their holdings, keeping them in trust for future generations, but they could always afford to be rootless, moving from country estate to town house to house parties. They could afford novelty and change. It was the way of things. The lives of the lower orders had to be rearranged, each life manipulated. Tin soldier beings sliding across a table map. She had accepted that too, before she lost her power.

"You think I would do this for money?" he asked, cold anger competing with the bite in the air.

She turned her face up, searching, and saw a vision of Malcolm Ross introducing her to his children—Ewan, Kathleen, and then his hand had cradled the back of Robbie's head. It was a gesture she had seen him make dozens of times since that day. He would set his strong hand between the world and the ones he loved. Always.

Penny walked a few paces, chafing her arms and missing the warmth.

"No," she answered, stopping in the shadow of the house, standing in a kind of no-man's land between the front entrance and the servant's path. He ought to turn his way and she ought to turn hers.

"It was unjust of me to say so. I was sorry for them—the villagers. Perhaps they will be longing for what was, wishing they might have a measure of it returned."

He let loose his own breath which told her he was not angry anymore, merely tired. "A measure of starvation, squalor and poverty, Miss Starling. I can't afford to dress it up to suit romantic notions. The old ways are dying here. It wasn't me who killed them off, and it'll be made all the worse by a year in which the wind blows the seed from the fields and the sun never shines." She heard the rasp of his palm rubbing against his jaw. "When hard times come, we can only look forward, not mourn for what we do not have."

Penny shivered and crossed her arms across her chest. His words were as neat and orderly as the lanes of his village.

"If they prefer the old ways?"

"They don't have that choice. They cannae grow families here and keep them. Not on plots so small. Their choices are between breaking their bodies in a Glasgow factory or scratching out a living in a polluted slum and working in a paper mill set in their own hills. Between emigrating to America and resettling here, it's not the perfect choice, heaven knows, but they would do better to deal with the world as 'tis instead of spending their days trying to find the way back to how it was, but never will be again."

Penny turned quickly, a lump of emotion scratching in her throat. Why did *she* want to cry about a paper mill? There were mills dotted up and down the British Isles, and Malcolm Ross would run one with as much compassion as any master. But there was something here she could not like.

"I understand," she said, and didn't. She turned to stalk towards the servant's entrance until his voice stopped her.

"I hope you're happy here, Miss Starling."

She nodded and watched him go, hating the name he called her, hating the lie. *Penny*, she longed to say. *Call me Penny or Pen, or even the hated Penelope. Call me by my name.*

The dim awareness that had been growing within her settled like a bird on a branch. She liked him.

Oh Penny.

Imagine being as silly as forming an attraction to a widowed Scotsman with difficult children, as tied to his land as ever a man was. It could not develop further.

Malcolm would not be as comfortable as an officer in the diplomatic corps. He would not be easy at all. She attempted to scowl the feeling away only to find it wouldn't budge as easily as that.

No one liked her here, and they would be happy to see her go. If she really had stepped from that ledge and plummeted to her death, she doubted there would even be a short homily before the celebratory cake in the schoolroom.

She would not like them. She would not.

She cut through the kitchens, and in her haste to climb to her bedroom, almost cannoned into Birdie who was holding a knife.

Penny bobbed. "Quite sorry, ma'am."

Birdie frowned and signaled for a footman to carry his tray to the dining room. Before she followed him, she glanced at Penny. There was the usual exasperation at Penny's Englishness, but her expression was not unkind. "Next time, Miss Starling, before you rush to your death, slow down."

"Yes, ma'am." Penny nodded.

Slow down. Slow down.

Her magic had abandoned her. She had almost died today. She felt she could ill afford to slow down. As she turned up the stairs, a thought hit her with the force of a beam striking between her shoulder blades.

Magic slowed me down.

Chapter Fifteen

Malcolm dismissed his overseer and curled a hand around the back of his neck, hunching over the ledger. For several minutes, his finger traced down the long list of sums, automatically checking and rechecking them. The estate was bleeding money and each mark on the carefully lined page was another cut.

His mouth tightened and he leaned back, closing his eyes. There she was, rendered by his traitorous mind in perfect detail—the waywardness of a curl brushing her neck, the face lighting with delight at some jest she had thought up but hadn't yet spoken, her strides lengthening because she was furious.

Last night in the twilight, she *had* been furious. Something about his village had touched her to the quick, and though she had not come out and accused him of pushing his tenants off their land, she had come damn near.

He shouldn't care about her opinion. It was the half-informed judgement of a young woman earning her wage. But here she was, claiming his awareness the moment he let his focus soften. He tried to sharpen it now.

The village. He applied himself to the ledger once more. At the rate his obligations were piling up, the village would be only half finished by fall.

It ought to be enough to consume a man. It was enough. He might admire the lass, but he would not nurture the attraction. He began to compose a list of necessary work for the coming week and pushed thoughts of Miss Starling from his mind.

Hire a few boys to collect river rock.

Her softness as he'd held her.

Arrange for a firm to transport the millworks.

His scent mingling with hers.

Begin clearing the cottages of refuse.

How her mouth might feel under his own.

The door slammed open as his heart hammered in his chest and Elspeth charged in. Thank God.

"I wish to speak to you about Miss Starling," Elspeth said, planting her hands on his desk. Malcolm groaned. Lord help him, he was trying.

"What's the woman done this time?" Malcom asked, tipping back in his chair with every appearance of welcome.

Elspeth frowned. "I'm not so unjust as to look for excuses to set myself against her. The girl was strange today—"

Malcolm's chair snapped upright. "I knew it. I knew she was still in pain. A fall like that—" he muttered, reaching to summon the footman. "I'll call Doctor Bell to ring a peal over her head."

Elspeth trapped his hand. "It's not that. She—" Elspeth darted the tip of her tongue across her lip. "She didn't invite me to take tea with her."

Malcolm's brows lowered in question. "Do you take tea often?" He almost smiled at a memory. Penny's tea would have been carted across the country, no doubt, to ward off the chill of a barbaric Scottish spring.

Elspeth took her time, settling into a chair and pleating the fabric of her skirts. "Well, noo," she began, "I cannae say as we do. I've...I've not had the time." Her chin angled aggressively. "She's English."

Malcolm knew she was English. It was the thing—almost the only thing—that kept him safe from her. The only thing that recalled him to his senses. "I don't understand your problem."

"She asks. She always asks. It's not always tea, but she treats me like I'm a castle to be seized." Her voice became higher and English-ish. "How was your day, Mrs Stuart? Can I offer you an oatcake, Mrs Stuart? Would you like a lap blanket, Mrs Stuart?"

His lips twitched. "The nerve."

Her expression was dry. "Your nanny should have spanked you more, boy."

He grinned. "Birdie never could bring herself to it. But Elspeth, you got what you wanted. She was pestering you, and now she stopped."

Elspeth lifted her disgruntled face to the shelves and Malcolm could have sworn there was some tense emotion hovering around her mouth. She flattened it away.

"She always tries with me, and she's stopped." When he failed to understand the import, she huffed, "Anyone could see that the solitude has done her in. Alone as she is, can it be a shock that the weak-minded English girl is touched in the head?"

Malcolm Ross beat Elspeth's words against the threshing floor, tossing them up again and again until the oats were divided from the chaff.

"You think she's lonely?"

"Aye. Haven't I been saying that? She takes her meals on her own. The servants do not make friends with her, and the walls of your fancy house are so thin," she said, buoyed high on a tide of outrage, "that I have heard her weeping."

Weeping? Malcolm had seen her cry when there was cause for it, when her arm had almost snapped in two. But the thought of secreting her tears away made him want to charge up the stairs and demand to know why.

Elspeth flung her skirts away and she looked queenly. "It upsets my digestion."

Another smile crossed his face, reflexive this time, unmoored to his heart. Pen was crying.

"Something must be done."

At last, they had come to it. "You want to help her in some way? Elspeth, you surprise me."

His mother-in-law scowled at him, a sign he had hit the mark. "I would not leave a dog penned up as she is. It will not do for the children to have a teacher so out of spirits. You should invite her to take her dinners with us."

"You may do as you wish, Elspeth. This fancy house with the too-thin walls is your home." It was spoken calmly enough, but his heart constricted at the prospect. Likely, it meant nothing but that older men were prone to apoplexy. It was Elspeth who wanted the girl. Not him.

She gave a curt nod. "I know you would prefer to be alone with your thoughts at the end of the day."

Malcolm was caught up short at the sudden understanding that wasn't true at all. In the last years, he had exhausted himself on solitude. Gorged himself on loneliness. But last night, walking down the lane with a lass, his heart almost in his throat, every nerve reacting to the merest twitch of her skirts, and seeing his village with new eyes because they were her eyes… He didn't want to be alone.

Mealtimes had become somber, but now he would have Penny to sit at his elbow every night he wished it. He traced a splotch of ink on his blotter. The idea of it pleased him so much his hand trembled. Chambers of his heart, long-since bolted up and left under the weight of Holland covers quickened with life. It wasn't too late to brush the cloth into smoothness once more, closing the doors with the sharp click of a lock, plunging the rooms into deep quiet.

He heard the steady thump of his heart in his ears.

When he said nothing, Elspeth stood. "She will join us this evening."

A smile tucked his cheek. Elspeth would not be so vulnerable as to ask. She would command it.

He arrived in the salon wearing his best coat and snowiest cravat, unwilling to examine the reason for either, and spent the ensuing minutes prowling from the mantel to the sofa to the window and back to the mantel again.

"You're restless tonight," Elspeth said when she joined him, watching his movements with a gleam in her eye.

"Business matters," he replied.

"I hope I have not kept you waiting."

They both turned to find Miss Starling standing in the doorway. She wore her fair hair in a knot, contrasting with the deep blue of her gown, and it seemed a wildly inspired choice. Blue wool and fair hair. Alert the presses. Someone tell Brummell.

"Not very long," Elspeth replied as the clock chimed the hour.

"Not at all," he corrected, shooting an admonishing glance at his mother-in-law.

"I'm a little excited," Penny admitted, glancing up at him, neither uncomfortable, nor uneasy, stealing the breath from his lungs.

"We hope we will not bore you."

Something flashed behind Penny's eyes he could not catch, and he wished he had the right to brush his hand down her arm to clasp her fingers and ask what it was. He did not. He paid her wage and tried to remember that. Instead, he offered Elspeth his arm and led her into the dining room as Miss Starling followed behind.

The mahogany woodwork gleamed under the soft candlelight and several landscapes of the Pentland Hills adorned the walls, the canvases under a thick patina of age that rendered them far more lovely than they were.

"Thank you," she murmured, as he pulled out her chair. She reached for her napkin and draped it across her lap as elegantly as his mother had ever done. He knew little of her life before she had come to *Coille na Cyarlin,* and a sudden need to remedy that fact took hold of him.

"Are your people from the country, Miss Starling?" he asked, as direct as a child and as heedless of the conventions.

She seemed to check and then picked up her knife. "I went to London once," she said, "long ago. The noise was appalling."

He could imagine her coming up from the country—starting her journey in the early hours of the morning and coming up in time for breakfast, her curious face under a plain, girlish hat, watching the bustle of Piccadilly or Pall Mall. She would have been holding onto someone's hand. "Your father, what is his profession?"

Penny sliced across a potato. "He is an instructor."

The picture he had of her sharpened. "Like his daughter. Did he teach you—"

"Papa's Latin is much better than mine," she cut in. Then she rested a forearm on the table. "Now that I have satisfied your rank curiosity, I have questions of my own. Weeks and weeks of questions."

So bold. His gaze met hers and warmth banded his neck, spreading under his collar. "Fire away."

Penny leaned forward and he found himself inclining towards her, watching the play of light and shadow over her clear features. "Were there ever real witches at *Coille na Cyarlin*?"

"Real witches?"

"The library has no record of any, and none of the artwork in the hallways depict—"

"Real witches, my lady?"

She tapped a finger impatiently on the table and a little sigh escaped her. "The rain has turned the entire world into a damp stocking. I can't afford to ignore my interests, sir."

“But witches, Miss Starling.” He held his mouth as solemn as a monk’s, but she wrinkled her nose at him when she saw he was laughing.

“I am answered. You may retire your patronization, sir. Fold it away and keep it for other company.” She smiled as she said it. “However, as you asked two impertinent questions, Mr Ross, I must be allowed to even the score.” He liked her best like this—when she had forgotten she was a servant here, favored enough to dine at the table with her master. He prayed she would not remember.

“You’ve instruments in the garden. A thermometer, a barometer.” Her brow wrinkled. “Something that—” She formed a circle with her fingers and thumb, sketching a tube.

“A rain gauge—a bad one, I fear, and a bit of silk to give me the direction of the wind.”

Her mouth. Lord, he loved how her mouth curved slowly when she was pleased.

“You measure the weather?”

“That makes two impertinent questions. I do. Though I have no happy news to report this year. Only bitter cold and glowing skies.”

“Do you hope to publish your findings?”

“Three.”

She laughed and he wanted to make her laugh again.

“Nothing so ambitious, Miss Starling,” he said, almost stumbling over her name. Damn. He must stop himself from lapsing into this habit he sometimes had of allowing himself to think of her as Penny or Pen. “Knowing the weather helps with the planting.”

“You do not rely on folklore or old wives’ tales?”

“Four. You are deeply in my debt.”

“How improvident of me. It only counts if you answer.”

“I prefer modern methods. I’ve been keeping a record since I was at university and hoped—” He shook his head. “Now I am kept busy with the village, with the farms, with Kathy and the boys. I keep a record for my own pleasure and information.”

Her eyes dimmed. “That’s a pity.”

“Is it?” He set down his fork and leaned back in his chair.

She lifted a hand. “I like interests to be nurtured.”

“Such as a curiosity for real witches.” She smiled. “I suppose it makes you an ideal governess, but you cannot split your soul and tread down every path. Some choices required me to give up other choices. If I am not destined to become a leading scientist of The Royal Society, at least I have not cut myself off from my enthusiasms. Are there not sacrifices you made when you formed the mad resolution to become a governess in Scotland?"

There was a curve in Penny's cheek and a smile on her mouth. He tensed, waiting for her response, hardly aware Elspeth was watching. Penny's eyes sparkled with unexpressed humor and then she blinked it away. Another blink and she caught her lip in her teeth. Still another and she exhaled, straightening away from him. As the breath left her body, she seemed to lose herself by degrees. Less Penny. Less cleverness and contending. Less matching him, word for word.

She had to answer, according to the rules of this foolish game.

"I am content with my position," she offered.

Liar.

Something unruly and wild raced through his chest, vibrating the anchors which kept him tethered to what was reasonable, to what was possible. She was lying and he knew it. He knew it as certainly as he knew the calluses on his palm. He knew her.

"Is your arm still feeling poorly?" Elspeth intruded, bursting the fragile threads binding them.

"We have returned to conventional questions," Malcolm declared.

"Much more comfortable," Miss Starling admonished him and turned to Elspeth. "I was only a little sore when I woke," she said, brushing two fingers softly up her arm. A picture formed in his mind of carrying out his own inspection, of being nestled together and reaching to enfold her more closely. Malcolm swallowed, and felt the narrowness of the path he had resolved upon grow more precise, more slender.

Penny stretched her arm in front of her, turning her neat wrist and shoulder unselfconsciously back and forth. He almost growled.

"Good as new."

Elspeth stood abruptly, her chair clattering back. "I'm finished," she declared, holding her hand out until Malcolm supplied his arm. He led her into the rose salon, a small, close room decorated for comfort rather than elegance, and seated Elspeth on a sofa, "You wanted her here," he whispered. "Be kind."

Instead of the crotchety assent he expected, Elspeth clutched at his sleeve. She spoke low, beyond the hearing of the girl arranging the tea tray. "I don't know how. I—" Her mouth clamped shut.

Understanding settled on Malcolm. He laid a hand over Elspeth as Miss Starling came to offer tea. The girl was young, as Jean had been. She guided the children as Jean had once done. Elspeth's antipathy wasn't roused by Penny's Englishness or anything else she was. It was who she was not.

While Elspeth gathered herself together, Malcolm turned.

"We are comfortable here, Miss Starling. We work on puzzles and dip into books." He indicated an instrument in the corner. "Are you musical?"

"I play the piano forte with all the delicacy of a herd of elephants on the march," she began, adding to the picture he had constructed in his mind of her upbringing. Pennies and pounds scraped together for a few formal lessons. Papa allowing her to sit alongside his scholars, dresses passed down and mended. Did she have sisters and brothers? The broad plain of all he did not know stretched out before him. "I can read aloud well enough, if you keep your hopes bridled."

"Too late," he said, handing her a few worn books of poetry. "They are running away already."

They sat in the soft glow of candlelight and fire, silent for long stretches while the wind howled without. They traded a verse now and again, exchanging opinions.

"Hear this one," she said, and he lifted his eyes from his book to take in his fill of her when she couldn't possibly know he was watching.

She began in a round, low voice.

At setting day and rising morn
Wi' soul that still shall love thee,
I'll visit aft the birken bush
Where first thou kindly tauld me
Sweet tales o' love, and hid my blush
Whilst round thou didst infauld me.
By vows you're mine, By love is yours
A heart that cannot wander.

Her words with their mangled accents died away though the magic of them wove around his ear. Elspeth cleared her throat, drawing his gaze, and smiled, a touch of knowingness to it, and he flushed.

"Did you hear the word I wanted you to?" Penny asked.

Vows. Aye. Love. Aye. Sweet. Heart. Aye, aye.

"Cannot."

At his look of confusion, she walked the book to him. "This is that poet of yours." She pointed to the stanzas she had read aloud, and he quelled a desire to wrap an arm around her waist. "Infauld" her as old Ramsay would say. To make vows and seal them.

"Well now," he looked up. Her eyes shone like the soft stones of a riverbed. "He's not mine."

She crouched down. "He says, 'A heart that cannot wander,' and I don't understand why."

As her scent drifted into his lungs, his own heart charged, a storm of emotion blew his carefully planted rows into disarray. His plans and intentions seemed to scatter in the face of it. There was no time for reflection, to take the meaning from the chaos. Penny was inches from his shoulder. Elspeth was watching them with dark eyes. He had no recourse but to shelter and wait until he could reflect.

Penny shot him an irritated look. "You are like those boys of yours. Not paying me any mind at all."

He grinned.

She swallowed and shook her head returning her gaze to the page. "He used 'cannot.' I know it's all English, but the Scots form is so often cannae and willnae, it is not? I…" Then she smiled. "I cannae make sense of it."

"Don't try to make sense of a Scotsman," Elspeth said, jerking them from their reverie. Malcolm looked up, pleased with her effort.

She was also perceptive. The smallest arch of her brows spoke volumes. Elspeth was laughing at him.

"Sometimes Scotsmen have an odd kick to their gallop," she said in her silkiest tone. "They like what they like. Even English things." Her eyelids flickered and now her eyes were fully on Penny. "You did well with those tricky words, Miss Starling."

Penny returned to her seat. "Thank you, ma'am. Perhaps Robbie's lessons have done me some good."

There was a taut silence before Elspeth acknowledged the topic. She nodded graciously. "I hope they have."

Penny closed the book and set it aside. "Is that your sewing table, Mrs Stuart?" she asked, turning the topic. Malcolm went to the tea service and felt rightness mooring him to this room. Elspeth had been cruel—unusually so—to taunt the girl about Robbie's trick, and Penny could feel herself justified in holding a grudge. But here she was, braving hurt and trying with Elspeth again.

Elspeth snorted. "I haven't used it in years." She lifted her hands as if in explanation.

"Can nothing be done?" Penny asked, taking the dish of tea Malcolm offered.

Malcolm waited for sourness. Bitterness. Waited for Elspeth to slap down a question that ventured far beyond the conventions.

"Heat helps. Rest. But it always comes back. I should content myself with feeling less pain for a time. It's greedy to hope for more.

"Hope isn't greedy," Penny replied, and Malcolm stared into the fire. He wasn't used to hope. In the last years he had moved grimly into the future, like a coal miner picking his way forward, inch by torturous inch. Lord, what if there might be an end to it?

He raised his teacup. "To you, Elspeth. May your hands be as strong as your heart."

"Oh, that is nice." Elspeth raised her own cup. "May you finish the village. To the glorious rise of New Pentland."

Remembering the long afternoon spent going over the numbers he gave a short laugh. "May money rain from the sky."

He was about to search for some more entertaining topic, one that might amuse their guest, but Penny spoke before he did. "Are there other investors?"

Malcolm grinned. More bold questions. Well, hadn't he started them off? He shook his head. "It's my land. Shouldn't I assume the risk myself?"

She didn't let it go at that. "The industry you hope to bring to these hills will benefit more than the Ross family, supplying farms with seasonal laborers, justifying better roads, providing a locus for a richer social life. If they advanced a certain sum, a stockholder could expect to reap tidy profits from the mill."

Of course, she had an opinion on the matter. Of course, she was sharing it. "You think I should actively seek more capital?"

Her eyes were level with his. "Exactly that."

"I would have to go to them hat in hand. Who would—"

"Hat in hand nothing," she scoffed. "If your village is a sound financial opportunity," he nodded, "then the next step is to find someone with deep pockets."

He laughed and looked to Elspeth who was already tapping her lip. "Leadburn," she suggested. "He might do. He's as clutch-fisted as a miser but would not pass up the chance to put money in his pocket."

Malcolm began to take the matter seriously. "Lord Berwick is at Penicuik all summer. I could invite the both of them to tour the site, see what they thought."

Unconsciously he looked to Penny, gauging her reaction.

"Are they married men?" she asked.

The shock of jealousy was like stepping into an icy stream, but Elspeth hooted. "Looking to make a match, Miss Starling?"

Her mobile brows snapped down, but she laughed. "And be trapped in a land so cold it frosts in June?"

The laugh was unequivocal, and in that moment, Malcolm knew himself, knew how high his hopes had flown.

"I only mean to say, in my experience, all business is contracted socially. In Vienna, every diplomatic coup was won in the ballroom before it was ever signed by dignitaries."

"Vienna," he said, the image of her beginning to dissolve with that one word.

Penny shook her head slightly. "A woman I knew went to the Congress of Vienna with her husband. She was good enough to share her stories."

The picture in his mind reformed, and beyond the modest cottage there were the gates of a large country estate, and a rambling house where the Misses Starlings were invited to take tea from time to time.

"Contracting business socially," he prodded. "What are you suggesting?"

"I wouldn't presume to suggest anything." Penny folded her hands in her lap.

He grinned. "It's too late to be so prim, Miss Starling. You have an idea. Don't hold it back on my account."

She inclined her head. "I suggest a soft approach. Perhaps Mrs Stuart could host the wives for tea. Perhaps you might throw a ball."

"The idea being that if the wives are won around—"

"Who better to win around the husbands?" she finished.

"I can't," Elspeth exclaimed. She held her hands up. Though the movement was supple, the skin was still pulled tight over swollen knuckles.

"What has that to do with the matter?" Penny asked.

Instead of bristling, Elspeth's face wore a look of patient explanation even as she waved a hand. Strange. She had never balked at acting as his hostess. "Miss Starling must do it."

Malcolm's gaze held Penny's wide, anxious eyes. "Are you wanting an invitation, lass?"

Penny froze. "Lass?"

Elspeth ignored it and Malcolm pretended to. He could not tell her it meant nothing, this informality.

Penny made a protest. "I have the children to give lessons to."

"It wouldn't be every day," Elspeth said, as crotchety as a dried willow branch. "A tea or two. Mary and I could oversee their instruction while you are about the business. Everyone knows I'm frail," she persevered, sounding anything but.

"I am a governess, ma'am."

"And I'm the widow of a clerk. You will brush along well enough, and we can hint to the high and mightiest you are gently bred and doing me a great favor acting as my factotum."

Penny suppressed a laugh. "Factotum."

"Factotum," Malcolm declared. "You cannae abandon us now."

Her lips twitched. "Cannae. I will help if you wish."

A slow smile lifted one side of his mouth. "I wish."

At the end of the evening, Malcolm tugged at his cravat, winding it around his hand.

If he wanted a woman, could he not have found a comfortable widow? The girl who sparked his fancy wasn't supposed to be English, wasn't supposed to be in his employ, and he wasn't supposed to feel anything for her.

A response came to him softly, wearing the voice of a lost love.

But you do.

This time, instead of fighting the realization, he surrendered. It marched through his body, demanding every part of him as if by right. Planting a flag and claiming him for England and St. George.

His laugh was low and rueful as he pulled off his boots and shrugged out of his coat. Was it wrong to fit so well with a lass who was so unlike Jean? A betrayal of her spritely, dark-eyed beauty to discover that fair hair and challenging grey eyes were all he could think of? To love her long-limbed body and mind that moved like quicksilver?

He sighed, tugging on his nightshirt, and slipped into his cold bed. It was not the simple love of a young boy gripping him now. He had spent that love—willingly, with great joy, watching it mature as they grew—and yet here was more.

His eyes drifted shut and he could hear the tap, tap, tap of rain against the glass. His palm rested heavily against his heart as he examined the new emotions, finding there was not less room for Jean now that Penny was here.

"She laughs like you did."

The words seemed to hang in the room before being absorbed into the old walls. Malcolm closed his eyes again. What would become of this love now that it had him? He gave a wry grunt—half pain, half believing he could talk himself into enough detachment he would not be shattered by it.

It didn't matter, he concluded before drifting off to sleep. Nothing could convince her to put down roots in Scotland.

Chapter Sixteen

It was silly to be here. Silly and presumptuous. Nevertheless, Penny scratched at the nursery door before she could think better of it.

Mary swung the door open in all her starched glory, and Penny took a hard breath. It was bad enough to tell Mary how to do her job. It was worse the idea had come in a dream. For more than a week, she had dreamed she was a tree and Robbie a shrub, his leaves dropping off one by one. It was obviously some sort of allegory and explaining it would make her sound like a loon.

"Yes, miss?"

Penny swallowed. Between the gnawing worry her magic would not return if she failed to fling herself from a cliff, the frequent notes flying to and from Foxglove Cottage containing inquiries and suggestions, and this idea tapping against her brain, it was possible she was turning into a loon.

She almost blurted the words. "I'd like to improve Master Robbie's schoolwork, Mary, and wondered if you might be willing to help."

Mary's brow buckled. "I'm no governess."

"You dress the boy?"

"Aye," Mary said, drawing out the word in confusion.

"I would like you to stop."

Stupid idea. Stupid. Where it had come from, only heaven knew. In her waking hours she could never piece the connection between Robbie's clothing and his scholarship. Yet the thought plagued her.

Mary began chewing the inside of her lip. "Kathy—"

"I'll take Kathleen each morning."

"She'll like that."

"But you have to train Robbie to dress himself."

"He won't like that." Then Mary giggled. "I'll be trading one grappling match for another. All those buttons and laces. It'll take hours."

Penny grimaced. "I'm upending your whole morning."

Mary nodded. "What do you hope it will do?"

Get the maggot out of my head.

Penny spread her palms. "I don't know for certain. I don't care if he looks like a rag and bone man when he gets to the schoolroom, but he must do it himself. It's only an idea,"

An idea wholly untethered to reason.

Mary agreed, and when Penny rang her bell to signal the start of school, Kathleen entered wearing a smile stretching from ear to ear. The child's hair had been trained into tight glossy braids, one ribbon half-dangling, and she looked so angelic Penny half-expected a heavenly choir to follow on her hem.

"I put your books and papers here." Penny tapped a spot at the end of the table, quite near Mrs Stuart. Ewan came over, and unprompted, began retying Kathleen's ribbon in a neat bow.

"I made a list of words that follow the alphabet," Penny murmured to Mrs Stuart, wondering how Ewan could have such a big heart and share not the smallest piece with his governess. Penny handed over a paper with clear, bold letters and simple line drawings. "Can you take her through them as I work with Ewan?"

Mrs Stuart glanced pointedly at Ewan, Kathy, and the empty doorway, but when Penny failed to supply an explanation she got on with her task. Within the last week Mrs Stuart's manner had subtly shifted, and Penny's mind sought to measure the precise nature of it.

The older woman wasn't so ready to pounce on Penny's missteps. The intensity of her gaze hadn't lifted, but now there was a degree of goodwill in it. They had moved into some indistinct place, past the boundaries of mere tolerance.

Penny turned to Ewan, first setting out mathematics. Without his brother to look out for, Ewan was inclined to be more mulish than usual, going through each subject as though he resented his own mastery of it.

Finally, she drew out a list of Latin phrases, testing his knowledge of past lessons.

"*Alea iacta est*," sighed Ewan, determined not to be interested. Then he supplied the meaning. "The die is cast. *Sapere aude*. Dare to know."

Sunlight warmed her neck and she turned to the shelves like a flower, dragging a finger across the spines, hesitating when she hooked a book of animal anatomy, the blue leather cover fitting her hand as though it were made for it. Unthinking, she pulled the book down to the table.

"What's that?" Ewan asked, stopping his task.

"I'm not certain," Penny replied, brushing dust from the blue, tooled cover. She swatted it with her handkerchief and then brushed more vigorously. The book was enormous, and a thought tugged at her fingertips. "It belongs on the floor, Ewan. In that patch of sunlight."

He didn't smile but his ears lifted hopefully. "Aye."

They lifted it down with a thump, kneeling side by side, and flipped open the cover. Instead of tight, cramped text covering each page, they found a world of rich, detailed drawings of native Scottish animals. Pen and ink depictions of talon and fur so precise they might have been real. Lithographs of birds rendered in vivid color next to descriptions of habitats and habits.

Penny opened her mouth to explain the treasure, but Ewan's face fairly glowed.

"Do you like animals?"

He blinked and some of the light went out of his eyes, even as he devoured a drawing of slick, silvery river lampreys weaving through rocks. "Robbie doesn't like dogs."

"Do you?"

In his silence was a whole ocean of longing.

This child had been nothing but a trial to her since she came to *Coille na Cyarlin,* but his answer sent the soft touch of sympathy through her.

"I have a dog. You've seen him with me. Fritz."

Ewan nodded. "Short-wiry fur. Brown and black patches over a cream-colored body. Was his dam so small?" he asked as he turned the pages, his eyes darting over each morsel of information. He probably didn't even realize he was speaking to her.

The memory of the fire flickered behind her eyes. She heard the screaming horses, the groan as the roof caved in on her back. The lancing pain and searing sense of grief were muted, as though she were observing a painting of a thing, rather than the thing itself. "He was the runt."

Ewan didn't answer her, but as he looked down at the book, she could see the elusive tail of a smile lift his cheek.

"There's Latin here," he said, running his fingers under a caption of a common kestrel. "*Falco tinnunculus*. What does it mean?"

Penny glanced to the table, at the abandoned Latin phrases Miss Starling had drilled into her. She ought to retrieve them, bring the lesson around to where it was supposed to be. But the sun was so curiously warm in this circle of light, brightening the hair on the top of her head, toasting her through the sober wool of her dress. It almost felt as if each muscle and nerve had taken a great breath, enjoining her to stay as she was.

She continued kneeling alongside Ewan in the patch of sun and began to sketch out binomial nomenclature in the animal kingdom. "Every living thing was given a name with two parts. The first is the genus…"

Time flew as Ewan absorbed the lesson, halting abruptly when Robbie sprang through the door. Mary followed him, her hair greatly disarranged, but she met Penny's eye and clasped her hands, shaking them high in the air. Victory.

Penny looked Robbie over as he strutted in a slow, cocky circle. His shirt tails were half tucked and his trousers, backward, made a funny puff of fabric over his front.

All the while, Penny was aware Ewan reverted to his habitual tense and watchful expression.

"Robbie Ross," she began, twirling her finger in the air so he might spin for her again, "I've never seen such a handsome devil in my whole life."

"I did all the buttons, myself. All of 'em."

"And a fine job you did," she exclaimed, conscious it'd taken a good deal more than an hour, and he'd lost time learning his sums and how to form his letters. How could it possibly be worth his while?

"You've come to take Kathleen?" Mrs Stuart asked Mary.

"You need another tiger," Kathy insisted.

Penny moved to her side and picked up a page.

Mrs Stuart looked over her shoulder. "Kathy said, 'How many trees do you want me to draw, Gran?' and I said, 'Six, Kathy' and then she said, 'A bird pooped two seeds Gran. You have eight trees now."

"Did she really?" Penny looked over the stack of papers.

Penny put a fist to her hip and a palm to her forehead. Her chest rose and fell in a gusty sigh.

"You cannae hold her back," Elspeth whispered. "Yon Robbie looks as pleased with himself as if he'd conquered a kingdom. Mebbe he won't notice his little sister is gaining on him. Heaven knows she will, whatever we do."

Penny invited Mary to stay, knitting on the sofa and carrying on a low conversation with Mrs Stuart while the three children got on with lessons until, finally, Penny called a halt.

"We have a little time before tea," Penny said, feeling the pleasant strain of happiness against her chest. "Why don't we let Robbie choose what we do until then? A game? A book—"

"Stories," Rob said.

"If you like." Penny swept her skirts aside and began to take a seat at the table, but he stopped her.

"Can't tell stories at a table." He walked to the fire and plopped down, the puff of fabric sticking out like the dome of a mushroom.

The others joined them, and Penny bade Mary stay where she was, electing to curl up on the floor with the children.

Ewan lay on his back. "Tell the one about Cyarlin the Witch, Rob."

"Which one?"

"The true one, Rob."

He rocked on his seat, his knees paddling the air until he settled. "They're all true...in one way a' the other. Now let me see…" His voice shifted and suddenly he was a bard, holding some ancient court in thrall.

"Cyarlin, the Old Hag of winter, held the hills in her icy grip, clawing valleys into the woods, carving stone wi' her frozen heart. It were bad that year. Badder than this'n. Cows—or what they then called cows—hideous horned beasts with long faces like sermons and flannel underthings—nosed the fields for grass and cracked their teeth against the rock-hard ground. Cyarlin ruled Scotland from Hadrian's Wall to the Great Glen where her castle lay."

Kathy climbed onto the sofa, wiggling into Mrs Stuart's lap. Ewan's eyes were closed, his face wearing a smile. Rob was a revelation.

"By and by, the Hag grew restless and sent her tent...tendrons.."

"Tentacles?" Penny prompted.

Robbie nodded and scooted himself into her lap as though it was his throne. “Aye. Tent-icicles stretching across to Glasgow and down into the soft belly of England.”

“England,” the children pretended to spit with a reflexiveness no one seemed to take notice of.

“Being weaker vessels, the puir English bas—”

“Rob,” Penny dropped her chin on his head.

“Being weak,” he amended, “the sickly English king begged Cyarlin to return to her homeland, to draw her sword against the stout men of Scotland. Now, it was no good time for a killin’ frost. The lowlanders had fields to harvest and barley waiting in the soil to push its bearded tops through the snow. So, they found themselves a witch.”

“What kinna witch, Rob?” Kathleen asked.

“A white witch. Brigid who would bring the spring back, sending the Old Hag home like a sot stumbling drunk from a pub.”

“Did she go, Rob?”

“Och, aye,” he said. “Don’t be so daft, Kathy. You can see there’s no ice now.”

“It’s awful cold, Rob. Won’t Brigid come this year?”

“Brigid will come,” he said, “beating back the Old Hag of winter and burying her in the earth.”

“That’s nice of her. What’s she like?”

“Bonny as a Scot. Trim ankles and strong. As bonny as Miss Starling, here, but not English, a’course.”

“A’course,” they echoed.

A voice came from the door. Malcolm, wearing the rough clothing she had met him in. “You’ll make your governess ashamed to be English, Robbie.”

“She can’t help being English, *Aither*. We know that well enough.”

Malcolm’s eyes danced as he assessed the schoolroom and nursery. When his gaze remained on her face, Penny’s throat tightened. “What will it be like when Brigid comes?” she asked.

“We’ll be happy again,” Rob said. “The hills will bloom, and every button will jump into their buttonholes…”

“Every sheep will bear twins,” Ewan said.

“Every day will be school,” Kathleen said.

"We'll beg her to stay and never go away again," Malcolm finished, his rough voice making Penny's face blush hot.

He didn't take his gaze from her even as the children began to swarm his limbs, pushing his thatch of hair around his forehead. He had Kathy up on one broad shoulder when he said, "I'm walking down to the village and wondered if you wished to come."

How had Beatrice managed it, Penny wondered, when she had fallen in love with her captain? Extreme emotion had always touched their abilities off. How had Beatrice stayed earthbound long enough to accomplish anything when a simple attraction seemed to lodge in Penny's throat and shake through her like a storm? If she had been able to rise, heaven knew she would be pressed against the ceiling now, making her apologies for magicking in mixed company.

A dimple lined Malcolm's cheek. "The ladies you hope to win around to my cause will want to know what all the fuss is about."

Penny scooted to her feet, brushing the back of her skirts. What a foolish thing to imagine walking into Malcolm's arms at this moment. What foolishness to feel it the most natural thing in the world.

She checked the clock on the mantel. "I suppose it's past time for the children's tea. Mary, may we continue as we did today?"

Mary nodded, ushering the children from the schoolroom. Malcolm held the door and Penny took a fortifying breath and began to join him. Mrs Stuart stopped her, and though her look was not cruel, it was amused as well as something else. Canny, the Scots called it.

"I will listen to recitations if you're not back on the hour," Elspeth said. "Take all the time you like."

It wouldn't take long, Penny thought, adjusting her bonnet atop her hair. An hour, maybe less, but she could not repress her delight. A whole hour in the fresh air—no matter that it still felt the grip of the Old Hag.

Most importantly, she would be with Malcolm.

The tingling sense of magic rose when he was about, calling forth her own magic. Small wonder she wanted to be with him.

Long puddles spread over the lane, but Penny skipped from one side to the other, earning an amused look from her companion who seemed impervious to the wind and the wet. He glanced across the wide track, taking in her red nose, no doubt. "Were you educated at home?" he asked, striding along.

She leapt another puddle and took a few steps, giving herself time to see her footing and where her path might lead. "Oh yes. My parents wanted to keep me close." True. Mama would never have run the risk of having Penny's magic observed and exposed.

He grunted. "And you've brothers and sisters?"

"No brothers. Only myself and two sisters."

"Both younger? I can imagine you ordering their amusements."

The thought that he imagined her at all made her stumble over a rut. "Both older. But I did order them about when I could."

"Like Kathy."

"Employing the same high-pitched wails when I didn't get my way. Mama would consider teaching Kathy my just deserts."

They passed fields brushed with fragile chartreuse green—the sprouts shivering in the elements—and made a slow steady descent on a good road that brought her to the bottom of the cliff she had contemplated not so long ago. She might have died. Like the sprouts, she shivered, hurrying after Malcolm.

At last, they came to the edge of a shallow river and Malcolm stood frowning at it. "The planks washed downstream."

It would be easy to cross if she could rise, to dig the toe of her boot into the muddy bank and push off, gliding over the frigid torrent until her feet touched down on the opposite side. Her power had been so strong she could have carried him. She would've tossed him over her shoulder and started out while he was still sputtering about impossibilities.

The thought almost touched off a grin. "A pity. Perhaps we might come another time."

He looked down, a gleam leaping into his eye. "You'll forgive me, I expect."

Before she could ask what for, he scooped her into his arms and strode into the water. She flung a hand to secure her bonnet and hoped she would not suffocate with pleasure or curiosity, or whichever base emotion gripped her now.

Malcolm Ross was holding her, and it was gorgeous and delicious, and enormously irritating. If anyone ought to have stirred her it should have been one of several, indefatigable Polish counts, a Spanish poet, or the junior officer in Papa's diplomatic corps who possessed the squarest chin in Christendom. Not a widower. Not a Scotsman. For the love of heaven, not this man.

"Do you have your feet?" he asked when he gained the opposite shore, setting her down with a noticeable hitch in his breath. He had been as stirred as she had.

"Yes," she whispered, her breath catching like a tangled knot of embroidery silks. She stepped away from him quickly, tugging at her cloak now there was no mountain of Scotsman to come between her and the sharp wind.

"Forgive me?" came his rough question, hardly penitential. Merely curious.

She swallowed thickly. "Nothing to forgive."

Turning, she staggered a few steps up the embankment to find herself standing on the beginnings of a village lane. A few more steps beyond that and she was already flanked by matching rows of neat, snug cottages.

The precipitousness of it caught her by surprise, and as he walked her up the road, her brows drew closer and closer together, her mouth screwing in confusion until she identified the source of her unease.

There was no impression of a hamlet growing in the landscape, edged by tufty fields which straggled when you approached and resolved into order at the center. The village was too abrupt for that.

She tried to ignore the disquiet feathering her mind. Even to her untrained eyes, the workmanship on the cottages was of a superior quality. There were no tumbledown walls or roofs sagging from neglect.

He began to point out things which elevated a village beyond a collection of cottages. The bakery. The grocer. A spacious plot set aside for the church. Wide, flat lanes. When they had toured the length of it, nodding to the workmen, poking her nose through every window he indicated, they found themselves in a cottage where she was called to inspect the stairs and sleeping quarters, a tidy front room and hearth.

Penny paced the length of the floor as Malcolm watched her, his brows lifted slightly. These homes were a little larger than the cottages on her father's estate—and those had been generously built. It was clean. The walls were plumb. She dreaded meeting his look, putting off the moment when her gaze would encounter his and she would be called upon to praise a village which had been mashed in place like an ill-fitting jigsaw puzzle piece.

He tugged at his lip with his thumb.

She turned to the window and stared into the garden area and then heard a boot scraping the floor as he crossed the room to stand behind her.

"Well?"

She turned to find him closer than she expected. "You've accomplished quite a lot."

His eyes moved swiftly over her face, seeing everything, or so it seemed.

"Do you approve of it? I've not designed a village before." His mouth curved into a self-deprecating smile and her fingers longed to brush his cheek.

"You studied it out quite carefully. Did it take a long time?" Her voice was bright.

His smile faded. "Is it so bad?"

Why couldn't she lie? Every moment she was in Scotland was a lie. Every time she answered to the name Miss Starling was a lie. Telling him Papa was an instructor when the only kind of instruction he did was standing nose to nose with the Earl of Clancarty, was as good as a lie. Maybe it hadn't mattered in the beginning, but it did now.

"I can see your care in every detail."

"Worse and worse. You had better tell me how bad it is," he said, leaning against a windowsill, hands on the ledge, finger hooked around the brim of his soft cap.

Her throat felt dry. "I can't see the heart of it."

"I couldn't very well add that to the plans," he said, a smile in his voice but he had somber eyes. She had hurt him. "I hope they'll see that I've done my best to make them comfortable."

"I'm sure that's so."

He drew a sharp breath. "What do you expect of me, Pen?" he asked, his voice a harsh rasp. Their eyes widened as her name slipped from his mouth. Not her name. Almost an endearment. She could not draw a breath and he looked away, rubbing the back of his neck.

There was no cravat there, covering his throat and the beat of his heart. She saw the finely molded collarbone and the strong muscle in the cleft of his neck and shoulder.

She touched his arm.

"You remember you gave me the freedom of your library, sir. You have several books about the history of these hills, and I read every one. Some of your cottagers will be gathered in from run-down little hamlets their families have occupied for hundreds of years and no careful planning can replicate the knobs and textures of what they leave behind."

He put a few feet of distance between them.

"I'm not trying to be presuming," she said as her fingers slipped from his arm.

He turned and stared at her so long she wondered what he was seeing. More than dark material. More than cheeks rosy with the chill. More than stubby eyelashes. No one had ever looked at her in such a way before and she shifted under its weight.

His mouth quirked up in a half smile. "You've no need to try presumption, Miss Starling. With you it comes naturally."

When he offered his arm, she threaded her hand through it and he led her into the afternoon sun, the distant echo of hammer and nail sounding at the end of the lane.

"Say I've come as far as I know how to with street plans and cottage construction," he began. "What more would you do to give this place a heart?"

She halted, enjoying the sight of his thoughtful face squinting up the street. "I wouldn't have the first notion."

He turned a look upon her. Both dimples. She was not proof against that smile, and felt her knees soften.

"So speaks the wily diplomat," he said, and a flick of shock traveled up her spine. "You'll never convince me you haven't thought of something already." He saw so much.

"The villagers—the women, particularly—will have ideas if they look over the building site."

"I thought the people will bring the heart of New Pentland with them when they come. No tour, no small changes, will replace that."

Penny lifted a shoulder. "You can't know until you ask."

He was silent for a long moment and she could not help but compare it to Papa's junior officers—bright young men who always knew the answer, and if they did not, filled every silence as though they did.

"You think I don't understand my people." He ran the back of his thumb against his bottom lip again and again. "But I do know what it feels like when one's life has been toppled over like a tower of blocks. I know how tempting it is to build it up again in the same way—to try and try only to discover there are bricks missing. The pieces don't fit. The tower is wobbly and unstable. I know it's far better to put the blocks away and find some other material to fashion a future out of."

She blinked rapidly, flicking the gathering moisture from her eyes. She looked at the branches of a tree, the rooftops, towards the distant hills. She looked anywhere but at him. His words reduced her to a child, scrambling under the rug and behind the sofa for lost bits of her magic. She wanted to clap her hands to her ears and run away. Instead, she struck out at him, blindly, unthinkingly.

"How tidy," she said in a voice that shook, "sweeping away the past into a bin as though it never was. Maybe you want to forget it, if you can. To turn your face to the future and become so caught up in some project grief cannot outrun you." A furious hand sketched an arc that encompassed the whole village.

"Tread warily, Miss Starling," he warned, his mouth settling into a grim line. "You trespass on personal matters. I know with painful experience grief is merciless, but this project, as you term it, will do good. If it helped me to keep from drowning during the long years after my wife died, all the better. I could not sit forever, nursing my misery."

Was it possible to stare with open-mouthed horror at one's self? Her accusations spent, Penny wished desperately to have the power to call them back again. To stuff them down so deeply all memory of them would be forgotten. Pungent curses—Russian, German, sailor—ran riot through her mind and her throat ached with the need to weep.

He touched her cheek with his calloused hand, thumb erasing one fugitive tear. How could he be kind to her?

"I'm sorry for saying that," she murmured.

"I know." He inhaled deeply and withdrew the warmth of his touch. "We went awry somehow but may we not begin again? You were telling me what you think these people will need. Putting me right." There was that smile of his. How could he be in charity with her after all she had said? The least she could do was banish her tears and meet him on a footing of good humor.

She sniffed inelegantly. "The villages are unique. I read that Skelpit Maun has a May festival each year, but the maypole is set up at the center of the village green all year round. In Wryborne the women paint their shutters red to ward off the Old Hag—Oh," she exclaimed. "I understand that now."

He smiled and she went on. "Scunner and Wee Scunner daub their sheep with contrasting patterns to keep them separate."

"And Lour?" he teased. "What can you tell me about that village?"

She flushed and spread her palms. "These alterations wouldn't be so expensive. The traditions have meaning. They might act as anchors as the foundations shift."

"You think they cannot fashion new anchors?"

She wanted to say no but he deserved a thoughtful answer.

"Perhaps. But what might be lost if we discard too much, too easily? Should there be no fight for the things that matter?"

"For maypoles and painted shutters?"

A flush climbed her cheeks.

He offered her his elbow again and they began to walk. "I am up to my neck in this business, Miss Starling—finding investors, building the mill. I don't know when I would—"

She reached for his hand and he stopped. As their skin touched, a frisson of magic twisted through her, the bands which seemed to hold her earthbound tightening. She was caught up in discomfort and struggle but knew, in a blinding moment of clarity, how to ease the constriction. "I could do it."

The bands seemed to slacken, coiled softly at her feet, and she wanted to scream as she looked down. There was nothing on the ground but her sturdy boots and bits of building material. What was this magic? Why was it elusive? Why, in the midst of it, did she never need to rise?

"Why?" Malcolm asked.

Penny could not tell him an invisible power seemed to grip her at the oddest times, inviting her to do the oddest things. But that wasn't the only reason.

She had always been curious. It had been the quality which had carried her from one end of the continent to the other with relative ease. It had helped her to adjust to her magic when the same discovery had almost turned her sister inside out. It drove her to learn everything about her gift that she could. To visit the sprawling city of London and feel as though every door and every book was open to her.

Without her powers, she was riding a storm without a sticking place. It was that, too, that drove her on. Some of the villagers who would settle in New Pentland would do so happily. Others— She knew what the others would feel.

When she didn't answer, his hand twisted under her own, fingers grasping hers for a brief moment. "You know about loss."

Her eyes shifted away. She didn't want him to see her so well. But he did not press for explanations or histories, simply allowed that it was so.

When they got to the stream, he lifted her into his strong embrace without any preambles. There was nowhere to put her hand that did not give her interesting terrain to explore, so she held it away from his back and neck and arm and shoulder and head like the spout of a teapot, rehearsing one of Mama's discourses on the Merits of Propriety.

Still, her fingers were perilously close to touching his dark head of hair when he let her down on the other side. Their glances caught and clung.

"Are your boots soaked through?" she asked when the silence had grown too full of things she had not given herself permission to think.

"Not too much. Hoby made these boots."

She chuckled and began up the lane. "An Englishman?"

"Aye, an Englishman." His cheek tucked though his mouth set in mock sobriety. "But I'm sure his mother was a Scot."

Chapter Seventeen

Penny reached a large globe down from the top of a shelf, as battered as everything else in the schoolroom, and placed it on the table. The strange object—common in the room but strange in the center of it—brought a brief hush.

Penny knew what she ought to do—what Miss Starling would do. She would begin in an orderly fashion, first teaching her pupils about their home, then county, then country, then the wider world. However, Penny knew precious little about Scotland and falling into Robbie's trap had been a reminder that she was shamefully ignorant of its ways and language.

Ewan eyed the globe doubtfully.

"Will you show Robbie where you live?" Penny asked him.

"Here, Rob." Ewan spun the globe until Scotland appeared under his finger. He stabbed at Scotland, the pad of his finger covering the Pentland Hills and the Firth of Forth.

"What do you know about *Coille na Cyarlin*?"

"I know how to say it," Ewan said, almost too low to be heard. Almost.

But it was Robbie who answered her in the piping Scots she could not help but find enchanting.

"The fortune of our house came from treasure. Long ago when men were giants and enormous mountains pierced the sky, the first Ross struck his lance in the ground of *Coille na Cyarlin*, prying up black diamonds."

"Diamonds, Rob? No—" said Ewan

"*Haud yer wheesht*, Ewan. Coal becomes diamonds," Robbie said, suddenly a boy in command of his facts. "If you give them enough time. They were rough and dirty, and dinnae look like much, but we are bred of men wise enough to find treasure where others find rubbish."

"Aye, aye," Ewan agreed.

Penny rubbed her fingertips, conscious of an animating tingle drawing her to the inkwell, the pen, the paper. The feeling was so common now that she heeded it almost without thought. She drew them to her and began to transcribe Rob's tale scratching the paper as quickly as he spoke. His account echoed the one she had gleaned from a dusty volume in the library, sketching out the history of the house and its masters. A young gentleman named John Ross had begun a coal mine, married an heiress, bought more land, and generation after generation built the house and served the monarch.

It wasn't a particularly distinguished story when matched against many of the other houses of Scotland and England, but when Rob told it, he placed the Rosses in the center of every event, the fulcrum and pivot.

Why shouldn't he, she mused, listening to his story of high adventure and great romance. His land and his people were at the heart of him, and she felt a shaft of envy. Had she ever felt so passionately about the safety of Thorndene with its well-tended land and gently rolling hills? Nae.

Her eyes crinkled. No. Perhaps it was the fault of her magic—the rising that allowed her to float high above the ground or to skim its surface. Never settled. Always rootless.

Rob's voice shifted a little and Penny became aware that she was hearing the story of Malcolm Ross. Her attention sharpened.

"He was a young man still, with time enough to look about him for a bride. When he returned from university in Edinburgh, one day he spied the only daughter of Magnus Stuart riding bareback on the road to Penicuik, missing a shoe, her hair a tangle." Rob hooked his thumbs around the lapels of his coat, standing like a lecturer, clipping each word for greater impact. "Did he pass her by, nose in the air like many a fine lad who thinks his own wind never stinks?"

"Nae," came the chorus of voices around the room. Elspeth knocked her knuckles against the woodwork of the sofa for emphasis, and Penny smothered a grin.

"Ross men are canny, plucking treasure out of black rock. He whisked her away on his saddle bow and vowed she would be his *jo* forevermore."

"Jo?" Penny asked, lifting her pen.

There was a rustle of movement at the door and Penny looked up to find Malcolm Ross watching her. For how long, she wondered.

Though she had heard his low, laughing tones through the walls of the nursery each night, she was always caught by surprise that the mere sight of him should send a quaver through her stomach. He had to be magic.

"I expected you to be finished by now," he said, "and the children ready for our ramble."

"It was my fault." Penny straightened, rubbing a hand against her sleeve, hoping the quicksilver prickling under her skin would grow more faint, hoping she could ignore it entirely. "We forgot the time."

That smile of his settled on her and widened a fraction. "That's a first."

"Tell Miss Starling what 'jo' means, *Aither*," Rob interjected, taking his father's hand and leaning his whole weight on it, swinging a little.

Malcolm's eyes shifted down for a few moments, as though the child had driven the question out of his mind. But when he looked at her, they were as bright as sapphires.

"Dearest. Joy."

He smiled and that smile meant danger. She could feel it in the way her stomach became weightless and the way her toes began to press into the floor, tilting her imperceptibly into his orbit. She could sense herself sending out roots whenever he was near, delving into this strange soil. Growing. Thriving.

She wasn't meant to. She glanced at the battered globe. There was the whole world waiting for her to discover. When she got her magic back, as surely she must, she would tear herself away and run. She prayed to God there was yet time to do it without dealing herself some mortal injury.

"See what you've done, Robbie?" She gripped the closely-written page and held it up. "Your words filled the whole of it without even trying."

She clipped off the desire to complete the thought. *If you work on your letters, Rob, you will fill it yourself.* He was a clever boy. He would work that out himself.

Rob tugged his father from the room, and Penny turned, replacing the globe on the high shelf.

"Was it like he said?" Penny asked, feeling that she might dare the question now.

For a moment Mrs Stuart sank more deeply into the sofa, her eyes intent on the fire. "Robbie is a disgraceful fabricator, but for all that, he caught the spirit of the thing. Malcolm met Jean at an assembly and asked her to dance. She lost a shoe coming down the line and he liked to say that he fell in love before the fiddle came away from the bow." A gentle smile curved her mouth and Penny held her breath, as she would if a butterfly landed on her finger.

"It could have spelled disaster for our girl—her father nothing but a clerk and Malcolm Ross the young man up at the great house—but he wouldn't take anything less than marriage. 'Whisked her away on his saddle bow'," she repeated with a laugh. "Young Rob knows how to find the kernel of the truth."

"He's a bright little boy," Penny surprised herself by saying. Her mind returned to that first day. To "slinch," and the letters that snaked across the page. Hardly anything had changed since that day but her opinions.

Mrs Stuart moved toward the door. "Malcolm is riding to Penicuik to take dinner with Lord Berwick and his family tonight."

Penny's blush rose and she wondered if Mrs Stuart saw her weakness for the tall, dark-haired master of *Coille na Cyarlin*. She looked for him everywhere, catching fleeting glimpses of him as he stalked the hills after hours with the children, hearing his voice from some other part of the house, looking forward each day to when they would meet and trade their thoughts, reading out short passages of poetry or items in the newspaper under Mrs Stuart's watchful gaze.

It narrowed on her now. "Berwick has three unmarried daughters. Malcolm won't be the only one hoping to spring a trap."

Penny's mouth dried up. "The Berwick girls are lovely?"

An imperceptible smile lit Mrs Stuart's eyes, and not for the first time, Penny began to wish she had the power to coax her ungovernable words from existence. The question hung between them when she wanted it to leap to the floor like a cat, its long feline body sliding along the shadows unnoticed until it slipped through the gap in the door.

"Not lovely," Mrs Stuart stated. "Beautiful, more like. Stunning."

"How advantageous," Penny murmured, gripping a composition book, the edges biting into her flesh. No match for the sudden flare of jealousy igniting in her stomach. The Berwick women might have the good grace to be hunch-backed and leprous at the very least.

Mrs Stuart's eyes bored into Penny's. "If Malcolm should wed an heiress, it would be the perfect solution to his financing problem."

No. No, it most certainly would not. The ferocity of the emotion jolted through her and she fought a pitched battle to maintain her composure. "Are they wealthy, too?"

"Rich as Midas. Lord Berwick owns collieries throughout the lowlands."

Damn and damn. Penny Thornton might be an heiress, able to buy several collieries of her own, if she could talk her papa around to releasing the funds, but Penny Starling was a simple governess, and it was that girl who must make her way in this land.

Penny shelved the materials, her hands working unconsciously. "Has he known them long?" she asked.

"He won't have seen them in years. The girls have been in Edinburgh being educated at a private seminary for girls, they say. Well, you can see how it will be." Mrs Stuart looked coy. "Them so suitable, and him so braw."

Penny could see. Oh, Lord. She could see it as clearly as if she were a serving girl, standing with a dish at his elbow, longing to dump the gravy boat on the heads of three misses. She sucked in a hard breath and looked for any escape. She found it in the strange Scots word.

"Braw. I've read that word a few times in the last weeks. What does it mean?"

Mrs Stuart stifled a laugh. "Fine. Exceedingly fine."

Penny swallowed, the act not quite enough to banish the invisible specter of three marriageable heiresses right at Malcolm Ross's fingertips.

"I must be going. Lady Ainsley invited me around for tea," she said. When Mrs Stuart frowned she asked, "Ought I to have refused, ma'am?"

Mrs Stuart's face was a perfect scowl. "I only meant to tease you about the Misses Berwick."

"I don't know how you should tease me about them. They sound like lovely young women, and if my station allowed it, no doubt I would enjoy their company."

"Your station," Mrs Stuart grumbled. "I would mind if the man I—" Penny lifted her chin and the older woman's voice clipped off as sharply as the corner of an ornamental shrub.

Mrs Stuart fumbled for the shawl and Penny rushed to tuck the loose end into the crook of her elbow. Once it was secured, the women froze, looking intently at one another for a long moment.

Mrs Stuart tugged the shawl closer and scowled. "I expect he thinks them three of the silliest widgeons ever to breathe. Horse mad, the lot of them."

Her words followed Penny all the way to Isabelle's cottage, repeating in her mind until even the thought of one of Isabelle's meager teas was a welcome distraction.

Instead of taking tea in the parlor, Isabelle waved Penny through the door of the still room and offered her a high stool next to the work bench, a far more pleasant prospect than being stared at for three quarters of an hour, each raw emotion having to be concealed from her hostess.

Isabelle gestured to a stack of books and Penny tipped up their spines: *Magicae Artes, The Lesser Book of Magic,* and *The Grimoire of Cornovii.*

"I'm halfway through this one," Isabelle said, tapping the last. "Read on and tell me what you think. Make a note if you come to anything of interest."

Penny folded back the pages and worked her way through spells for conjuring a wall of flame, and receipts for curing capriciousness until a maid brought a tea tray.

"Shall I pour?" Penny asked, but Isabelle waved her back to her book. At length, she set a cup at Penny's elbow which contained a murky blend brightened with a tiny slice of shriveled lemon rind.

Penny took a polite swallow and cleared her throat. Isabelle left hers untouched as she finished her preparation, a straw-colored liquid in a small vial.

"Is that one of your tonics?" Penny asked.

Isabelle nodded, stopping it up with a cork and handing it over. "For my little cousins. It wouldn't do to have them getting sick in such weather."

Penny slipped the bottle into her pocket. "It's good of you to think of them."

Isabelle shook her head slightly. "It's nothing. I wondered if you had observed any magic in that quarter. The children are with you constantly."

"No magic," Penny replied, giving Isabelle the truth, if not the whole of it. Isabelle would surely expect the magic to be something beyond fanciful dreams and tingling palms. Still, uneasy gooseflesh raised on Penny's arm at Isabelle's question. Malcolm protected his children and guarded their privacy. Isabelle was their cousin. Penny scrubbed the bristling flesh away knowing her information amounted to nothing. "They come to the schoolroom and I try, with no great success, to stuff knowledge into them."

Isabelle wiped her hands on her apron and cleared away her distillation tools, working in neat methods. She brought out a knife.

"Have you found anything of use in there?" she asked, pointing to the grimoire with the tip of the blade.

"Possibly. Here's a passage, which has me thinking. "Magic is nothing more than a parasite in need of a host. No attempt to romanticize its origins negates this basic idea. When a shock or disturbance jars a magic from its nestled home, it may be collected—like mistletoe is collected from a low-hanging branch. If one seeks magic, one must wait for shocks, and act with decision."

Penny turned the page and released an outraged grunt. She flopped her head into her hand. "Remedy for a Costive Cow."

Isabelle laughed, but Penny threw up her hands in frustration. "Magic is like a seed. Magic is like mistletoe."

"Don't let your impatience blind you. The passage had a good notion. Waiting for shocks and acting with decision. Does that ring true?"

Penny's teeth fretted along her lip. "Having faith in my magic and putting it to the test rang true, but I almost broke my neck."

Isabelle's brow tented in concern. "You must never do such a thing without me. You might have been killed."

"I have to do something."

"Travelling to Scotland, hunting all over *Coille na* Cyarlin, practicing… You are doing something."

"Then where is it?"

Isabelle squeezed Penny's hand. "You did say that remnants of your magic slowed your fall."

"Should I fling myself from a cliff and find out for certain? No, thank you. My power will have to find me some other way." Penny's chin tightened as she held back the tide that threatened to engulf her. What if her magic never really came back?

Isabelle leaned across the worktable and tapped the grimoire. "Finding another source of magic and reaping it after a shock. That is your way."

"How could I plan for such a thing? How could I reap magic if I happened to be nearby? How would I know if someone had magic to lose?"

"You're asking the right questions," Isabelle said. "We could solve that last problem. I am able to detect magic and could tell you which one of the children has it."

Isabelle reached for a handful of stalks, laying them crosswise over the table. "You could bring the children to my cottage. If you gave me an uninterrupted hour or two..."

Restiveness bloomed in Penny's belly and she had the sensation that she had wandered down some dark, forbidden path. How easy it would be to continue on. How difficult to find her way back.

Isabelle gave Penny a sympathetic look. "I want to do my best for you."

Penny nodded but took temporary refuge in her employer's dictates. "I'm not allowed to be with the children on my own."

"Still?" A soft veil of confusion settled over Isabelle's brow. "I was of the understanding a governess had children constantly under foot and you've been at the house for some time. Don't they trust you?"

Did they? There was a sting to Isabelle's question, which undermined the simple pleasure she was beginning to take in Mrs Stuart's company, and shattered the fragile confidence she was winning from the children. It called into question every visit to the schoolroom by the master of the house. It reminded her of all the lies she had already told to gain their trust.

"We will think on the problem," Isabelle encouraged, scooping up discarded roots and dropping them into the waste bin. "The other questions can be dealt with, I think. I must find you a way to absorb magic. You must prepare yourself to stand nearby if an event or an illness occurs to jar some wayward magic loose."

Penny wrinkled her nose. The path was dark, indeed. "You mean I should hover ghoulishly at a sick child's bedside?"

Isabelle grimaced. "Is that what I made it sound like? I am sorry." She placed her knife against the stalks and drew a hard slice backwards, severing the flowery heads and tossing them away. "I meant, if the magic is unmoored, I would hate to waste it. Accidents and illnesses happen to children every day of the year. If you were not there to catch the magic, perhaps it would be lost forever."

Penny furrowed her brows. She had been searching the library for weeks, testing her old powers by leaping from her bed, from chairs, even from the table in the schoolroom. She had been feeling the strange remnants hum beneath her fingertips, feeling the pressure beginning to build as she lived day after day under the same roof as Malcolm Ross, and worried over what it meant. She ought to grasp Isabelle's help with both hands. But she stood, scraping the stool back, and heard herself say, "I dislike the idea of taking the children's magic."

"I told you, you would not be taking." Isabelle's voice was civilized. "Consider it salvaging."

"I'm only interested in my own magic. In rising again."

"I have a suspicion," Isabelle said, tipping her head "Magic is like water. It takes the shape of its holder."

"I thought it was like a seed." Penny's laugh was blessedly normal, beating back the shadows.

"Penny," Isabelle rebuked lightly. "Within you, it's likely that magic will always be rising magic. Fundamentally, we can't change who we are."

Penny caught her breath. Oh, how she wished that were true. It might be. If she could reap any kind of magic it would manifest in her as she was used to. The thought tasted like sugar on her tongue.

Isabelle began splitting long stalks, running the back side of the knife up the center to collect the milk, scraping it into a jar.

"Do you know what else?" she asked, bundling the stalks when she was finished, bending them in half and stuffing them into the bin after the heads. "I think you would never have come all the way to Scotland if you weren't half-mad with grief. I think if there was the smallest sliver of hope you could get your magic back, you would not hesitate to be ruthless. You would lie and cheat—"

Penny's mouth fell ajar. It wasn't like that. "I wouldn't—"

"No?" There was such pity in Isabelle's eyes, such understanding Penny wanted to weep. Even her sister Beatrice, who had risen as high as Penny ever had, could never fathom the loss which lived in Penny's bones. But Isabelle—living far from London and far below her station—seemed to comprehend it.

There was a long silence between the women and Isabelle rolled her cuffs down, buttoning them. "I see how you long for the sky, my friend. Your loyalty to your charges and to my cousin, do you credit." Her words were gentle. "But I can see that you were a magnificent creature once. Full of power and lightness. It would grieve me to see you balk at the final hurdle."

Chapter Eighteen

Malcolm galloped down the narrow servant's stairs towards the kitchens. On a bend, somewhere in the middle, Penny appeared suddenly, colliding into his waistcoat and jerking back in astonishment. Her hands thrashed as she struggled to maintain her balance until he snaked an arm about her waist and hauled her against his chest, nerves tightening in alarm and sudden wanting.

Her back rose and fell with large, shaking breaths, her hands flattened against him, but when she looked up, her grey eyes were as distant as if they were chance-met acquaintances nodding across parkland. She rolled her shoulders and he released her.

"You prevented me from sailing top over tail down the length of the stairs, sir. Thank you."

The passage was narrow, but he wished her far closer. It was madness to long for a girl who spoke of returning to England. To want one who could not settle in their ways.

"It will not happen again," she added, as she would if she had been a servant he had scolded. In these last few days there had been a shift in her attitude towards him. She did not offer her opinions so readily. She did not challenge his. There was caution in her eyes and the set of her chin.

She bobbed a brief curtsey and gathered her skirts to proceed on her way. He stopped her with the softest touch of his fingers grazing her arm. The brief contact sent sparks arcing up his hand, leaping to his chest.

She glanced at him, her eyes on the same level as his. Her mouth—

"Yes?"

"You won't stop racing around on my account." His voice was rough, but he could not seem to do anything about it. "I was looking for you," he said.

"I was with Fritz. We ran along the boundary of the nearest oat fields."

"Those seedlings are doing better than they have any right to be. Berwick reports incalculable losses. Leadburn too."

A spark of interest animated her expression, but she snuffed it out. "You were looking for me, you said. Did you need anything?"

His eyes narrowed and suddenly he saw the humor in the situation. Crusty Scots Widower Requires English Governess with a View to Matrimony. He chuckled. "Aye. I hope you're thirsty. I invited a couple villagers, Mrs Johnston and Mrs Hunter, to take tea with you. I thought you would want to talk about changes—minor changes—they might suggest for the settlement. They elected to drop by this afternoon."

"They're here now?" Penny was already turning down the stairs.

He caught at her hand and she paused, glancing back. The movement had taken them both by surprise and he had the fleeting impression of soft skin against the irregular calluses on his palm, of how his hand enveloped hers even though she was not a small woman.

"I'll stay as long as you need." He released her hand and let a smile steal over his mouth. "I'd not throw you to a pair of Scottish she-wolves. Though they are far kinder than the cursed Rosses, and you manage us well enough."

Penny poised below him, tilted her chin up until their gazes locked. He'd roused her at last. "You don't think I'm scared, do you?"

He laughed. "You're never scared."

She spun on her heel and raced down the stairs, he following after, his long stride barely keeping up.

He had thought to ease Penny into an awkward situation, bridging the gap between these merchants and one they might view as a mere servant, between Scottish and English. He had no sooner performed the introductions than he saw that he was in the presence of a master.

"How kind of you to struggle through my shocking accent," Penny said to the women. "I pray the tea makes it worth your while."

Mrs Hunter gave a merry laugh and reached a hand to Mrs Johnston. "Tae. We call it tae an' it tastes a' the better for it. But *dinnae fash yersel'*, lass."

Penny had an adorable pucker between her brows, and he touched the back of her hand so that she glanced at him.

"Fuss," he translated. "It means that you aren't to bother."

"Excellent," she answered, easing herself one pace away from him. Then she tilted her head up and a wicked gleam came into her eyes. It was hard to breathe suddenly, and he thanked heaven he wasn't still on that private stair with her. She would have found herself soundly kissed and kissed and kissed.

"There's no need to...*fash yersel'*, Mr Ross," she said, glancing inquiringly to Mrs Hunter who beamed, nodding her approval. "You must have much to do, and the ladies and I will get on together." She turned to them with an appealing vulnerability. "You will put me right if I say the wrong thing, and bear with my lamentable ignorance, I hope?"

Then he found himself shooed out of the room as though he had been caught swiping buns from Mrs Johnston's bakery. When the door closed, he stared at it for a perplexed moment.

In the end, he wandered to the library where he ought to have settled down to his accounts, wringing pennies and pounds from the intractable numbers stacked in his books. His heart was not in the battle. It was across the hall in the salon with the children's governess.

He picked up a pen and stared unseeing at his books, the tip hovering a whisker above the paper. He worked with half a mind and tossed it aside as Penny entered less than an hour later.

"Well?"

She gave a satisfied smile and he answered it, glad she was not wasting time pretending she was a docile, washed-out governess still. "They were charming."

He unfolded himself out of the chair and came around the desk, leaning against it.

"Mrs Hunter informed me that she and her husband are the grocers and that Mrs Johnston is the baker's wife."

"Aye. In their way they will have more to do with the success of New Pentland as anyone else. You were right to suggest I have them inspect the work and assure themselves it is all being done properly."

She wore a look on her face, which reminded him of Kathleen caught trying to cut her braids off with a pen knife. "They are assured of that."

"But?" he prodded, feeling a blaze of warmth when she smiled up at him.

"I made some promises."

It didn't matter she was in no position to do so. He could not deny her anything. "How expensive are they going to be?"

"Spoken like a Scotsman," she laughed. "Some of them won't cost you a pound." She leaned against the desk as he did.

"Some."

Her brows lowered in mock irritation, and he slid a scrap of foolscap closer, picking up a pencil. "What did you promise?"

"Paint for the shutters."

Easy enough. He scratched the words out on paper.

"And?"

"Rowan trees. There is one rowan already, along the upper ridge of the village, but Mrs Johnston hopes there is room to plant an entire walk."

"Rowan trees," he spelled out with a laugh. "Is she superstitious enough to believe they will grant her protection against an ill-natured fairy?"

"She wants a lover's walk," Penny said, twisting the end of her little finger. "If the young people are to enjoy the courtship rites of Wryborne, a rowan walk is essential."

"I never took Mrs Johnston for a romantic." He watched Penny flush, finding it the most enchanting thing he had ever seen. "What rites are these?"

She lifted her chin, her voice no more than instructive. "A young maiden collects berries from a rowan tree and thinks of the man she loves when she tastes the fruit. If the berry is bitter, he is not the man to woo her. If the berry is sweet, he will love her forever." Then a puzzled line creased her brow. "It's a wonder there was any wooing in Wryborne at all. The raw fruit is horribly tart."

He chuckled. "That's only because you haven't met the lover who will turn it sweet."

Her eyes widened. "That must be it."

Malcolm cleared his throat and looked down, writing. "Find some rowan saplings around the estate…"

She touched his hand and he stopped. She could not know what she was doing to him. "Would it be possible to find saplings around Wryborne? The extra care—"

It would mean a long day of travel, weeks of careful nurturing. Malcolm had watched Penny as Robbie had woven his stories her eyes alight. This lass loved tales, and this one would make a good story, weaving the old ways into the new.

"Aye."

She smiled and then shifted slightly. "I—I don't expect you can do the next thing, but I did promise to ask."

He could almost feel the pounds and pence fly from his purse. "Best have it out at once."

"It's about the bridge. You had the architect's drawings laid out for inspection and—"

"Do they wish it relocated? That's the only reasonable place to ford the river for miles."

"They don't want it moved."

He gave a relieved sigh. Thank heaven for small miracles. However, his hopes of financial solvency were dashed in the next moment.

"Mrs Hunter spoke with great fondness for the bridge at Lour. It had a series of gentle arches—"

Another sigh, but this time not so happy. His architect had added no embellishment or decoration to the bridge, drawing the lines with efficiency and cost uppermost in mind. He would find himself promising to fund handcrafted abutments if this little witch continued to look at him with that expression of hopeful expectancy. Utterly impractical. It couldn't be done.

"I'll see what can be done," he heard himself say. "Anything more?"

"Only the tiniest thing." One eye closed as her features twisted. "It won't cost you a penny."

His look narrowed with suspicion. "What is it?"

"The name of the village. It's a little..."

"What's wrong with New Pentland? It's a fine name."

"Nothing at all, of course. They find it quite noble." She shook a bracing, warrior's fist over her chest. Was she laughing at him? "Elegant, classical…"

"But?" With some difficulty, he restrained the impulse to gather her up in his arms and let her have her own way.

"They wondered if they might have the naming of it for themselves."

“But it’s my village.”

A gentle elbow nudged his side. “You won’t have to live in it. I said that if every adult had a say in the naming that you would abide—”

“I don’t want to abide.”

She laughed. “You sound like one of the children.” Her eyes danced, but the longer he looked, the more amusement seemed to give way to constraint. She blinked and took a breath, pivoting around to stand as she ought to. He would not’ve believed the transformation could be wrought in such small gestures if he hadn’t seen it himself. No more Penny—his Penny. She was Miss Starling again, a governess with a job to do and information to impart.

He crossed his arms over his chest. “I like New Pentland.”

“This is such a small thing. It would bind the villagers more fully to the place if they have a say.”

He shot her an irritated look she didn’t even have the grace to laugh at and wrote, “Rename the village.”

Chapter Nineteen

Penny walked a circuit around the schoolroom as the children worked, bending over slates and books, making corrections. Her hand smoothed Robbie's hair as she came to him. Ewan checked, watching her, but Rob did not.

The boy was wearing the correct number of garments, buttoned up in the ordinary way, turned the right way around It had taken him only a quarter of an hour more than the other children. Weeks of patient toil were paying off; the restless nights when ideas had seemed to rush through her were bearing fruit.

One morning had her facing Robbie across his bed.

"Mary makes my bed. Always."

"Does she do Ewan's?" Penny had asked. Ewan and Kathleen were already in the schoolroom seeing to their lessons. Rob need not worry he was being watched.

"No. But she likes the corners sharp."

"I bet you could get your corners sharp."

His eyes dropped open with a dry skepticism as he tugged the sheet up, pulling it free from its anchor on the opposite corner. The coverlet was flipped atop that with no effort made to smooth the foundation linens. The pillow was whacked for good measure.

"Done."

"Oh, that's very good. You made it look so easy. May I try? What does Mary do first?" Penny asked, fluttering her hands ineffectually over the linens.

"Don't you know how?"

"I've never done it before."

"Are the English as doltish as that?" he asked.

"Terribly doltish," she answered, lifting the linens—stirring them—the corner of the bright fabric pinched between two delicate fingers.

He pushed his shirt sleeves past his elbows and tugged them from her hands. "It's laundry day so we strip it clean."

"Like this?" Penny yanked on the sheets, tumbling onto her backside in comedic ineptitude.

"That's rubbish, Miss Starling. Let me explain it from t' beginning."

Then he began to teach her the correct way, pushing his childish hands under the mattress, tugging the corners. He did not move quickly, but with the patient perseverance of an overseer correcting ignorance and sloth.

On another day, he was repairing Penny's quill with a pen knife and reading her an exhaustive lecture on maintaining her writing implements correctly.

"You'll never get anywhere, Miss Starling, if you keep a shoddy pen," he said.

"No, Robbie. I can see you're right," she said, looking up to find Malcolm standing in the doorway with a quizzical look on his face. "Do you think you've got it?"

"In a minute," Robbie muttered, his tongue jutting out as he positioned his thumb to catch the blade. "You're only going to ruin it again if I give it back."

"I promise I won't," she vowed, finding herself short of breath as Malcolm's gaze rested on her.

"This is the fifth pen today," Rob admonished.

"What if I break it twice more?"

He stopped for a long think. "You break eight pens and I'll have to tell *Aither*."

Eight. Penny sighed. Progress came slow.

"Tell *Aither* what, Rob?" came the deep voice from the door.

Rob lifted his head and set his work down, swinging off his stool and into his father's arms. "That you should hire a Scottish governess. The English are expensive."

"Is *Aither* Scots for father?" she'd asked Malcolm as they played a lazy game of piquet in the small parlor at the end of the day, the room lit in the warm glow of candlelight. Mrs Stuart snored lightly by the fire. "Or have I been fooled again?"

Malcolm turned his card and won the trick, collecting it and placing it face down. His lips tightened. "An old Scots pronunciation of 'other.'"

He laid another card down and she tilted her head in question.

"One parent is gone but he still has the *aither*."

Now Penny shook her head, banishing the memory to a forbidden corner of her mind—an area she inspected closely on more than one occasion—and picked up Robbie's cloth, wiping away the extra consonants strung from the end of his painstakingly spelled "becaussz." Then she chalked on an e.

"E is a rotten sneak," he explained.

Penny turned at the sound of the door and a maid appeared with a square of paper in her hand. "A note, miss, sent over from Lady Ainsley."

Penny took the missive and unfolded it near the watery light of the window.

"Dearest Penny," Isabelle began, the strong hand slanting across the page. "The weather has been miserable, but not so bad as all that. Have the servants hitch up the coach and come. Our books are full of interesting information I wish to impart."

Penny glanced up to see her charges. Robbie stared at the ceiling blankly, head tipped all the way back. He would resume his work if she called to him, but there was another hour until his lessons would be over. Ewan was kicking the table leg as he always did when the topic of study was not to his liking. That couldn't be helped. Fractions weren't to anybody's liking.

"Do bring the children who, I am sure, must be fit for bedlam after all this rain. Affectionately yours, Isabelle"

It was a careful note, but pregnant with Isabelle's wishes. Penny folded the paper and dragged a fingernail along the crease. It was not the first such invitation in these last weeks. The excuse Penny always made—she would not be trusted to be alone with the children—was wearing threadbare.

She had finished her close inspection of the library, and though her knowledge of *Coille na Cyarlin* had increased, the exploration had proved fruitless. If she did not find answers soon, she might never get away.

She didn't need to ask herself why. The gravity to the place was Malcolm. Every evening she sat at his side as they took their meal together. Every evening she listened to his voice read out a scrap of poetry, a passage in a book, or an article in the newspaper. Only last week he had spoken Papa's name, relating some information about the riots in East Anglia. He'd smacked the paper and groused, of course Liverpool couldn't be bothered sending an emissary—especially the precious Sir Charles Thornton—into the dark and barbaric wilderness of Scotland.

"Useless. The lot of them," he'd grumbled, and Elspeth had laughed.

Now Penny glanced from Isabelle's letter to Mrs Stuart sitting by the fire, her knitting needles working slowly. She imagined asking to take the children. Imagined suspicion lighting Mrs Stuart's gaze, erasing the amusement or curiosity the woman often expressed now. A sour slickness coated Penny's throat. Didn't she want her magic? How much?

A gust of wind rattled the windows, blowing smoke into the room and making her decision for her. It was unwise to drag the children out on a day such as this. She must defer the discovery of her magic and suffer Malcolm's company a little longer. It was no hardship. Penny could not stand near him without feeling shivery and responsive, like the straining eyes of a garden snail reacting to the slightest touch.

She stifled a laugh. Garden snail. *Cornu aspersum.* She shut Ewan's large book of animals with a heavy thump.

"I cannot bear this a second more," she said, and the boys lifted their heads from their slates. Mrs Stuart paused her knitting and glanced up. Mary and Kathleen, building a tower of blocks in the corner, stilled. "We've been cooped up too long in this room. Don't you agree?"

Robbie cast down his chalk and gave a gusty sigh. "Oh yes."

"Are you sending us away?" Ewan asked, his chin tilted at an angle that said *he knew it* and had been waiting for her to tire of them. Penny sighed. Ewan expected so little of her he would never be disappointed.

"I want some adventure. Perhaps you can show me your favorite spot in the house," she said, expecting they would trot her off to the kitchens or some bricked-up chimney, which vaguely resembled a priest hole.

"The gallery," Robbie said, sharing a glance with Ewan. "You've not met our ghosts."

Ghosts? A smile spread over Penny's features, surprise lighting her eyes. "Lead on."

The boys raced ahead, but Penny caught up Kathleen in her arms, calling, "tallyho", as Kathy shrieked with laughter. They ran down the stairs and raced to the end of the hall, an area of the house Penny had not yet trespassed. She lurched to a halt, bent to set Kathleen on her feet, and felt the child's small hand slip into hers.

"*Aither* doesn't come here," Robbie breathed as Ewan pushed the doors wide.

There was barely a second to wonder why *Aither* stayed away before her eyes took in the whole sight. A long wall of windows glowing with soft light ran along one side of the room and, on the wall facing it, every inch of space was stuffed with paintings, scores of them, each gilded frame rubbing up against its neighbor.

The arrangement wasn't tasteful or elegant but looked if this room were an ark, and the Ross family had decided that each one of them would be saved from the great flood together.

Penny ran the length of the room with the children several times, finally casting herself next to Mrs Stuart on a long bench.

"Who is this? "Penny gasped, waving at a portrait of a tall, dashing fellow with Malcolm's strong nose. As Mrs Stuart had her back to the room, staring out the window, the children must be her guides.

Robbie flopped onto the carpet, wadding his coat under his head, and pointed. "That's our adventurer. Do you like his *swidge* of hair?"

"Swidge?"

"Scots for swoop," he said, sending his hand into an inverted arc away from his hairline.

A falsehood, she was sure. But there was no malice in it.

"He sailed to Brazil and Italy, and once went to America, hunting for timber to make masts. He found trees so large you could unroll them and cover a whole floor. That's what's under here," he said, reaching back and knocking the rug with his knuckle.

Penny looked down, inspecting the wide planks of wood peeking out along the edge of the carpet. She glanced at Mrs Stuart who nodded a confirmation of the tale.

Robbie rolled over several turns and came to rest under a portrait of a woman with a high ruff collar and a jeweled bodice. "An' that's our lady of ill repute."

"Robbie Ross—" Penny scolded, mentally amending her lessons to touch on topics far more delicate than spelling and botany.

He blithely continued. "Reputed to spy for the French. Though in Scotland that doesn't make you so very bad." He tipped his head backward. "Right, Ewan?"

Ewan grunted. "Only sometimes."

"And this one?" Penny laughed, pointing to the next portrait—a merry-faced lady with youthful curves. "Is there a secret elopement in her history or a daring escape from a highwayman?"

"That's Mam," Ewan replied, his voice gruff. The smile died in Penny's eyes, but before she could speak Ewan jabbed at Robbie and Kathy, rousing them all to race down the length of the room again.

Jean Ross.

Penny felt Mrs Stuart stiffen beside her but couldn't tear her eyes from the painting—a half portrait of the smiling young bride whose departure created such a cavity it had not been filled even years after her death. The artist had caught something around her mouth, which gave an impression of restlessness and good humor. Penny wished she could ask if it was a true likeness.

For a few moments, they were alone together, Jean looking down at Penny and weighing her up, calling forth an accounting. Isabelle's letter scratched against Penny's dress and the memory of it made her want to shift and look away from the fine, clear eyes of the children's mother.

Only little lies. Allowing Isabelle nothing more than a few uninterrupted hours with her young cousins. What could it hurt?

But Jean's eyes.

Tightness formed in Penny's throat. The face seemed to require more of her than being an adequate, if temporary, governess. More than using a false name and having hidden motives.

Why couldn't her expression say she found all of this a bit of a lark, or she secretly admired Penny's derring-do? Penny glanced away from the sensitive face to find Mrs Stuart wiping at her cheeks. "What—"

"The oats should be dead," the older woman said in a hard voice demanding Penny ignore the streaks of damp trailing over her face. She lifted a hand to the window where, beyond it, dense woods swirled between green fields full of waving grass, high enough to brush the belly of a dog.

"Ma'am?"

Mrs Stuart's voice was rough, crotchetier than it had been in weeks. "The snow ought to have finished off the seedlings. If not that, then the pounding hail which came after, or the killing frost. These weeks and months of rain should have wrapped up the job."

The children at the end of the gallery had found a game in aping the poses of their ancestors, collapsing into fits.

"It's a resilient crop," Penny said.

"It shouldn't be."

Penny glanced back to the portrait of Jean Ross and felt as though her palms were brushing the tops of the leaf sheaths, the grasses bending and twisting under her hand. She felt her magic.

Within herself, Penny scrambled for her rising, stumbling over thoughts to remember the steps that would send her soaring into the air. *Gather, radiate, rise. Gather, radiate*... Damn. There was nothing to gather, nothing to do. Merely this prickling liveliness that seemed to wind itself in one direction. She followed it.

"She's much like you," Penny said, her voice soft. The prickling disappeared and she heard Mrs Stuart's sharply indrawn breath. "Your hair—"

Mrs Stuart tightened her shawl. "She didn't have any gray when she went. She didn't have any lines on her face. She didn't ache like I do…"

It sounded like a snub, but Mrs Stuart twisted around on the bench, her features hardly less contorted than her body. Her eyes bore into the painting of her daughter.

"She caught a stupid chill, which didn't go away." The sound from her throat was inarticulate, shaking grief bound up with the shame of a child, too old to be caught crying. "Now she's a painting, frozen on a wall until kingdom come."

Penny turned her eyes away from the grief. She didn't need tickling palms or the quickening sensation in her veins to realize the woman would resent her for witnessing it. "Was she fun? She looks it."

Mrs Stuart stared out the windows, her eyes unseeing, on the oat fields that should be dead. Pain tumbled out of her mouth but so did a short laugh. "I could never teach her not to bellow up the stairs like a common fishwife. We weren't so fine as the people of *Coille na Cyarlin and* must take care with our manners. She'd shake her head at me and call for Malcolm as though there weren't an any number of servants to do her bidding. She told stories."

"That's where Robbie gets it."

"Aye. She liked her own way. Liked to keep us dancing to her tune. Still, if she slammed a door, she was as quick to open it again and make amends."

Penny's gaze returned to Jean, and she knew as deeply as one could know a thing that Jean would have stood in front of her children like a sword-bearing Valkyrie if she thought they were in danger.

They were in no danger from her, she assured the image. Here in this long gallery with the hard rain pounding against the windowpanes, they were in danger of nothing more than knocking their heads together.

Chapter Twenty

"I cannot disobey orders," Penny insisted.

Isabelle looked about the richly appointed salon. "I'm not sure that's true anymore. Do you know what they say about you? You've been called upon to act as Malcolm Ross's hostess, receiving Lady Berwick and Mrs Leadburn for tea. Receiving them like a gentlewoman." She selected a crisp almond biscuit from the tray and smiled widely. "I cannot believe you haven't managed to relax the rules."

Penny recalled Jean's clear eyes and straightened her own shoulders. "As I have said, only Mary is allowed to accompany the children from the house."

"But Mary's only a nursery maid."

"Mary is a respected member of the staff," Penny corrected.

Isabelle's smile broadened. "That was spoken like the mistress of *Coille na Cyarlin*. But, really Penny, a governess must be in a position to bend the rules." She leaned forward, examining Penny's face. As she did, Penny looked Isabelle over too.

Naturally, the lady could hardly help taking an interest in Penny's search for her lost power. She was a gentlewoman living far outside of her natural sphere, whose abilities were wider than a little cottage and the lop and chop of home-brewed tisanes and tonics. How frustrated she must be. How bored. How lonesome.

"You are kind to consider my needs, Isabelle. But the prior governess behaved like the Russian army burning down Moscow. The ground has been scorched black. How much trust do you suppose the Mr Ross has left?"

"You are right, of course, and it presents a difficult problem." Isabelle gave Penny a long, considering look. "Have you thought that Cousin Malcolm might be interested in female company? An attraction might be just the thing to distract him." Her eyes narrowed. "Though it's a pity you have such plain gowns."

Isabelle had arrived in a light pony cart, wearing a midnight blue habit with black frogging across the bodice and a hat set at a jaunty angle. The fabric on her elbows was worn and Penny noticed a small tear in her skirts had been mended with nearly invisible stitches. Still, the lady had taste. Her ensemble would not look too out of place in London or Vienna. In rural Scotland, such magnificence was suffocating.

Penny smoothed the fabric of her dress across her knees, fighting a moment of wild rebellion, which kicked against the back of her teeth. Each morning she chose from brown, blue and grey. She longed to feel like herself again, to tell the only story about herself that was true. Here is Miss Penelope Thornton, youngest daughter of Sir Charles and Lady Sarah Thornton, wearer of glorious silks, wielder of sky magic.

She gave no hint of her turmoil. "These are appropriate to my station."

Isabelle sighed like an overwrought lover in a bad play. "It's such a pity. In a proper gown you could have had Malcolm eating from your palm."

"You can't imagine he would trust me better if I looked more polished."

"There you are wrong," Isabelle giggled. She was only teasing. "Men are simple creatures. A man who imagines himself in love has given you all the power you need."

A shiver ran up Penny's back. "Why haven't you tried this tactic with Mr Ross? You've had plenty of time."

Isabelle wore a *Come now, do be serious* expression. "And risk being stuck in Scotland forever? No, no, dearest, I think not. When I hunt for a husband, it will be for far bigger game than my poor cousin."

Game. For all the Thornton wealth and position, Penny's family had not been in the habit of speaking this way. Her oldest sister Deborah had had the pick of London and settled on the son of a near neighbor. Beatrice wed a penniless captain. Mama was wildly ambitious, but not for sons-in-law.

"Will you try capturing his interest?" Isabelle asked, glancing about the room. "You are a charming girl. I vow you're half there already if you're hosting his tea parties."

Penny's smile stretched so tight that it was in danger of becoming a grimace. The topic was painful somehow, laced with hidden barbs and thorns, which caught her tender flesh. She chose an answer to end the torment. "Only to be trapped here? Heaven forbid I capture the heart of a Scottish rustic."

Isabelle left shortly after, but it had been an exhausting exercise and left Penny in no state to settle the children into Botany and Mathematics. She could not blame them for their high spirits. The worse the weather was, the more restless the children became.

The idea for respite crept and clung into her mind the way a trailing plant hung onto the crevices of a brick wall. They should play hide and seek. Her mind traversed the twisting ringlets of the vine. She even knew the perfect hiding spot.

Mary volunteered to count with Kathleen, and they began a slow chant to one hundred as Penny and the others scattered through the house.

After the oppressiveness of Isabelle's visit, Penny had to stifle the urge to laugh as she pelted down the stairs like a child. She knew exactly where she ought to go, though how she should be so certain caused a little puzzlement. It was the perfect spot—hidden, but not too hidden—the precise compromise for playing with a little girl who would flop on her backside in the hall and howl after five minutes of slapdash hunting. Kathleen, for all her winsome ways, was not a good sport.

Penny pushed into the library and swept behind the curtains and held her breath, listening to the sounds of Ewan and Robbie claiming their spots in the direction of the ballroom.

The heavy curtains were stuffy and dark, and she stifled a sneeze as someone entered the library. Definitely not Kathleen who would be bellowing her name.

These steps were heavy and furtive. Penny jumped when the curtain was lifted back and Malcolm darted in, bumping into her, treading on her toes.

"Out," she hissed in the close, dark place. "Out. This isn't sardines."

His eyes crinkled. "Sanctuary," he said, laughter breaking his words. "I claim sanctuary. If you kick me out, Kathleen has vowed to put me in Newgate Gaol, and I do not know where that could mean."

Penny smiled. "Second stair down from the landing. Mary only puts her there when she's called the boys cork-brained."

Laughter shook through him—shook through her at every point of contact—but the sound of Kathleen searching grew louder and Penny clapped a hand over his mouth. The jostle knocked him off balance slightly and he reached a steadying arm about her waist, pressing his other hand against the wood paneling at her back.

"Shhh," she whispered, laughing. "If *I* get found first, I'll have to write lines for an hour. An entire hour. Don't you dare get us found."

She released him, but the smile she expected to see had disappeared. The light was curious here. In the half-dark she ought to have noticed fewer things, but instead, it brought a heightened awareness to her senses.

She heard the control of his breath, the steady inhale and exhale stirring the curls beside her ear. How it checked when their gazes met. Her nose filled with the mellow tang of his shaving powder, and the other scent, beneath that one, which she would have known blindfolded. Her fingers held the memory of the slight scratch of his skin where her hand had rested against his mouth.

She shouldn't be here. Kathy's punishments be damned. She should run.

Her eyes traced the trespassing light shifting over his skin. It looked like a sunrise over a pond. She would leave now. She saw herself do it—flip back the curtain and race away on a laugh. Unchanged. As she always was. That Penny was safe already.

This Penny, rooted to the ground, too curious to move, was not.

Malcolm drew a jagged breath and captured her hand in his, pressing them both against his chest where his heart pounded—timeless, constant. She hadn't been the only one, it seemed, who had stayed up nights, plucking the coverlet and thinking about this awareness between them. Wondering if such a delicate, astonishing thing could blossom and bear fruit in the midst of the storms blowing in from the hills.

They froze for several heartbeats and then he dipped his head. He moved slowly, giving her an eternity to draw back, to pretend she didn't want this, to remember her resolutions about a life that would take her far from Scotland.

She ignored the voices calling her to temperance and wisdom. She lifted her chin, her breath mingling with his.

She had been kissed before.

The atmosphere had been aided by a warm summer night, a garden full of flowers, and the strains of an Austrian waltz floating on the air. The whole thing had had a tinge of inevitability.

She had been dressed in rose-colored lutestring and the man—what was his name? If she had been offered a fortune, she could not remember his name now. She had a vague memory he looked dashing in his formal clothes, and when they came together it had been as orderly as a slight crescendo in a second-rate piece of music. Something to dance to. Not to lose your soul in.

That was nothing like this. Malcolm's gaze brushed over her and there was nothing loverlike in it. No softness. No attempt to coax something from her. It was plain with wanting. Surely, he would find an echo of that in her eyes.

How it could be that the distant sound of children laughing could accompany this moment far better than music? She went up on her toes, exactly as she did when she unleashed her power and rose into the night sky. His thumb traced the pointed, half-moon edge of her chin and his mouth claimed hers.

The contact was slight at first, and then enveloping as a ruffle of magic, as strong as an ancient oak glorying in the wind, every leaf fluttering and shaking within an immovable bower, setting each nerve alight. She tugged a steel button of his waistcoat, bringing him closer, and he deepened the kiss.

"Pen." His rough whisper scratched her heart as he drew back a fraction, his breath warming her skin. She could die here and be happy. "What are you doing to me, Penny Starling?"

The name doused her in the icy chill of mortification, strong enough to yank her away from him when every hope and wish was to curl against his tall frame.

She stumbled back and his arms dropped away from her. "No," she whispered, speaking around the large breaths she took, praying he would not regard them. "We can't."

She whirled from the heavy drape and into the room, blinking against the sudden light. He lifted his hand to catch her back, but she turned away, rushing for the door.

"Pen, wait," he said, repeating a name she had only heard from people who loved her. "We must speak."

She disciplined to her expression, hiding the confusion she knew would be there. Only then she turned, thankful he was still several paces away. Any closer and her composure would evaporate. “No need, Mr Ross.” Her voice sounded as it did when she gave lessons on multiplication charts. Firm and filling the whole room with certainty so everyone would hear. Her eyes darted to the unsettled drapes, slowly swinging into stillness; her mind replayed the events, which set them in motion.

“That was a mistake,” she declared and watched a muscle jump in his jaw. “I don’t blame you. I—I—” She exhaled sharply. “Think nothing of it.”

“That I cannot do.” He pushed a hand through his hair, thatching it.

Like Kathleen, she wanted to scrunch her eyes up tightly to convince herself she’d disappeared. Imagine the foolhardiness of acting on an attraction with a man she had to see every single day—a man who could not even call her by her true name.

The feeling of mortification felt like being crawled over by beetles.

Malcolm fisted his hands at his side and inclined his head. “I’ve taken gross advantage of my position, and you must, at least, allow me to apologize.”

Penny flinched and she caught the suddenness of it in a mirror. Her face was white, the color competing with the snowy cotton cambric at her neck. Her lips were rosy. He was apologizing because he thought he’d been a cad? A poor employer?

Perhaps that might explain why he’d kissed her. She was near at hand and he had an itch to scratch. Couldn’t he remember how she’d—she’d— A flush climbed her cheek as she remembered exactly how much she’d helped him. The whole thing made her want to read herself one of Mama’s more brimstone-y sermons.

“It’s already forgotten,” she lied.

“Scared to love a rustic Scotsman?” he asked, and her mouth dropped open to hear her words—her own lies—repeated back.

“Were you listening at the keyhole?” Oh heavens, what else might he have heard?

He coughed, shifting. “I caught that much in passing.”

“Were you trying to punish me? Is that why you followed me into hiding?”

"Of course not, Pen. I—"

She didn't wait to hear the rest. She turned on her heel and raced towards the ballroom, every stride marking her out as a coward.

"There you are," Robbie shouted from under the piano forte when she rushed through the door, at which Kathleen burst into tears insisting that she must find Miss Starling on her own. Ewan peeped his head out of the orchestra gallery.

"Come, Kathy," Penny said, taking the little girl by the hand and then scooping her up like a shield. "You have your captive and may decide my ransom."

She walked past Malcolm under heavy guard, avoiding her employer's hard gaze.

Chapter Twenty-One

When she reached the safety of the schoolroom, Kathy pronounced her punishment for being found so easily. Ewan thrust a pen into her hand. Robbie had her transcribe what he claimed was an old Scots proverb, *Sasse mhour vesteg ur a mslain Sasse*, which he declared meant, "An Englishman fried in butter is still an Englishman."

For an hour she wrote, though her hand cramped and the children giggled when they came to check her progress. The rote monotony of the task allowed her feelings to prey on her.

Stupid Scotland. Stupid Malcolm. Stupid game of hide-and-seek. She wiped the heel of her hand against her cheek. Stupid tears.

She hadn't been entirely lying to Isabelle when she'd spoken about the danger of falling in love with Malcolm. It would be lunacy.

Her hand scratched words across the page. Penny was playing with fire. She could not do anything so unforgivably foolish as to regain her magic only to lose her heart. Especially to a man who'd apologized for kissing her.

Her hand stilled and the letters blurred before she blinked them back into focus with a sharp sniff. Why had he done it?

It hadn't felt like punishment at the time. Perhaps he felt like a tea kettle kept near enough to the fire to warm the water, but not so near that any release might be found in boiling and steaming. It had been years since his wife had gone, and he was still a young man.

Two young people under the same roof had succumbed to the kind of temptation proximity wrought. Proximity. That explained it. Her hand wobbled and the neat line under her pen trailed drunkenly.

Even so, the man knew how to properly kiss a woman. Two kisses to her name and she had already deduced that much. Officer What's-his-name had balanced her on the end of one knuckle, tucked gently under her chin, while Malcolm Ross held her as though she was his and he would never let her go.

Then he had.

Better he had, she sniffed. She was an English girl. She was lying about everything. She would have to leave sometime.

Her eyes dropped to the page and some of the sun seemed to leach from the room.

"*Sasse mhour vesteg ur a mslain Sasse*," she sounded out as she wrote.

***

The following week, as she resumed her normal routine with visits to Penicuik, and tea with Lady Berwick, her mind returned again and again to the kiss. She popped in on Mrs Hunter and Mrs Johnston, pleased to find, despite Malcolm's chilly demeanor, the master of *Coille na Cyarlin* was not neglecting his promises—her promises—to make his tenants as comfortable as he could.

Isabelle visited the great house often, but, to Penny's relief, said no more about making Malcolm fall in love or gaining access to the children.

"I am trying to learn the trick of rooting my magic in place," Penny had told her. If her rising had once been conjured by meditating on lightness and weightlessness, perhaps rooting her magic might respond to the same methods.

"Are you still having vague flutterings?" Isabelle asked, and suddenly Penny felt like an old woman afflicted with nerves.

Perhaps she was. She could not know if the shivering along her veins amounted to the return of her power until she began to see a pattern in its comings and goings.

Penny's head and hand moved equivocally. Yes, there were flutterings—often when she thought up some idea for the schoolroom. But sometimes the ideas—odd ones like taking the children into the garden to scratch their lessons in the dirt, or having Robbie collect twigs and stones to shape his letters—seemed to come from her mind. Who could tell if it meant anything?

"Have you discovered any way to reap magic?" Penny asked.

Isabelle bobbled her head in the same ambiguous way.

When it came to Malcolm: weather from that quarter blew with a decided chill.

Penny sighed, holding her hand above her brow and looking out on the garden where the children raced and skipped. The sun glinted bravely through the grittiness of the pale blue sky.

It was too cold for farming, but the fields around *Coille na Cyarlin* seemed to thrive even as news came from Edinburgh and beyond, crops were failing, beggars rioting, and unrest crawled through rural communities like a contagion.

Here she was, handing Ewan a pen knife to dissect a flower and nodding as he named the parts—pistil, stamen, petal, leaf—before calling for tea to be brought out on the terrace.

Malcolm joined them, bringing with him that familiar magical delight, which brushed over her when he was near. No busyness readying the tea things or directing the servants could drown out the sound of his laughter as he played with the children. Nor could it take away her pleasure at hearing it.

She thought she had been careful not to look at him. However, she didn't need Ewan's shout he'd killed his father to make her hitch up her skirts and tear across the lawn. She'd seen with her own eyes the shuttlecock ricocheting off Ewan's battledore, dropping Malcolm on the ground.

"It's nothing," Malcolm said, when she knelt over him. He squinted up at her, brushing her hands away from his face.

She gripped his hands firmly and shoved them to his side. "Let me see," she commanded, too anxious to worry about his role and hers.

There was little blood, thank heavens, but the wound was too near his eye.

"It'll be a bruise," he scowled. "I don't need fussing."

She ignored him, lifting his eyelid with her thumb. Gently she touched the site where his skin was darkening and a familiar shiver passed through her, leaving in its wake a strange, calm certainty about what she must do.

"Mary, continue with the children. I'll see to Mr Ross."

Under the noise of the nursery party resuming their game with a gruesome lack of concern for their father, Malcolm propped himself up on one elbow bringing his face in proximity to hers. "See to me? How can you see to me? You haven't looked at me in days."

Her cheeks flushed, but she helped him to his feet.

"Come," she said, scanning the near meadow for what she sought. Her eye lit on the tiny yellow blossoms of her quarry. Sweet clover.

She led him along to the tea table. "Sit," she ordered, scurrying away. She returned with a clump of the herb in her hands.

"What are you doing?" he asked as she chafed and wadded the greens in the folds of a fresh handkerchief, wrecking it beyond repair.

"Making a poultice," she answered. Then, less confidently, "I think." Had she read this somewhere? Perhaps in one of Isabelle's grimoires, she thought, though that didn't seem right. She tended to skim the pages about folk medicines. Those didn't contain magic.

She poured a small amount of the hot water from the tea pot onto her handkerchief and screwed the bundle tightly, pressing it against his head.

His hand reached up to cover hers and she caught her breath, loving the feel of his warm fingers lacing with hers, knowing she shouldn't.

"Better?" she asked.

"Too soon to tell," he rasped.

When she would have withdrawn her hand, he caught it closer and fastened her gaze with his good eye.

"I'm sorry, Pen," he said, not retreating as she had expected him to, behind a stilted armor of formality or ambiguity. "I didn't mean any dishonor. I was—" He crashed to a halt. "I wasn't thinking of punishment when I kissed you. I wasn't thinking at all."

She didn't pretend to be ignorant. All week she had been tending a wall between them, carefully stacking her stones one atop the other, hoping he could not glimpse her tender heart on the other side.

"I didn't mean that, either. About you being a rustic Scotsman."

He gave a low roll of laughter she felt more than heard. "I *am* a rustic Scotsman," he replied, his accent kicking up.

How colorless other men of her acquaintance appeared beside him. Like tea brewed from thrice-boiled leaves next to strong Scots spirits.

"I'm not waiting for you to give me leave to use your Christian name, Pen. You're never Miss Starling in my head and I won't pretend you are."

"Manners are not silly," she replied.

"Do they teach governesses to spout such bromides before they loose you on an unsuspecting world?" he grunted, and her mouth twitched into a smile. "I wish you would call me Malcolm."

"You know I cannot. It is one thing if I allowed you to use my name," she said, guilt spiraling through her belly. Penny was the only honest name she could own, and she could not halt the sharp desire to hear him use it. "It's quite another to address my employer in such easy terms."

"What an unchristian view, Pen. Are we not all equal before the Lord?"

Penny choked back a laugh.

"Anyway, you're far better than I am," Malcolm pressed his case. "You found me in a sorry condition—crusty, too caught up in finishing the village to consult my people. They will have a better time of it because of you. The children—"

"You cannot credit me with virtue on their account. I nearly failed there. I nearly fail every day." She looked down the garden, to Ewan holding Fritz's lead, Rob playing as far away as possible, not taking his eyes from the beast.

"You don't give up," Malcolm said, his gaze dwelling on her. Then a twinkle lit his eyes. "I will confine myself to using your name when there are no others to disapprove. You may use mine when you cannae help it."

There would never be such a time.

"Agreed," she said, slipping her hand free and wiping it dry on a napkin. "We can return to our easy ways and pretend the...the incident in the library never happened."

He leaned back on the delicate chair and stretched his booted feet out, crossing the ankles, his accent thick and rich. "I'll no' be doing any such thing. Don't think I could if I tried." He lifted the poultice and gave a roguish smile, which played havoc with her stomach. The bruise—and it was a good one—had not altered his attractions a whit.

"I would have us be friends, Miss Starling," he said, suddenly grave. Silence stretched out as she weighed the risks. Then his light of deviltry returned. "Miss Starling, Pen. Do you see what a pattern-card of virtue I am, observing the proprieties?"

A burst of laughter overcame her. She could not help it. "Terribly proper. Quite decorous."

"Then we are agreed," he said, repeating her words. "We are friends, not easily given to discord and mistrust."

Friends. That might be as dangerous as kisses. But these last few days had been lonely and the temptation to have him near was stronger than the risk he posed.

"As you say."

***

He was as good as his word. They acted as friends and sometimes she forgot there had been a time when a broad-shouldered Scotsman hadn't taken the lion's share of her attention.

They spent their evenings solving riddles as Mrs Stuart's knitting clicked away, reading aloud some novel or bit of poetry. They tracked her parents' progress around the counties from dispatches in the newspaper. Cambridgeshire, north to Loughborough.

"Unrest and famine," Malcolm said, slapping the paper down one night. "Calamity and violence. What sort of man is Sir Charles to hold it back?"

Penny knew exactly what kind of man her father was. "He must have some abilities, sir, or Lord Liverpool would not have appointed him."

"Liverpool. That noted specimen of Tory mediocrity," he said, much to Penny's amusement. "His agent will be no better," he added.

Unable to mount a defense of her kind and brilliant father, Penny trounced Malcolm at piquet, all the while making frequent references to the reign of James the First.

"James the Sixth," Malcolm fulminated from time to time, which put her in a lovely mood.

It was in the parlor by the fire she began to feel her choices narrowing. After Malcolm would make some jest, their glances would meet, and the laughter would die away in his face. She would see some question in his expression and knew it would demand an answer at some later date.

She began to lie to herself in a new way, telling herself the date would never come, pushed off endlessly by the disorder of managing the children and attending to the tasks required of her by the village.

One July afternoon had combined the two. Accompanied by Mary, she set out towards the green on the edge of the new village to give the children a lesson in suffrage.

"Every man and woman who is planning to move to New Pentland will have the right to vote on another name, if they wish. There will be speeches and a picnic to follow. Your father has promised to have nothing to do with the outcome."

They passed the track, which would take them to Isabelle's cottage, and she gripped Kathy and Rob's hands more tightly. This errand had nothing to do with Isabelle, and the children had nothing to do with gaining her magic.

Penny had never seen any of them exercise the smallest speck of it. It was kindness, really, to save Isabelle a good deal of bother and wasted time. Nevertheless, Penny called Ewan to come along with Fritz and walked a little faster.

The day had been exhilarating, noisy and great fun, but it was an exhausted, apprehensive Penny who presented herself to Malcolm a little before dinner. She knocked on the library door, determined to grasp the nettle.

"Enter," came his low voice and she peeked around the corner.

Malcolm flung down his pen and laced his hands. A light danced in his eyes. "You have such a look on your face. Who have you killed? We take feuds quite seriously here in the north, and we'll stand with you. All of *Coille na Cyarlin* is prepared to wreak eternal vengeance for your cause."

She tucked her lips into her mouth, trying to prevent a smile. "You won't like it," she said when he moved swiftly from his seat.

His eyes glittered as he advanced. "Won't like what?"

"I did as I promised." Penny swallowed down the laugh and turned to the bookshelf, drumming her fingers along the spines, walking briskly away from him. "It was completely democratic. Every adult in the village got a say about the name."

"You told me they would change it if they could. I'm not surprised they have."

She halted when her gaze touched the heavy curtains, suddenly wishing he would drag her within them, kiss her senseless and call her by her name.

"I won't be mad."

She turned. The laughter in her throat almost bubbling up. "Do you promise me?"

"A Ross never breaks a promise."

She bit her lower lip, giggles escaping, and he gripped her arms. "How bad is it?"

"Robbie enjoyed the entire process—he understood it at once—got up on the back of a cart and started giving a speech. They humored him. You know how persuasive the lad is…" Penny covered her grin with her hand. "Now you promised not to be mad, Malcolm Ross, you promised."

He gave her a little shake. "Tell."

"Slinch Bickey."

There was a moment of blank incomprehension before Malcolm gripped Penny's arms and threw back his head, the sound of his laughter filling the room. "How am I going to write that in an advertisement?" he asked when he had recovered enough to lean against the bookcase, one arm thrown along the shelves over Penny's shoulder. He arced his other hand across the air. "'Welcome to the village Slinch Bickey. Cottages to let.' Lord, I'll be a laughingstock."

"It's no stranger than Boghead or Auchenshuggle."

His lips quirked. "Your English accent—"

"You won't make them change it, will you?" She could not dim the pleasure in Mrs Johnston's eyes when she had counted out the ballots. Such an honest feeling ought to be nurtured.

He looked down at her, his eyes closing while he shook his head. He had inched closer. "How can I? It's perfect. The name has more wrinkles than a walnut. What stories they'll tell of how it came to be."

She smiled up at him and realized her fingers rested lightly on his waistcoat, absently tracing the rim of a button. She was this close to pulling him behind the curtain herself. "You'll have the sign painted?" she asked, dropping her hand.

"I'll do one better and have it engraved in stone. Slinch Bickey," he laughed again. "Pen, we are raising a reprobate."

A tide of pleasure washed through her cheeks only to have it leach out again, leaving her cold and confused. She was not raising Rob. She would board a ship to England as soon as she got her magic back and never stay long enough to see the lanes of Slinch

Bickey busy with people. Never see what became of her charges. Never see if learning to make his bed properly ever mattered to the lad.

Something of her confusion must have shown on her face because Malcolm reached up to touch her, running light fingers over the high ridge of her cheek, following it past her ear and cupping the back of her jaw. She leaned into his hand for a second, closing her eyes.

"What's the matter?"

She swallowed thickly, hardly understanding her feelings. She was going to discover how to root her magic, return to her life in England, and finish her story as it was always meant to be written. *Penny Thornton. Bearer of sky magic. Englishwoman. Traveler.*

"Nothing," she breathed. She lifted her eyes to his. "We'll have to get the spelling right."

Mrs Stuart entered, lifting her brow. Malcolm dropped his hands and Penny slipped from his side.

"The town is named," he said, moving forward to escort Mrs Stuart into a chair. "Slinch Bickey."

She chuckled when Penny told the tale. "Robbie ought to have a future as a politician. Why don't we throw a ball to celebrate?"

"Do you think so?" Malcolm asked, handing her a drink.

"Of course. We'll invite Doctor Bell, some of the tradesmen and their wives, your investors..." She brushed her hands together as though dusting them off. "This year has been miserable. We should kick up our heels when there are reasons to do so."

"The expense. Won't that be too much for you to plan?" he asked.

"I'll have Miss Starling to help, and between us we can find a way to do it up without so much money."

Penny nodded. "Of course. I'm happy to set anything you wish in motion."

"You will dance with us too." Mrs Stuart slipped the words in as though they could not excite comment. "What merry figures we will cut."

Penny looked away and encountered Malcolm's blue eyes, his tense form. She was only a governess. No matter how often she drummed that fact into her head, the gentlest glance from her employer seemed to send the thought winging. *Only a governess.*

"I can assist you in trimming out your gown, ma'am."

Mrs Stuart's eyes narrowed. "As I could help you."

"I don't think—"

"I insist," Mrs Stuart pressed. "You must be prepared to step into my shoes if my energy flags. You'll be my... What's the word I want, Malcolm? Proxy? Secretary?"

"With that look on your face?" he chuckled. "The word is victim."

Chapter Twenty-Two

Delicious wind tore at Penny's hair, pulling the breath from her lungs and wrapping her in sighs. Clad only in a thin night rail, her cheeks were apple bright as she floated in an ash black sky. Laughter burst from her lips, the sound drifting in a hollow stream towards the stars.

A sudden gust sent her sailing along an air current like a kite, and she breathed in the magic. It was strong, coursing through her on familiar pathways, the sound of it a song of which she knew every note.

Distant lights signaled the only sign of human habitation. How far she was from the worry down there—the confusion and turmoil. There was safety in the sky. Comfort. She closed her eyes and tipped her head back, weightless.

Penny woke on a sudden gasp of breath.

The pitched ceiling of her room confused her for a moment, and she sat up, glancing over her shoulder to inspect the shallow depression her body had made in the mattress. Her mouth tightened.

She hugged her knees and pushed away the grief. She closed her eyes again. Staying perfectly quiet, breathing slowly, she imagined her magic as—her nose wrinkled in thought—a potato with knobby green sprouts. She imagined hoeing a long furrow of rich dark earth and placing the pieces within—one, two, three—mounding it over again. If she stayed perfectly still, the delicate roots might begin to anchor into whichever innermost part her magic had been ripped from.

A dull thump followed by a piercing squeal rang out and her eyes shot open. The Ross children were awake. Penny swung her feet to the floor, hitting the bare wood with as much force and weight as ever. Another day without any magic at all.

There was no magic in listening to Ewan explain the bones in the foot to Robbie. No magic in Kathleen burning her finger on the hot end of the toasting fork and declaring she would die. No magic in glancing from the window and seeing Malcolm Ross returning home, his brimmed hat whacked into shapelessness against his dusty breeches. No magic at all.

"How was your day," Malcolm asked when she sat at his table at the end of the day.

"I sent the invitations off with the morning post," she said, sampling the wine.

"The more I consider the party, the more I like it." Malcolm said, tilting his glass to his lips. "It will give Leadburn and Berwick a chance to see the progress on the village."

"Aye," Mrs Stuart agreed, her eyes bright. "And it will give you a chance to see Berwick's pretty daughters again."

Penny's chin didn't dip or lift or tilt or do anything that might indicate she knew or cared about the Berwick girls.

Malcolm's glance flicked to Penny—too quickly for Mrs Stuart to catch it, surely—and in it was a warmth that sent her frozen sinews thawing.

He murmured, "You're not to meddle, Elspeth."

After dinner, Malcolm begged off from joining them in the parlor, claiming his accounts had become a tangle. An offer to join him trembled on Penny's tongue, but Mrs Stuart whisked towards the door. "Are you coming, girl?"

A small, banked fire glowed in the hearth and Birdie brought in a tea tray, setting it, for once, at Penny's elbow without any sign she regarded the young woman as much of an interloper. Penny stared after her.

"Don't look so surprised, young woman," Mrs Stuart laughed. "Birdie was bound to come around when she understood you meant no harm to her wee chick."

"Robbie?" Penny wondered.

Mrs Stuart snorted. "No. Malcolm."

Penny laughed that a man as vast and unconquerable as Malcolm Ross should be described as anyone's wee chick.

"A bare fortnight until the ball," Mrs Stuart said as Penny passed over her tea. "Have you decided what to wear?"

Penny opened her mouth. Shut it. Opened it.

The older woman spoke with characteristic bluntness. "You've nothing grand enough."

That wasn't true. Penny's clothes press at Thorndene was bursting with confections that made her hair glow as bright as a copper penny, lace overskirts, which highlighted the flecks of silver in her eyes, silks so delicate they might be pulled through a ring.

What a fool she was. Hopping from ledges, meditating on imaginary potatoes rooting in the ground, watching for wayward magic and listening to every theory Isabelle presented for absorbing powers ought to be enough to occupy her mind.

But presently her mind was envisioning the ballroom of *Coille na Cyarlin*, herself clad in sober gray cut right up to her neck as Malcolm danced with every gently bred female within ten miles. The idea of it made her restless and grumpy.

"I don't wish to go at all," she lied.

Mrs Stuart's brow lifted in a way that immediately made Penny feel she had been silly. "I have something for you," she said, reaching for a parcel and tossing it into Penny's lap. "Open it."

Penny folded back the tissue paper to discover the dull shine of blue silk—impossibly smooth and lustrous in the candlelight.

"It's not a dress," Mrs Stuart said, her somewhat anxious gaze resting on Penny's face. "Not yet."

"Such lovely silk," Penny breathed, stroking her hand over the folds. "Where did you get it?"

A tiny pause and then, "I bought it for Jean. I saw the length in Edinburgh, the autumn before she passed, and meant it as a New Year's gift. But—"

A hard lump formed in Penny's throat, sharp and dense as a pebble. "You can't— It's far too lovely, Mrs Stuart."

Mrs Stuart's voice was blunt, almost rude, as though Penny had been getting it wrong this long while. "Elspeth."

There was no magic today. But she was having difficulty remembering it as the woman's clear, determined eyes held her own.

Penny nodded. "Elspeth. You must call me Penny. Penelope if you're cross. Mama always does." She rubbed her thumb over the fabric and imagined Malcolm. The silk was the color of his eyes. "I couldn't possibly accept it."

"Why should I give you a choice?" Elspeth grumped. "My companion at such an event should not shame me. If I commanded, you'd have to obey."

Penny smiled. "I would."

"I won't command you, and well you know it." Elspeth expelled an irritated breath. "Take the dress length and make something nice for yourself."

"Why?"

Elspeth made a sound from the back of her throat. "To please an old woman. Or in payment for all you've done for the children." She waved her hand. "Because your hair is perfect for this color. Pick any reason you like."

Penny dropped her eyes to the silk spilling like blue waters over her lap.

"Come, now. Every girl wants to cut a dash, and it's within my power to make it possible."

"A governess has no business cutting a dash," Penny murmured.

Elspeth snorted. "You think yourself a mere governess in this household? I didn't think you were as stupid as he is."

"I'll accept it," Penny blurted, silencing Elspeth's runaway mouth before it carried her over the cliff.

Elspeth beamed. She actually beamed. "Excellent."

"On one condition," Penny added.

Elspeth's familiar scowl returned, comforting Penny like the familiar feel of Fritz's head under her hand. "Which is?"

"I've never sewn a dress before. I'll need help."

Elspeth's eyebrows notched and Penny bit down on her lip. Blast and blast. As the months wore on, it was easy to forget she was playing a role. To forget that she wasn't who she said she was. It was hardly any wonder the performance was fraying around the edge.

Of course, a penniless governess would have known how to sew for herself. She would have to make do with inferior materials and make what she had last and last with careful mending.

"Do you not know anything about needlework?" Elspeth's voice was careful. She hid her shock poorly.

Penny brushed her tongue along her lip. She knew plenty about plying a needle, her expertise honed at her mother's side. No matter which foreign capital they resided in, or what pressing social engagements awaited her that evening, Mama had been careful to set aside a half hour of quiet and repose to spend with her daughter, chatting easily about every topic Penny cared to find as embroidered flowers bloomed beneath their hands.

She swallowed away the sudden lump of homesickness, her gaze returning to Elspeth's.

Should she admit that she was expert in the kind of ornamental work which embellished handkerchiefs and slippers? Well-versed in decorative needlework? "There are gaps in my knowledge. I could use someone to—"

Suddenly Elspeth's puckish smile returned. "You need a governess."

With that, they began to debate essential points of design.

"It must be plain. We'd never get it finished in time otherwise," Penny pleaded in response to Elspeth's sudden burst of enthusiasm.

They began to work, bringing out their project in some unspoken accord during times when they were alone. In the evening after Malcolm had gone to the library, or after Mary had taken the children into the garden. Victim, indeed. Friend, perhaps, Penny began to hope.

"I am worried about your droopy bodice," Elspeth commented one evening in her private sitting room.

The firelight turned the blue into the sinuous curves of a river and the simplicity of the cut presented a problem Penny had not foreseen. Every flaw or failure would be on full display, not hidden under a mountain of trim.

She lifted her arm with a frown. "I could take it in—"

"Let me fit you," Elspeth said before Penny could object. Elspeth's hands moved nimbly to the silk, pinching the fabric and tacking it down.

"Elspeth," Penny breathed, hardly daring to move as she bristled with pins. "Your hands."

Elspeth's dour expression was ringed with smug, satisfied pleasure. "Thought I was past it, did you?"

"Is it the weather? It's been warmer this week." Penny's voice was full of wonder. It seemed not so long ago that Elspeth had been a hunched figure, each limb and joint twisted out of place.

"I've been getting better for months," Elspeth answered, carefully working Penny out of the dress.

Penny stood perfectly still until Elspeth was done and carefully stepped from the gown, setting it over a chair before throwing her arms around Elspeth in an embrace she returned, hesitantly, at first, and then with her full strength.

Finally, Elspeth withdrew, handing Penny a wrap. "I dare not hope it will last."

"You mustn't think that." Penny plucked up the soft blue dress, examining the care with which Elspeth had executed the fitting, and felt a shiver of joy run through her spine. Miracles were possible. "You've returned to your old self."

Elspeth shook her head. "My old self didn't know I could lose the use of my limbs. My old self could not understand suffering. My old self thought I would go on and on as I was. My old self was an idiot. I don't want my old self back." She spread her hands. "I'll take this season of healing and store up enough gratitude to hold back the bitterness when the healing goes again."

"You're so sure it will?"

"The future makes no promises."

Frustration churned Penny's simple pleasure. She wanted Elspeth's healing to be less complicated, easier, more like a child's tale in which dragons died and stayed dead. She fretted her teeth against her lips and tried to mold Elspeth's news into the shape she wished it to be. "How lovely to feel yourself again."

Elspeth caught her hand and Penny looked at her own smooth, youthful fingers laced in Elspeth's spotted ones. "I was always myself. No pain could change that. It showed me facets of my character ease and comfort could not unearth. There are times when you find a piece of yourself you could not find any other way."

Elspeth began folding away her sewing tools and Penny swallowed, settling on the sofa. Could she ever be thankful she lost her magic, lost the world of tearing wind, biting cold, and glorious weightlessness? What joy had come of that?

The answer came so swiftly she drew her breath. If she had not lost her magic for a season, she would not have met Elspeth, met the children, or journeyed to this wild country. She would not have loved Malcolm.

There. Time and past to admit it.

She had not planned to love anything in Scotland. The sojourn here was supposed to be an unavoidable stop on her journey home. No different than that greasy inn at Bruges. She had only meant to retrieve her truant magic and drag it home by the ear.

The future made no promises.

Penny wrapped her arms around herself, staring into the fire, the flames blurring in the grate. Her heart had given itself to Malcolm Ross. When?

Not at the inn. Not in the shepherd's cottage. Her mind supplied an image. Ewan hanging from his neck, Kathy on his boot. Malcolm reaching his large hand to cup Rob's head. She choked back a watery laugh.

She was supposed to fall in love in a ballroom with a young man who would send her posies and leave his calling card, promising her a future in snow-brushed Oslo and the fragrant reaches of the Orient. She was supposed to travel everywhere, consuming the whole world in tiny morsels.

Malcolm, however, was not a man capable of skipping or skimming over the surface. He was planted here at *Coille na Cyarlin,* and it would be a sacrilege to uproot him. Penny shivered at the thought, suddenly wanting it to be easier. Wanting to find a man whose loving would not require sacrifice.

Her cheeks warmed and her lungs tightened. There would be compensations. The memory of fitting against him in a close embrace, of looking up to see the warm question in his eyes—a question she hadn't allowed herself to understand until now.

"Now, I can help you sew," Elspeth said, jerking Penny back to the present.

"No. You mustn't." Penny stood, pulling herself from the warm nest she'd made by the fire, wondering if Elspeth's sharp eyes could see it in her face—her love for Malcolm, and she wondered if Elspeth had seen it all along.

Penny looked away. "I want you to do what you've been longing to do. Pull the grandchildren up on your lap. Walk the garden path. I don't want you to waste any of your healing on me."

Elspeth gave her a scowl. "Not wasted. Nothing is wasted."

Chapter Twenty-Three

Malcolm moved swiftly along the passage until he stopped outside the schoolroom. The low murmur of voices met him in the hall, and he touched the door enough to open up a narrow sliver. The nursery party was too loud to hear him, but he held his breath, nonetheless.

"Turn it, turn it," Elspeth shouted and Ewan, who was toasting his bread over the fire, put one hand on Robbie's fork, turning them both. Penny held her hands outstretched to Kathleen. "You may hold it, but you'll sit in my lap."

"I won't burn my finger," Kathy insisted.

Penny caught the finger and kissed it, hauling the child by the waist. "Into my lap."

Little elbows and limbs crowded onto the gray skirts.

"Finish your story, Elspeth?" she asked, and Malcolm's brows lifted. Elspeth?

"Aye, where was I?"

"Mam was stuck up a tree, Gran."

"Och, aye. When I bid her get down, her boot wedged in the notch of a branch and she flipped top over tail, exposing her bare backside for God and all of creation. Well, who'd ya think rides by at that very moment?"

The children began to guess and then Elspeth declared in a dramatic flourish, "The minister."

There erupted a shocked gasp and flurry of shouted questions until, finally, the firm tones of Miss Starling settled them down. The noise was replaced with the low-humming delight which accompanied hot buttered toast being consumed and dishes of tea being passed around. He watched them for a few minutes, and then a tiny, stifled giggle jerked him upright. He turned his head to find Mary standing with her hand over her mouth.

"I'm not spying," he declared in affronted whisper.

"No, sir," she laughed.

Fighting down a flush, he straightened his waistcoat and entered the room as he ought to have from the start.

They did not see him until Kathleen rolled off Penny's lap with a thump and he scooped her up. Penny's hands were full of toast, butter, and a knife, and she tipped them into Ewan's hands and got to her feet, brushing out her skirts and scattering crumbs.

"Have I interrupted?" he asked, holding Kathleen close, the comfort and familiarity of it contrasting against the bristling awareness he felt every time Penny was near.

Months of proximity had served to heighten the feeling, no matter what he had said about friendship. So now, even when she stood so far from him, she had only to glance, or twitch her skirts, and he would feel it.

"Not at all." Penny's color was high, and she turned to tidy the nursery picnic, scooting the boys off the floor, whisking the toasting prongs to the table. His chest lifted and fell in a silent sigh.

What did he want? For her to feel so comfortable in his presence she treated him like one of the children? Or for this constraint to spring up whenever he caught her anywhere but at his dinner table, safely divided by lace and mahogany?

He set Kathleen down and walked to the table, swiping a piece of bread and sticking it on a fork. He settled his large frame in front of the fire as the women watched elegantly from the sofa. "What have you been up to, Kathy?" he asked.

She barged onto his lap and craned her head around. "Sums. Papa, do you even know how many boards are in the floor if you count crosswise? Seventy-two."

He looked at Penny who gave her head a tiny shake. Her lips pursed in half a smile. Shc mouthed "Twenty-seven."

He grinned. "What a first-rate mind you have." He turned his toasting fork and glanced at the ladies. "How are preparations for the ball coming?"

Elspeth glanced at Penny, taking her in confidence. "Isn't it like a man to ask such a question when it is far too late to do a thing about it?"

Penny's mouth screwed shut, but her soft grey eyes were dancing.

"We have it well in hand," Elspeth continued. "Penny had every one of us scouring the forest for greenery. Cook has made oceans of white soup. The farm has slaughtered a pig and Doctor Bell brought us several game fowl. There is nothing left to be done."

"All arranged without me having to lift a finger."

"Your task is Herculean enough," Penny added somberly. "You'll have to make pleasant conversation for the entire night."

"Wretch."

He felt Kathy twist around in his lap. "Wretch?"

He laughed and caught Penny's amused expression. Then the light in her eyes shifted and she cleared her throat. "I have to give Fritz a run. Would anyone like to come with me?"

He would.

Kathy jumped to her feet and Penny looked suddenly thoughtful. "Wouldn't you like a walk, Rob?"

"He won't come if you bring that dog of yours," Ewan broke in.

Malcolm opened his mouth to rebuke the boy—his tone had been bordering on rude—but Penny silenced him with the smallest flick of her finger. How had she known he would see it?

"You would come if Fritz were on a lead, yes?" she asked Rob and he nodded. "It's a great deal to ask Ewan, but would you manage the dog for me so that Rob may come?"

As though doing a great service at enormous personal cost under conditions of greatest duress, Ewan assented, and the children raced off to collect their outside clothes.

Malcolm frowned after his son. "You handled that well, Miss Starling," he said. "Ewan is a doubtful, hard-won child."

She laughed. "Some are born curmudgeonly. Some achieve curmudgeonliness. Some have curmudgeonliness thrust upon them," she misquoted, lifting her shoulders. "I like the crosspatch. His feelings are honest."

She excused herself, but at the door, turned again. He was struck anew by the queenliness of her tall figure, and his heart felt too large for his chest. She smiled. Not for Elspeth. Not for the children. For him.

"You're burning your toast."

He yanked the fork, juggling the hot bread in one hand as he scraped away the blackened bits. The door closed behind Pen, and he soon felt the weight of Elspeth's speculative gaze.

"Were you thinking of other things?" she asked, her voice dry and knowing.

"The village," he began. "Rowan trees and bridges. I've been busy putting things in order for Lord Berwick and Leadburn. It was a long morning out at," there was the barest hesitation, "Slinch Bickey."

"Hmm." Elspeth sipped her tea. "And yet you spared a quarter of an hour to stand in the doorway listening in on the nursery party."

"Not a quarter of an hour," he corrected, biting into the crusty bread, the acridness of the burnt toast blending with the smooth melted butter. "Hardly more than five minutes."

"It's nice to see you so often," Elsbeth said.

"We agreed that the children would need careful watching."

"You're doing far more than I expected." Her words were bland but there was something in the way she said them that prickled his senses. "Especially for one so busy. I wondered if it had anything to do with Penny Starling?"

The trap was sprung. He fought to keep his hands steady. "Calling her by her given name is new," he said, gambling on deflection.

Elspeth gave one of her thin smiles. "She's got a way with her. Don't you think?"

He could feel the jaws of the trap ratcheting open again, the spring being delicately set. His answer was careful. "The children are enjoying their governess. It's as I hoped."

"I'm excited for the ball," she said, and he began to relax. To think himself out of danger. "What an excellent time for you to look about you for a good Scots woman."

He choked on a bite of bread. "You think it's time for me to marry again?"

She cocked a brow. "It's always time for a widower to marry. There is a shortage of men."

He focused on the steady in and out of his breath. "Mmmm."

"Of course," her voice was brisk again, "you could save yourself the trouble of looking and make do with a choice under your nose. Have I mentioned how deft Penny is with the children?"

Make do. Penny was not "make do." She was not someone to be wed for the sake of the children.

"She has a life in England. A home," he said, repeating the words he'd spoken to himself again and again since Penny Starling came to *Coille na Cyarlin* and turned over the tables of his well-ordered life. "She is cold here."

"So warm her up." Her words were as good as a cuff on the back of the head.

He smiled but stabbed another piece of bread on the fork and held it toward the flames, crisping the pitted surface of it, patience and skill turning it into what he wanted it to be. You could not do that with a person, no matter how long you waited.

"She never wanted to be a governess. She won't want to look after someone else's children her whole life."

"Who said anything about being a governess?" Elspeth frowned at the fire. "You've come back to life this spring."

Malcolm's heart ached in his chest, stretching its confines. "She's English."

"Aye, I cannae help but hear it every time she mangles the name of the house." Elspeth poked his shoulder. "You have a habit of loving where you shouldn't."

Elspeth knew. He wondered how long she had known.

The sound of the fire popping in the grate jerked him back to the toast and he turned it, narrowly avoiding the fate of the first. Penny must know he wanted her, but she made no sign. "Love doesn't mean you get what you want."

Elspeth's words came like a sharp-edged plow, turning over the earth. "No. It doesn't. Love didn't save our Jean, but that emotion wasn't buried with her. Four years gone and you've forgotten how brave you had to be to marry her. Facing down your own father when he wanted you to look higher." She exhaled and a smile flitted over her mouth, her eyes bright and glittering. "You were sure-footed and daring, then. But, Malcolm Ross, I'm telling you this. If you don't take a chance for Penny, my daughter wouldn't know you."

"Hell, Elspeth," he exhaled. "Next time knife me between the ribs. It would be kinder."

Elspeth snuffed. "You'll live, lad. You were the best of husbands to Jean. I'm not worried you'll forget her," she said, releasing him from a burden he had not known he was carrying. "She'd want you to be happy. Do you love the girl enough to wed?"

He pulled the toast from the fire. Just in time. “Aye, if she’s fool enough to take me. It’s the only kind of loving I know.” All or nothing at all.

Elspeth cracked a satisfied smile. “She’s fool enough. You should speak.”

Lord, he felt like a stripling again. The same reckless excesses of energy rising within him. The same impulse to break his neck to impress a girl. He grinned. “Even though she’s English?”

Elspeth nodded. “I daresay we can teach her to salt her porridge quicker than you can learn how to live without her.”

Chapter Twenty-Four

Penny donned the blue silk dress, pinning the bodice in place as Mary tied the sash. Each seam had been carefully pressed under Elspeth's exacting instruction, and though Penny had put the frock on a number of times during its construction, exhilaration bloomed under her skin.

She smiled at the dim reflection mirrored from the window. There was no warm hip bath or scented powders tonight. No array of tasteful jewels suitable for a young woman to choose from. No posies from hopeful suitors. Only Mary to attend her and a narrow bed on which to sit as she pinned a spray of purple heather to her hair. Still, she knew she had never looked better.

Elspeth gave a hoot of triumph when Penny met her in the hall.

"You're full of deviltry, Elspeth," she said, gripping the woman's hands.

"I'm not up to anything, child." Then, taking Penny by the elbow she tipped her head. "Shall we go down and dazzle Malcolm?"

Penny grew warm under Elspeth's inspection. "It's enough to dazzle you."

Elspeth snorted. "That would be a terrible waste of a beautiful gown."

From the drawing room they heard Isabelle's high, chiming laughter, Malcolm's deep murmur, and other voices, less familiar. Penny's slippers rooted to the floor.

"Chin up, girl. They won't eat you."

Penny shook her head a little as if to say, "Of course not." She took a sharp breath. She was the daughter of Sir Charles Thornton, knighted for his service to the Crown. She was the daughter of Lady Sarah Thornton, who could stare the Queen out of countenance if she wished. She had met Grand Dukes and Marshalls, Kings and Emperors. She moved forward, her back straight, her face calm, prepared to do her mother proud.

They were greeted by Mrs Hunter, wearing an exuberant display of ruffles from hem to bust, and Mrs Johnston, clad in elegant mauve. They swept their gazes over Penny's radiance, taking it for granted she should look her best, clucking delightedly and turning her around, behavior far too warm-hearted and impetuous for London.

Mrs Hunter embraced her, jerking almost immediately out of Penny's arms.

"Oh," she exclaimed. "Bless my soul."

"What did I do?" Penny asked.

Mrs Hunter flapped a hand. "You? Nothing. I had a pain in my side, just here," she said, pointing at her ribs. "I fell off a chair reaching for a book. I know I shouldn't have, Anne. It's too late for scolds." She turned a radiant smile on Penny. "Thought I'd broken a rib, bless me. Almost didn't come."

"I'm so sorry, ma'am," Penny exclaimed. "I can find you a quiet room and send for Doctor Bell."

"But that's it." She prodded her fingers roughly into the third tier of ruffles. "It's gone—disappeared."

The women moved on and Penny looked up, encountering Malcolm's gaze cutting across the room, taking in every part of her. She wanted to touch his face; to twitch the folds of his cravat. She had never seen him in clothes so formal, and she wasted precious seconds reconciling the two men into one. The first who greeted her in the common room of an inn looking like a down-at-heel farm laborer, and the other man, lending half an ear to Isabelle, looking like he was on his way to a dinner at Carlton House.

Elspeth steered her towards the small group, laughing as she reached the Doctor Bell's side. "I've not seen you look so elegant in years, Donald," she said, her eyes travelling over the doctor's kilted figure, pausing to take in his rather surprisingly shapely calves. "Nor you, Malcolm." She turned her face up, receiving his salute with an easy acceptance of affection Penny longed to mimic. "Terribly handsome. Don't you agree, lass?" she added.

Penny's mouth dried up. "Yes," she managed, holding back a flood of words and straining with the effort. He looked so good she wanted to disgrace herself. "Kathy would be quite impressed."

He crossed his arms, blue eyes dancing. "Only Kathy?"

"Ewan and Rob, too, of course."

"Of course."

"And our Miss Starling," Elspeth prompted. "We contrived the loveliest gown for her, have we not?"

His eyes lit with a sudden fire and he plucked his lip with the pad of his thumb. Isabelle filled the silence.

"What a kind thing to do, Mrs Stuart. I fretted and fretted dear Miss Starling would have to come to the ball in one of her workaday gowns, but now look at her," she smiled. Penny was jarred to see that she bared her teeth, "putting the rest of us in the shade."

"My lady, you have no fear of being cast in the shade," Penny assured her.

Isabelle had abandoned her widow's weeds and wore a new gown, or one that had been carefully preserved and reworked from better days. Gauzy pink with twining green trim, which set off her ivory complexion and smooth, dark hair to perfection. Tonight, her looks had a sharp, glittery edge.

Was it possible that Penny had angered her friend in some way? She tried to work out the reason. Was she hunting for a husband? Penny was no threat there. Even in a pretty dress, she was taller than most of the men in the room. Her lineage, as far as anyone knew, was obscure, and her fortune unknown.

Isabelle brushed her finger over a cunningly turned sleeve. It was not a costly detail but one that had taken time. "The hours you must have spent, Mrs Stuart. Penny is lucky to have a benefactor so generous with her time."

There it was. This was about trust, and Penny's precarious place in the *Coille na Cyarlin* household. She had been repeating Malcolm's rules to Isabelle for months, never giving any hint those rules had relaxed. Obviously, they had. No wonder Isabelle was hurt.

Of course, she was. Working away at Foxglove Cottage, Isabelle was as lonely as Penny had been. She had promised to help restore Penny's lost magic, expecting nothing in return, and this is how Penny had treated her—putting off meetings again and again, skeptical of suggestions. Ruffled feathers would have to be soothed.

The dinner bell chimed, and Penny took her seat according to her station, in the middle of the table. After a sumptuous feast, she caught Birdie's triumphant smile when she brought in the nougat almond cake Cook had been pessimistic about. Was this what Mama felt when she brought off a party? Weeks of managing difficulties praying it would appear effortless.

When it came time to open the ball, Elspeth declared her intention to observe from a distance.

"I'm too fatigued," Elspeth said, sitting heavily into a chair. Penny crouched, inspecting the Elspeth's face. Her color was good, and her deep breaths put Penny in mind of a theatrical performance.

"You must stand in for me." Elspeth aimed a glance over Penny's shoulder. "You'll lead out Miss Starling, won't you lad?"

Penny stood, her stomach coiling into a tight knot even before Malcolm spoke. She knew it was him in the way the air moved differently when he was near. His proximity brushing the fine hair on her arms, and at the back of her neck.

Heat bloomed in her cheeks as she turned, she caught the amused narrowing of his eyes when he glanced at Elspeth, the tug of his gloves and the band of deep brown skin glimpsed at his wrist.

"You'll partner me, Miss Starling?" he asked, a laugh coloring his deep voice, reminding her of the times he had called her Pen. Didn't he understand this was not the same as stealing a kiss in some hidden corner of the house? Something between them would shift if he led her out into the center of a ballroom, no matter how much it made Elspeth laugh.

"You're courting danger," she said.

If anything, he looked more roguish. "I know exactly what I'm courting."

"Well, do you know there are other choices to be had?"

His azure eyes seemed to sharpen as he grasped her hand, tugging. "I've made my choice."

She lifted her chin and followed at his side. She would not embarrass them. The servants at *Coille na Cyarlin* had toiled for weeks to make this possible. She would not shame Malcolm, who carried the future of the village and his people on his broad shoulders. Nor could she resist her own desires—desires felt so deeply she could not see a beginning or an end to them.

Turning into her place with the soft swish of petticoats, she glanced over the hard lines of her partner from the corner of her eye.

"Satisfied?" he asked, amused, and her chin jerked away as the music began.

The men of the diplomatic corps had been so deadly serious, they'd never dream of teasing her over protocol. Such young men stroked their patchy whiskers and nodded sagely about the precise boundaries of German states, thinking they were the only men capable of holding calamity at bay.

She set her fingertips against his palm and marked out their steps. "I did not mean to...to—" she began, too full of wonder to laugh at herself, and her impertinent perusal. *Lord, if there is a way I could stay with him forever, let me see it.*

"You make me blush, Pen," he whispered as he crossed at arm behind her waist, meeting her touch, wrapping her within the wholly frustrating half-intimacy of a dance.

Warmth crept up her neck, but their movement swept away the troubling questions tripping on her heels; obscured them in the exhilaration of dancing with him, of skipping breathlessly down the line and twining her fingers in his as a rush of couples threaded under the arch.

He turned her in a wide arc, his hand burning on the curve of her waist for a too-brief moment. "You've worked miracles," he murmured, nodding at the arranged branches and boughs, which decorated the ballroom. "I would not have thought the house could look so grand." Lines fanned from the edge of his eyes and his accent thickened. "For so little money, lass. You've been careful with the pounds and pence."

He laid a hand over his chest, the glove bright against his dark coat. "There's nothing that pleases the heart of a Scotsman more than sobriety in the matter of money. Faith, Penny, I've kept the accounts. If I told the assembly what you had accomplished, some man would fight me for your hand and try to carry you off this night."

She glowed with pleasure, eyes dancing under the light of the chandeliers.

"It would be a pity to lose a governess," she said, sliding through the narrow space created when his arm and hers stretched over her head, hands clinging, twisting. Their palms kissed and dropped away.

His voice lowered. "I said 'try,' Pen. I wouldn't lose you."

She missed a step and he righted her in one smooth motion. "I did only a little organizing," she demurred. "It's your people, from

Birdie all the way down to the smallest tweeny, that did all this. They did it for love."

"Oh? And what did you do it for?"

Love. But she was saved from having to lie when the figure broke them apart for a few moments, bringing them together at last for the final curtsy.

"I hope," she said, striving for some sense of normalcy as he escorted her to a seat, "I was an adequate proxy."

He leaned close, his voice rumbling in her ear. "Is this how the English go courting, Pen? Must a man fight through a thicket of manners?"

His words were thick with meaning. What would he have said if they were not in a crowded ballroom with the duties of being a host hemming him in from every angle?

Penny could have backed away. She could have laughed and inched out of reach. Another girl might have done so. But she stood perfectly still and tilted her eyes up to his.

He took a sharp-drawn breath and then Isabelle's voice shattered any illusion of privacy. "Cousin, I believe this dance is yours."

Malcolm fixed Penny with one final look before turning, straightening his coat and striding off with the same efficiency he used when roofing a cottage, or building a wall. The message in his eyes stayed with her for a long time.

Throughout the night, her gaze kept straying to Malcolm's tall figure as he escorted ladies, young and old, through the figures of a dance. During an interval, Penny glanced up at the clock and slipped unnoticed through the door. She hurried through halls, which seemed more silent when contrasted with the bright gaiety of the party, anxious to keep her promise.

Hearing the faint, thin strains of music resume in the ballroom, she rapped a soft knuckle on the nursery door and waited for Mary to peep her head out. "Are they fast asleep?" she whispered. "I hate to wake them for this."

"They're wild to see your dress," she said, swinging the door back for Penny to enter.

The children were in their beds, though the younger two were the wrong way around, lying on their stomachs.

"I told them they have to stay in the bed," Mary murmured.

Ewan gave her a cursory glance but held himself aloof from the excitements of the younger children, training his eyes on the window. Pig-headed, Penny sighed. She had been a pig-headed child too.

She made her way between Kathleen and Rob's beds, allowing them closer inspection. Though plainness was her preference, she regretted her choice now to refuse Elspeth's offer of lace and ribbon. Regretted she hadn't the speed for some of the finishes one might work with a needle and thread.

Kathleen didn't seem disappointed as she let the silken sash slide through her pudgy fingers. "You're a queen."

Robbie surveyed her more critically. "You look funny," he said, and she held her hands out. He leapt into her embrace, surprising her. She laughed into his warm neck, knowing, but uncaring, the carefully pressed frock was creasing.

"Not funny, Rob," Malcolm said, filling the doorframe. "You don't tell a lady she looks funny."

There it was again. He had only to speak and her heart dropped from its perch, racing around the confines of her chest like a duckling in a too-small pail of water. It was hammering away, and Robbie must have felt her stiffen because he wriggled, and she let him go. He burrowed into his covers. "I meant funny, *Aither*. She doesn't look like herself."

"Doesn't she?" Malcolm asked, stepping past Mary who sat by the fire with a basket of mending at her feet.

"No, Papa. She always looks like a bickey, black cloud with a rim of goldy sunset at the top."

"Sunset," he said, sitting on Rob's bed and giving him a poke.

"You're the king, Papa," Kathleen pronounced over the noise of her brother's shriek.

"Are you all quite satisfied now?" Penny asked, her eyes skirting over the back of Ewan's head for a moment. "Will you allow Mary to settle you to sleep?"

Kathleen reached out with her hands and Penny sat at her side, stroking her dark hair back from her brow. Mama used to do this when she was little. It had always felt nice and she puzzled over the feeling it gave her to be performing her mother's ways with these children.

"'Night, Kathy," she said, bending to kiss her forehead.

"I will have one," Robbie said. Penny kept the surprise from showing on her face.

"Thank you, Rob," she murmured, kissing him too.

"You're welcome," he declared, turning over to his stomach and rubbing his nose. "Ladies like kissing."

She smiled but said nothing, making her way from the room as Malcolm tugged the coverlets up and kissed his children. He soon followed her, drawing the door closed. They stood, as they often had, across the width of the hall. But instead of sunlight streaming through the far window, there was a pale strip of silvery moonlight.

"You left," he said, voice husky.

"I promised to show them my dress." Maybe if she continued to speak this knot that had formed in her throat would dissipate. "Your guests will be missing you. You should go back."

"Not yet."

The darkness seemed to deepen, filling the hall with sable shadows, which pressed close. The strains of a country dance wove from the ballroom, a counterpoint to the veil of decision which clung like cobwebs over them both. This was no children's game, as it had been last time when they caught one another in an embrace.

She waited for him to say more but he remained silent, precisely when she wanted to kick the dam loose, tumbling the planks downstream and unleashing the torrent of speech which would make sense of her heart.

"I have three children," he said, strain bracketing his mouth.

Her heart, which had started to fail her, began to burn, and her fingers tingled as though she were leaping from a ledge and trying to grasp a hold on the other side: unsure, hoping. She wanted him so badly, the strength of it crowded out thoughts of her deception, of how he might feel to know she was not who she said she was.

There were no considerations of Scotland and the ties that bound him here. She only looked and wanted—wanted as high as she had ever risen. Higher.

"So many?" She took a step towards him, through the thickening shadows.

"Aye. I've spent a young man's first love."

Another step. If she wished to, she could lift her hand and brush the lapel of his coat. They carried so much inside, the two of them—

so much unspoken. What would be the harm of turning the earth over, digging up the things laid buried between them?

She ought to stop him from speaking, but this longing was like the turn of a screw, tightening and tightening all the time, causing exquisite pain at each quarter turn. This could not wait.

"Is this how the Scottish court, Malcolm?" she whispered, an odd constraint closing her throat as she spoke his given name aloud. He had given her leave to use it when she could not help herself. She could not help herself now. "Must a woman tell a man when she wants to be kissed?"

He narrowed the gap between them.

Blazing hot fire burned through her veins. She could turn back if she wished. Nothing had been said that could not be taken back and palmed off as the aftereffects of a romantic evening and too much wine. A simple attraction had travelled beyond its boundaries...but it was nothing of the kind.

His breath broke from his chest and he pulled her to him, his hands encircling her waist, lifting her up on her toes. "Pen." Her name was a ragged growl, and then his lips settled on hers, hot and certain.

Chapter Twenty-Five

Malcolm kissed her as though he might never have the chance again, his control slipping when her hand slid around his neck, her fingers tangling in his hair, tightening into a fist. He lifted his head. Moonlight clung to the curves of Penny's face. His fingertips traced the same path over her cheekbone.

A laugh shook through him and he dropped his forehead against hers, breathing deeply, filling his nose with her scent. His breath came out raggedly and he closed his eyes. He was no halfling. No young man chasing after a girl, but there was no use telling his heart. The organ acted as though this was the first woman he had ever held in his arms. The first woman he had ever loved.

"I mean this, Pen." His voice was rough with emotion and he touched her face, running his fingers along trails his eyes had taken a thousand times. "I can't love by half measures."

She nodded, her breathing as unsteady as her hands. She dropped the one in his hair and he plucked it up again, pressing a kiss to it and placing it against his heart. "You have a choice. Mine is already made."

She lifted her clear eyes to his and he was almost undone. Going up on her tiptoes she kissed him on the mouth, her warm lips clinging for a too-brief moment. Doubt and uncertainty fled, replaced with exultancy. He would belong to this woman as soon as he could make his pledge. She would belong to him.

"Is your father yet living?" he asked. "I must write to him."

Her face shadowed, and she dropped her gaze. "I—"

He was asking too much. He could not expect her to race along as impatiently as he did. He enfolded her and laid his cheek against her hair, feeling the heavy sigh that went through her frame.

"Dallying with the governess. Malcolm, you shock me."

Isabelle.

Malcolm released Penny slowly and she stepped from him, turning towards the shadows to tuck strands of hair into the knot at the back. He faced Isabelle, shielding Penny the best that he could.

When Penny had collected herself, she slid past him, touching his hand as she went.

"What are you doing up here?" Malcolm asked when she had gone. "The children are abed."

Isabelle glanced over her shoulder, watching Penny disappear around the bend in the stairs. She gave Malcolm a mocking look. "A good thing they are, too. What an example you've set them, Cousin, consorting with the hired help in a darkened hallway."

"I don't know what you think you saw—"

She laughed, the malice of it grating on his raw nerves. "I have eyes in my head."

"I asked what your business is here."

She drew a bottle from her pocket. "No need to act the fearsome Scot with me. Penny mentioned your nursery maid was under the weather and I brought a healing tonic."

He straightened his coat where kissing had disordered it and ran fingers through his hair where kissing had accomplished a similar disarray. "I must return to the ball," he said, offering his cousin a stiff bow and leaving her in the dark hall.

He entered the room and immediately pulled Penny into the figures of a dance, aware of the knowing looks and whispers following his actions. Good. Let them see.

This was a country dance, splitting them up as often as not, and each new figure brought more dissatisfaction. "There's a dance on the Continent," he murmured. "Recently arrived in London, they say. It's a scandal, but now I wish I knew it. I want you to myself."

"The waltz," she smiled. "Are you admiring something that isn't Scottish?"

His laugh boomed across the room and the figure of the dance split them yet again. "We ought to learn," he said, when she returned to his arms. "If only for the sake of fashion."

Her nose crinkled in laughter and it was all he could do not to scoop her up into his arms. "With the children counting out the time?"

Yes. That's how it would be. It would never be only them. He brought three unruly children, a mother-in-law, and all the ghosts of

Coille na Cyarlin riding pillion. Would his lass feel cheated of a proper wooing?

There would not be time for more. He would declare their union in another minute if he did not let her go and pin her down to the particulars of where and when she would give her promises, and he would make his in return.

"Walk out with me tomorrow?" he asked, the thought of waiting to see her in the evening with Elspeth looking on suddenly unendurable.

Her lips twitched. "I have lessons to supervise."

He held her closer, far too close for politeness, and felt the noise in the room rise. Good. Let them talk. "After dinner, then. I have a passion to iron out the details."

She grinned.

Chapter Twenty-Six

As she danced and drank and chatted with his guests, Penny was conscious of Malcolm's gaze resting on her. Her own attention was as fixed as his, returning again and again to his broad form like a falcon to its perch.

Now, as guests waited for carriages and stood about in the great hall, he was gathered with a knot of men—investors—his dark head bent in conversation. Then he glanced up and his blue gaze met her own, sure and certain of her. How could he be otherwise? She had rushed headlong into answering his unspoken questions. Can you love me? Will you marry me? Will you stay by my side? Yes. Yes. Yes.

"*Coille na Cyarlin* is so easy to reach," she said, almost absentmindedly forwarding Malcolm's cause as Lady Berwick and Mrs Leadburn chatted about the excellence of the ball. "The roads are so good."

She jerked her gaze away from Malcolm to the ladies who were busy exchanging knowing smiles.

Had she been reckless to answer him?

No. It was not reckless to love a man as fine as Malcolm Ross. It was not reckless to want him with every part of her. But to give him her heart before he knew all? Her stomach slid uneasily. There would be a reckoning tomorrow and she had not yet worked out the best way to tell him.

Malcolm, I'm magic. I used to be.

Malcolm, there is a funny story about my name.

Malcolm, would you like a seventh glass of wine?

Her gaze drifted towards him again and she felt certain about one thing. She did love him. The thought of returning to Dorset with her magic, of writing to her parents and joining them in Yorkshire or Norfolk, of finding a suitor when they returned to London. Her stomach lurched again.

Any wedding bereft of Kathleen tumbling down the aisle seemed insupportable. Any life without bright green vistas. Any home without an overstuffed portrait gallery. Anyone tugging her into his arms who wasn't him.

Mrs Leadburn touched her hand. "Miss Starling, I am forming a charitable committee in the next few weeks to address some of the shortfalls caused by this miserable growing season. I would be pleased to have you join us."

Penny colored. "I'm only the governess. Perhaps Mrs Stuart—"

"I spoke with Elspeth. She assured me you were precisely the lady to ask." Mrs Leadburn looked up as Malcolm approached with Lord Berwick. "Say she may come to tea again, Mr Ross?"

Malcolm took her hand and slid it possessively under and around his elbow, his eyes laughing. The man must know it looked like he was making a declaration.

Then he made it far more obvious.

"What do you say, Pen?"

The flutter of inarticulate feminine interest was like a covey of birds taking flight at the sound of a gunshot.

"It sounds delightful," she answered, shooting Malcolm a look promising to charge him for his high handedness.

Isabelle stood at the edge of the circle and Penny wondered if she was sad or merely tired. Her mouth was in the form of a smile, but it didn't sparkle in her eyes. "Miss Thornton is such an asset here."

Thornton. Penny tensed, her mouth flooding with the taste of fear. There wasn't even a shadow of confusion among the assembly yet. Isabelle had misspoken. The gathered guests had almost dismissed the incident until Isabelle gasped and clapped her hands over her mouth, large eyes brimming with tears.

"Oh, Lord. Oh, Penny." Isabelle's voice was frantic, scrambling. "I didn't mean it."

"What's this?" Lord Berwick grumbled.

Penny felt the flush creep into her cheeks, the color creeping higher. She began to slip her hand from Malcolm's grasp. He gripped it all the tighter. She swallowed, praying Isabelle would have the sense to play off her blunder. Instead, Isabelle dug into her mistake as a sawbones would dig into cankered flesh.

"I didn't mean to expose your—your charade. I sincerely didn't. Please forgive me."

Malcolm's hand had turned to stone in her grip, and this time when Penny tugged her own it came free. All her hopes seemed to wither like an autumn leaf. A little wind would tear her from her mooring and send her skittering away from all she loved.

She lifted her chin. This was no time to entertain the grief or violence knocking against her heart.

"What's this?" his lordship barked.

Penny turned a cool smile to Isabelle. "Don't upset yourself, Lady Ainsley," she said as embers of fury erupting under her skin begged for release. She tamped them out, her thoughts trained on saying whatever needed to be said to keep Malcolm's fragile plans for his village together. "My pretense is no longer necessary."

"Pretense? Charade? Did you know of it, Ross?"

Penny could feel the fate of the mill and the cottages hanging by a thread; could feel the itch in her palm where it longed to slap Isabelle's teeth down her throat. Damn, that woman and her carelessness.

Penny darted a look at Malcolm, his face too stern to play this off. If he wanted to sail through unscathed, he must follow where she led. She reached her hand to his and squeezed his fingers, keeping her composure when he flinched away.

"Of course, he knew," Penny said, turning a smile upon him, willing him to understand what she wanted. "Not a thing happens at *Coille na Cyarlin* that is unknown to its master."

Lord Berwick's beetle brows lowered. "Then why this havey-cavey nonsense? If a governess be called Starling or Thornton, nobody gives a rat's—"

"Berwick," his lady scolded, silencing the man, but not cowing him.

Lies—good ones—marshalled on her tongue and she began to deploy them alongside half-truths. "I am Miss Penelope Thornton, sir. If you have been following the London papers, perhaps you have read of my father who is serving as Lord Liverpool's agent and advisor to His Royal Highness." His Royal Highness was an insufferable clodpoll, as Papa always called him, but his title was impressive.

Now for the lies. Penny smiled as she redoubled her efforts to awe, knowing all the while every word would damn her in Malcolm's estimation.

"While they were on His Royal Highness's business, the attentions of a particularly persistent suitor became unwelcome to me." She paused as though the topic were a delicate one, still painful. "My parents could not leave their duties, but agreed it would be best if I could remove myself from Society until the gentleman was posted abroad."

Elspeth, mouth clamped like a trap, watched the recitation, and Penny said a silent prayer. *Don't be difficult, Elspeth.*

"Mrs Stuart was kind enough to offer me a position." Penny was a single lady of uncertain fortune in the employ of a marriageable man. It was better not to speak of Malcolm at all.

She wove her story like fine cloth, cutting and piecing the fabric with unpracticed hands, trusting no one would inspect the seams too carefully.

"I could not do less for old family friends," Elspeth declared. Relief washed through Penny and she began to breathe.

Nevertheless, Lord Berwick's face was still knotted in confusion, a faint wash of irritation coloring his expression.

Malcolm revived. "You know what young ladies are," he said, clapping the man on the shoulder. "Spectacle and drama wherever they go. No doubt her father could have managed to sweep away the mess if she'd heed him."

His lordship looked to his daughters and grunted knowingly.

"It will be a great loss to *Coille na Cyarlin* when Miss Thornton returns home," Malcolm pronounced, turning Lord Berwick toward his waiting carriage.

"When shall that be?" Mrs Leadburn asked.

"Soon," Penny answered, her heart like glass.

"Little more than a fortnight," Malcolm confirmed.

The guests began to disperse, Malcolm standing on the front steps as they went. Other guests with farther to go followed Birdie and a small gaggle of housemaids to rooms, which had been prepared for the night.

Isabelle stepped to Penny's side. "I could not think." Her voice was strained, her hands twisting. She appeared sick with guilt, but Penny could not look her in the face. "You must forgive me, dear friend. You must."

Penny turned, a hard ache hollowing out her chest and throat. She pasted a tight smile on her lips. "No matter. It was bound to come out sometime."

"I'm feeling exhausted," Elspeth scowled, pushing between them. "You'll help me to my room, Miss Thornton," she declared, her tone carrying for lingering guests, Penny supposed.

Penny nodded, lending her arm as Elspeth made her stately way up the stairs. At her door, Elspeth pushed inside. "We will talk." She waved her maid away and stirred the fire, wrapping her finery in a humble shawl. She stared at the muted glow of firelight.

"Penny Thornton," she said. "Is that your true name?"

"Yes," Penny answered, standing with her hands clasped behind her back.

Elspeth frowned. "Sit down, girl. You're making me anxious."

As she had countless times in the schoolroom, Penny settled on the rug, her skirts billowing around her. Reflected flame made azure rivers on the cloth and she traced the ripples with clouded eyes.

"You are what you said? Pestered by a suitor, daughter to one of Prinny's men…" Elspeth twirled her fingers in the air, spinning the tale on and on.

"I have no suitor. That was an invention of the moment. Papa does work for the government. We've been reading reports of him for weeks—Sir Charles and Lady Sarah Thornton."

"Oh hell," Elspeth breathed. Silence reigned for a time. "Now I know why you cannae do good, plain sewing. I don't suppose you had to."

"Mama's lessons were ornamental, rather than practical." Penny fumbled with the end of her sash, rolling it around her wrist, over her palm. "Thank you for supporting the lie."

Elspeth grunted, but there was a laugh in it too. "If they believed it, they deserve to be fooled. As though I would have offered refuge to an English chit, hardly able to manage the children. Do you have a good reason?"

The flames in the grate danced and blurred before Penny's eyes. "He won't think so." He. Malcolm. What could she tell him about magic he would believe? She had none to show him.

Elspeth waited for her explanations, but when none came, she said, "He's furious. For all his smoothness—"

"I know."

Elspeth nodded. "Do you want to bother making amends? Or have you got what you came for?"

Penny's heart stopped. Her breathing stopped. If she had been rising, she would have dropped from the sky. Her words came in a whisper. "Mrs Stuart—"

"Elspeth."

What else the woman might have said was choked off when a servant knocked, carrying a message from the master.

"Here's your reckoning, lass. He will not be put off until morning." Elspeth stood and murmured something about checking on the children, giving Penny a sympathetic look as she went.

Penny made her way to the library and took a bracing breath before pushing the door open. Malcolm—Mr Ross as she must begin to think of him—was still wearing his formal dress, staring out at the moonlit garden. He turned and she swallowed a lump at his look, as cold and forbidding as a Scottish wind.

"I will not keep you long, Miss Thornton."

There was the faintest pause and question at her name, and she gave a little nod, taking her seat by the fire, feeling ridiculous in the liquid blue dress, which had swirled about her ankles when he kissed her in the hall. How much easier she could bear this in serviceable grey wool.

He strode closer to the fire, standing between it and her, cutting her off from the heat and light, his dark shadow now rimmed in molten flame.

"Who are you?" his voice rasped.

She straightened her shoulders. "Miss Penelope Thornton, daughter of Sir Charles and Lady Sarah Thornton—" He let out a sharp, low exclamation. "Of Thorndene in Dorsetshire."

"Your father has a title?"

"It's only a knighthood," she explained and knew by the look on his face it was the wrong thing to have said. "I mean, it isn't an old title. Papa got it for having money enough to pay Prinny's debts."

Another exclamation escaped through gritted teeth. "You're an heiress? Is that why you have suitors pestering you? They're fortune hunters?"

"I have no suitors," she said, beginning to be irritated with his irritation. "That was a lie. I spent last year in Vienna. I'm not ashamed of my father."

He lifted a brow. "I never suggested you should be. If I were you, I would tell everyone I met exactly who he was and what service he performs. It might even be the first thing I mentioned after his credentials as an instructor. You must forgive me, Miss Thornton," he said, his fury hardly contained. "I'm merely attempting to discover what parts of you are counterfeit and what parts are true. You lie so well."

Her lips tightened against the trembling. She had never seen Malcolm so angry.

"Are you a governess? Have you ever been one?" he asked, a muscle jumping in his jaw.

"Never before. Though I am qualified."

"Where is the Miss Starling who came with such a glowing recommendation from my cousin? Did you beat her over the head and throw her down a well?"

She gave him a rebuking glare, brows leveling.

"There she is. There's the governess," he said, mocking. "I can see her now. Maybe you swallowed her."

"I took her place."

"Nobody noticed?"

"Nobody. Have you ever seen a game of thimblerig?" she asked, too tired to argue. "A dried pea is secreted under one of three thimbles and then you have to guess which one it is. I merely—"

"While a knave tries to cheat you," he finished, his nostrils flaring. "Aye. So, your parents didn't send you away from a fortune hunter or approve of this Gothic scheme." He stepped close and the air seemed to shimmer with tension. This was the man who had whispered to her *I mean this, Pen*.

"Instead, they're staring at empty thimbles, caught up in a foolish schoolgirl's game."

"It wasn't a game," she countered, furious now. Oh, if he knew, if he only knew all she had lost. "You've read the papers. My parents are in Yorkshire, no doubt hearing the complaints of mill owners, passing them to the government. They think I'm in Sussex with my sister. They won't have missed me."

Malcolm crossed his arms. "If it wasn't a game, why did you do this? I'm waiting to hear."

Her mouth opened to tell him, but the shape and the scope of the words would not fit past her lips. *Magic. Rising. Lightness. Fire.*

What could she tell him when there was nothing that could prove her words? She would sound like a madwoman.

"I am not at liberty to say."

"Not at liberty." Malcolm's eyes shuttered. "Unless you lied about your age too, I've no right to harbor you under my roof without your parents' consent. English heiresses don't wind up on the wrong side of Hadrian's Wall without exciting some notice. I could be accused of abduction. You've put all of us in a dangerous position."

"No, I haven't." How silly did he think she was? "If they take the time to inquire, my parents will know I'm safe. I left a letter with the real Miss Starling in the event they begin wondering where I am and included my intentions and general whereabouts."

His exhale was sharp and disbelieving. "General whereabouts." He turned from the mantelpiece, growling. "Would it be enough for you if Ewan ran off, leaving a note telling you he was well? How would you feel if he was gone for a whole night? A month? Six months? Would it matter if he were eight or eighteen?"

Imagining Ewan somewhere beyond her reach or knowledge clutched at Penny's stomach in a shocking and alien way. Would she be content to wait for communication? No. She would be beside herself. God in heaven, is this what her mother would be feeling?

She shrank from the emotion, from the unbearableness of examining it. "My mother will not worry. She knows I can look after myself."

"You don't understand the smallest part of what a mother feels," Malcolm roared, plowing fingers through his hair. "She won't rest the moment she knows you've gone."

Penny wanted to lift her chin and fight him. Mama would not worry over her. Mama would know how important her magic was. Mama would know.

Penny's chest tightened painfully, and she blinked back tears. "What are you going to do?"

He sighed, looking every day of his age and more. "Two weeks will be enough to settle the gossip in these hills. People will think your time was spent, and we knew all along who you were. In the meantime, I will write to your parents to collect you."

"I'll go on teaching?"

His mouth was rigid, as though it was learning new, harsh forms for the first time and resisted settling into them.

"Do you think I can trust you with my children?"

Chapter Twenty-Seven

What Penny might have answered was lost as Elspeth threw back the door with a hard, gouging clatter. “Mary,” she gasped. “Come quick. She’s having a fit.”

Malcolm moved first, dashing for the stairs and Penny raced after him, leaping steps two at a time to keep up. They found Mary in the hall, hunched against the wall and gasping for air, the wind squeaking in and out of her lungs like opening an ill-fitting drawer. Penny fell to her knees and lifted Mary’s shaking hand.

“Mary?” She ran a palm over the girl’s damp brow, lifted her heavy lids. “What’s wrong?”

Mary’s dull eyes met hers and she shook her head slowly.

Penny tugged the ties of a chemisette from the girl’s throat and Malcolm scooped her up in his arms, head swiveling for a lost moment.

“This way.” Penny pushed through the door of her own room and stepped aside. She lit the small candle and set it back from the bed lest the tense, seizing body overturned it.

Malcolm eased Mary onto the mattress, her tight form spasming in his arms as he released her.

Though the commotion had been muted, it must’ve been enough to draw Isabelle from her room. Her shadowed form stood in the doorway, fist wrapped over her locket, eyes riveted on Mary. “How may I help?”

“Send a footman for Doctor Bell,” Penny ordered.

“May I not see to the children?” Isabelle asked, a note of anxiety in her eyes. “Are the children well?”

Elspeth, brushing past her, muttered, “They have not stirred. I will sit with them.”

“You are too tired, Mrs Stuart,” Isabelle said. “They are my cousins—”

Elspeth snapped, "They are my grandchildren. Get the footman as you were asked."

The voices receded and Penny and Malcolm worked at each other's elbows to settle Mary. The girl thrashed and Malcolm anchored her legs. Was there nothing to do but wait until the doctor might come? It was then the thought arrived, unfurling in her mind like the petals of a sunrise flower, opening at the first touch of morning light.

"Charcoal," Penny whispered, then gripped the thought tighter. "Get me some charcoal."

Despite his distrust, Malcolm responded to her command, rushing away as Penny held the girl down, crooning gentle words into her ear. He returned quickly with a few lumps and they transferred the charcoal and the girl.

Penny grasped her pewter cup, crushing the particles in the bowl with the handle of her brush until the grit had turned to rough powder. Tipping out a small measure of water from the ewer at her bedside, she swirled it with her finger. Instinct pulled her now.

"Sit her up?"

"Aye." Tenderly, he lifted Mary, and Penny tilted the cup to her lips. Mary flailed, bashing the cup away. For one precarious heartbeat, Penny thought she might drop it.

Malcolm anticipated her needs, pinning down Mary's arms, and Penny leapt forward, pinching Mary's nose and draining the contents down the girl's throat. Mary choked and sputtered. Half the charcoal sludge went down Mary's throat and the other splattered across the blue dress.

Penny waited for a heartbeat, long enough to search her mind for anymore inexplicable ideas and sank to her knees. Mary pushed Malcolm roughly back, grappling Penny as close as she could.

For long minutes, Penny held the position, twisted on the floor as Mary sweated and thrashed, and finally lost consciousness. When she could hardly bear the agony of her pose for another second, Penny heard Malcolm move across the room. He unpegged one of her gowns and rolled it into a pillow. Crouching low, their breath mingled as he pushed the wad of fabric under Penny's arm, his hand finding every gap and filling it. He raised his brows, and she nodded her relief. Then he kept looking, his countenance grave.

“How did you know to do all that?” he asked, his whisper as rough as the charcoal grit.

“I don’t know.”

His face hardened, but she wasn’t lying. Mary had been dying, and perhaps, given the steady rise and fall of her chest, now she had a chance, all because Penny had a thought she could not explain.

He stayed with her, sitting on the end of the bed until the doctor came. Penny got to her feet so quickly that she stumbled slightly and stifled a whimper. Malcolm put a steadying grip under her arm but did not look at her as Doctor Bell made his examination, listening to Mary’s chest, feeling her pulse, lifting her eyelids, checking her fingernails.

“Tired but well,” he pronounced, peeling the spectacles from his head. “That trick of using charcoal, Miss Starling. Forgive me. Miss Thornton,” he corrected with wry amusement. “What made you think of it? Have you been reading French medical journals, miss? Did you think she’d been poisoned?”

Penny blinked heavily as a cloud of frustration settled over her. She didn’t understand the knowledge or its origins. Perhaps she had heard it on the Continent?

Doctor Bell waited and then said, “No? I really thought you had. There was a French chemist who took it into his head to swallow charcoal and an arsenic compound. He lived to tell the tale, but no one has been fool enough to try it again. In any event, Mary took no harm from the stuff.”

“What do you think it was that had her?” Malcolm asked, taking more than his share of the room with his bulk.

“Bad fish, a stomach complaint.” Doctor Bell supplied, lifting his hands. “I’ll come again tomorrow, and she may be able to tell us, herself.”

Malcolm saw him out, and when he returned, he said in a formal tone, “Shall I fetch a kitchen maid to sit with her?”

“No. I wouldn’t dream of it. The servants have had a long day, preparing for the party and your guests. They’ve earned their rest. I will sit with Mary if a chair might be found.”

He did not bring her a hard stool but fetched one of the low bergère chairs from the nursery, the fabric worn in parts. He hefted it through the door, placing it at Mary’s side, took a final, encompassing glance around the room, and departed.

Thank heavens she had Mary through her long vigil. Penny returned to minding the steady rise and fall of the girl's chest, the warm hand gripping her own, the words she whispered when restlessness threatened to wake the sick girl. Her own sorrow was too heavy to lift.

At sunrise, Mary's eyes blinked open. "Who's with the children?"

A shadow of a smile passed Penny's lips. "Mrs Stuart spent the night with them."

Mary, deep smudges of sickness darkening her eyes, struggled to find the border of her coverlet.

"Settle down, Mary. You're much too ill to shift."

"But—"

"The children are in good hands." She pressed a hand to Mary's damp brow. "It's you who has us worried. Have you ever been sick like that before?"

A Mary's look of confusion, Penny supplied, "Shaking, vomiting, joints that would not obey. You were gasping for breath and your heart was fit to beat right out of your chest. We called Doctor Bell—"

Mary's eyes goggled. Doctors were beyond her experience, likely. She would have had good cottage nursing from her mother or a woman in the village, and even that would have been scant.

"He could not explain the fit," Penny continued, her eyes investigating the girl's face. "Can you?"

"My nose was drippy," Mary said, closing her eyes again with a heaviness that told Penny sleep was not far off. "So, I took a tonic." Her lips turned up. "The drip is gone."

When Mary turned over, her breath came in the deep even cycle of health-giving sleep, and Penny slipped out of the room. She caught her reflection in a mirror and sighed. Her hair was a crow's nest and the dress, so carefully made, was stained and crushed. The splatters might never come clean, but Mary was well. Penny could push through the nursery door with a smile.

Elspeth was letting chaos reign, looking on benignly as feathers wafted onto the floor. Penny plucked up a pillow and beaned Ewan in the back of the head.

"Your nursemaid is resting," she said when the three faces turned to hers. She pitched her voice lower, "So we'll whisper today."

"Is she very sick?" Robbie asked.

Penny lifted her eyes and met Elspeth's. "She is, but she's doing much better." She regarded the children. "She is much too tired to tidy this room, however."

Ewan tugged his sister's hand, and they began to put the nursery to rights, Kathleen stirring up as many feathers as she collected in her skirts. Robbie was determinedly making his bed, hauling the covers back and forth. Where Ewan went, order and neatness followed in his wake.

Elspeth, making no effort to protect the children from Penny's presence, excused herself to her own room and Penny wandered into the alcove Mary slept in, tidying the bed. She turned and saw an empty bottle on the bureau, the pressed glass catching the light and striking an incongruous chord alongside the other items.

Penny picked the bottle up and sniffed it, recoiling from the scent of… She wrinkled her nose and coughed. What was that smell? Another reluctant sniff identified a fragrance that carried the bitter waft of mouse droppings.

A rap on the nursery door preceded Isabelle swinging through it and Penny slipped the bottle into her pocket.

"I came to see how Mary is faring," Isabelle said, offering Penny a tentative smile. She swung her locket back and forth on her chain. "I was terribly worried about her."

"What do you mean?" Robbie began, a note of worry creeping into his voice. Penny shook her head quickly at Isabelle in a sharp, unspoken command to shut her mouth. So much had happened last night to make Isabelle's mistake a lesser concern, but Penny was prepared to split skulls rather than have her tongue upset anyone further.

"She is looking well this morning," Penny insisted, leading her a little away from the children. "It was only an upset stomach."

A look of surprise crossed Isabelle's face. "You think she snuck something too decadent from the party?"

Penny's eyes narrowed and she held the bottle out for Isabelle's inspection. "No need to blame her common birth," Penny said and watched Isabelle's skin leach of color.

"You can't think my tonic caused it," she declared, eyes wide with shock. "It's harmless."

"It smelled vile," Penny cut in, pitching her harsh question low enough so the children would not hear. "Think, Isabelle. Could some dangerous clipping have been collected alongside the yarrow and tansy?"

Isabelle's brow wrinkled, distress in every line of her face. "I got a message last week about cases of whooping cough up in the hills. I gathered some hemlock for the crofters, for their little ones, but I was careful," she insisted when Penny gripped her arm. "The roots can be used safely if one knows how to handle it. I never even brought it into the house with the other herbs."

Penny flung Isabelle's arm away. "That knife you carry. If you cut the hemlock and then you cut whatever went into your tonic, it wouldn't matter. You didn't clean it properly. You will not be so careless again."

Isabelle's lips tightened, but when she took the bottle, there was a wash of relief on her face. She sniffed the bottle and jerked her head back with a low exclamation. "I'll throw out the lot and start afresh. Lord," she breathed, bracing herself against the window.

Isabelle stared blindly into the garden for a few moments. "Mary will recover?"

"Yes. We were lucky though. If it had been one of the children..." A shiver ran across Penny's shoulders.

"It is a miracle." Isabelle straightened, took a cleansing breath, and nodded. "I'm surprised to find you still here."

Penny scooped up a pillow, punching it before she tossed it to a chair. The children began making Kathy's bed together. "Did you think Mr Ross would throw me out on my ear?"

"Mr Ross?" Isabelle gave a light laugh. Penny was not ready for laughter, her own or Isabelle's, and she frowned. "I thought you were on warmer terms than that. From what I witnessed in the hall—"

"I am to remain for a short time until I am sent packing."

Isabelle touched her arm softly. "I am sorry, Penny. It's impressive what you've managed in so little time. Elspeth never used to abide the English, she hasn't been more than civil to me in all the years I've lived at Foxglove Cottage, and Malcolm can't abide deception, not after that last governess. Did you use magic to win them somehow?" Her nostrils flared as she sniffed. "It's covering this room, practically painting the floor."

"No," Penny said, rolling her neck and working away the stiffness. Magic had not won these people over. Love had. There were limits to even that, evidently. "What magic I have, remains as much a mystery as ever."

Chapter Twenty-Eight

She was halfway through her morning instruction when Malcolm entered the schoolroom and asked to see Elspeth in the hall. Penny overheard them. Of course, she did. The walls were thin.

"We haven't decided yet if Miss...Thornton is fit to teach the children," he murmured. "We came to no decision."

Penny set Ewan to reading a book aloud to his siblings and drifted nearer the door. Were Elspeth and Malcolm standing on the same little square of sacred ground where he had kissed her and she had kissed him back? Had it only been last night?

"Fit," Elspeth spat. "Fit. What do ye mean, lad? Fit."

His voice deepened into a growl. "I mean that the children know her as Miss Starling and now she declares she is Miss Thornton. Even her name we must take on faith. We cannot afford to take chances with the children, Elspeth."

Elspeth, bless her, sputtered. "I've taken nothing on faith, Malcolm. I've spent nearly every hour with that lass since she came all those months ago. Long enough to see the children give her hell. Long enough to give her hell of my own. Long enough to know she tries and tries no matter how many times we knock her down. She would no more hurt the children then she would parade through the village in a state of nature."

"We don't know why she came. She will not speak of it. Is that trustworthy? Is that honest?"

The silence was so long, so heavy, Penny began to wish she could see through walls. There would be a handy magic to possess. Far better than these ungovernable nudges, which sprung up without reason.

Then Elspeth said, "Why don't you admit, Malcolm Ross, you're the only one of us hurt. She's wounded your pride, no doubt, but you know as well as I do, she isn't any threat to the children."

"I'm sending her away," he said.

“Fool,” Elspeth breathed.

Fool or not, Penny was allowed to keep on teaching the children without anyone telling her otherwise. Perhaps it was because there was no one else to watch the children while Mary recovered. Penny was granted the right to shift her things to Mary’s alcove, leaving her private room to the convalescing girl. She grew accustomed to listening to the nursery fire and Robbie’s whispered stories before drifting off herself.

Fritz no longer settled in the crook of Penny’s legs, giving companionship and comfort to his mistress. He had abandoned her to curl up on the end of Ewan’s bed. Some instinct told her not to remark upon it. Robbie tolerated Fritz as part of the nursery, but he shifted his bed away from his brother and put Kathy in between, sitting on top of his headboard each morning until Fritz was handed off to a maid.

Kathy had taken to burrowing into Penny’s arms when she woke each morning, the wispy curls tickling Penny’s neck and the elbows and juts of her bones sinking into Penny’s softness. Time seemed to take on a greater significance as each day dropped away in its turn.

“Time to wake,” she called one morning, pinning the front of her dress closed. She tilted her head around the corner of her alcove and prodded the children to make their beds. Rob fumbled with the coverlet, and she resisted the impulse to help him. Why had her magic prodded her to teach him this? It hadn’t brought him any closer to spelling things properly.

“What are we doing today?” Ewan asked, his voice muffled as put his bedding in order.

Penny slid a glance out the window. The sun was out, and the clouds were banked over the hills. One more sunrise. One more day gone. Her throat tightened. “It’s much too nice for slates and numbers. What do you say about a picnic?”

A chorus greeted her, and even silent Ewan allowed a smile to rest briefly on his lips.

“A learning picnic,” she amended. Robbie flopped dramatically on his back and she nudged him aside. “I’ll talk to Birdie and we can be out in the sunshine as long as it lasts.”

When the children finished their morning ablutions, they joined her outside the kitchen door like hopeful tradesmen, giggling as

Birdie greeted them as she would a travelling tinker, asking to see their wares.

"What are 'wares'?" Kathy tugged on Penny's hand and whispered into her ear.

"Special things to sell, pet." Kathy nodded, leaving her hand tucked in the warmth of Penny's grip. Penny smoothed the dark, crooked braids on Kathy's head with a rueful smile. They were nowhere nearly as neat as Mary's efforts.

Her gaze travelled up the line of children. She would never be mistaken for their mother. The coloring was all wrong. The eyes. Yet, her hands performed the same offices for them her mother's had once performed for her.

A fortnight was all she had been promised. Again, the thought of how little time remained produced a physical reaction, tightening her throat and causing an ache in her stomach. She had once been anxious to leave this place, certain when she kicked its dust from her boots she would never look back.

Birdie handed the basket off to the boys who carried it between them, leading her away from the house. They skirted fields of bright green barley and made towards the twisted oak, which grew so near the cliffside.

The silhouette of the tree was picked out against a sky full of clouds and she caught her breath. Instead of the blackened, writhing trunk she expected, there was a branch half obscured by vibrant leaves, shivering in the breeze.

"Here?" she asked, hesitantly. "It's so near the edge."

"We've come here loads of times with Mary and Papa," Ewan said. "Kathy knows not to go beyond the tree."

Penny frowned up at the branches as she shook out a blanket. Her gaze returning to the strange sight again and again. When she had climbed those barren branches, she'd had such hope her magic would be restored.

The thick layer of leaves frisked in the breeze. If a tree could return to what it had been, perhaps she could too. She waited for the first stirrings to fill her breast, waiting as sunlight filtering through the leaves. Instead, a sharp, bitter thought came.

The magic doesn't matter.

She caught her lip, biting into the soft flesh as she fought off the realization. It mattered. *It mattered.* Her magic was the only thing that would make any of this worth it: the lies and losing Malcolm.

Nothing could compare to the freedom of lifting into the cold night sky, her frame weightless, the soft tingle of magic sparking through her veins.

Nothing.

A childish laugh jerked her from her thoughts, and she called the children to her, spreading open a book of local flora she had taken from the library. The sun warmed her neck and heat collected against her stays.

"Now then," she said, setting aside the book, "your task is to find wildflowers and leaves. Bring them back and then we can look up the properties. Mind you stay well back from the drop and don't wander too far."

She looked after them as they pelted across the lush ground, counting their heads. One, two, three, one, two, three—like the rhythmic beat of a waltz. They dove into the woods, their voices carrying back to her, and emerged as a group. In their wake came Isabelle, making her way up the rise, a wicker basket hanging from her arm, filled with the usual roots and stalks. Tansy and heather.

Isabelle dropped her basket and settled next to Penny on the blanket, spreading her skirts next to Penny's workaday brown. She snapped open a parasol, shading her eyes from the sun, peeking from behind the clouds.

"I felt it," Isabelle said, her hand shaking, voice full of wonder, "coming through the woods. It's stronger now than it used to be, or more rooted within him. He wasn't so near the others."

"Him? He? What do you mean?" Penny rubbed her arms.

"It's not the little girl who has magic." Isabelle was trembling with excitement. "That much I can be certain of now. It's one of the boys." She gave a short, incredulous laugh. "Ewan probably."

Why Ewan?

Isabelle clasped Penny's hand and have it a short shake. "Why aren't you more excited? We can send you home with your magic. With your help, I can reap it—"

The magic doesn't matter. Penny had no time for more complicated feelings to surface before there came a high-pitched squeal. She shot to her feet, shading her eyes and scanning the field.

One, two, three. "Kathleen," she muttered, her tone long-suffering. "Trust her to find the mud."

Isabelle bubbled over with laughter. "Better you than me."

Penny strode past Rob and waded into the tall grass, stopping when the ground became dark and squishy. None of the words bouncing on her tongue gained release. *Did you have to Kathleen? You'll be the death of me. Why can you never be easy?* Instead, she unlaced her boots and tore off her stockings, stuffing them into the pocket tied under her gown.

"I'm coming, Kathy," she soothed the child who flapped her hands, specks of mud flinging every which way. Fat tears rolled down her cheeks. "I'll have you out in a trice."

Penny draped her skirts over an arm, rather liking the sensation of viscous muck oozing between her toes. She laughed, careful not to fall on her backside as she pulled Kathleen up, her feet making a sucking noise as they broke free. This would make a funny memory, she thought, and then Ewan bellowed.

It was not a playful shout but frantic, drenched in terror. He screamed Robbie's name over and over and over. Penny didn't stop for her shoes but commanded Kathleen to hold on as she ran, her eyes trained on Ewan's thin figure pacing against the sky. Too near the cliff. God. The little girl lifted her muddy feet and hooked them around Penny's middle and Penny tore across the field, her legs pumping faster than her heart.

"Where is he?" Penny shouted, long before she stopped.

"He's going to die," Isabelle shrieked, leaning over the cliff, her parasol abandoned. "He's going to slip."

Penny dumped Kathy on the blanket. "Stay," she warned, her eyes shifting to Ewan, flat on the ground and drawing his thin leg over the edge.

"Don't you dare, Ewan Ross," she roared. He froze, staring at her with wide, red-rimmed eyes. "I'll murder you myself if you move an inch."

"I can reach him," he cried but she wasn't listening. She had moved way beyond uttering sharp foreign curses and could only pray as she neared the edge.

God help him. God help him. Be alive. Anything, God. I'll give anything.

She was on her knees when she rocked forward, looking over the lip of the cliff, knowing how far down it was, raging at herself for coming at all. God forgive her because Malcolm wouldn't. She thought the children knew to stay away from the cliff. She thought this was safe.

She choked off a cry when she saw him, slithered fifteen feet down and perched on the narrowest ledge, the toes of his tiny boots caught on a rim of rock, a couple inches deep. No more. His short pants had not protected his trembling knees, which were smeared with dirt and blood. Grit bounced from under the soles of his shoes, all the way to the valley floor.

"Are you mad, miss?" His white face was pressed against the rock, but he turned his frightened eyes up to her. His dark hair was caught by a feathering of wind and he screwed his eyes shut until it passed. Only the smallest slip and he would tumble another thirty feet. Oh, Lord. Terror clawed at her throat and she wanted to cry out for Malcolm, Elspeth, her mother, anyone who could fix this for her.

"Not mad, Rob." Her voice shook and she swallowed, willing it to stop.

Isabelle leaned over the edge, near hysterics, her necklace dangling over the precipice. "How could you, Robert Ross? I warned to away from the cliff. Told you you'd break your neck."

Rob chin crumpled and Penny whirled on Isabelle, shoving her onto her backside. "Shut up," Penny roared. Isabelle's eyes were wide with shock. "Can't you see that you're making it worse?"

Penny's gaze focused on Kathy, covered in mud and Ewan who wept, his head turned shamefacedly away. "Ewan, you have to take Kathy home. I'll keep Rob safe."

"Papa told me to watch after him."

She glanced at Isabelle. Useless. The woman was weeping into her hands. "Take Kathy. Tell your Papa to bring a stout rope when he comes. Some footmen, too. Hurry."

He spun away, the noise of Kathy's tears going with them.

Penny sat on her heels and suddenly Rob howled her name.

"I'm here," she said, scrambling forward again. "I'm here. I have to get into my climbing costume, Rob."

Shrugging the gown from her shoulders, Penny kicked it off. Then, scooping the fullness of her petticoat between her legs, she tucked the end in the ribbon of her pocket. Isabelle was quiet now, holding a fist to her chest, murmuring prayers quietly under her breath. Penny would need them.

She looked over the edge and wanted to squeeze her own eyes shut, to blot out the fear and terror this view held. She took a breath and began to map a perilous course to Robbie. The mere thought of taking it set her hands and feet tingling, her chest tightening painfully. It was so far down. Fifty feet from top to bottom, and then more, sweeping away at the base in a rocky slope, which dropped into the river. Terror and anguish skittered through her bones. If she had her magic, fifty feet would be nothing.

It wasn't nothing now.

"I'm coming," she called, turning around, and levering her legs over, feeling the horror when nothing met her probing toes. The hard, rocky lip bit into her stomach as she eased herself down, inch by terrifying inch.

Any farther and she would not be able to pull herself back up again. She kept moving until, finally, a seam of rock caught under her bare foot. Her stomach slithered into place. "Hold tight for me," she said, sounding like she was taking Rob through his sums instead of hanging from a cliff. It was well only God could see her face.

A gust of wind tugged at her hair and she gripped the rock, digging into the earth with scraped fingers. A shadow passed overhead, and she looked up to see while she had been focused on Rob, thick clouds had multiplied over the sky. Penny risked a look down. Nearer Rob, the handholds were fewer, the ledges narrower. She closed her eyes and released a long, shaky breath.

"How did you get there, Rob?" she asked, when she could trust her voice again. Talk would distract him—distract them both—as she lifted her foot into uncharted territory. Her palms were slick with sweat and she cursed her lost magic. She had never needed it as she did now. She'd never been so desperate for its familiar power.

If sheer wanting would return some portion, she would be rising now, cleaving through the air like an arrow, catching hold of Rob and carrying him up, up, and over the lip.

Safe, safe, safe.

Wishing she had her power would only waste time. She had only the power to make her way to him one agonizing inch at a time.

“I was reaching for a flower. It only grows on cliffs, is what she said. It was going to be the best one, wouldn’t it?” he gasped, and she filled the silence before it flooded with his fear.

“Yes, yes, of course. The best.”

“Ewan didn’t help me at all. I did it myself.”

“Very brave, but cliffs are dangerous, Rob,” she said, feeling the ball of her foot slip from underneath her. She scrambled wildly for a moment, heard rocks skittering down to the valley below and a sob shook from her lungs, dying in her throat. Once stable, she looked down. Robbie’s trembling form was plastered to the rock. This time she noticed he was clasping a scrubby yellow flower in his fist. A common weed.

“I was allowed,” was all he said.

Almost there now. She was parallel to him and she sent up another silent prayer as she swung out around him, blindly grasping for a root, a rock, anything. Luck was with her. Or Brigid. Or God. Or all of them because she fisted a snarl of roots, trapping Robbie in her embrace.

Safe. She wedged her knees in a line under his arms, silent tears falling on his hair. Safe. He was safe.

Chapter Twenty-Nine

The heavens opened with a low rumble of thunder and an icy rain tore across Penny's face. She hunched her body protectively over Robbie while rivulets of rainwater wove down her back, turning her stays into a prison. Bits of cliffside softened and sloughed away under her hand.

"Where's *Aither*?" Robbie whimpered. Penny redoubled her hold on the roots, her fingers numb with the strain, even as her shoulders burned.

Time passed unevenly, but still she tried to measure it out. A quarter of an hour for Ewan to return to the house, time to find his father, more time to rally the footmen and find what he needed. Another length of time to return. Could she do this for an hour?

A spasm of pain shot through her twisted hand. "Ride a cock-horse to Banbury Cross, to see what Robbie can buy…" she sang, for the fifth or sixth time, her voice thready.

Rob could no longer be distracted by nursery rhymes. "Is he here yet?"

"Not yet, love. Soon." Isabelle had begun wailing at the top of the cliff and God help them if she did not stop.

When Malcolm finally came, his voice was softer than she expected. No sudden shout, merely, "Penny".

She looked up, rain pelting her skin, his stern face blurring and resolving as she blinked the drops away. The clamor of Isabelle's weeping had stopped somehow, replaced with a calmness radiating from Malcolm's solid presence.

All would be well.

She wasn't alone anymore.

She dragged air into her lungs. "He's all right, Malcolm. I've got him." Her face broke, half-twisting in pain or relief. "I won't let him go."

His certainty sunk into her bones. "I know. I know. Steady on."

A servant handed Malcolm the end of a rope and when he disappeared for a moment she wanted to cry out. *Come back. Come back.*

Only when he reappeared did her breathing ease, catching again as he stepped over the ledge. He moved deliberately, bracing his feet against the rim of the cliff, calling for slack.

Down he came, the storm soaking him to the skin. She watched him as though her gaze bore his weight, carrying him to the next foothold as he descended, tracking the strong hands gripping the rope, the soundness of knot holding him secure, the slip and catch of each step.

Then he was at her side, his shoulder almost brushing her own. His voice was steady, but his glance did its own inspection, brushing over her face, down her bare arm, the legs holding Robbie against the cliffside, to her hands; gauging the strength of her grip.

"I have to slide an arm between you and Rob, under his shoulders. I'll get my knee up under him before he turns to hold my neck. Understand?" he asked, his voice hardly above a whisper.

"Yes," she answered, choking with relief. Of course. Get him to safety. Let him have decades more to lie to Mary about washing his teeth and lie to governesses and tutors about doing his sums. Leave me on this cliffside forever. Only let him be safe.

She felt his hand slide past her belly, easing Rob from the protection of her body. She felt the breathless agony of it until he was securely delivered into Malcolm's arms. Malcolm, his blue eyes grave, gave her a final look. Then, he wrapped a forearm about a length of the rope and whistled sharply. Creaking and groaning, the ropes seemed to twist through every sinew in her body as men hoisted them to safety.

They skidded over the lip of the precipice and she cried out with thanksgiving and relief and fear in one breath. Malcolm reappeared, making his way down the cliff once more.

"Your turn now, Pen," he breathed.

She looked at him, certain he would see the fear in her eyes. It was only a little distance, but her fist would not unclench from the roots, her mind magnifying the drop beneath her until she could only imagine her broken body.

"I won't let you go," he promised. He slipped a hand around her waist, holding her so tightly the roots became a hindrance, and he became the refuge, the anchor. She clung to his shoulders and wondered if he could feel her shaking.

A sudden jerk pulled them higher, and soon they snaked over the edge like fish landing on the bottom of a boat. She rolled free of him, breathing in the smell of the grass, thanking God for gravity and dirt, and flatness.

Malcolm gave a shout, ordering the footmen back to the house, and she took another few, bone-shaking breaths before tearing the end of her petticoat from her waist, untucking the sodden fabric, and flinging it over her bare legs. She felt the prickle of turf under her palm and the remorseless rain on her arms.

Never in her life had she felt so depleted, struggling even to rise to her knees. There was a coltish clumsiness to it, but when the position was achieved, she cast a glance around the meadow. Her dress was gone. The basket of food. The book of native plants. The blanket she had shaken out. Isabelle and her parasol. It was as though they had not been here at all.

Malcolm's coat settled over her shoulders with a heavy drape, and she clutched the lapels. "Where's Rob?"

"A footman took him back. I sent Isabelle off to her cottage." Malcolm fell to his knees at her side, hands fisted on the ground.

She heard the gentle drumming of cold rain beating the earth and heard him take a hard breath. Then he pulled her into his embrace, lifting her flush against himself and burying his face in her neck, a feral howl ripping from his throat.

Though hesitant, Penny slid her hand up his neck and pushed her fingers through his hair, conscious of his arms wrapped fiercely around her, the shaking rise and fall of his chest. He had been calm, stoic even, when he had coaxed Rob from her arms.

Inexplicably, she remembered the farmer stumbling from the blazing barn, grief and loss in every line, his wife covering him with her soft woolen shawl. It was a plain image. There was nothing of hot passion or cool manners about it.

She could do this much for Malcolm.

Penny closed her eyes, fitting herself against his heart.

In the end, when he had blunted the bright edge of emotion, he took in a deep, shuddering breath and lifted his head beyond the reach of her touch. Her fingers slid free of him.

Would that be the last time she held him in such a way?

"You'll catch a chill," he said, adjusting the coat to sit more securely on her shoulders. His hand lingered on the roll of the collar, tracing the line of her chin, fingers lifting briefly to touch her sodden curls. "Let's get you home."

She staggered to her feet and he saw her bare toes, the indecent length of petticoat clinging to her legs.

"You climbed down without shoes," he said, almost stupidly.

"I had to fish Kathy out of the mud first," she began, but he lifted her into his arms and began walking, turning up the collar to give her more protection from the elements.

He walked through the informal knot of servants gathered in the great hall, up the grand staircase, up the less-grand staircase and down the nursery hall, never releasing her until she stood at her own door. Her toes slipped to the floor and puddle of rainwater began to pool at her feet.

His expression was intent, but there were no easy words on their lips. What was the proper protocol for thanking someone for saving one's life? Or for receiving thanks for saving another?

It might be declaring their debts to one another had been discharged equally.

It might be decorous words, followed by a bow and a sodden curtsey.

It might be flinging herself back into his arms and kissing him as she feared she would never be allowed to do again.

She stood, looking at him with her tongue frozen in her mouth, and felt her balance shift slightly.

Her door swung back, and her heels dropped firmly onto the floor.

"I've got you a steaming bath," Birdie announced, beaming. The housekeeper looked over Penny from head to bare toes. "We have to peel you out of those clothes."

Malcolm must've made some noise because Birdie's face suddenly squared off. "Hurry along, Master Malcolm. Here is no place for you."

A ghost of a smile drifted over Malcolm's mouth as he took himself off.

Penny was treated to such luxuries as a long soak and tray for dinner, after which, Birdie tucked her up in bed. "Mary declared herself well enough to manage the children, Miss...Ah," Birdie said, murmuring with great diplomacy over the irregularities of Penny's identity. "You're to have a good lie-in."

To her surprise, Penny slept deeply, only waking to find Malcolm leaning on the door jam, watching her as though their days together had no number. He blinked and the look was gone. Two weeks was all she had been given and those were half over.

"Where's Robbie?" she asked, pushing her hair back from her face and sitting up.

He came forward quickly and wedged a pillow behind her back, her hands briefly tangling in his. She froze.

"He's still abed. Your nose is red," he said, placing his callused hand to her brow. His eyebrows knitted. "And you've a fever."

Penny flipped the flat of her fingers against her cheeks. "A tiny one."

She was breaking her heart over him, and he was simply checking for symptoms.

"Why are you frowning?" he asked, running a knuckle along the volume of Ramsay poems she kept returning and nicking back from the library.

Her color rose and she rubbed at her cheek. "You're unforgivably tall."

His lips curved in a half smile, the first she had seen since he'd banished her. "You're tall too, Miss Thornton."

Miss Thornton. The name was like crossing some invisible threshold.

"Mr Ross?" Penny took no liberties and felt him tense. "You have my deepest apologies. I had no notion—"

His smile was gone. "I've had the story from Isabelle. She arrived early this morning to explain how it all came about. You must know no blame could possibly attach to you. Indeed, Isabelle told me how you sprang into action, calming Rob long enough to get to him."

Isabelle. Penny plucked at her bedclothes, bubbling with guilt. It hadn't been Isabelle's fault she had been beside herself when Robbie slipped from the cliff, and what had Penny done? Shouted abuse and shoved her into the dirt like they were schoolchildren. What had Isabelle done to repay her? Traversed the boggy path first thing in the morning to assure Malcolm Penny had been a heroine.

Malcolm continued. "Elspeth and I thank you for your sacrifice."

What else did she want? Penny stared down at her hands, fisted around her coverlet and when she made no answer he moved to the door.

"Mal—"

He checked the set of his shoulders an unbending line.

"Mr Ross," she corrected. Only then did he turn, his face a mask. She reached for her hairpins and began to wind her hair. "Will you be good enough to send your cousin to me?"

"Aye." His closed fist tapped the door jamb several times and he went.

Isabelle entered a short time later, the sharp tang of some perfume filling the small space. Her eyes darted around the room. "Oh, I thought nothing could be worse than my pitiful hovel."

"It's not been so bad," Penny countered. She had been happy here, at least.

Isabelle perched on the chair. "You got nothing more than a soaking? I expected worse. I expected everyone to be all to pieces. I worried that Malcolm was going to murder you."

"That's why you spoke to him on my behalf."

A brisk nod. "I had to. I know how Malcolm could have seen it. A governess endangering the life of his child again, almost killing him." Bile started to gather under Penny's jaw, but Isabelle continued. "You did the impossible, climbing down that cliff. I have never seen anything so brave. I was impressed."

"You should be furious. I treated you abominably."

"I cannot blame you for that. I was insensible."

"Well, in any case, I wanted to thank you," Penny added. "It was good of you to smooth things over with Mr Ross."

Isabelle laid a cool hand over Penny's. "I wish you would allow me to help you in a more substantive way. I know what you must have felt down there to be so frightened, vulnerable. It's hard enough to be a woman in this world. Far more difficult to be one without magic. Your powers are near at hand, and there is time to get them back."

What could Isabelle do now? "I have only another week, maybe a little more, before I leave for England. Mr Ross has not been able to accept me as Miss Thornton."

"Did you expect otherwise? No man likes to feel a woman has bested him." Her eyes dulled, but she shook her head suddenly, "If you help me, a week is all you need."

The fever warmed Penny's eyes, weighting the lids, but she strove to sit up straight, think clearly.

Isabelle reached into her reticule. "I've been carrying this around in case you needed it," she said, pulling her locket, swinging on a rolled gold chain. She placed it into Penny's open palm, coiling the chain and dropping it.

"This only senses magic."

"Not only that. I've been hard at work bending the gold to my will."

Penny's eyes widened. "What did that involve?"

"Persistence. Need. A few potions. It will capture loose, unrooted fragments of magic if you are close enough to the source. If you wear it always and say the ancient words, I believe you will have collected enough to stitch together your own power."

"Words?" Penny's nose wrinkled, recalling words for foot rot and virulent rashes. The grimoires were full of words. "A spell? Are spells real?"

"Says the girl whose powers would shock the ton." Isabelle's eyes twinkled in a wicked smile. "When you harvest magic, you must say *áuferant eam*."

"Latin." Penny laughed. It would have to be Latin. The foreign tongue would insulate her from its bald, English meaning. *Take it.* "This will allow me to rise again?"

Isabelle released an amused, exasperated sigh. "Your precious rising."

Penny dropped her eyes to her coverlet. "Robbie could have died yesterday. Slipped into the gully and been broken. Without my power I have nothing." No. She shook her head, the sting of tears in her nose. That wasn't right. The story she'd told herself again and again since coming to Scotland didn't feel true any longer. "Without my power I felt helpless," she amended, tracing the delicate scrolling metalwork on the face of the locket. "Only, I must know it's not stealing."

Isabelle's expression was serene, certain. "If magic is not rooted, it doesn't belong to anyone."

Penny's questions were smaller than the memory of Robbie's thin hands gripping the rock, the abyss stretching below.

"I'll wear it," she said, slipping the chain around her neck.

She did not say anything for a long time, but searched along the familiar veins of her magic, willing them to fill again, holding her breath. She only felt tired and hot. She felt dry lips and heavy eyelids. She fumbled for her handkerchief and sneezed.

Isabelle stood. "Do tell me if you sense a change. I have confidence in this magic, but it is experimental. I worry the authors of all those magical texts were leaning over kitchen fires and inhaling far too much smoke."

When she left, Penny slept the morning away and woke, feeling worse than ever. Mary touched her forehead.

"Where's Robbie," Penny asked, yawning into her hand. The girl looked away and Penny flipped back her blanket, conscious when she had asked before, she had been palmed off. She stood, leaning heavily against the wall as a sudden dizzy spell hit behind the eyes.

"He's resting," Mary whispered.

"Where is he," Penny repeated, not bothering with her slippers. Her feet were like ice, but she feared she might collapse if she spent the energy to put them on.

Mary slipped an arm around Penny's waist. "Can you manage the stairs?"

Penny gave her best affronted look, which was difficult to maintain as her head wobbled heavily atop her neck. When they came to the head of the stairs, Penny glared down at them. It was too much. Her muscles would not hold her steady.

"I'll scoot," she declared. She sat hard on the top step and took an eon traversing the distance, jarring her backside as she went.

"Why is he so far?"

"The master wanted him nearby. They put him in the old mistress's room, away from the other children."

One of the children had escaped the nursery. When they came to the family wing, she found Ewan sitting on the carpet facing his brother's door, eyes hard and red all the way around, knees pulled up under his chin. Fritz, standing sentinel at his side, watched her pass without the least interest.

Mary released her and Penny pushed open the door, leaning hard on the handle. Rob was in the center of the wide bed, lying much too still. Stumbling to the edge, she leaned over him, combing hair away from his brow. "Rob," she said. Every second she seemed to feel weaker and weaker.

"You shouldn't be here." Her head came around, brain bouncing roughly against her skull. Malcolm stood at the threshold of the door, open between his own room and this.

A hot tear rolled down her cheek. "No one would tell me about Rob. You didn't," she accused.

He came around the bed, supporting her gently into a chair. There was nothing loverlike in his embrace but, even if she held onto him forever, he would not fail her. He would not fail Rob.

"He's so warm," she said and could detect a wailing come from the pit of her, pressing against her heart and eyes, searching for release.

"He's taken a chill."

"What's been done?" she asked, wading through her own exhaustion as though she were wading through an ocean tide, her skirts dragging her back. "Has the doctor been? What medicine has he brought? Malcolm, has he been?" As her voice became more frantic his hand began to stroke her back in long easy passes. Settling her.

"Doctor Bell left powders and will call again tonight. He's confident the fever will pass."

She slipped from him, and climbed onto the great bed, kneeling next to Robbie and taking his hand. There was heat deep under his skin, a grey-pink pallor to his cheeks, and dark smudges below his long lashes.

She pressed a fist hard against her chest, holding herself together. Her heart had been stolen away piece by piece until it was not her own anymore. Malcolm had stolen it, Kathy, too. Ewan, despite wanting nothing of her, had it as well. Robbie carried it and if he failed—

She swallowed, tucking her bare feet under her nightdress.

"Don't send me away," she said, pleading.

A muscle in Malcolm's jaw clenched. "I've already written to your parents."

Shock and embarrassment swam through her veins in tandem. He'd thought she was begging to stay with him, and he was rejecting her once again. "No." She shook her head in a firm, face-saving gesture. "I mean, don't send me back to my room. I can stay and nurse him."

"There is no need for that. *Coille na Cyarlin* owes you much for saving the life of our boy. We would not claim any more of you." Each word seemed to hold her at arm's length. He'd give nothing of himself for her to hold on to.

"If I hadn't taken them—"

"You must stop blaming yourself, Pen," he rasped.

Her name slipped from his lips and she caught it, holding it in her grip like Rob and his common weed, clinging to the edge of a cliff. Malcolm froze at her look and seemed to grapple with the stupidity of saying it again, this time in the proper way, as though their breath had not mingled and their touch had not explored beyond the threshold of lovers.

His head dipped. "You're in no condition."

"I can't get him sicker than he is. Let me stay. Please."

"It's difficult to say no to you when you ask something of me." He wasn't teasing her with a light smile. Rather, he looked like a man navigating an impenetrable maze. Then his fingers brushed her hairline. She closed her eyes and caught this treasure, too. "You need your rest."

"Let me rest here."

He dropped his hand and held her gaze.

At last, he nodded.

Chapter Thirty

Penny wasn't getting better. Though she wished to attend Rob, each day her eyes ached no matter how little light filtered through the heavy drapes, each night she sank so far into sleep that she wondered when she would touch the silty bottom of her illness and swim up again. Three days of this.

On the third night, she stirred on her simple pallet. Malcom had insisted she have a bed of her own but left her in the room with Rob. Had she ever been so sick? The memory of the fire and its aftermath burned through her mind, her mother's crooning voice and constant presence.

Yes, once she had been this sick. She'd found her way out then by the slimmest thread, and there were two to find their way now—her and Rob. No matter how she searched, there was nothing to guide her.

The sound of treads on the carpet tugged her into wakefulness. Malcolm, standing in a dark shadow by the bed. His head bent and she heard the tearing sound of grief break from his throat.

Penny closed her eyes tight and cried the long while with him, keeping secret vigil. At length, she heard his careful steps. His figure stopped by her cot. His fingers brushed her hair, lingered on the rim of her ear, and moved away.

Were they dying? Was that the truth behind the heartiness and bright smiles furnishing the sickroom? She worried over the thought when the house had fallen into silence once more. She worried about it like a recusant with her rosary, hands returning again and again for solace, and answers.

When no answers came, she kicked off damp covers and faltered towards the bed, expending the last of her energies to pull herself onto the coverlet.

Rob's breath was harsh, loud in the quiet night, and she sounded almost as bad. The locket thumped heavily against her heart and she gripped the almond shape in her fist. If Rob was magic, she could take it now. Pull it from his body and add it to her own. She had the locket. She had the words. If she had her magic, she thought, her mind groggy with fever. If she had her magic, then she could…

Her fingers brushed the papery skin of Rob's cheek. Rising wouldn't help this. Rising wouldn't restore him in these last hours. Yet, that is what consumed her. A sudden self-revulsion shook her frame, muscles tightening painfully.

How many lies had she told to find herself precisely where she was now? Not only lies about who she was and what she had been trained to do, but lies to herself, as well.

How many soft, placating justifications had she entertained—that she was only taking back what was her own, hurting no one—when the whole of it had been a scheme to get what she wanted. Even now, she had been tempted to collect Robbie's magic. Take.

Rob would need every gift he could lay claim to. Penny's breath came like a knife and with a small cry she twisted up her hand and ripped the locket free, flinging it away. It hit the ground with a sharp whack and ricocheted from the wall. The moonlight caught it as it skittered into the center of the floor, spinning, spinning.

When it halted, Penny gave a short, breaking sigh. The future made no promises, Elspeth had said. Penny was so weak, and Rob's breathing so strained, death seemed to hover like a shade in the corner. Fretting over her magic had no place here.

Slipping her hand into Rob's, she laid her head on a pillow and slept.

Morning brought light and light brought pain. Penny was still alive and Rob—she heard a reassuring snore. She heard, too, the sound of Malcolm's footsteps entering the room. Then there was a sudden crunch and muttered exclamation.

He stooped, picking the locket up by the broken hinge, the little window hanging drunkenly open, an apology in his eyes when he looked at her.

She should say something, excuse him, tell him it was nothing.

Her eyes widened as the thousands and hundreds of thousands of tiny threads binding her to the ground sang with magic. Oh Lord, she was going to rise. She could feel it.

Penny couldn't fight this; she could not hold herself down even if she wanted to. Malcolm would see it. Robbie might, too. She didn't care. She swung her feet over the side of the bed and sat up. Here it came. Closing her eyes, she prepared to watch the miracle within.

She gathered magic—that's how it always began. A line formed between her brow as she tried to interpret what was happening. Her magic shivered and sang in a language she had never heard before, rushing through the filaments like the wind from Slinch Bickey, through the barley fields, stirring the bearded tops like a flight of birds. This was not gathering. Her magic was misbehaving, spreading, sending out roots and feelers.

Distantly she heard her name on Malcolm's lips, and his hands banded her arms, anxiety on his face. Magic rushed through her like a vine racing over a trellis, reaching curling shoots to catch the first rays of the sun. His touch against her cheek was soft and she leaned into it, savoring the contact.

Then his hand shifted to her forehead, the back of her neck, and, with a shaking laugh of relief he leaned his head against hers. Her mind whirled and whirled with confusion. The magic had failed her, after all. She hadn't risen, not a fraction. But this feeling. She rubbed her fingertips together, no longer burning with fever.

Penny stood, bringing him up too, right against her. She gave a breathy laugh and fought the urge to wrap her arms around his chest, holding him as tightly as she could. When he gripped her elbows, balancing her, magic roared in her ears. It was like flying on a winter's night, sharp and bracing, every nerve alive.

"Do you have a mirror?"

He inclined his head to the doorway, and she brushed past him, conscious his hand had slipped from her, down her arm, fingers clinging as she left him.

There was a simple shaving mirror on his bureau, and she turned her head this way and that, pulling at her eyelids, sticking out her tongue. She looked as though she had rested at the mineral baths near Vienna rather than spent three nights tossing on a small cot, illness gripping her body.

She skimmed fingers across her cheekbones, stirring the invisible filaments. They had been there all along, but she'd understood them to be fetters, restraints that must be broken.

Malcolm stood in the doorway, watching her. "What is it?"

She swallowed, hardly able to make an answer while she stood in her loose night rail, her hair a tangle down her back. "I'm well. Can you see?"

She held onto the bureau and closed her eyes, harvesting the lightness, reaching for it. There. There it was. Gathering like a bead of water, thickening, pooling in her midsection.

Rise, she commanded.

No response.

Thistledown, bickey clouds...Rise.

Nothing.

Each time she reached for her magic, centering it around her will, she felt its playful tendrils curling outward, felt the sensation of roots growing from her heels and sending searching fibers delving into the ground.

With a laugh she lifted her feet and inspected the high arches. What was this magic? What did it do? She itched to find out, vistas of exploration opening wide before her. It was enormous, this chance for discovery.

"What are you doing?" Malcolm asked. He moved forward and his hand curled around her own, the pad of his thumb over her wrist.

She closed her eyes. "I'm trying to think."

Penny felt his amused grunt as she turned her mind to her most inward parts and started, as Adam had in Eden, to put names to things she didn't know, transforming the foreign into the familiar.

She had felt these sensations already. Not the sudden, undeniable rush of magic, but as the same kind of frisson shivering lightly through her veins.

When?

She felt for clues, shining stones on a moon-brightened path. She'd felt it in the schoolroom. There was that day with Ewan when she knew, without knowing how she knew, she must reach for the illustrated book of animals.

She felt it again when she dreamed of having Rob begin to dress himself. Then too, there was the moment when she'd ordered Malcolm to fetch charcoal for Mary. The feeling had driven through her mind, telling her the way to healing.

Oh, and every time Malcolm touched her. Every time.

Penny searched the common thread that wove these things together. This magic wasn't as straightforward as rising. One knew quite quickly, if one was bouncing against the ceiling, precisely what one was dealing with. But she did know that Mary lived because of her magic. And she lived too.

Rob. Penny nipped around Malcolm, into the other room, and scrambled onto the bed. She had magic again, but she must discover how to give it away.

Her mind began to churn with possibilities—spilling his blood, entering his dreams, wrapping him in an invisible vine cocoon—discarding several as soon as they came into her mind. What felt correct? She reached for the old tools of her magic. Thinking thoughts of lightness and tipping them away. She gathered Robbie into her arms, cradling his warm face in her palm, and thought healing thoughts. *Tonics. Clean water. Limbs running full tilt down the gallery.*

A quickening gathered in her shoulder, winding down her arm like water from a slowly seeping pot.

Robbie stirred in her arms. Malcolm gripped her at the elbows, closing a circle around his son, and looked hopefully into her face. It was a good sign, but the magic was not coming fast enough.

Then the magic reached for a thought, a memory, really, of Rob telling the story of Brigid, beating back the Old Hag of winter. How the white witch brought spring, of bud and root and new beginnings.

Brigid.

Magic left her in a whoosh, like tumbling down a hill in a flurry of petticoats and laughter. Malcolm squeezed her hand, but her thoughts were all for Robbie.

“Wake up, Robbie Ross. Wake up,” she commanded in a whisper.

Delicate pink chased away the grey in his cheeks and the hard rasping breaths smoothed. Still, his face was immobile. Her gaze roved back and forth over his form like a sheepdog guarding his flock. *Wake up.* When the sun broke free of the clouds, a slanting ray crossed his face. Rob’s nose wrinkled and his eyelids lifted. He swallowed thickly.

“Morning, Rob,” Malcolm said, his tone was easy, but he was crushing Penny’s hand in his own.

“Morning, *Aither*.” Rob glanced at Penny, and more pointedly, at her and Malcolm’s hands entwined.

A broken laugh escaped Malcolm, and he scooped his son into his arms. Penny slid from the bed and opened the door, nodding when Ewan raised his head. She stood to one side and he bolted past her, Fritz on his heels.

The room overflowed with light and noise as Kathy, Mary, and Elspeth joined them, hurrying down the hall. There were no hushed tones as befitted a sickroom, no soft footfalls.

Penny watched from inside the door, backed up against the wall, her lips trembling as a smile chased across her face. Seeing this family whole again was different than the pleasure of climbing into the night sky and claiming it for herself. Different than riding the waves of the Channel, alive with the prospect of adventure and new horizons.

Months ago, Penny would have been railing at God, Nature, or at whatever source she owed her magic, to take back these powers and return what had been lost, down to the last measure.

Later, she would have been pleased any magic had returned at all. Having discovered it, she would be busy with plans to return home and pick up the orderly threads she had set down. To carry on with her life, find a uniform to marry, and discover what her powers could do in India or Canada, or Canton.

Now, tendrils of her magic raced along the smooth oak floor and climbed the bedpost, curling over the carved wood, twining, and flowering as they twisted higher. She could almost see them forming a protective bower. Her eyes crinkled.

This tremulous contentment had little to do with magic, and whether she had it, whether it was the same.

She loved, and her loved ones were safe and happy. Her magic, though barely understood, had been strong enough to lift the heaviest veil of sickness off Rob. If she never did another magical thing, this was enough. Forever enough.

The relief and boisterousness soon tired the lad, and before long, Mary was ushering the noise and laughter away. Silence fell and Penny watched as Malcolm brushed Rob's hair back, tugging the coverlet up to his chin. He looked up and moved towards her, tugging her hand as he walked through the door, pulling her into the hall and a little way down.

He wore an intent expression and she wondered what he would say if he could see her climbing shoots of honeysuckle and wild rose winding about him now, her roots driving so deeply into *Coille na Cyarlin* she would leave a portion of herself behind when she tore herself from this place.

He wove his hand between them. "You did something to help Rob and I felt—" His features twisted, and he looked down, splaying his fingers and tracing the lines of his work-roughened palm. "And then he woke up."

His words went from certainty to certainty like a man crossing a stream, stepping from stone to stone, trying not to wet his feet with the unexplainable. The thought of answering him with the truth knotted her stomach. Thorntons, by long habit, hid their magic. They did not speak of it.

"Will you describe it?" she asked.

Malcolm's brows gathered as he searched for words. He closed his hand and pressed the knuckles against his chest, his voice thickened by wonder and confusion. "It felt like Rob was being put back together piece by piece. It felt like he was being called back home. It felt like spring when the oats push up through the earth and I know we'll have a harvest."

"Spring." Penny nodded, tasting the word on her tongue, liking it. spring was renewal, beginning. "Yes."

"You knew that was going to happen."

She shook her head and felt her plait loosen, felt the bareness of her feet, and pulled the shawl more tightly around her shoulders. Her magic reached for him, feeling along the unseen threshold dividing them, wanting to bridge and bind them.

What did this bit of magic have to do with Rob's recovery? Hers?

"I didn't know what was going to happen. I hadn't ever done that before. Not on purpose."

Why hadn't she been able to direct it before now? That was a question waiting for a quiet hour and close examination.

"But the power came from you. How?"

Penny darted a tongue across her lip. "What you felt was magic."

"You're magic?"

"Yes." The word arrived on a narrow breath and she repeated it. "Yes. I came to Scotland because I lost it for a time." She cupped her neck, but the only thing under her searching fingers was smooth skin. There was not even a scar to show him.

Malcolm was breathing carefully, his frame so still it hardly stirred the air. "Why Scotland?"

"I don't know. My mother received a letter from my sister, asking for a governess. She was simply holding the missive in her hand, and I knew I had to come. That was the first time in months I'd had any trace of magic," she replied, willing him to accept impossible things.

At her words, the distance between them grew, almost imperceptibly. Her magic rioted between them like a garden in midsummer, but she was powerless to make him draw near, to make him believe her.

"Magic." He repeated the word as a store clerk might repeat an order, wanting to make sure he had heard her aright, possibly to tell her that, no, Madam. There was no magic to be got today. None to be had at any price.

"I must come to Scotland was the only sure thing I knew." She wanted to laugh, then. Not Scotland. Here. To his house. To him. Why?

His expression was troubled, the lines carving his face deepening. He opened his mouth, looked down and away, then back with an intent blue gaze. "I begged you to tell me why you'd lied about your name. Did you think I wouldn't believe you?"

Her head dipped to one side. "Would you? I don't do parlor tricks and had no proof. If I had told you I had stolen the crown jewels, you would want to see them. Having lost my magic, I had nothing to exhibit and could not expect you to believe me. You were furious."

He gave a short nod.

Penny tented her brows and tipped her palm towards him. "Why do you believe me now?"

He lifted his hand and she gasped softly as he placed his palm directly over hers, hovering above it an inch or two, the air between them heavy with a glasshouse warmth in the narrow channel. "I have to. I felt it with my own hands, saw it with my own eyes, and could no more deny it than I could deny the sun rose today. I don't understand magic, only enough to be glad yours returned. You were a healer?"

At the word, the filaments of magic brushed, bent over like a field of long grass. Healer.

"No," she said, not sharing anymore. She must have time to put away the magic she lost now that her new magic had taken root. Time to mourn it. Not now. Not when the joy of Rob's recovery made her heart ache. She gave a low laugh. "It seems I am now."

He nodded, dropping his hand at his side. "We thank you."

We. Her smile dimmed.

"I should be thanking you. I came to get magic and *Coille na Cyarlin* restored it to me." Her eyes blurred. How to tell him what it meant? She had magic again and Rob was going to be well. A smile gusted over her mouth.

He stretched his hand to tuck a tumbledown lock of hair behind her ear and her magic sang, aching for an outlet.

His expression sobered. "The Scots like a fair trade. You got something and we got something. No one has to feel cheated you when you go."

Chapter Thirty-One

Penny notched her brows and ran the back of her hand along Robbie's pink cheek. Dusk had come again and there was a low fire banked under his skin. She held his hand, wishing that her magic might weave him all the way together again. S*eedlings. A bracing spring.* She gave a small sigh when no invisible tendrils wound from her hands. No unseen thistledown drifted across his brow. Her power was spent, and no careful gleaning would yield her the result she wished for.

She rubbed her eyes and remembered her first lessons in magic so many years ago when Beatrice had instructed her about dangers and limits. Penny had thought it a load of nonsense. It was difficult to think about limitations when she had been gifted the sky, and when the advice had seemed so calculated to anchor her magic to practicalities.

Practice each day.

Build up endurance.

Rest.

She leaned a hand onto the counterpane and closed her eyes like a child trying to cast a spell. She was resting, sort of, allowing her mind to sort and file all she knew about this magic.

She could heal, in some measure. Inspecting her own person, Penny could find no trace of illness. The magic had done that, she was certain, but not until the locket was dashed to pieces.

Then, her magic had powered through her like a steam engine pumping water from a flooded mine. Were it not for Isabelle's misguided magic—her quackery—Penny might never have noticed the subtle shifts within herself.

But such an explosion of power was impossible to ignore.

Had her magic been at work before she controlled it? Oh, yes. Elspeth had taken no powders, and no potions. There had been no Turkish bath treatments to help her along. There was nothing but

Penny's daily company, her passive magic pulling away the fibrous husk choking at aged joints.

A bubbling happiness spread through Penny's veins. What else had she done?

Mary. That puzzling episode could now find an explanation. Penny's magic had likely healed her too, though in a different fashion by carving a channel of intuition through Penny's mind to make way for the idea of grinding charcoal for Mary's draught and forcing it down her throat. She never would have thought of that on her own.

What had healing to do with the other instances of magic?

Had Ewan needed to learn about animals in the same way a child needed a splinter pulled from his knee?

Penny stifled a yawn. Beatrice had warned her about the cost of magic. How rising too much would leave her body shaking and weak. How there was always a price exacted. She curled a hand around Robbie's, heard the gentle snoring of his deep sleep.

Another yawn. This was a cost. If she wished for healing, it must be meted out with caution or it would be missing when she needed it. She had wasted the lion's share of her healing on herself and must wait until her stores were replenished.

Her last thought before sleep claimed her was to wonder how long.

When dawn arrived, Robbie stirred and Penny turned on the bed, an expanse of rumpled coverlet between them, abandoned land over which their hands met.

"How are you, Rob?" she whispered, sunlight making the white linen glow yellow.

"Right as rain," he croaked, coughing into her face. "Never better."

"Lies." She wanted to grab him up and hug him. "Are you mending?"

"Aye." Rob's eyes drifted closed and he said, "*Aither* says you'll leave us when I am well again."

"Is that what he says?" she murmured, her tone a soft contrast to the sharp pain in her breast. "Well, your papa always tells the truth."

She stretched, kissing his forehead, and stared up at the canopy, her eyes clouded with tears, their pinky fingers wound together.

"Do you want to leave?" Robbie asked.

She opened her mouth to say she had obligations at home. A mother and father who worried over her and nieces and nephews to spoil. She meant to say she was homesick. Something a small child would understand and forgive her for. Instead, she felt her face twist in pain, and she heard herself say the plain truth.

"It will tear me in two to leave, Rob. I'll cry as soon as the ship weighs the anchor, and I'm frightened I'll never stop."

Her eyes widened, bringing every finely wrought detail in the plasterwork into focus. This was not the gentle fiction one was supposed to peddle to children. This was nothing like her plan to get him used to the idea of another governess whom he would like as well as he liked her. Probably more. Lies like that would be kind.

"I'll cry too, miss," he said, his voice matter of fact. "Promise. Will you miss *Aither*?"

She felt the strangest sensation brush along the surface of her skin, as though her cropped store of magic was being buffeted by a sudden gust. *Tell him the truth.*

"Yes," she admitted, skidding to a stop like a runaway horse—a bucking, flinching animal ready to cast itself over a cliff.

Magic. Not hers. She knew now what that felt like. All reaching branches and plunging roots, and the pressure of tight seeds breaking free. This was friendly, creeping magic. A magic of white mice running along floors, drafts stirring a fire, and the snick of a lock springing open. It could only be coming from him.

"Robbie, quick, ask me another question. Ask me what I think about oat cakes."

"No need to ask that, miss. I know you love 'em. Birdie says how you finish a whole plate for tea. You know what I wonder? I wonder what you think of the witch in the woods?"

"Hmmm?"

"Lady Ainsley. You gave her a sound thrashing the other day and I wondered."

The other day. The other day he had been hanging from a cliff.

"Oh." Her heart began to pound as the otherworldly breeze picked up. Would she have noticed it if her own magic didn't shiver like a pond of bulrushes? No. To anyone not ready for it, the powerful command to tell the truth might not be noticed, only acted upon.

"On the night of the party, she called me by my name on purpose." Penny frowned at the note of certainty in her voice. How had she known a thing and not known it? "I hurt her—spending so much time with Elspeth—and I think she must be lonely."

"Och, I understand," he answered, sounding so much like Malcolm Penny laughed.

She rolled over onto her stomach, slipping fingers free from Robbie's. "Ask me again."

His patience with the game was sliding away and he yawned, muttering, "What you think of Lady Ainsley?"

Now it was easy to parcel out half-truths. "She is an elegant lady and wears her clothes beautifully."

Rob closed his eyes and Penny tried for an out-and-out lie.

"Lady Ainsley is a purple elephant with ballet slippers and performs at Astley's every night and twice on Saturdays."

"'S'nice," he murmured, slipping into sleep once more.

Robbie had magic.

Penny wondered what it would mean for him and fell to parsing out the implications. Her thoughts were interrupted a few minutes later, when Birdie, scratching at the door and spilling through it like a cat rubbed up the wrong way. The morning sun cast long slanting patches across the room.

"'er ladyship begs to see ye," the housekeeper grumped.

"Lady Ainsley? Here?"

"That's 'er," Birdie confirmed. "Don't see what call she has to come pestering a sickroom."

"We won't let her pester us. I'll come to the drawing room and we can keep her from Rob."

"We ought to keep her from you too," Birdie frowned. "You should be resting, young miss, instead of scampering about the house with no regard for your health."

Penny smiled. This is what it must be like when Birdie decided you were her people. Lovely and cozy, and a little stifling. Penny swung from the bed and looked to Rob, noting his still-warm skin and gentle snore. Nature and rest were repairing him, if slowly. Magic would finish the job.

"Tell her I'll join her in a quarter of an hour, Birdie?"

When Penny entered the drawing room, it was obvious a quarter of an hour had not been enough time to meet Isabelle on equal ground.

"Darling, you look a wreck," Isabelle said, kissing her cheek, her eyes roving over Penny's face, checking slightly when they dipped to her bare neck, innocent of the locket. "Did you even run a comb through your hair before you pinned it up?"

Penny raked a smoothing hand over her head. "Robbie is on the mend. It doesn't matter what I look like."

Isabelle face puckered. "Dr Bell called and said the lad had gone through a bad patch, and you, with him." She laid a gentle hand on Penny's arm. "I'm sure he'll be well before long."

Penny trapped the hand, unable to contain her relief, her joy. It must find expression. "Isabelle, I must tell you. He is well. I healed him."

Isabelle raised her brow.

Penny sketched an equivocating line through the air. "Not entirely healed, but I had never done such a thing before, and he was very sick. Still, I did it."

"Are you a healer now?" came the tentative question.

Penny was too pleased for discretion. She drummed excited fingers on the cushions of the sofa. "I think so. It was magic."

At this Isabelle's eyes widened. "Magic? The locket worked?"

Penny chewed on her lip, pulling the locket from her pocket and handing over the crushed gold medallion, its little hinge hanging like the broken wing of a bird.

Isabelle uttered a tiny cry and Penny rushed on. "It didn't work as we'd hoped. The locket was trapping my magic, and it wasn't until Malcolm stepped on it that—"

"Stepped on it?" Isabelle paled, her fingers tracing the shattered lines of the jewelry. "Penny, this locket is priceless. It was my most powerful magic."

"I know. I am dreadfully sorry. Papa will understand it is a debt of honor and will advance me the sum to repair it."

Isabelle slipped it into her reticule, her mouth set in a hard line. Lord, she looked as though she might cry.

"I didn't mean it to happen," Penny went on, clasping her hands "but I'm glad it did. The gold was harvesting my magic and when it broke—" There was no vocabulary for what had happened. Penny's hands burst apart like an artillery shell. The memory of it spread a banked smile across her features. “My magic has rooted again.”

“Rising?”

“No. Something better.”

“You mean it changed?” As Penny had hoped, Isabelle was too excited to be upset anymore. “I wondered if that was possible.”

Penny nodded. “I have healing magic.”

Isabelle’s head tilted. She looked like an inquisitive little bird. “Fevers, cuts, broken bones, and things?”

Penny nodded, and Isabelle tossed her dark curls, giving her a bright smile. “It’s marvelous for you. I suppose healing can be quite useful.”

“You suppose?” Penny choked on a laugh, thinking of all she might do. The possibilities stretched on as far as she could see.

“Well, you must understand I never dreamed the magic would come back differently. I wonder you’re not downcast, you loved your rising so.”

“I have magic again. That’s all I wanted.”

“Not quite the same though, is it? You came to Scotland determined to find your old magic, cudgel it over the head, and drag it back home with you. You were determined to rise again. Now you are accepting whatever scraps have been tossed your way, so easily turned from what you want. What happened?”

Penny sucked in a breath. “Rob happened. My rising would have been powerless to help him. But this—” Her pleasure, so strong before, felt fragile now, as if it were liable to shatter like a butter biscuit.

“I am happy it was useful,” Isabelle added.

Penny was saved having to respond when Birdie entered with a tea tray, aiming a scowl at Isabelle’s head as she departed. Penny grinned and reached for the teapot.

“Don’t you dare,” Isabelle said, waving her back. “You must be exhausted after your ordeal. You were too near death’s door for my liking, and though you have been too kind to say it, I gather that my locket was no help at all. Pouring out is the least I can do.”

Penny nodded and sank against the cushions, running a hand over her face.

How could Penny explain about her magic? Though she dearly longed to rise once more, the powerful rush of magic which had bloomed from her to Robbie, had been no less exhilarating.

Watching the return of soft pink to his cheeks, and his lungs clear had filled her with as much wonder as floating in the buffeting wind high above Thorndene. How could she hope to make Isabelle understand it when she herself hardly could?

Penny shook away the heavy thoughts and reached for the tea Isabelle offered, taking a swallow, and wrinkling her nose. Musty. Was there no tea Isabelle could not manage to ruin in some way?

"I expect there are all sorts of things about your magic you haven't told me," Isabelle said.

Oh, there were, and curiously the barrier that made up all her reasons for discretion, for the silence which had wrapped up Penny's magic safely from the moment of its inception all those years ago, seemed to become soft and tissue thin.

"You will laugh when I tell you about the other magic," she said, feeling muzzy-headed and giddy. She ought to rest. Three nights of fever and only one of healing. She knew hardly anything about her new gifts—the costs and limitations, the strange consequences. Nothing of Robbie's. "You will laugh."

"Other magic?" The question came so softly.

Robbie's touch had given her an affable, friendly feeling—like drinking down champagne— This… Penny closed her eyes as the room began to tilt and her senses to slow. "You were correct that one of the children has magic, though you were wrong about which one."

Isabelle set her dish of tea down. "That is a delicious bit of news. It's Robert?"

"Aye," Penny answered, detached but amused at the way the Scots expression felt at home on her tongue. "He'll be a menace if we don't teach him to be careful with it."

Isabelle waited.

"Your mouth looks like a day-old scone," Penny said, wandering after another stray thought. "Hard and square. Your tea is dreadful, I always wanted to tell you." She exhaled a big breath.

"I'm not sure you should tell me about his magic," Isabelle said. "You look like you need a good rest."

Oh yes, the magic. "He can make people tell the truth, even when they don't wish to."

"Well," Isabelle exclaimed, saying nothing more as her eyes shifted along the plasterwork on the ceiling, as though she were working out a difficult sum. Then, "How did you discover it? Were you trying to lie?"

Penny waved a dismissing hand. What funny things hands were. Five fingers even if the smallest was next to useless.

"Were you trying to lie?" Isabelle repeated.

"Little lies one tells children, but he got the truth out of me without even trying. I doubt if I would have even noticed it if I had no magic myself." Penny rubbed her temple. "My head aches abominably."

Isabelle tapped the bowl of her teaspoon to her lips. "That will be a great boon to him."

Penny smiled at that, holding onto the thought of Robbie like an anchor in a whirlwind. "Something should come easy for Robbie. Something should be natural and simple. In one thing he should have the advantage over little Kathy who has taken to her sums as a duck to water." Her brow furrowed. She couldn't seem to hold any thought in her head for long before it tripped past her tongue. "It won't be as fun for him as rising."

"Fun," Isabelle snorted. "Where is the fun in having magic you have to spend your whole life hiding? But his. Get that into a room with politicians or bankers or cent-per-centers, making people say what they really think? Well."

Penny's head wobbled. "Oh dear, an excellent point. I'll have to talk to Malcolm about his moral instruction."

"Just so," Isabelle said, standing to go. She was elegant in her widow's weeds. A black rose. "You look tired, dear. Why don't you put your feet up and have a rest?"

When Birdie found her later, Penny's hair had slipped out of its pins and her mouth tasted of cotton.

She could hardly remember Isabelle's visit at all.

Chapter Thirty-Two

The days could not be held back, filled to the brim with tradesman's accounts and unexpected disasters, and plans for the celebration, which would signal the first official day of Slinch Bickey. There ought to be enough to keep Malcolm's mind from a certain governess, but his thoughts returned to her again and again.

Malcolm tipped the letter toward the library fire, scanning the polite, apologetic phrases poorly concealing Sir Charles and Lady Sarah Thornton's shock in discovering their youngest daughter was five hundred miles from where they had put her.

"...we arrived Newcastle after a fortnight in the country and found your distressing letter...the roads were impassable...It was, no doubt, a childish whim...Our deepest gratitude for your care, sheltering our daughter as though she were your own…urgency does credit to your feelings as a father...our hope that this short, unhappy episode may be forgotten…"

Malcolm dropped his hand, having already committed the letter to memory. He didn't need to read the words again to have them emblazoned under his eyelids.

Urgency. There had been an excess of it. Malcolm had written on the night of the ball when all his loss, all the sudden, violent hollowing of his ambitions and hope to marry a young woman of no account and be happy with her for the rest of his life had gone into the missive, the hard, unbending text of which amounted to, "You must come and collect your wayward daughter at once."

It served him right he was getting what he asked for.

Malcolm ran his thumb over the script and attempted the rough calculations. A few days to gather reports and send them on to Lord Liverpool. Another day to pack their belongings and take their leave. "We will follow this communication shortly," Malcolm repeated the phrase, remembering the rest with a dark smile.

Penny's parents had expressed their thanks to Mrs Stuart, a lady's whose moral compass he had assured them was "instructive and undeviating," and begged his patience for a little while only.

Two days, perhaps three, is all he had.

At the scrape of the door, he bolted upright, presenting an appearance of a man hard at work, going over his accounts. Penny would not find him lost or aimless. She would not find him—

"Elspeth," he breathed, feeling the full weight of disappointment as he cast down his pen. How long would it be before he stopped expecting it would be Penny? Hoping. Far longer than two days, perhaps three. "You are well?' he asked, noting her walking stick.

She waved his concern away as she took a chair near the fire and he joined her, sitting opposite. "A little stiffness. No matter."

He doubled over the letter, creasing the fold with his fingernail. Already, the paper had grown soft. "Is there anything you need?"

"I need to tell you a story," she said smoothly, folding her knobby hands in her lap and regarding him with sharp eyes. Sitting next to the fire she looked like a goddess of the hearth. There was a danger in being fooled by such a domestic picture. In his experience, wise women with lined faces and steel-grey hair claimed the right to order the world as they wished.

He nodded for her to continue.

"Once there was a bear with a sore paw, but the bear was too stupid to find a remedy, so he died miserable and alone. The end."

A smile lit his eyes. "An excellent story. Rob's?"

"It's of my own invention, lad. Let me explain the meaning, for those too daft and blind to see. You are the bear. Our Miss Thornton has caused the sore paw."

He tried not to lose his smile on his face or in his voice, but the effort was enormous. "I'm going to be miserable, too. Is that it?"

"You already are, lad," she said, staring him down until his smile unbent by degrees. "You've been neglecting the nursery, have been silent at dinner, and you're back to your account books the moment we dismiss ourselves." Elspeth glanced to the desk. "They cannae be that bad."

"They're not bad," he admitted. "The idea for investors was a godsend."

"The idea wasn't the only thing that was a godsend."

Malcolm lifted the page. "I've a letter from Sir Charles and Lady Sarah," he informed her. "They will be here tomorrow or the day after."

To collect Penny. To pull her out of the Pentland Hills, out of Scotland, and out of his life forever. A childish whim, her mother had called her journey, making no sign it had anything to do with magic, which was a fight for Penny to reclaim the very foundation stones of who she was.

Perhaps it would be best if he accepted Lady Sarah's construction. Penny would be recast in his mind as an immature youth. One would forget her folly, and any pain it caused, quickly, and he might ease into the role of the avuncular, temporary guardian Lady Sarah had convinced herself he was.

His grunt was one of bitter amusement. Elspeth was right. He was miserable.

"Mrs Johnston called," Elspeth said, and he was grateful for the change of topic. "She needed to tell someone about the decorations for the ceremony tomorrow. Buntings and things. Her nose was quite out of joint because she had to report her triumphs to me."

Malcolm frowned. "Was she not giving you proper respect?" he asked.

She gave an irritated shake of the head. "Can't you see? She's listened to them, settled petty matters of dispute, put their concerns in front of you. Your people have claimed Penny Thornton as the mistress of *Coille na Cyarlin,* no matter she doesn't bear your name or share your bed."

"Elspeth."

Her eyes flashed. "It's time for plain language. Who was it that raked Mary back from the edge of death? Penny. Who was it that held on to a cliffside by her fingernails and saved Rob's life? Penny," Elspeth declared, warming to her theme. "Aye, she lied to you about her name, heaven knows why, but if you want to know who she is, open your damned eyes.

"Your people have realized the fastest way to your ear is straight through hers. The lass is the mistress here, even if you're too much of a fool to make it so in fact." Her speech slowed. "*Are* ye too much of a fool?"

Malcolm lifted the letter, his breath seeming to tear from his throat. "Her parents are coming. I set it in motion and cannot turn them back. Anyway, it's far more complicated than wanting."

A gleam lit Elspeth's eyes and a smile spread across her wide mouth. Jean's mouth. "Complicated," she repeated, holding one hand up and then the other, "You love her. She loves you." She clapped her palms together. "Not so complicated."

Malcolm stood, pacing to the mantel, his gaze drawn to the glowing embers of the fire. "She came to Scotland for a particular purpose, and having achieved it, she must return home."

"Home," Elspeth snorted, snatching up her walking stick and jabbing the back of his leg. "This is her home. We are not loveable people," she declared, swinging the stick up and back, pointing it in the direction of the private rooms. "It is your great good luck she doesn't seem to know that. In the beginning, aye, she wanted to pitch the lot of us down the nearest privy hole, I will admit." She gave a wry smile, bringing her cane down with a thump. "We might have deserved it. But it's been some time since we made peace here. Even Ewan is bending. Can you not make her stay?"

He crushed the letter in his outstretched hand. "We have a day, maybe less, until her parents arrive."

Elspeth's eyes narrowed. "I might have expected such helplessness from an Englishman. I thought you had resolved to do it."

"I thought I was asking a poor governess without any better prospects—" He cut the words off. "I would be asking her to take on the burdens of three children and an estate which can hardly pay when she is an heiress, used to travelling abroad."

"Scotland is abroad," Elspeth muttered. "We are a whole other country."

Malcolm shook his head. "So foreign we speak the same language."

"She hasn't mastered it yet."

Malcolm crossed his arms over his chest. "Her father is an agent to the Prime Minister. Do you know what kind of match a woman like Penny might expect? Titled, wealthy, young, unencumbered. Her future could be anything. How could I take that away?"

"You remind me of Jean," she said, surprising him. She smiled at the memory. "Before you wed, all she did was worry you were throwing away some chance with an imaginary girl dressed in gold cloth with diamonds stitched into her stays."

"Elspeth," he groaned, hand at his neck. She must understand. "You should have seen Pen's face when she thought Rob might die. I've never seen anyone so shaken. She was desperately ill, hair all about her head, face grey with grief."

"You would spare her that?"

"Shouldn't I, if I can?"

Elspeth made a rude noise and reached out her hand, so Malcolm crouched before her. She drew him close. "Children are magic," she began, and he tightened his grip at the word.

"They can do anything," she said. "Might be capable of anything. I watch Ewan, Rob and Kathy, and they're like endless possibilities plonked down in the middle of a compass. The fun is finding out which way they will go. No one makes their home in a compass. Having all the choices and never making any is not real."

Elspeth harrumphed. "Penny made a choice when she ran away from England. Foolish, perhaps, but she had to strike off in one direction and take the rewards as well as the sacrifices that came along." She reached a hand and tugged his ear. "That look on her face you described? Grey and anxious? I know that look. I've worn it. Birdie, too. You have worn it again and again since Ewan was born. It's the price of love. Would you spare her that?"

Malcolm looked down at their clasped hands, his thumb brushing over the ridges of her knuckles, thinking of the costs Elspeth had paid.

She touched his hair and he looked up into her stern, determined face. "Don't imagine you're saving her from pain and hardship. Don't imagine she will travel the world and won't ever encounter anything that will wring her heart. Most of all, you Scottish daftie, don't imagine she will thank you for driving her away from *Coille na Cyarlin*. Her heart is here."

A fire began to kindle in Malcolm's chest, warmth spreading to the tips of his fingers, and his gaze followed the line Elspeth's cane had taken.

If Penny would meet with hardship anywhere, who better to meet it with than with someone who would love her with every part of him? Penny was not gone. She hadn't yet dipped him a stiff curtsey, called him Mr Ross, and followed her parents into a coach.

Did he have the power, even after the hot words which flowed between them, to meet that lass across the width of a hall and coax her to close the gap?

A grin eased over his mouth. He was a Scotsman, wasn't he?

Malcolm seized Elspeth and gave her cheek a hard kiss.

"You have a plan," Elspeth declared, a narrow gleam in her eyes. "How do you have a plan already?"

"I've done nothing but think for days, hoping where I shouldn't. Aye, I have a plan, but I'll have to wait. Today there are children underfoot and the lessons to manage. I have business in the village. Tomorrow we'll dedicate Slinch Bickey."

"The buntings, I can assure you, will be a masterpiece."

Malcolm laughed. "As long as they're festive enough to overcome the better judgment of an Englishwoman."

"That's not a very high threshold."

"Elspeth," he reproved. Malcolm stood, straightening his waistcoat. The outcome was too important to chance to a moment of impulse. He could wait. He hoped he could wait.

"You should rest. I would hate to see you laid up for the celebrations."

Elspeth laughed, and a surge of gratitude rushed through him at the sound.

"Soon," she replied. He touched her hands, and he went from the house, walking the road to the village. He closed his eyes against the bright sun and a scrap of Ramsay's poems came to him:

When e'er the sun grows high and warm,
We'll to the cauller shade remove...

A smile lit his mouth.

***

"Elspeth," Penny said, glancing up from her book. "The children are off taking Fritz for a run," she explained.

Elspeth scooted a chair and sat at the table. "I came from Malcolm. He tells me your parents have written. Two days, he said, before they come to collect you."

Penny's hand pressed against the pages. Two. Well, she had known it was coming.

"You'll be glad to return," Elspeth assured her. "You can trade those plain wool frocks for something a bit more fitting. Go back to filling your days with…" Her imagination must have escaped her, and she wielded the back of her hand like an invisible broom, sweeping away the lessons Penny had toiled at, tea with Lady Berwick or Mrs Hunter, the children, Malcolm. All of it.

"You'll have a Season in London?"

Penny nodded. Once Mama's fury cooled, she supposed so. Dress fittings with Madame, rides in the park. Beatrice would bring her family up for a few weeks to enjoy the novelties, tactfully avoiding the topic of her magic until she knew about Penny's.

Meg, the present Lady Ainsley, would watch out for Penny, steering her toward the kind of man Beatrice would not find it a punishment to spend holidays with. Penny's throat ached at the prospect.

"You'll find a young man," Elspeth went on, digging the knife into her flesh. The woman didn't even have the delicacy to wear her customary scowl, instead, looking positively gleeful over the idea of Penny, far removed from *Coille na Cyarlin.*

She wouldn't find a young man in London. She wouldn't find him anywhere. Malcolm was what she wanted, and he was sending her away.

"He doesn't trust me," Penny said, not explaining the sudden digression. "He said as much."

"Nonsense." Elspeth's reassuring scowl was back, not pretending ignorance of the speech which had flowed silently beneath the one of Seasons and beaux. "His fears on that score were put to rest when you risked your neck for our boy. He loves you."

"Then why hasn't he spoken?" Penny sprang from her chair, holding her arms about her waist.

Elspeth reached out her hand and Penny grasped it, magic winding down her arm, like roots working their way around an immense boulder. At the boundary between their skin, Penny halted the magic, fighting to keep it from leaping the divide to begin its work of wholeness and healing.

Her stores were reserved for Rob, to get him entirely well before Mama and Papa came to claim Penny and return her to a life she must accustom herself to.

Elspeth swung Penny's hand lightly. "I didn't want to love you, and I didn't want the children to love you," she said, her words as simple and plain as the flip of an oatcake. As before, the real communication composed a river below the words she spoke, carving deeper courses. "You're not much like my girl."

"I love you, too."

"Then don't leave us. We need you."

"Need a girl who likes her own way too much? Who has never been overfond of children?"

"You love ours."

Penny made a final effort at sense. "He's not asked me to stay."

Elspeth lifted her shoulders in a mighty, aggrieved breath.

"Well, that is a puzzle."

Chapter Thirty-Three

The morning sun was brighter than it had been all summer. Along with Mary, Penny took a noisy breakfast with the children and oversaw their preparations, stumbling over Kathleen who had taken to walking in her shadow. Finally, the requisite number of cheeks, hands, and ears had been scrubbed clean, and Ewan jogged from the nursery along with Fritz whose long tongue lolled out of his mouth, his eyes fastened on Ewan's face.

Fritz. For a moment Penny imagined sailing from Edinburgh, the sound of the sea mingling with the plaintive, high-pitched whine of a dog without his true master. She would be tracing the line of the southern hills as the sails snapped.

Tears threatened to spill now, prickling behind her eyes, and she fiercely swiped them back. This might be her last day. She would not ruin it with weeping.

"Miss?" Mary prodded.

Penny jerked her head. "Sorry, yes. Why don't you go ahead with Kathy?"

Penny turned to Rob as the others bustled from the room and held out a hand. When he took it she felt her magic unfurl.

"Your boot," she said, sinking to her knees. He hitched a shoe up, and sorting out the laces, she encountered a knot. She slipped the tines of a fork in the tangle and worked it loose, tying them properly. There hadn't been enough time to teach him this. There wasn't time now.

A wave of grief slipped through the closed chambers of her heart, washing the walls, flooding them. Rob would walk around with his laces tripping him up, getting a split chin and bleeding all over his clothes. She imagined the uproar, the consternation of the laundress, his father holding him as Mary dashed off for a bandage.

She swallowed, resisting the temptation to catch Rob up in an embrace, instead taking him by the hands. He looked at her with eyes that were the soft brown of rich earth freshly spaded, and she could sense the faint sickness lingering from the way her magic wanted to spool out of her. She relaxed her grip on it and let it flow, impossibly happy as it rushed out, working miracles.

His skin pinkened and the faint shadows under his eyes disappeared. For the first time in days, there was still some of her magic left, dregs only but he needed no more. She would leave him in perfect health, anxious already about how he would fare the next time he fell ill and none of her magic was at hand.

"Are you done?" he asked, rubbing his nose with the flat of his hand, a touch of ordinariness that would always live alongside any high drama at *Coille na Cyarlin*.

"Yes," she replied, swatting his bottom as he raced away.

She followed on his heels, down and down the stairs, into the hazy sunshine to where Malcolm waited by the carriage, a spacious, old-fashioned barouche with the top turned down for the occasion.

It was good of Malcolm to look so handsome, today, of all days. The starched linen at his neck was anchored by the restrained elegance of a steel cravat pin. She took in his well-tailored bottle green coat and shining boots, the ones from an Englishman whose mother was surely Scottish.

Though, as ever, his hair defied order, looking as if he had come in from a tramp on the hills, or had stolen a kiss on the stairs. He hadn't, of course, and she was tempted to reach up on her toes remedy the oversight. Her parents would be here tomorrow or the day after. He couldn't sack her now.

"Cold?" Malcolm asked, and her eyes widened.

Penny shook her head a little too vehemently and glanced to the collapsed carriage hood. "That's a risk."

"I'm feeling brave," Malcolm laughed, his eyes boldly holding hers as though it had never been decided she must leave *Coille na Cyarlin* forever. She touched Elspeth as she climbed in, sending the last of her healing to the woman who had become such a friend.

Kathleen climbed into Penny's lap and Malcolm squeezed in next to her, contact stretching from her shoulder to her knee. The trip to the village was going to be torturous. The driver gave a whistle, a shake of the reins, and they were off.

"The fields have no business looking so well," Malcolm murmured as they skirted thick-grown barley and oat fields, crossing paths she had traversed again and again with Fritz. “Not when you consider the rain we’ve had and the killing frosts. My daily records show a summer that never arrived.”

He had lifted an arm, inching into her space, and she inhaled the scent of sweet tobacco and soap. She would get a reputation for eccentricity as she haunted every tobacconist shop in London until she found that blend and scoured booksellers for every volume of poetry Ramsay ever produced, too.

The carriage began the long descent to the river, passing the oak, blackened but waving a banner of bright green leaves, almost at the top. She dragged her focus from Malcolm’s arm running along the back of the bench and spared some for the curious sight.

Was it possible her magic done all this? Had it rescued the heart of a tree so broken that branches, brittle with age and ruin, snapped off and clattered on the ground? It was growing again, in the precise spot where she had stood, longing for magic. Such a thing could not be a coincidence.

Gusts of wind chased around the tops of the barley, turning the meadow into a ripple of green and yellow. It should be dead, Malcolm had said, not thriving. The harsh, inhospitable conditions they had weathered this spring and summer should have withered them at the root. It was a miracle.

Insatiable curiosity had seized her when she first got her magic, and here it was again, greeting her like an old friend. *Come discover my secrets. Play with me.* A soft smile danced on her mouth. She had thought healing a worthy gift. Good. Virtuous.

Now came the possibility of more. Her gaze flew across the vista and she imagined cultivating a variety of plants here, which did not belong in the lowlands of Scotland. Gardens as vivid as the finely worked flowers she had learned to embroider from her Mama bloomed in her mind’s eye, each coiling bed bright with color. The square, spare lines of *Coille na Cyarlin* needed— She checked. Mama would be here tomorrow. Papa too.

She subsided against the squabs, feeling thoughtful. Then, amidst the hurly-burly of the carriage ride, the noise of the children and the general jostling, she felt a touch on her shoulder. Malcolm’s gloved fingers, grazing her arm briefly from the back of the bench. She looked up and he looked down in silent communication.

Are you well?

It was nothing.

I'm not sure I believe you.

A pity.

She smiled. He echoed it. Then the noise of the celebration claimed their attention.

The carriage rumbled over the shallow water crossing and Penny craned her neck around Malcolm's bulk, gaping at the gently curving arches of a stone bridge being picked out above a wood scaffold. Pleasure spilled through her, erupting in a delighted gasp. "You said you couldn't do it. Said I was a beast to ask. When—"

Lines fanned from his eyes. "When you weren't looking. With the investors, we had more flexibility in the budget. It cost—" Laughter rumbled through him and she could feel it trembling in her own chest. He dropped his voice. "No, lass. You'll sleep better if you don't know how much it cost us."

Us.

The word was horribly vague and might mean anything from the investors to the people of *Coille na* Cyarlin. It might mean Malcolm Ross and Penny Thornton.

Malcolm's look warmed her cheeks. Then Ewan tugged on his sleeve and he looked away, the carriage jolting up the short, steep bank into the village.

The sound of music greeted them, and the children spilled from the carriage, diving into the festive crowd filling High Street without waiting for permission.

"I can't blame them. They're excited," she told Malcolm, looking after them. *One, two, three.*

"*I'm* excited," he answered.

She looked up at him, breath catching at his expression. She parted her lips to speak but Mrs Hunter and Mrs Johnston descended upon her, each looping an arm around her elbow, sweeping her up the lane. Penny glanced back, but Malcolm waved her along with a look that seemed to say, "Later."

It was a look that made her want to double back at once and say, "Now."

She allowed the women to lead her past wooden trestles groaning with food, guide her over to inspect the bran basin Kathy was busy trying to climb into, show her the maypole planted in the green, and point out the festive bunting crisscrossing the sky from house to house.

"The bunting is exceptional," Penny said.

"I was certain you would think so." Mrs Johnston beamed.

At each stop, Mrs Hunter introduced her to the matrons in the village as though she would still be here the day after tomorrow. Suddenly she looked feverishly for Malcolm, discovering him leaning against a barrel in the middle of a knot of men, arguing some point. As though aware of her watching him, he paused and glanced up. Even from here the bright blue of his eyes shone.

A knot formed in her stomach. Good or bad, happy or disconsolate, she could not tell. She knew only that her heart had chosen this place, these people, that man. It would go on choosing him when she landed in Dorset, suffering whatever punishments her parents cared to mete out, or whether she spent the next seventy springs in London, searching for a husband.

When the sun reached its zenith, the festivities paused to give a place to the enchanted words of prayers and speeches, which would call this village into existence. A low dais had been erected on the green and Elspeth mounted it to stand at Malcolm's side. He scanned the crowd for a long moment, halting when he spotted Penny, and grinned.

Even as far back as she was situated, Penny knew the look was for her. Her cheeks pinked as heads swiveled in her direction, faces wore knowing looks, elbows nudged neighbors.

Incorrigible.

His eyes danced as he lifted his arms to settle the crowd. Penny, at the back, took in the whole scene like a butterfly hunter intent on pinning bright memories to a mounting board for minute perusal at some later date.

Malcolm's voice was clear, his strong Scottish accent making the words a poem. "We thought we had no choices. That we must lose each other to the mills down in Edinburgh. Or to Glasgow or England."

Penny smiled when a discontented murmur rolled through the crowd.

"We thought we would lose each other to settlements in Canada or America. Some friends and loved ones, some familiar paths, were lost. But here at Slinch Bickey—" A laugh rolled through the crowd at the name and Penny wanted to whoop with them. It was ridiculous, that name. God willing, it would never cease to make them laugh. "We're going to lay a new foundation. We are going to hold fast to the things that give us strength, and forge new traditions. Here we are going to become people we could never have been anywhere else."

He stepped aside for the reverend and there was an uproarious cheer. It swirled down every alleyway, skated along each window frame, twined over the neat rock walls and tumbled through the doors. The magic of hope kissing each surface.

Reverend McNair bowed his head, and the men of the gathering doffed their caps to seal these promises.

It was as her head was bent Penny heard a familiar noise, a small exclamation. One of the children. Lord in heaven, when they were about, she was never able to properly close her eyes to observe a prayer. They seemed to sense it was the best time for naughtiness.

She lifted her eyes, scanning the crowd, counting heads. One, Ewan. Two, Kathy… Where are you, Rob? What mischief are you up to now?

Her glance swept up the street and she caught a glimpse of a boot with a trailing lace whisking around a distant corner. Holding her breath, she crept silently back from the gathering. The reverend's prayer promised to be thorough, blessing every rock and rill within miles.

Though she scurried after him, Penny turned the corner too late to catch the lad. "Robbie," she whispered, low-voiced but insistent. Following the scuttling noise through the last of the dwellings and paddocks she jogged up the rise toward the rowan trees.

"Robbie," she called, and then spotted a dark figure climbing awkwardly up the hill, Rob in tow.

Penny trebled her speed and the figure turned, glancing back.

Penny breathed a laugh, pressing a fist into the stitch in her side. "Thank goodness, Isabelle. The lad got away from us. Was he trying to—"

Then she looked more closely, and her words dried up like the blackened petals of a withered flower. Isabelle was gripping Robbie by the arm, roughly holding his thin wrist so high that only the tips of his boots touched the ground, slipping over the dirt.

Penny's senses sharpened. Isabelle stood too near a short, deadly precipice where the path wound around an outcropping of rock. The hem of her frock was covered in splatters of mud and grit, her cap hanging down her back. She was missing a glove.

It looked as though she had been grappling on the ground, and it looked as though Rob had given her hell.

"What's happened?" Penny asked, striding forward with the bright governess-y voice that would sort out the meaning of these strange details and dispense understanding and good-hearted justice. If it was false, if panic coiled tightly in Penny's belly and beads of perspiration collected on the edges of her hair, she did not let it color her tone. "Did you find him in a pigsty?"

Isabelle slithered backward, yanking Rob dangerously near the drop and Penny halted, her hand half-raised, her heart in her throat. There was no hiding her panic now.

"I stole him," Isabelle declared, her cool tones at odds with her eyes, which were suddenly wide with shock. She clapped a hand over her mouth and continued up the path, her skirts rattling through the dirt and debris as she dragged Robbie along, his feet and laces tangling.

The sounds of the celebration down in the village picked up once more. Bows and pipes and singing. Damn it. Damn it. A simple shout would have brought help before. But now?

Penny inched nearer the pair her hands. spread as though she were herding a skittish stallion into a pen. Lord help her if Isabelle had gone mad.

"Stole? What do you mean?"

Rob chose that moment to aim a kick at Isabelle's shins and Isabelle roared like a lioness.

"She snatched me," he cried.

Isabelle twisted Rob's arm, and the howl this time was Penny's, outrage clawing from her throat.

"I found him with his greedy nose pressed to the baker's window," Isabelle spat, a flare of incredulity and fury forking through her eyes, "so I grabbed him."

Murderous rage erupted in Penny and she jerked it back, binding it down until it might find release. "Why?" she asked, her voice deadly calm and full of purpose.

What Isabelle might answer was unimportant. That she must have been lying to Penny, almost from the moment they met, was unimportant. Rob was in danger. Penny's entire being narrowed on that one, fragile fact, and she played for time, watching for a chance to tell the boy—her boy—to run.

"I want his magic," Isabelle shrieked, frustrated and furious, Rob's power dragging the truth from her lips.

A grim smile settled on Penny's features. Isabelle was weak. Rob's gift revealed her, stripped her bare in all her ugliness.

Penny narrowed her eyes. "You've never cared about magic, only in helping me get my own back. You said you were content. That was a lie, wasn't it?"

Isabelle fought for control, her lips clamping shut, her neck twisting, the tendons straining. Her eyes rolled and then her chin snapped down, attention sharply fixed on Penny. "Yes. I had power, little girl. Beyond anything you could ever imagine. I could unlock the darkest secret of your heart, simply by brushing your arm. I could hold your handkerchief and make you walk off a cliff."

Penny's chest hurt. Rob was by a ledge now. So close. "You can force people to do what you want. Is that what you did to me?"

"No. I lost my powers." It was Isabelle's turn to smile, evil and slick. She wore the expression so naturally Penny wondered how she had ever seen any other. "Once you've tasted power, you don't give it up without a fight." Her lip curled. "Well, you do."

"You did something to me. I know it. What?"

"I used an old potion, barely enough to loosen your tongue. Would it make you feel better if I had pushed you to come around the cottage and listen to my lies? If you were forced into it? You'd be innocent, then. Helpless. Instead, you came to me as a desperate, pitiful child begging for your magic back. You would have done anything for it."

Isabelle's words sunk into Penny with the force of an arrow. Yes, she had been feeble, like a baby crying for lost comforts. For a time, she had become a person willing to ignore the slippery grey bogland of Isabelle's moral calculations, but that Penny had vanished forever at a child's sickbed.

"I listened, you cow, but I never let you near the children," Penny spat.

Isabelle jerked Rob's arm, wearing a dark, glittering grin. "No, I really think you learned to love them."

Isabelle would make a weapon of it if she could.

Penny wetted dry lips. "I have power," she said, so clearly that Isabelle could not misunderstand her. "You don't need the boy. Take mine."

"Healing," Isabelle scoffed. "What can I do with healing? It's a nursery maid kind of magic. But this?" She jerked Robbie's arm viciously and he whimpered, his brown eyes pleading for Penny to help him. "This is something I can use."

Isabelle's wild expression told Penny time was running out. "I broke the locket," she stated. "You won't be able to collect any magic until it's mended."

Isabelle ripped her cap away and tossed it to the ground, dark hair tumbling around her shoulders. "The locket was merely a vessel. Quite useful if I could not get near the source of magic on my own," she said, giving Rob a jerk. "Perfect if a mewling governess were somehow convinced to carry it into his sickroom for me."

Penny's cheeks drained of color, bile churning in her gut. All that time for so many days, she had been making Rob sicker. God, she had begged to be at his side.

"But if I'm right here, next to him," Isabelle continued. "I need no go-between."

"Then take his power now," Penny said. Isabelle was too dangerous, and Penny began to bargain with the priceless. Rob would still be Rob without his magic. "Then give him back to me."

"Oh, but it's not that simple. I'm afraid it's got to hurt." Isabelle's lips pursed in mock-sympathy and Penny felt a sudden desire to scratch her eyes out, to tear her limb from limb. "As it did when a barn knocked your magic loose. As it did when my sister ripped my magic from my body and flung me away to Scotland."

"Your sister?" Penny shook her head. She spared Isabelle a portion of her attention and watched Rob, holding on to his captor's wrist.

"Rooted magic," she said, fist to her stomach, "hurts when it's torn away. I have to get it back. Making do with those feeble potions the grimoires taught me to brew—"

Oh Lord. "It was you. Mary and the tonic." Isabelle was capable of murder.

Penny breathed hard, seeing a hundred ways Isabelle might hurt Rob. Dashing him against the rocky ground, hurtling him down the steep incline. "It wasn't an accident." Sudden clarity hit her. "And it wasn't for Mary."

Isabelle gave a mocking sketch of acknowledgment, dipping her head. "Not my finest plan. Any one of the children could have taken the draught, not necessarily the magical one. I'm afraid the surprise of discovering you were an enemy made me incautious."

"Enemy?"

"How many hours did Elspeth slave over your dress? Malcolm could barely keep his hands off you. That's when I knew you'd been lying. You could have brought the children to me anytime."

"The cliff."

Isabelle gave another gracious nod. "Now, that *was* some of my best work."

Isabelle dragged Rob onward a few steps, but despite the terror in his eyes, he never took his gaze from Penny. He looked certain that she would help him, and Penny's mind wheeled desperately through the possibilities.

Penny suddenly cried out, pleading now, "What I can offer?" stumbling into the hill. In her frantic haste, she appeared clumsy but when she found her feet she was positioned on higher ground. A slight edge.

Isabelle fumbled with her bodice and drew a glass vial out, flicking the cork off with her thumb. "We can do this here." She grimaced. "Poor child is in for a nasty day, I'm afraid. This won't be a dilution, but you're welcome to put him back together with that trick of yours when I'm finished."

The blood drained from Penny's face. She scraped her body for magic, willing it to twine and grow, sending out tendrils and roots. No, no, no. She had spent all her magic only this morning, and now here was nothing to stand between Robbie and a killing dose.

Nothing but herself. In that, Penny found the last advantage she would be offered. Of the two combatants, Penny would be willing to fight to the death for Rob.

Penny's face hardened. "Let him go, Isabelle. This is the only warning you'll get."

Isabelle grabbed Robbie tighter. "I simply won't—"

Penny's eyes jerked to Rob, expending the precious store of trust she had put by these many months, and shouted. "Run."

At the sound of her voice, Rob obeyed, pulling free as Penny launched herself at Isabelle, hitting her square in the midsection and shoving her arm away. The vial slipped from her grasp, tumbling, splashing across Isabelle's gaping mouth like ink spilling from its well. Penny propelled Isabelle onto her back, but she rolled, the wild scramble for supremacy as vicious as animals, skirts and petticoats wrapping around their limbs, trapping them.

At last Penny caught her, pinning a leg across her thighs, gripping a wrist, and slamming it onto the ground. Isabelle writhed and spit, dragging her mouth across her shoulder.

"Fool," she screamed, plunging her free hand into her skirts, fumbling until she whipped her old pruning knife free, raising it to Penny's face.

Penny scrambled off her and Isabelle staggered to her feet, holding the hooked blade with the confidence of long practice. "You can give me your magic, or I can take it," she said, waving the knife between them.

"I have none left," Penny said, breathing hard as she circled around Isabelle, wishing suddenly for the power to rise, to strike off into the air and find safety.

Isabelle lunged sharply, plunging the blade to the hilt into Penny's stomach, spilling her warm blood.

Penny felt the sharp sting of pain and bile begin to fill her throat. She felt the jagged backwards tug of the blade as Isabelle pulled it free. Her body hunched protectively over itself, waves of weakness breaking over her, stronger and stronger. There was Isabelle, standing next to her, pale and shaking, repeating unintelligible words.

There was pure sensation. The hot rush of nausea, sweat, and shaking, which seemed to reach all the way to her heart and break it. Penny fell to her knees as poisonous magic invaded her body, pressing its palms blindly on every surface, looking, looking. Poking long witch-like fingers into every hidden chamber of her mind.

Penny slipped sideways, a deck of playing cards cascading to the ground.

Isabelle would find nothing. The last of her healing was gone, spent worthily. She could not regret it. Time slowed and bent.

Malcolm. Damn it. She would miss him most, she thought, on the heels of the cold realization she was going to die here, blood soaking into the roots of the rowan trees.

Her vision clouded, colors blurring, smudging like lights in a fog. She heard a desperate, rage-filled scream and the rustle of grass as Isabelle staggered away.

The howl became agony, the panicked suffocation of a dying beast.

Chapter Thirty-Four

Malcolm walked up the village street, craning his neck above the crowd. Where is the lass? Later, he had promised, and it was later now. Too late, by his reckoning. He ought to have settled the thing long ago.

He didn't see Rob until he felt the small body of his son crashing into him, clamping on his hand and tugging him forward. The cuff of Rob's sleeve had inched back, exposing an arm covered in bright bruises.

"What is this?" Malcolm asked, narrowing his gaze. He tugged on Rob, attempting to find a place for questions and answers. "Who—"

"I'm fine," the lad insisted, his little face wearing the expression of a warrior. He jerked Malcolm forward with his whole strength, hardly moving him at all. "Miss needs you to help her. Hurry."

"Where?" Malcolm barked, already moving forward.

"Up near the rowans," Rob pointed, and Malcolm broke into a run, deaf to the exclamations following as he passed.

He wove through the cottages and crested the hill where he seemed to see everything at once. The clusters of unripe rowan berries hanging heavily on spindly branches that rode the breeze. Dappled sunlight shifting over two bodies lying on the ground. Isabelle, further on, her black hair matted with leaves, gripped in a fit which twisted her limbs like the black oak tree.

And Penny.

He went to her at once, hands brushing over her shoulder and hip. He jostled her.

"Have you been falling out of trees, then?" he teased, his voice rough, hardly disguising the desperate edge of it. Would this woman never stay safe? He probed her spine and she moaned, shrinking from his touch as it neared the small of her back. Thank God. He released a tight breath.

He bent forward to pick her up, encountering the wet slick of sweat beneath her neck. It covered her face, dampening the loose hair above her brow.

"Look at me," he commanded. "Look at me, love."

Her grey eyes drifted open, rolling unnaturally, unable to focus. Lord, she was cold. So cold, her trembling lips leached of color.

Other men from the village began to arrive and dimly he heard their shouts and commotion, felt them slide past him to tend Isabelle. He slipped an arm under Penny's knees when a spasm shook her, and he glanced down at her hands covering her midsection.

Blood. So much blood soaking the grey wool until it looked as dark as a black band of mourning. He pulled Penny close and strode down the hill, making an evil bargain, trading gentleness for speed, and shouted instructions. A path cleared all the way to Mrs Johnston's stone cottage.

"In here," she called, and he squeezed through the freshly painted door to find the doctor standing before the table, already rolling up his cuffs.

"Careful," Doctor Bell warned as Malcolm laid Penny out.

He expected some protest as he stretched her along the hard surface, but her silence was worse. Empty and cold, he could not take his eyes from the way her slippered feet hung off the end. She was tall for a woman.

The doctor began to cut away the fabric and Malcolm crouched by her ear, by the bright curls brushing the tops. He reached for her hand, twining her fingers with his own.

"Pen," he whispered, begging for something more than the shallow, infrequent sound of her breathing. "Pen, I don't give you leave to abandon us. You can't."

Damn and blast. He'd waited too late for later, and now this was the later they had.

Her eyelashes didn't twitch, even when the doctor reached for a fresh cloth, pressing it into the wound. Doctor Bell glanced at Malcolm, tense lines marking his face.

"Don't stand there, Donald," Elspeth cried into the stillness of the room, her voice fracturing. "Do something."

"This is beyond me, Elspeth." Doctor Bell lifted one blood-soaked hand. "I could stitch all day and never close the wound."

Malcolm shook his head, the movement labored.

God in heaven, were the shoe on the other foot, Penny wouldn't let him die. She wouldn't give up before she'd thrown herself into the fight. How would she begin to solve this?

Penny would try. She would try and she would fail. Then she would try something new, poking at the problem until it gave way. As though she were shaking him by the shoulder, he could her hear say, *Think of something. Save me.*

He stood. His fingers still laced in Penny's. "You can't cauterize it?" he asked, sick to think of the doctor plunging hot metal into her soft flesh.

"No," Bell shook his head, giving the cloth more pressure. Mrs Johnston's floors slicked with her blood. "A wound that size? It would kill her.

Malcolm raked a hand through his hair. What else? There had to be another way forward. "Is there no way to give her more blood? I would give mine."

Bell's expression faltered. "A transfusion? That's the stuff of medical journals. I haven't the training or the tools."

Malcolm stared at her hand in his, at the blue veins running through his wrist, so near her pale skin. It seemed such a simple thing to give some measure of himself to make her live. Yet, science could not help him.

His head snapped up.

Penny was magic. A healer. He had felt her healing touch swim through his veins. Why couldn't she heal herself?

"Elspeth," he rasped, "get Rob." His brows tented. "Mary, too. Come back and hurry."

Elspeth touched his arm, her eyes hooded with pity. "We cannae make her wake to such pain, only to say goodbye. We know she loved us."

"We're not saying goodbye," he growled. He jerked his head, sending her on her way, and turned to find Doctor Bell's sober expression.

"You'll do everything to keep her alive along as you can."

What do you expect—?"

"You do it," he snapped.

Elspeth returned, towing Rob and Mary behind her. Ewan slipped through the door and scraped himself up against a wall.

There was no hope in Elspeth's eyes. She stared at Penny's body with glassy, burned over emptiness.

"She's not going to die," Malcolm insisted. He regarded each of the gathering with steady, serious eyes. "Penny came to us because she lost her magic."

At the word, the doctor grunted, but Malcolm plunged on, hurrying.

"When she found it, it came to her as healing." He looked at Mary. "She kept you from slipping away when she forced that charcoal down your throat. Who would have thought of that? It was the damnedest thing. I asked her how she knew what to do, and wouldn't believe her when she said she didn't. Elspeth." Elspeth's brow was furrowed. "Your joints are easy because you sat near her all spring."

"They aren't easy now," she countered.

Malcolm breathed a laugh. "Because she has been spending her power on Rob. I felt it when she plucked him back from the edge of death. She's been filling him with healing for days."

Elspeth looked shocked, but Robbie nodded with such faith Malcolm kissed the top of his head. "We need to return that magic to her."

Dr Bell stood with locked arms pressing a mound of wadded linen, the snowy peak giving way to grim realities nearer the base. Penny was yet breathing, though a deathly grey pallor infused her cheeks.

Malcolm recalled the rush of magic that went through him when she brought Robbie out of his fever. It felt like shoots pushing up through the dark soil. As fresh as a spring wind. Doctor Bell did not have the tools to transmit blood, but Penny's magic had not worked in such a way. As soon as she'd touched Rob, channels had opened for her.

How could he dare to use her power in such a way? He was not magic. He pushed the uncertainty aside.

"Take her hand. Touch her face. Anywhere you can reach."

They arrayed around Penny, each commanding a spot as he began feeling his way along the unfamiliar rite. Ewan, too, though he had not received Penny's healing, put his small hand on her ankle.

"Think of how you want her to get better," he said. Robbie screwed his eyes shut tight and Malcolm closed his own, waiting.

She had never given him any magic. There would be no magic he could return to her care. Still, her touch consoled him, as did the light pulse under his fingertips.

"What's it supposed to feel like?" Elspeth asked after some time. "I don't feel anything."

Malcolm's eyelids lifted and he watched the shallow breaths come fitfully from Penny's chest, battling back the terrible fear each might be the last.

"Does anyone feel anything?"

None of them answered and an animal-like cry tore from Malcolm's throat. He bent his head over their hands.

She could not leave him. He had thought himself happy enough before she came to *Coille na Cyarlin*. Happy when he'd only been marking time, hiding away from the past, consuming each hour with well-laid plans. How easily she had upset them.

Was there ever the makings of a worse governess than Penelope Thornton? He'd been so certain she would beg him to pack her off to England on the first boat. But the weeks turned into months, and his amusement had shifted into respect, and then into love. As different as she was—the kind of creature who dressed in silks and sailed for the Continent—somehow, she belonged to him.

How had he resisted her when love had been there all the time? She'd given him back himself. He was again a man who dared things, laid down his plans, and changed them. A man who laughed. There had been magic in that. She had restored his heart, making it whole again.

There had been magic in that.

Malcolm's hand ached, as though it was a hard, unbroken seed. He looked at it, twined in Penny's smaller palm, their fingers laced together. Then the magic accelerated, bursting through the border between their beings.

"What's that?" Mary wondered aloud.

"Magic," Elspeth gasped. Malcolm raised his head to meet her shocked eyes.

"Rob?" he asked.

Robbie looked up his face drowsy. He smothered a cough in his hand.

"Not too much, Rob. We can't have you sick again."

"I'll do. We must get Miss back on her feet."

"Whatever it is, keep doing it," Doctorr Bell instructed, tipping the sodden cloth back, tossing the lump and applying a wad of fresh linen. Red seeped around the bottom but not so quickly as it had before. Magic rolled from Malcolm like an endless stream and the process repeated. New cloth, seepage, discard, new cloth. Finally, the doctor began wetting the rags and wiping her skin clean, the only fresh damage appearing to be the ragged wool of Penny's dress.

Her face was drawn, but color had come back into her cheeks, and she emitted a light snore which had Malcolm grinning.

"I wouldn't—" Bell stammered, pushing his glasses onto the top of his head forehead. "I never—"

Malcolm was on his knees, too exhausted for speech.

Too pleased.

He looked down the table.

Ewan smiled.

Chapter Thirty-Five

Penny dreamt of barley fields, of thin, elegant stalks balancing rows of ripening grain on their ends, of the quick slice of a short-handled sickle, felling them at a stroke, and of practiced hands bundling the sheaves. She dreamt of the satisfaction of bringing the harvest safely in before the rains came. Of dancing and being held in arms that belonged around her waist.

She rubbed a hand across her abdomen and smiled, turning on her side with a contented sigh. Yellow light slanted over her eyelids and she blinked. Dawn. What was so important about it? A moment of fumbling found the right piece of information. There it was. Today her parents would come and collect their daughter. She would no longer be a governess. The dream of golden barley disappeared, and her thoughts slid like a horse on icy cobbles.

Though her lazy view was half-obscured by a goose-down pillow, she could see this was her room, within hearing of the schoolroom and nursery, bare, save for her few things, easily packed up into trunks.

Her stomach rumbled and she slid her hand over her stomach again. Memory caught up to her and her hand stopped. This was where she was cut.

Penny sat up, throwing the covers back, reaching for a small hand mirror as she gathered up the hem of her night rail. She tipped the mirror, looking for the mark, livid red against pale skin. Though she had half expected it, still she gasped. Her fingers brushed the spot where her skin knit together. Sensitive, yet she was alive.

She remembered so little after Isabelle's thrust. The pain, Isabelle stumbling back, Malcolm's voice, his arms.

Anxious for answers, she stumbled out of bed and reached for her blue gown, throwing it on quickly and feeling the tug of new flesh over her belly. She scooped up several hairpins, holding them between her lips. Then, twisting her hair, she smoothed the curls as she put it up.

A soft rap came at the door.

"Come in," she called, speaking around the pins. She slipped another free and jabbed it into her knot.

It wasn't Mary, as she had expected, but Malcolm.

"I came to see if you were up," he said, setting a vase full of half-ripe rowan berries onto a ledge.

He regarded her from the door and though his mouth was as solemn as a churchman's, his blue eyes lit on her features. She felt his gaze skim over her hair, across her cheek, down her neck, and it set her skin tingling like magic.

There was no magic in her now. Or rather, it had better things to do than spool outward towards this man, tugging her body nearer his to tell her something she already knew.

She belonged here. She belonged to him.

"How is it that I don't even have a bandage," she breathed, stabbing at her hair in a haphazard manner until it no longer threatened to topple down her back, "when I thought I was going to die?"

She dropped her hands decorously to her side and waited for his answer. Malcolm was silent as he stepped closer and the room seemed to shrink. He took her hand, the other reaching up to trace the line of her jaw. Penny held herself perfectly still, longing to lean into his hand, to turn her head and kiss his palm.

His fingers slipped from her face.

"Isabelle. Lady Ainsley," she amended, frowning. It didn't seem correct to use the Christian name of someone who tried to murder her, "attacked me, but I didn't have any magic to heal myself. Isabelle would've stolen it if there had been a pennyworth left." The memory of crabbed, poisonous hands pawing through her innermost parts, finding nothing... Penny shivered. "She tried to."

"You weren't healing. The blood—" A muscle in his neck jumped and he bit off the words. His thumb began brushing along her palm in soft, rhythmic strokes, as though to reassure himself she was still alive, her flesh still warm under his fingers.

"Rob had a croupy rasp in his throat. I gave him the last of my magic," she said, the tiny motions making it difficult to speak. "To top him up with a little left over for Elspeth."

A smile carved grooves in his cheek. "It was only a cough."

"I didn't like the sound of it."

His smile deepened. "So, you gave away your magic and left none for yourself? You cannae do that anymore."

"None for Lady Ainsley when she wanted it." Her brow furrowed. "What happened to her?"

His thumb stopped its lazy path and he inhaled sharply. "We found the knife. It is the only one to make a cut like that." His free hand reached near her stomach, halted, withdrew. "She thought to cut your magic from you. Why?"

Why? The image of Isabelle fluttered before Penny's eyes. Beautiful, clever, heaped about with her rotting grimoires. The woman had been on a path as dark as the one that led to Foxglove Cottage. How comforting it would be to think of her only as a monster.

Penny's mouth shook with sudden knowledge. They had wanted the same things. She had walked that twisted track with Isabelle, for a time, only saved from being dragged into darkness because *Coille na Cyarlin* had called her from it. The noise of the household, the clamor and busyness of the schoolroom. Malcolm and his burdens.

"She lost her magic, not as I had, but still, and she never reconciled herself to the loss. I was a shortcut to what she wanted."

Malcolm's thumb began to mark a trail across her skin once more. "There wasn't time to call the magistrate and bring her up on charges. The doctor did what he could. He tried charcoal like you used on Mary, but the poison was too strong. She died."

Her own poison. Penny shivered and brought her palm flat against her stomach. "How did this happen?"

Malcolm's fingers touched the back of her hand, rested there, his callouses gently scraping her skin. "All these months you were healing every one of us at *Coille na Cyarlin*. Elspeth, Mary, Rob," his eyes gleamed, "me. I thought if we could sort of tip it back into you..."

"What?" She smiled. "Like a wheelbarrow full of dirt?"

He gave her a slow grin with those two dimples, which were at the right depth to set a seed in and pull the dirt over. "Elspeth is feeling a bit stiff. It exhausted me. I got you home and fell hard asleep."

"Robbie," she yelped. "You didn't make him sick again. Not for me."

"It's only a little cough."

She pulled her hand from his and tried to navigate around his tall frame, but he caught her by the arms, bringing her far closer than was strictly necessary for a conversation about whys and wherefores. Malcolm was already shaking his head from side to side.

"No, Pen. He's proud of himself. He fancies himself a hero. It's no worse than a cold. I had the good doctor up and everything. Mary is tending him in the nursery, and I am supposed to be tending you." The blue of his eyes was brighter than the sky.

She raised her brow, her heartbeat roaring in her veins. "You call this tending? Mr Ross, you promised me you never chased women around the furniture."

"Mr Ross," he scorned. "Pen, I—"

"Papa," Ewan spoke from the doorway, his eyes going from his father to Penny, to his father and back to Penny. He reached his hand to scratch at Fritz's head. "I came to see if Miss Thornton was well."

Malcolm released her so she might undergo Ewan's inspection with a degree of dignity, but when she clasped her hands behind her back, Malcolm hooked his fingers carelessly over the knot.

"Good morning, Ewan," she managed, her voice only a little strained.

"Morning, Miss Thornton. I've been tending your dog. As you see, Fritz has been brushed and exercised." He darted another glance between Penny and his father. "He will be in good shape for your journey."

"That's very good of you," she answered, feeling a sudden tightness around her heart. Malcolm hadn't spoken a word about her going or staying. Merely touched her hand as though she was supposed to know.

"I don't intend to bring Fritz with me when I go." See what Malcolm made of that. He only gave her hands a squeeze.

Ewan's small shoulders straightened, his eyes lifting hopefully.

"Thorndene is far too tame for him," she went on. "I'm afraid nothing will ever be as satisfying as *Coille na Cyarlin* is."

Her pronunciation of the name was almost perfect now, learned one sound at a time. Learned by listening. Learned by loving practice.

Penny smiled. It wasn't magic leading her on now. "I hoped you would let him be yours."

Ewan's hand rested on Fritz's head, teeth fretting his lip as he looked down at his dog. Then he nodded, his ears a bright red. "Do you have to go?"

Penny didn't dare look at Malcolm.

"I was seeing to that, son," Malcolm said, exasperated. "You run along to the nursery and tell them Miss Thornton is awake and fighting fit." He turned to Penny, never taking his eyes from her, even as he called to his son. "Strike that. Give me a quarter of an hour before you tell them."

Penny's heart was in her eyes. She knew it.

"Strike that," he called again. "Half an hour."

"Yes, sir."

Then the door clicked shut and he slid his arms around Penny drawing her close. She was poised on her tiptoes. "Not even nine o'clock and we've had such a thrilling day." He looked at her a long time. "Do you really feel well?"

Laughter was bubbling through Penny, shimmering through her veins. Across her skin, the tiniest seedlings of magic began to rustle in the wind. "Well enough for what?"

His mouth eased into a smile. "I'm trying to decide if you can have more upsets or not."

She said in an imitation of perfect innocence, "*Are* you going to chase me around the furniture?" She glanced exaggeratedly around the tiny space. "Or am I going to have to chase you?"

"Pen," he laughed. "You wouldn't cheat me of my speeches."

"Heaven forbid."

"When Rob found me yesterday, I had been looking for you to settle what lies between us at last. I was going to draw you away to do a spot of dedicating up at the lover's walk and ask you to tell me if the berries were sweet."

Penny's eyes shone. Isabelle's malevolence had no part of this, no power to haunt any corner of *Coille na Cyarlin* save the dark shadows of Foxglove Cottage. Penny found herself recalling she'd asked Malcolm to collect rowan cuttings from Wryborne, and he had done it for her, when he had precious little time to waste.

"I brought you sweet rowan," he said, and she glanced over to see that the clusters still had dew drops clinging to the stalks. He would have gone at first light.

"Sweet? Green, unripe rowans are inedible."

"Not so, my love." Malcolm touched her face. "A knowledgeable governess once assured me the berries have a magical property. They will turn sweet if a lass has found true love. Pen, will you end this torment and tell me if the berries are sweet or not?"

In truth, the berries would be hard as pebbles, making her lips pucker and eyes water. He didn't wait for an answer before he began nuzzling her neck in a proprietary way, taking it as his right. She tilted her head to give him better access, noticing the curious way her toes wanted to curl as his lips traced the sensitive path below her jaw.

Her hand cupped the back of his head, her fingers carding through his hair. Why had her magic led her to *Coille na Cyarlin*? Was it that these people—her people—had needed healing?

That wasn't it. The world was wide and full of brokenness and suffering. She could have halted not five miles from Thorndene and spent her healing again and again and again for the rest of her life. No, whatever else her magic could do, it wanted healing and wholeness. Somehow, her magic led her to a place where she would learn, and go on learning, how to exist in a world when she wasn't the most powerful thing in it. How to rise again when she fell, and how to take the bitter and make it sweet.

When she didn't answer, he drew back, his brows tenting in mock-irritation. "Are you too scared to marry me?"

A tremor of magic blossomed through her and she grinned. Reaching up, she rubbed her cheek against his, savoring the contrast. Her mouth was near his ear.

"I'm never scared."

He lifted her off her toes, covering her laughing mouth with his own, and when they parted, she leaned into him, their breath breaking with laughter and wanting.

"Would you look at that?" she smiled touching the edge of his mouth. "The berries are sweet. The sweetest I've ever tasted."

That earned her another kiss.

"Your parents are coming today," he murmured, leaning back against the door and holding her close. "How are we going to convince your father to let you wed an unknown Scot?"

"Papa?" she scoffed as her lips explored along his warm jaw, liking the way it made him shiver. "Papa will take one look at my face and know I belong here. If that doesn't do it, you'll show him the village and millworks, and he'll clamber all over them, inspecting. Anyway," she said, "it's Mama you'll have to manage."

Chapter Thirty-Six

In the end, it was Robbie who did the managing.

When a rosy-faced Penny and a slightly disarranged Malcolm adjourned to the schoolroom slightly more than a half an hour later, Penny felt the twining tug of her magic.

"Birdie," she said, Kathy's arms wrapped so tightly around her neck she was in great danger of losing consciousness, "if my parents arrive, don't put them in the sitting room. Escort them directly up."

Malcolm raised his brows slightly and she whispered across the disappearing gap between them on the sofa, "The magic wants me here, and it's better than my other plan of shouting down the stairs *I will have Malcolm Ross to wed and no othe*r, *and I'll elope with him to the nearest blacksmith if you deny me.*" Her brows furrowed. "Is that perfectly legal?" she asked, and he kissed her on the mouth in front of Elspeth and the children.

Her parents arrived at teatime, as Penny was handing around toasting forks and slices of bread, managing the general melee easily. Their commotion was welcome. The fire crackled in the grate and a sense of contentedness filled the room.

Penny introduced the company and watched as Mama's gaze sharpened when she came to Malcolm. Penny could hear Mama's thoughts: *Too young. Too handsome. Too near her daughter.*

Penny seated them on the hard-backed chairs near Elspeth, and they exchanged the particulars of their journey. Storms along the coast, and the roads were in barbaric conditions.

"Far better than the ones through Salzburg, dearest," Papa said. Mama gave him a withering smile. Her father had a gift for scenting intrigue, and assured his daughter was safe, blithely entered into the teatime ritual as though nothing whatsoever was unusual.

At length, Penny exchanged a silent look with Malcolm, and they began to tidy away the disorder. Their hands brushed briefly as saucers and teacups were passed along, the slightest touch communicating affection, reassurance, courage.

Penny stood next to Malcolm, tense and waiting for Mama and Papa to ask their questions and pronounce their judgments.

Fully sated on toast and marmalade, Kathleen tugged on Papa's whiskers, flipping off his lap as though she had been doing it for years. Mama gave a tight, diplomat's smile and opened her mouth to speak. Before she uttered a word, Robbie climbed into Mama's lap, holding her face in his jam-smeared hands.

"Why have you come?" he asked.

Mama scowled. "To drag my daughter back to England and lock her in a tower for thirty years." Penny's eyes widened. Oh Lord. Robbie's magic. She hadn't told Malcolm. She hadn't warned her parents.

"You cannae do that," Rob said. "Not when she'll be our *Eile*."

Penny's brow crinkled.

"It means 'other,'" Malcolm whispered, taking Penny's hand in his. He raised it to his mouth and kissed it. "But in Scots' Gaelic."

Penny glowed. *Eile.*

Then Malcolm raised his voice, drawing her parents' attention. "We've had a busy morning, sir. I asked your daughter to be my wife and she consented." He directed a look to Rob. "I meant to tell you myself."

"I'm shocked," came Papa's dry reply. There was a twinkle in his eye telling her he was well on his way to being won already.

Mama was not. "Outrageous," she sputtered. "You disappeared like a willful child and expect—"

"Would you like to hear the legend of *Coille na Cyarlin*?" Rob asked, tilting his head.

"No," she answered, frowning.

"Well, here 'tis then."

Malcolm drew Penny back against his chest, wrapping his arms about her, resting his cheek against her hair. Rob did not begin in the proper place with the men who wrested coal from the ground. He started with himself in a voice dipping and swaying with Scottish pride.

"Now listen. Cyarlin, the Hag of Winter, had killed us dead inside. We dinnae smell so bad, 'cept Ewan who always smells a bit. We were in a poor way. The clouds were heavy. Nothing would grow. The wind blew and blew, and the old oak on the cliff reached to the sky with the claws of Old Nick."

"Conditions have been dreadful all over," Mama conceded.

"But worse here because we had no heart. The Old Hag gripped us in her icy hand and would not let us go."

Penny's lips curved in recognition and gave a deep contented sigh. The Old Hag had gripped her too, frozen her heart in her chest. Malcolm's arms tightened and he gave her a neck a soft kiss.

"Then what happened?" Ewan asked, sitting cross-legged at their feet, stroking Fritz's head.

"Then the white witch came. Brigid. Spring and healing wrapped in one, to give us a proper mending."

"Brigid?" Mama asked, a pucker in her brow. "Who's Brigid."

"Your daughter, in yon clinch with *Aither*," Robbie said, pointing to the battered table. Penny tensed as Mama and Papa swiveled around, but Malcolm held fast.

"You're mine, little witch," Malcolm whispered, sending a shiver down her arms. If Mama was not persuaded to relent, Penny would drag this man off tonight and find the nearest blacksmith. She was almost certain it *was* legal.

"And," Rob continued, drawing their attention back, "she healed Mary from poison. Healed our Nan from being turned into a brick. Healed me when my lungs wanted to jump from my throat. Healed the land so it gave up our grain. And *Aither*... She healed him, too. It's magical, you agree?"

Papa laughed and gave Kathleen a sound kiss, won over, even without the complexity of the millworks.

Mama murmured. The truth wrung from her. "I agree. This is not the same Penny I left so many months ago. She appears healed too."

"Fine," Rob answered, swiveling through the word as only a true Scotsman could do. "Then you'll agree that you cannae take her from us. It would be monstrous."

"She was supposed to marry one of the young gentlemen in the Foreign Service," Mama fussed.

"She don't like none a' them. She likes us." Rob stared up at Mama with his brown eyes.

Mama's gaze drifted to Penny, frowning, no doubt over the liberties Malcolm was taking. Mama sighed. "You are an interesting person. It will serve her right to have a hand in raising you. Tell me," she said, settling him more securely on her lap, “did you know she was a sort of…Brigid right away?”

“No,” Ewan answered. “Who would expect Brigid to be English?”

Three little mouths pretended to spit.

Heavens, would Penny ever train them out of that?

“Oh, but she’s ours now.”

ABOUT THE AUTHOR

Keira graduated from BYU with a B.A. in Humanities, and now lives in Portland, Oregon with her husband and five children.

Over the last decade, she has authored three Regency Romances, and has co-authored *The Uncrushable Jersey Dress* – a blog and Facebook page dedicated to mid-century author, Betty Neels. Cultivating this corner of fandom confirmed Keira's suspicion: people who like sweet romances are as smart, funny, and are as interesting as readers of any other sub-genre.

When she is not busy avoiding volunteerism at her kids' schools like it is the literal plague, Keira enjoys scoring a deal at Goodwill, repainting her rooms an unnecessary amount of times, and being seized by sudden enthusiasms.

Take Tea with Keira at:
keiradominguez.com
facebook.com/keiradominguez8
twitter.com/keira_dominguez
instagram.com/keiradominguezwrites

www.BOROUGHSPUBLISHINGGROUP.com

If you enjoyed this book, please write a review. Our authors appreciate the feedback, and it helps future readers find books they love. We welcome your comments and invite you to send them to info@boroughspublishinggroup.com. Follow us on Facebook, Twitter and Instagram, and be sure to sign up for our newsletter for surprises and new releases from your favorite authors.

Are you an aspiring writer? Check out www.boroughspublishinggroup.com/submit and see if we can help you make your dreams come true.

Made in the USA
Monee, IL
05 May 2022